WOLF'S PACK

A Moonlight Universe Novel

WOLVES NEXT DOOR
BOOK III

AURYN HADLEY

Spotted Horse Productions

Cover Art by DAZED designs

Edited by Sarah Williams

DEDICATION

*This is for my Sisterhood of Being Too Old for That Shit. Well,
I call you my Enablers, but it's the same thing, right?
Thank you, Kitty, Kylie, and Lizzy for putting up with the
panic rants, for talking me off the cliff (a few times too many),
and for always being all-in.*

*When writing a book about family, that doesn't always mean
the blood relations. Sometimes, family is what we find along the
way, stumbling into them face first. You ladies are my rock.
Thank you for always being there when I need you most. <3*

But I'm still keeping those contracts y'all signed in blood.

Potentially Sensitive Content

The *Wolves Next Door* series contains profanity, consensual sex, and one adult woman who falls for multiple love interests.

CHAPTER 1

I braced both hands on the bathroom counter and stared into the mirror. My eyes were no longer the dark, rich color they'd always been. I glanced down at my phone, then back to my reflection, trying to match the new color with the "shades of brown" image I'd pulled up. Caramel seemed to be closest, but it wasn't quite right.

Then I found it. Not on the brown scale, but as an orange. The color was called cider, and it was a little darker than amber. Just one shade more brown than Seth's pretty cognac-colored eyes - but I'd expected that. They'd explained that the more time we spent as a human, the less yellow our eyes were. It was also why Lane's were so golden, and the natural-born wolves weren't that far off.

I still liked it. I also liked how my skin felt a little softer, almost younger. The pair of creases that I'd been fretting about in my brow were now barely noticeable. Sadly, my grey hairs were still there, but I could handle that. My only issue with this whole new wolf body thing was how much I still hurt. One day was clearly not enough time to recover from what I'd done to myself.

"Elena?" Seth's voice was soft, considerate of my new super-hearing. "You ok in there?"

Reaching over, I opened the bathroom door to find him waiting on the other side. "Willing to give a second opinion?" I asked. "Cider or more caramel?" And I held up the color chart.

A grin took over his mouth, and he glanced away. "I'd call them tawny, but I'm not really a color expert." Then he stepped in behind me, wrapping his arms around my waist. "How do you feel?"

"Like my body was twisted up into a pretzel and left like that for a while." I leaned back against him. "The muscle relaxers help, though."

"So stay home?" he suggested before leaning in to kiss my neck. "Ashley doesn't need you in the office. We're all willing to help if it gets busy. Stay here one more day and recover, Elena. Even Gabby slept off her change for a few days."

"Yeah, but I can't get used to my new senses if I'm at home and all of you are talking softly and being so considerate." I turned to face him. "I ache, but I really am ok, Seth."

"I'm just..." He smiled again, struggling to hide it. "This is me being overly protective."

"And this is me thinking it's cute." I leaned in to brush a kiss across his lips. "But Gabby's *quinceañera* is a week away. Next Saturday, actually. My parents are coming into town, there's going to be a lot of music and people, and that is not the time or place for me to realize that I'm overwhelmed because I can now smell and hear everything."

He just palmed my cheek. "Ok." Then his thumb swiped across the side of my face. "But I'm telling Lane, and he'll talk to Ashley. If you can't take it, you'd better expect all of us to show up."

"I know," I assured him. "But I'll be sitting down all day, so that counts as resting, and I've already taken too much time off. So, I don't know, work on that stuff Ian was talking about with foxes and the other shifters?"

"We have been," he assured me, pausing for a moment.

The best part was that I heard it too. It now sounded like my kitchen was right beside me, and someone was clattering around for pans. I could hear male voices mumbling. I was pretty sure that was Lane and Ian. My eyes narrowed as I stared at Seth.

"That's cheating, you know."

He chuckled. "It's kinda not. How else did you think we always knew when someone else was here?"

"Uh, because they said they were coming over and you heard something? Not *that* clearly!" And then my heart stalled. "Oh, shit. Does this mean Gabby can hear... you know... us? At night?"

"She asked for earbuds for Christmas for a reason," he admitted. "We made sure she got a really good set for that exact same reason. Yes, she sleeps with them in. No, it won't ruin her ears. She also won't want to go to many concerts, so there's that. Dunno how to break it to you, Elena, but your nearly fifteen-year-old daughter understands that people have sex. She also has no interest in knowing when you do."

Oh my. Yes, my face was getting warmer, but I also

knew he was right. "Ok," I said, stepping away from him to head into my bedroom. "I need to get dressed, and you need to make sure those guys don't try to stop me from going to work."

"I was chosen to talk you out of it, actually," Seth admitted. "Lane was worried you'd say he couldn't understand since he's always heard like this."

"And Ian?" I asked as I pulled on my shirt.

Seth shoved a hand across his mouth. "Um, he didn't want to make it a dominance thing, and he knows you're still getting used to those pack urges."

"That's actually kinda cute," I admitted.

Seth just nodded. "Yeah. But Trent and Pax might be over at the office already, adjusting the phone settings for you and, um, warning Ashley." Then he shrugged. "We're trying very hard not to smother you, so don't get mad?"

Next, I pulled on a pair of slacks. My most comfortable pair, because I was going very office-casual today. "I'm not," I promised. "But can you check on Gabby today? The subtle kind?"

"Because she's allowed to date Roman again, you'll be out of the house, and you have a feeling she's going to try something with her boyfriend," he guessed. "Sure. I can do that."

I groaned. "And sneak some of those condoms into the upstairs bathroom or something?" I begged. "Just, you know, in case? I'd rather she waited, but if she's not going to, I'd prefer she doesn't end up pregnant because of it."

"Promise," he said, backing toward the door. "And you're dawdling." Then he winked. "Breakfast will be ready soon."

When he opened the door to leave, I could smell it. My

stomach growled, reminding me that the broth and soup I'd had the last two days - while good - didn't count as a real meal. The scent of eggs, bacon, and sausage was even more amazing now, and I was suddenly craving it. I also needed to put on enough makeup to make myself feel presentable.

I hurried through that, knowing I didn't need to impress anyone. The entire pack had basically seen me naked on Wednesday night. Sure, I'd had a pair of wolves lying on me - and a rather large man - but still. This meant I had nothing left to worry about. Nudity was necessary for changing forms, they always said. Running as a wolf wasn't exactly the best way to "look good." Styled hair and painted faces didn't shift with us, so I would need to get used to looking like a werewolf sometimes.

Because I *was* one. I'd done it, I'd survived, and I was happy about it, but I was still getting used to all the nuances. Gabby had made this all look so easy. Then again, my daughter was fourteen - almost fifteen now. Her birthday was officially on Monday, and her big *quinceañera* to celebrate her becoming a woman was in a week. I still hadn't managed to get her a dress, either!

I'd planned to, but having a kid shoot up my daughter's school had shifted my priorities a little. Now, I was going to need to scramble a bit. Thankfully, Roman and Olivia would be willing to take Gabby around to look, narrowing down the options. My five boyfriends - no, mates - had offered to help pay for it, which meant tailoring was covered. This could still happen. It was going to be ok.

And I was actually a wolf. I couldn't stop thinking about it, as if my mind kept repeating that like a mantra. It felt good, like some guilty secret, except that there was nothing to hide. At least, not from my pack. So when I walked into the kitchen, following the scent of breakfast, there was a little extra spring in my step. It was almost enough to make up for the drag of my aching muscles.

"You look happy," Lane said as I rounded the corner.

I just grinned, and yep, my mind replayed my mantra. "I feel good," I told him. "Like a whole new woman, although I still ache all over."

His eyes just slid down my body. "If you stay home, I'll give you a long and very thorough massage."

"No." I laughed to take the sting out of that. "Guys, seriously. I need to get used to hearing more than just all of you being extra quiet. I need to smell the air outside. I have to get used to this, but I'm not going to push too hard. Promise."

"So..." Ian set a plate of eggs, toast, bacon, hash browns, and sausage before me. "Are we allowed to hover and worry too much, or would that bruise your newfound wolfish pride?"

"You can hover," I assured him. "After all, you are my mates." And I looked up to meet his perfectly golden eyes.

His mouth curled higher. "I like that."

"Hm?"

Seth claimed the chair beside me, gesturing for Lane to pass him some food. "Most wolves can't meet his eyes that easily," he explained. "Dominance, Elena. You have it, and not many converts can say the same."

"Gabby did too," Lane told me. "Pretty sure she didn't get it from her father." And he lifted a brow, making it clear he meant she'd inherited - or learned - it from me.

"I'm not dominant," I reminded them. "Guys, I'm the happy housewife type."

"Not as much as you think," Ian assured me. "Elena, three alphas couldn't force you to shift, but Lane *asking* could?"

"No," I said. We'd talked about this, but I felt like he still didn't understand. "I was just trying too hard. Lane begged, and he's the one who told me to stop pushing or fighting. I'd never considered that trying too hard could be fighting it, so I gave up and let you do your thing, Ian."

"I didn't do anything," he said, adding a glass of orange juice beside my coffee. "You changed back on your own. We tried. Me, Ashley, and even Kim. Henry was making his way over when you figured it out and just..." He huffed, clearly at a loss for words. "You just did it."

"Because I trusted my pack. And Gabby needs me, so I had to make it work." I took a bite, pausing to appreciate how good real food tasted. Not that my taste buds had changed, but it had been a bit since I'd felt up to chewing. "And this is very good."

"She's not going to believe you," Lane told Ian. "Just let it go."

"But - "

"No," Lane warned. "She figured it out. It doesn't matter if she ignored your dominance. She's your mate, she figured it out, and she'll be stronger for it. Leave it alone, Ian."

Seth just pointed his fork at Lane. "Wouldn't really push him. He was up all night."

"Why?" I asked around another mouthful of real food.

Lane leaned over the kitchen side of the counter, right

toward me. "Because my mate hurts. She may have needed me."

"And Seth was with me," I reminded him. "You could've crawled in bed and slept."

"Can't," Seth mumbled. "He's been a mess with worry since he bit you." He grabbed a piece of toast and shoved that into his face. "And Ian had to order him to sleep. So if you want to make sure he passes out, you're going to have to throw him in bed."

"I'm good with that," Lane agreed, a devious little smile curling his lips.

Ian just chuckled, turning back to the coffee pot to hide it. "So, if any of this gets to be too much for you, Elena, what are you going to do today?"

"Um, walk home?" I guessed.

"No," Lane said.

"How about call one of you?" Because that always seemed to be the right answer.

"No," Lane said again, proving me wrong.

"Tell Ashley?" I guessed, unable to think of anything else.

"Yes," Lane finally said. "She will call me. I will come get you and make sure you aren't scared."

"I'm not *scared*," I told him. "A little mortified to realize just how well my daughter can hear, and refusing to think about how I'm going to handle all of you spending the night now that I'm no longer in the dark, but I'm not scared. Lane, I'm a wolf. I survived. I look better than I have in a decade, and I'm excited to figure out all the new tricks that come with this. Nothing about that is scary."

"But what if the sounds are?" he asked. "Or the smells?

Seth said it was different, and sometimes he'd have to pause because it confused him."

"Disoriented," Seth corrected, "and it's because the volume and distance have to be relearned. It's not scary, Lane. Sometimes it's painful, but if Trent and Pax are adjusting the phone sounds in the office, she'll be fine."

"I don't like it," Lane grumbled.

Ian just reached over to clasp his shoulder. "Trust our mate, Lane. Elena's got this. She's one of the strongest converts I've ever seen."

Seth's head twitched. "Huh," he muttered.

Lane immediately looked at him. "What?" he demanded.

"Nothing bad," Seth assured him. "I was just thinking that you were stuck as a wolf for years. Elena was stuck as a human, in a life she didn't want. Maybe that's why you ended up fated for her? Like, some way for you to inherently understand each other?"

"Personally," Ian said, "I think it's because she's the perfect balance to him. Nice enough to make him be gentle but brave enough to not run away." His eyes shifted to me. "And determined enough to never give up. Kinda why we all have a thing for her."

Yep, I was smiling. It felt like my transformation from human to wolf had been the thing that finally took our relationship to a new level. Not sex. Not dealing with trauma or other issues. Now that I was a wolf, I could finally understand them, and my mates were no longer holding back, worried about my human sensibilities.

Because I was no longer a human, and it was the best decision I'd ever made.

CHAPTER 2

L ane walked me to the office. It wasn't even half a block away, but I could tell he was worried. Besides, it was kinda cute. However, Trent and Pax were waiting inside. The pair of them had done a lot more than just adjust the phones. The carpet in the lobby was clean. My little trash can had been emptied. A candle was burning at the side of the room, smelling like laundry detergent, and it was a lot more impressive than I remembered.

"Smells and sounds have been minimized," Pax announced as soon as I walked in. "It should be new-wolf safe, but tell us if anything's too much."

"The candle?" Trent asked.

I shook my head. "I actually like that one. It's the same scent I have at my house."

"My favorite," Lane said, leaving my side to make a lap around the room. He didn't even try to hide that he was sniffing at things. "You tell Ashley?"

"I did," Trent assured him. "And Henry's coming over later. Said he's going to be available just in case she needs anything."

Then a door down the hall clicked, opening a second later. The fact that I heard the latch release was actually rather amazing, but all three men looked at me, almost as if they expected me to flinch. I just rolled my eyes and headed to my desk. By the time I made it into my seat, Ashley walked into the room.

"How do you feel?" she asked, her voice completely and totally normal.

I sighed with relief. "Thank God. There's one person in the world who isn't whispering at me."

"Not whispering," Lane grumbled.

Ashley just laughed. "Out, you three. Elena's fine. She's not dying, and if she is, I'll call Dr. Bridget. Believe it or not, you really do have jobs to do." Then she flicked both hands at them, shooing them out.

"If you need anything..." Lane said as he headed to the door.

"I'll tell Ashley," I promised, "and she'll tell you. I'm *fine,* Lane."

Ashley moved to lean on my desk, and the pair of us watched my mates leave in silence. The door closed, and I heard that latch click for the first time. A moment later, the sound of doors to Trent's truck could be heard opening, and then closing not long after. When it started, it sounded as if the office windows were open, but it wasn't obnoxious.

Still, I could see how a person without a pack to explain all of this would be confused. There were so many new details that I could hear. Just little things, and I knew what they were, but my ears had never been this efficient in my life. At forty years old, my hearing shouldn't be *quite* as good as it had been when I was younger. Not that I'd ever noticed - until now.

"So?" Ashley asked, finally breaking the silence. "You want to kill them yet?"

"They're cute," I assured her. "Now, if I'd stayed home today, I probably would've ended up wringing Lane's neck, but they're cute now that they're gone."

Laughing, she moved around my desk to grab one of the chairs and drag it over. "How bad do you hurt?"

"I'm using some pills Bridget sent for me," I admitted. "And I still ache, but like a bad workout, not like I'm dying. I just wanted to make sure I really could handle all of this, and I'm tired of feeling like a burden."

"You are not a burden," Ashley promised, leaning toward me. "You ran hard, Elena. There was one point when only Seth could keep up, and that's saying a lot."

"What do I look like as a wolf?" I asked her. "Lane says I'm beautiful. Seth said I'm black. But what do I actually look like?"

She grinned at me. "Well, you're definitely black. Not that dark brown that's almost black, like Gabby. Your coat is completely black except for the little tawny lines under your eyes. I'm pretty sure there's some of that coffee-colored undercoat on your shoulders, but I only saw it when we had you pinned down."

"Do I look like Gabby?"

She nodded. "A darker, bigger, more mature version, but yeah. Definitely a family resemblance." She paused for a moment, struggling not to smirk, but failing. "And pretty much the entire pack wanted to do something nice for you. Sampson sent more venison. I had to talk Dad out of making some stupidly over the top gesture - "

"What did he want to do?" I interrupted.

"Give you the house." Ashley shrugged. "I told him you'd feel pressured to stay if you decided to find a new pack. We both know you won't, but I figured you'd hate that. But if you want it, I can tell him to go ahead."

"No." I waved her off. "As much as he's already done?"

"Kinda what I figured." But she still looked a little smug. "And the rest of your Sisterhood? Yep, we've made it clear that next week, every night at seven p.m., there will be wolf lessons. That it would be rude to laugh at you learning to walk, but that any wolf who needs some help mastering their canine body is welcome to join us."

"Wolf lessons?" Because that was my next concern. "Thank you!"

"Caveat," she warned me. "Your mates insisted on helping. I know David's going to be there. For moral support, he said, because you can't be as bad as he is. Gabby's little pack of betas will be running 'patrols' to keep the gawkers away, so you won't even need to be embarrassed."

"Did they gawk at her when she was first learning?"

Ashley shook her head. "Nope, but she's not the second in charge of our pack, either. Although, speaking of that, I'm assuming that her *quinceañera* would be a bad time for Ian to announce her as his heir?"

"My parents will be there," I reminded her. "So, humans. How is it usually done?"

"He's kinda been doing it," she admitted. "Every moon, Gabby's at his side. That's a position of honor, of sorts. The Alpha won't let just anyone invade his space, but it's subtle. Right now, it's just him claiming her as family - which she is. I hope that's not crossing a line?"

I shook my head. "No, I've always known that those guys think of her as their pup, and the truth is, I like it. They don't try to overrule my decisions, but they honestly care about her."

"But are you really ready for the rest of the pack to see them as her stepfathers?"

I pushed out a breath, because that was a big step. And yet, at the same time, it really wasn't. Ian had been calling her 'ours' for months now. Seth adored Gabby. Trent and Pax went out of their way to help her with one thing or another, and Lane was adamant that if anything happened to me, he'd be raising her. If that wasn't stepfather material, then I didn't know what was.

Granted, this new virus in my brain had me thinking differently. Before, I knew I would've been worried about it. As a mother, I would've wondered if it was too soon, or how to handle this if our relationship didn't pan out. The simple fact that they'd never asked should've bothered me, and yet they kinda had. They'd checked with me every single step of the way, and I'd always told them it was ok.

Because we were pack, and this was what pack did. Ian was the Alpha, and he was responsible for *all* of the pups in Wolf's Run. Was it really odd to think that he'd care for my daughter any less? Plus, he wanted Gabby to be the next Alpha, and he was offering to teach her how to take over if anything happened to him. Showing her how to lead instead of rule, basically.

For a moment, I sat there thinking about it. Not whether or not I approved - because I already did. It was more the change in my thinking. I could remember how I would've felt about this a week ago, and yet I just couldn't make those emotions work like that. This was my pack. Wolf's Run was my family in a way I'd never been able to understand before. It was home and belonging and safety all rolled into one. That Ian was not only the Alpha but also a man I loved? That made it easy to accept him honestly caring about my child.

"It's a wolf thing," I breathed, lifting my eyes to meet Ashley's.

For a few seconds, she just stared me right in the eye. "It is," she agreed, refusing to look away. "But can you feel the dominance when you do that?"

"No," I admitted.

That made her head twitch. "Really? Most new wolves find looking me in the eye to be uncomfortable. I think awkward might be a better term."

"No," I said again. "I did the same thing to Ian this morning, and he noticed too."

"Because you are not a weak wolf," she assured me. "You're also not an aggressive one, which is a little confusing, but I'm more than willing to go with it." Then she patted my desk. "Ok! Work stuff."

The gesture made my eyes jump over, which broke the gaze without forcing me to look away. I actually laughed at that, and Ashley's smile made it clear it had been intentional. Evidently, my best friend had quite a few subtle tricks up her sleeve.

"Teach me how to do that?" I asked. "I mean, if I'm supposed to be the second in charge of this pack, and this is a thing..." I paused, unsure how to explain what I was asking.

But Ashley understood. "You don't want to be rude

about it," she finished for me. "Yeah, I can do that. Since I stepped down as Dad's heir a while ago, I've picked up a few things to keep others from realizing that not wanting to lead the pack isn't the same as becoming submissive. So, we'll add that to the list, and I have a feeling the Sisterhood will help you practice." Then she pointed at the phone. "That and emails are your only concerns today. Pax turned down the volume as low as it can go. Adjust it from there. If you get overwhelmed, just put them on hold and let me know."

"I think I've got this," I assured her.

Ashley just leaned over to clasp my knee. "I know you do. I also know that you're a new wolf, this is going to wear on you eventually, and there is no reason for you to push through it. Elena, you're my best friend. More than that, you're one of my Alphas. I am going to take good care of you, whether you like it or not. Now, I'm not as annoying as your mates, but I'm just as fucking loyal, ok? Comes with the disease."

I caught her hand. "Thank you, Ash. For the job, the understanding, and all the help over the last few months. Most of all? Thank you for bringing a little magic into my life."

"It's still science," she teased.

"And still very magical," I countered. "Now go work. I got the phones, and I promise I'll whimper or something if I can't take it. I just really want to expose myself to real life now so I won't make a mess of Gabby's big day."

"Ok," she relented, standing up just to put her chair back where it belonged. "I just have one condition, ok?"

I almost groaned. "What's that?"

"Anything confuses you, bothers you, or needs to be

explained, and you let me know. Not my little brother. Not his betas. Me, Elena. No pride, no dominance, and no worries about what anyone else will think. My best friend just became a wolf, and I'm kinda happy about it."

"Promise," I swore. "Although I might actually need a little help with something."

"Anything," she promised.

"I didn't buy Gabby a present and her birthday is Monday - and I do *not* feel like I'm good enough to walk around a mall!"

She rolled her eyes and headed up the hall to her office, calling back, "I'm going out with Bridget on Saturday. We'll handle it. Get me a list!"

"Owe you one," I called after her.

"Call it a turning present," she said, not even needing to raise her voice much to be heard clearly. "Now finish those emails, Alpha."

"I still can't get used to that," I said. "In my mind, 'Alpha' means Ian."

"And now you are too," Ashley said. "Look, both terms are short for something. Pack Alpha or Alpha Mate. But, at the same time, you're his equal in the eyes of the pack. The other half of him. That's why we call you that, because anything you say can and will be backed up by him - or vice versa."

"But it's kinda weird, isn't it?" I insisted.

She just shook her head. "Not to me. Elena, wolves don't own their partners. One gender is not more powerful than the other. And of course there's the reality that Alpha Female is just a formal mouthful."

"Ok, but I didn't *earn* this position," I pointed out.

She looked at me as if I was a moron. "No, you just

tamed the most powerful wolf in the pack and made him all but submit to you. Maybe you didn't have a knockdown fight for it, but I promise that to all of *us,* you've earned it."

It was still weird, but in a good sort of way. In truth, there were a lot of things about the way these wolves ran their pack that went against everything I'd ever read in those paranormal romances I loved. Not that it was a bad thing, though. In truth, I kinda liked it.

Yet that didn't help with the list. So I turned on my computer and got started on that, thankful to finally have something to do besides just laying in bed. I also felt a little better about replying to the obvious shifters asking about the facilities because I was now one of them. I was sure this feeling would go away soon, but I was enjoying it. I'd upgraded from being the boring human friend to being one of the magical creatures that existed in the shadows of society, just like in some of those books I read.

By ten a.m., the feeling had already faded. Eighty-one unanswered emails had a way of erasing all the fantasy from my daydreams, slamming me back into the reality of running the leasing office. Thankfully, there'd only been three phone calls, and I'd actually had to increase the volume a little because my ears weren't that sensitive, but I was doing this.

Then the little chime on the front door sounded, making me jerk in my chair. It was much louder than I expected. The smell that wafted in right after made me sit up. And on the heels of that, a man walked into the lobby.

A large man. With two large friends right behind him.

They smelled like sweet grass and freshly-tilled earth. My eyes immediately jumped to theirs, wondering if this was how all humans smelled. The first guy was the biggest - both tall and wide. His hair was brown, his beard was thick, and his eyes? They were black with a flare of mahogany in the center. The color was just strange enough to stand out, but it was certainly not yellow, amber, honey, or any shade of wolf eyes.

Then I looked at the guy behind him. He was about an inch shorter, black, and looked nothing like the first guy, yet his eyes were the same. Guy number three was the shortest of the bunch, but almost as wide as the first, he was a very stoutly-built man, probably still six feet tall, though, or close to it. Like the rest, his eyes were exactly the same.

That was what made me shove to my feet. "Can I help you?" I asked, hoping like hell that whatever these men were, they'd come in peace.

CHAPTER 3

The biggest guy - the first one - stepped forward as if he was in charge. My heart was pounding in my chest, and that smell only got stronger as he came closer. The guys had mentioned that my perception of color would change. Did that mean I'd see human eyes differently too? Why hadn't they mentioned it? And if not, what was I supposed to be doing?

So, no, I was going to pretend that everything was normal. If they really were humans, I didn't want to expose us. If they weren't, maybe they'd think I was? My eyes were within the human shade of brown still. Barely, but I'd spent long enough staring at the mirror this morning to know that much at least.

Then the big guy stopped just out of reach. "Yeah, um, I heard you had houses for lease? I was kinda curious about the rules."

I swallowed. "Certainly." Damn it, my voice was a little

too high pitched. "Were the three of you all looking for a place?"

"We're with him," the Black guy said, adding a little smile, but his eyes were narrowed as if he was trying hard to figure me out.

Well, the feeling's mutual, bud, I thought. "So, I assume you're looking for a three-bedroom? Um..." I didn't bother sitting back down to type at my keyboard, pulling up our limited amount of available houses. "Ok, we have a couple of those left. So, if you'd like to fill out some paperwork, we can start the approval process. And while you do that, I'll get you some brochures that show the floor plan options."

My hands were shaking as I gathered up the necessary paperwork. Hopefully, they wouldn't notice, but something about this was not right. I should've listened to my mates when they'd warned me to take it slow. If this was how I reacted to a group of humans? Maybe I should just call Ashley? No, I had this. I would not back out now.

So I stacked four different floor plans and a leasing application together and put them on a clipboard. Snagging a pen from my desk, I held it all out for whichever man wanted to take it. "Here you go. If you'll just fill this out, I'll see if someone's available to - "

The door chimed again, and I visibly flinched, but when my eyes jumped to the latest person entering, my breath rushed out. That was Ian. He'd take over, right?

But his feet froze just inside the door. "Bears," he growled, his head swiveling from one man to the other. "Get away from my mate!"

"Move," the smaller man snapped, pushing the Black guy away from me.

The largest one just turned to face Ian. "Alpha, I presume?"

The tension in the room was thick enough to cut. My heart was hammering so hard I could hear it. My breathing was coming just a little too fast. Both of my hands were clenching the edge of my desk, and I desperately wanted to flee, but I couldn't. I had nowhere to run, and I would not leave Ian alone to deal with these men.

Which was when Ashley stormed into the room. "Ian, stop!" she snapped.

Everyone in the room turned to look at her. For a moment, it was quiet enough to hear a pin drop, and then the biggest guy's face broke into a grin. "Ashley!"

"Hey, Vic," she said, crossing the distance to give him a very friendly hug. "I see you found us."

"You know him?" Ian asked.

From my angle, I caught Ashley giving Vic a look of warning, and then she let go of his neck to face her brother. "I do. Now calm down, Alpha."

Ian just pointed at me. "Not until she does."

"I'm ok," I promised. Not that I was, but I wasn't about to admit how nervous those men made me.

"Shit," Ashley breathed. "Elena, sit down. It's ok. I know your instincts are screaming, but I promise they're ok. I know Victor, and he's a friend." The whole time she spoke, she was making a straight line for me until she'd grabbed my arms and was easing me back into my chair. "He's not going to hurt you."

"Guys," the shortest guy said, "back off. The lady's nervous."

"Never seen a bear before?" the Black guy asked.

Ashley's head snapped back. "She's just turned. She's never seen shit before, and she should be at home right now learning her senses, but she's the Alpha Female and too damned stubborn to let us help." Then she looked back at me. "Slow breaths. They smell sweet, and that's ok. They're big, but they're not real bears. That's your survival instinct warning you of a bigger, nastier predator, but it's primal and doesn't know what it's talking about."

"Fucking bears, Ash?" I breathed. "You could've warned me!"

"Uh..." The big guy leaned around his friends to see me. "She kinda didn't know we were coming." Then he looked at Ian. "So, I guessed right? You are the guy in charge?"

"I am," Ian said, refusing to budge.

"Yeah, so, we came to beg." Vic tilted his head to the door. "We're happy to step outside if that makes it easier on your mate?"

"No," I said before they could walk away. "I'm fine. I'm sorry. I just... I thought you were human."

And I gestured for Ashley to lay off, because I really was ok now that I knew what they were. A little freaked out, and my pulse was still racing, but that was just normal nerves. I could handle it. Knowing that I wasn't overreacting for no reason helped more than I wanted to admit.

Just to prove my case - and make Ian relax - I stood and made my way toward the bears with my hand out. "Welcome to Wolf's Run. How can we help?"

The shorter man accepted my hand first. "Scott," he introduced himself. "Black bear."

Then the Black man offered his hand next. "Jax, grizzly."

And finally, it was Vic. "Victor, a friend of Ashley's, and Kodiak."

"Elena," I told them. "I'm Ian's mate, and the leasing manager here." I checked Ian again. "I'm fine."

"Not gonna hurt your mate," Vic said again.

Ian just looked at Ashley. "*How* do you know bears?"

"Funny story, actually..." She crossed her arms as if bracing for a fight. "Met Vic at a bar. We were both slumming it and on neutral territory."

"Yeah," Vic said, picking up the story. "Bought her a drink and asked if there were wolves in town. She told me about this place. I mean, I'd heard the ads on the radio, but didn't think anyone would be that blatant. Then, what, a couple weeks ago?"

"The shooting," Ian realized. "And the video."

"Yep," Vic agreed. "No way that video was a hoax. I've seen plenty of wolves shift in my life, and that was a perfect recreation. Then there's some human kid saying she made the video? I mean, that girl's eyes were darker than a bear's. She's the real deal. So, figured that if Wolf's Run is locked down that well, then maybe we should come begging."

"For?" Ian asked.

Vic blew out a breath, but Jax was the one who answered. "Shelter," he said. "Look, Alpha, it's getting harder to survive in the real world, ok? Even in these hillbilly towns in the middle of nowhere, everyone has a phone with an impressive camera. The only way to keep from getting caught is to work in groups. The three of us have been moving together for..." He looked at the smaller guy.

"Five years," Scott answered. "Give or take. We tried a

hunting cabin in the mountains, and hunters noticed a Kodiak bear in Colorado. We couldn't stay."

"Native to Alaska," Vic explained. "And Jax here shouldn't be that far south either. Scott's the only one who can blend. So basically, we're fucked unless we move to Canada, and, uh..." He glanced at the others. "Human governments are just as bad as the shifter ones."

"It's hard out there for the rest of us," Jax said. "All we want is a place where we can live, stay out of the way, and not wonder if our neighbors will come after us with guns blazing."

"Why here?" Ian asked.

"Because you made a sanctuary," Vic told him. "You just went through every shifter's nightmare. You had a member of your kind caught on camera, and you made it work. And coming in here? The walls? The gates? This place is a damned fortress!"

"Makes it safe when one of ours turns," Ian admitted, finally gesturing for the guys to take a seat. "The thing is, this is a wolf pack, and wolves don't really play well with bears." He tilted his head at me to prove the point.

"Ian, she didn't know," Ashley insisted.

But I had an even better argument. "I thought we'd already agreed to talk about this?"

"To *talk*," Ian admitted. "But I didn't expect to have three bears walk into the office your first day on your feet, Elena."

"And I'm fine," I reminded him. "I'm guessing that 'other shifters' was going to be a lesson for next week."

"Probably the week after," Ashley fake-whispered. "Next week's walking."

"Haven't even made your first voluntary shift?" Scott asked.

I shook my head. "No. Today's actually my first day out of the house."

"Of bed," Ian clarified. "She ran hard."

"We do it too," Scott told him. "Tidal forces of the virus and all that. Ours is just a mutation of yours, so we feel the pull to hunt the moon too."

"That's going to be a problem," Ian told them. "Our pack runs every moon. Together. The nature trails we've got aren't big enough to avoid three bears."

"We work as a group now," Jax told him. "Got over the isolation thing a while ago. We could make it work."

"Don't know that we can," Ian countered. "If Elena was that shocked, then what about the pups? I've got children here, guys! Kids whose parents shift them for the night so they can learn their legs."

"So we meet them before the runs," Vic offered. "We're more than willing to make this work. And before you can say it, if you have a new convert, we're willing to help. Ian - Alpha, we are *desperate.* We will obey any rule you set because we don't have any other option. Right now, the three of us have an apartment in the middle of town with exactly one plant in the house. Wednesday? We locked our front door, closed the blinds, and got drunk so we wouldn't shift. We. Are. Desperate."

"I can't promise anything," Ian told them, but it was clear he was no longer as adamantly against it.

I claimed the chair beside him. "We can find a way to make this work, can't we?"

"Elena, what if Lane had walked in here?" he asked.

Ashley told the guys, "Her fated mate."

"We're not going to fight," Vic assured us. "We already talked about that before we came in the door. We knew we might not be welcome, but we're here to beg. We will not fight you, and we have no interest in hurting anyone. We just want a home, Alpha, and we aren't the only ones."

"What you have with Wolf's Run is a dream to most of the non-pack shifters," Scott said. "Bears, large cats, and the birds?"

"There are *bird* shifters?" I asked.

Jax chuckled. "Yeah, mostly eagles. They stand out, though. A little too big to be real, if you know what I mean."

"Let us prove ourselves?" Vic begged. "Ashley can vouch for me. At least, I hope she can?"

"I can," Ashley promised. "Ian, Vic's a good guy. I've heard about Scott and Jax, but I've never met them before. I think we need to at least consider it."

"When are you guys looking to move in?" I asked. "Assuming we let you, that is?"

"If you say now, we'll be hauling over boxes this evening," Vic told me. "I haven't been in my bear form in months. We can't live like this, so we're willing to do anything you ask, even if that's locking ourselves away on the full moon."

"No," Ashley said, looking at her brother. "Ian, you can't ask anyone to do that. And if this isn't exactly what you wanted, then I don't know what is."

"But we have to figure out how to make this work with the pack," Ian countered.

"So we talk to them," I said, turning my attention to the bears. "Can you three get me a list of anything you'd need, and then another of what you'd like to have but can live

27

without?" Then I groaned, realizing how bad that sounded. "Look, I've only known about shifters since the end of October, so please don't take this wrong, but this is our pack. It's our family, and they have to come first. I know exactly nothing about bears, but if we want to even have a chance of this not becoming a bigger problem, we need you to be honest with us, so we can be honest with you."

"Does this mean you'll consider it?" Vic asked.

Scott, however, was scribbling on the back of one of the floor plans. "Even if they don't, man, we have to try. Worst case, we're right back where we started."

"And we can help," Jax told me. "Kid gets stuck in a tree? Bears climb. We're strong. We're also a lot more calm than you'd expect. We're more than willing to work as a little muscle." He flashed me a smile. "Like, say, helping a new wolf learn to use her legs?"

"That's my job," Ashley told him. "Leave my almost-sister-in-law out of this."

"Just sayin'," Jax told her. "Ashley, Vic said you're kinda in charge of this, right?"

"Yeah..." She glanced at her brother. "It's complicated, guys."

"All I'm saying," Jax insisted, "is that we aren't looking for a handout. You're a pack, and while I don't really get that urge, we're willing to learn how to be a part of that. Believe it or not, bears have families too. I also kinda like doggies."

Her eyes narrowed as she watched him. "I am no dog, Teddy Ruxpin."

"Well, I *am* a teddy bear," Jax assured her.

Then Scott pulled out the paper and offered it to me.

"A list, just like you asked," he said. "And I'm sorry that I don't know your title - "

"Alpha," Ashley told him.

"Uh..." Scott flicked a finger at Ian. "And him?"

"Also Alpha," Ashley said. "My little brother leads the pack. His mate is kinda like the vice president of the pack. The Pack Alpha and the Alpha Mate are the positions. Alpha Male for him and Alpha Female to her, but could be any gender, and Alpha Mate is a genderless term. Both leaders of the pack are simply called Alpha - for short - as a sign of respect."

"Elena is fine," I assured him.

Scott smiled at me in appreciation. "Yeah, cuz that whole thing is kinda confusing. Well, if you have any questions, I put our numbers at the bottom. Talk it over. Ask us anything you want. And we can also pass as humans, due to our darker eye color. Yeah, we just want to help out."

"No," Vic said. "We want a place where we can live safely. A lot of us do, and with that video going around, Wolf's Run is the talk of the shifter world. I would've assumed a lot more of us would've come forward."

"They have," Ian admitted. "We just haven't had the chance to come to a decision."

Vic licked his lips even as his eyes darted between the three of us. "Please?" he breathed. "We're dying out there, and I don't know what else to do. Just... consider it?"

"We will," I said, "but I can't promise more than that."

"It's a start," Vic decided, but something in his tone sounded defeated, and it grabbed my heart and twisted it in a way I really didn't like.

CHAPTER 4

The three bears stood to leave, so I pushed to my feet and offered them my hand. I was a little ashamed that my mate had been brave enough to do it when I hadn't, so I was correcting that now. Still, the size of these men was more intimidating than I wanted to admit. The smallest of the lot was only an inch shorter than me, and the guy probably had a good fifty pounds or more of muscle on him.

In other words, one of them could kick my ass without trying. All three of them together? Myself and my betas combined wouldn't stand a chance. I didn't like that. The idea of allowing other shifters to live in Wolf's Run sounded nice in theory, but seeing those guys made me realize how easy it would be for them to simply take over.

And yet, the fact that Elena was invested made me want to find a way to make this work. Still, they'd terrified her. Granted, she'd never smelled a bear before, let alone anything else. Her enhanced senses were still new. She should be home, sitting in front of the TV, being spoiled for a few more days - which was my biggest issue. Every protective urge in my body was telling me to keep those threats as far as possible from my vulnerable mate.

"I'm trying to be rational," I admitted once the bears were truly gone, "but I don't think we can do this."

"We have to," Elena said before Ashley could even talk.

My sister's mouth hung open, making it clear her best friend had stolen the words from her mouth. So she tried a new line. "Ian, Vic's a good guy. He found a way to make living with two other bears work, so I think he's a great trial for our idea of integrating other shifters."

"So..." Elena turned her full attention on Ashley. "Anything else we should know about them?"

"Not with my brother sitting beside you, nope."

My eyes narrowed. "What did you do, Ash?"

"Nothing!" she insisted. "Look, you're the one who keeps telling me I need to meet someone. So I went to a bar to meet someone. And when I went to buy myself a shot, a man paid for it. I turned around, thinking I was going to tell him off, and I got a faceful of bear. Vic made it clear that he was just happy to see another shifter, and then we ended up talking."

"Uh huh," Elena teased, a little smile twisting her lips like she was fighting it.

"Just talk?" I asked.

Ashley shrugged that off. "He asked where the local wolf pack was. I told him there are two. Wolf's Run in town, and Hidden Forest just outside. He asked which one I was with, so I told him I ran the office here. That was almost a month ago. Maybe more, and well before the video came out. He's nice, Ian. A lot calmer than you are, and that says a lot."

"He terrified Elena," I snapped.

My mate dropped her hand on my arm. "Ian, I'm fine. I was having a panic attack because I could smell something, and their eyes weren't like wolves, but you'd all said that colors changed, and I was wondering if I'd even be able to recognize a human. So I was trying to figure out how to handle these people who I couldn't identify, but being bears makes sense. I'm fine. I'm just learning, ok?"

I just dropped my head to massage my brow. "Lane is going to end up attacking one of them."

"I'll make sure he doesn't," Elena promised. "Ian, we have to help them. Didn't you hear him? Vic said that they haven't been able to shift!"

"Uh..." Ashley sucked a breath through her teeth. "Yeah, that's not as uncommon as you'd think. Before we had the community, we'd need to make sure the hunters weren't out, and certain times of year - like deer season - were not safe times to run."

"But we have this place," Elena insisted, "so shouldn't we help others? I mean, isn't that the point?"

"It's to help *wolves*," Ashley said. "That's why it's Wolf's Run. Elena, it's taken generations for us to finally be able to make this happen. Most shifters move so often they don't have the chance to get good jobs, get promotions, and invest in a project like this. Is it really fair for us to use our pack's resources to help others instead of all those wolves out there who are still struggling?"

"And the bears aren't?" she asked. "Or the foxes, or whatever other things have already asked about it? Why does it only have to be one?" Her head whipped around to look at me. "Just the White people? Just the Asians? Just the Jewish or Christians, or whatever category you're going to claim you're a part of? Why can't we help those who need it most?"

"And where do we draw the line?" I asked her.

"At the boundary of the land," she told me. "Look, those who live here already? Great. But why should we take a self-sufficient wolf when there's a group of bears who are struggling? And why can't those guys become a part of a bigger pack? Why shouldn't we try to accept that their culture can complement ours?"

Ashley was smiling at her proudly. "That," she told me, "is why I said she should move here. We've spent our entire lives being raised to think only about wolves and what wolves need. Elena didn't. She's had to struggle, she's found success, and she's felt the persecution those bears are running from. Ian, I actually agree with her."

I blew out a breath, knowing I was already defeated. Oddly, I wasn't that upset by it, but I was trying hard to think of my pack first, not just the desperation on those men's faces. So, refusing to give in yet, I gestured to the paper Elena still held.

"Well, let's see their requirements."

She passed it over, and I scanned the hastily-scrawled notes. The bears wanted a house with modern facilities so they could be presentable for a job. They asked for access to at least one tree, preferably three. A set schedule when they would be allowed to be outside shifted, and a request to use the trails for at least the end of the full moon's course. An hour, they'd asked for. That was it.

I had to read it again, because that wasn't much. No, it was pathetic. If this was a list for my pack, I would've added in ten times that as simple necessities, but those bears were asking for only the bare minimum for their survival. Reading through it again, I felt tingles in my fingers as it dawned on me exactly how desperate they really were.

"What if the other wolves won't tolerate them?" I asked, the words coming out as little more than a breath.

"We'll convince them to," Elena assured me. "Ian, this pack trusts you. If you, your betas, and your family all accept them, then the other wolves will too."

"And the Sisterhood," Ashley said.

Wait, that was the first I was hearing of this. "What sisterhood?"

"Our Thursday night wine club," Ashley clarified. "Me, Elena, Kim, Heather, and Bridget. Kim's an alpha, Bridget's the pack's doctor - "

"Crap," Elena breathed. "We need to make sure she's on board with this." And she headed over to her desk.

I watched her while still talking to Ashley. "Ok, so basically the pillars of the pack. Ash, do you really think we can do this?"

"We have to," Elena said.

Ashley just thrust a hand back toward her. "What she said."

"There has never been a mixed-species community before," I reminded her.

"And there's never been a pack willing to make its

home in the middle of a modern, bustling town either," she countered. "You tackled the first, so why not the rest?"

"Rest?"

Ashley nodded. "Yeah. Bears, cats, foxes, birds... What about Gabby's covenant? I mean, wouldn't that help? We are shifters living in a world where we're bound to be discovered. A mixed-species community would give us all a chance if we're ever discovered. This place gives us protection from the hordes if they try to kill us. And, wolves are the most social of all the shifters. Sure, foxes have their... Are they skulks?"

"Yeah," I said.

She nodded and kept going. "But foxes live in smaller family groups. Wolves bring in families until the area can't support us. It only makes sense for us to handle this. We already have a social structure in place for organizing it. You, Alpha. Elena, as the community liaison. Me, for business management. We have a doctor; we have assistants to help you - the betas. It's already in place just because of our very nature. Those bears would have to start from nothing and fumble through all of it."

"And," Elena said, holding up her phone, "Bridget said that she's worked on non-wolf shifters before, but only a few. I think we need to have a little meeting and start working this out."

"When?" I asked. "You have Gabby's party next weekend."

Elena smiled at me a little too sweetly. "Tonight?"

Which was the moment that I realized this was definitely happening. She had no interest in putting this off, not even for a day. Elena felt it was serious. Ashley was on her side. I had a funny feeling that Gabby would be even more emphatic. Lane would go with anything that mattered to Elena. Seth had already made it clear that he was for integrating the other shifters. So, at best, it would be me, Pax, Trent, and possibly my father trying to stand against them.

And I knew that all of us would give in.

This was happening. One way or another, we were going to end up with bears living with us. The only question now was how to make that happen as smoothly as possible. Oh, I already knew we'd end up with mistakes, and possibly some critical ones. I only hoped that we could work it all out in theory before having to suffer through trial by fire.

"Ok," I told them both. "Ashley, you talk to Dad. Elena, tell Bridget we're going to need her expertise tonight. Let's say dinner at my house. Um, seven?"

"Dinner?" she asked.

I just nodded. "I have a feeling this is going to be a long talk, and it's not a decision I want to make on my own. Bring Gabby. Ash will bring Dad. Myself, my betas... Bridget. Who else do we need?"

"It would be easier if we could talk to the bears," Ashley admitted.

"One of them," I told her. "Probably Vic, because I get the impression that he's the one in charge."

"Largest," she corrected. "Ian, bears don't have alphas. They don't do dominance. Vic takes charge because he can, not because he's responsible. But sure, I can ask him to come alone. I can't promise he'll like it, though."

"I'm not going to pick a fight," I promised.

She just tilted her head to the side and glared at me. "Would you do it? Walk into another wolf pack without your betas at your side?"

Damn it, but she had a point. "Ok. Tell him I'd prefer he comes alone, but if he doesn't feel safe, then he can bring his... friends?"

"We're going to need a lot of food," Elena mumbled.

"You," I told her, "are not cooking. You're still recovering. I have no intention of keeping you away, but can you *please* take it easy?"

"Dad and I will handle the food," Ashley promised. "Trent and Pax can cook. Lane can worry about you, Elena, and Seth can explain everything to Gabby so she doesn't have a meltdown when she's face to face with the bears."

"Which means I need to at least clean my house," I grumbled. "Baby, I'm sending Lane over to spend lunch with you. Just..." I sighed. "Please don't push yourself?"

"And make sure he knows that my senses have me reacting to new things but that I'm not worried about it?" Elena nodded to show she'd guessed what I'd ask for next - although I'd planned to ask that of Ashley. "I'll make sure he knows," she continued, "because this is a good thing, Ian. It really is."

I closed the distance between us and wrapped my arms around her. "I really hope you're right, because I don't want to let my pack down."

"No," she mumbled against my chest. "You're making it stronger. Believe it or not, diversity is a good thing. Ask Seth if you don't believe me."

I intended to do just that. Oh, I wouldn't tell her, but I

37

was going to spend the rest of the afternoon learning every single thing I could about bears, about integrating communities, and then I'd see where that took me. Because when my mate wanted something, I had this overwhelming desire to find a way to make it happen. Mostly because she had a habit of being right.

CHAPTER 5

I an left eventually. Ashley headed back to her office to "look something up," she said. I went back to finishing that insane amount of email inquiries, but then I noticed the clipboard. One of the guys had managed to fill it out in the middle of our talk. Beside it, Ian had left the floor plan with the bears' list of requirements on the back.

I read through it. The part about the trees gutted me. They wanted access to a tree, preferably three? That was it?! For a long moment, I just sat there, staring at the words and fighting this feeling in my chest. It took me much too long to figure out the name for it, but it felt the same as when I made rules for my daughter.

Protective.

Once, Ian had mentioned that seeing me mowing my lawn with a broken mower had set off his protective instincts, and I had a funny feeling I was getting a crash course in how those worked. I wanted to make things easier for those men. The way they'd stepped back when they realized I was stressed out? How defeated Vic had looked just before they'd left?

On impulse, I dug in my purse for my phone and called in my secret weapon. The phone only rang twice before it was answered with a rushed, "Mom, are you ok?"

"I'm fine, Gabby," I promised. "But I need my Alpha-pup's help. Get in touch with your friends, and find out everything you can about the other shifters, would you? Specifically bears, but I have a feeling we'll need to know about all of them. Add foxes to the list because they've been mentioned. And then we're having dinner at Ian's tonight to deal with some pack stuff."

"What stuff?" she asked.

I pushed out a breath. "Gabby, a group of bears came in today, and they asked if we'd consider letting them live here. I want to find a way to make that work, but the wolves think like wolves."

"And we think like Latinas," she realized. "Ok. You cool with my friends all coming over? We can hit this hard. Wait, what time is dinner?"

"Seven," I told her. "And I want to make sure that Ian can't say no. I don't think he wants to, but I get this feeling that he assumes he has to. Let's change his mind?"

"On it, Mom," she promised. "And tell Seth that the counter is not a subtle place for condoms? Seriously?"

I groaned. "Look - "

But she cut me off. "I don't need condoms, ok? Not doing that."

"I'd rather they were there if you need them, *mija*, because I'm not ready to be a grandmother. That is not permission to use them, just a backup plan."

"Well, when you find them by the tampons, don't think the wrong thing. I don't need Roman coming over and getting the wrong idea!" She honestly sounded mortified.

"Put them in the tampon box," I suggested. "He won't look there. And Gabby? I'm proud of you for waiting."

"And now I'm feeling sick," she teased. "No more sex talks, Mom! I'm going to dive into bears so I can pretend like this never happened!"

And she hung up on me, but I was trying hard not to laugh. Over the last six months, I felt like my relationship with my little girl had gotten so much better. The fact that we could even have that talk? To me, it was pretty amazing. I also didn't believe that she'd wait as long as she thought. Not my child - but I didn't want her sexuality to be treated like a prize for a boy to win. I wanted it to be a trophy that *she* could be proud of, and it seemed my fumbling attempts might even be working.

But speaking of sex, I pushed back my chair and headed into Ashley's office. My muscles were already feeling a bit better for moving around, but I still moved like an old woman. It also didn't matter, because I had every intention of sitting down for this chat. Tapping at Ashley's office door, I stepped in without waiting for an answer to find my best friend scouring a very old book.

"Hey," she greeted me. "Everything still ok?"

"What's in the book?" I asked as I took the chair across from her desk.

She stuck a slip of paper between the pages and closed it so I could see the cover. "It's a very old history of shapeshifters. The first copy was written about the time of the Spanish Inquisition, and I have no idea how many times it's been translated, but it's mostly correct. It was also written by a human, and is treated as medieval bunk, but I was hoping for a few tips on bears."

"Mhm." I was struggling not to smirk at her. "And you didn't figure anything out when you screwed him?"

"Didn't really spend a lot of time talking," she admitted, looking up with a devious twinkle in her eye. "And thanks for not making that too obvious to my brother."

"Is that a line that shouldn't be crossed or something?"

She just shrugged. "It's kinda taboo, but I honestly don't know if there's an actual problem with it." Then she moved the book back to one of her desk drawers. "The truth is that most of us don't really mingle with the others. We're all predators, and one species tends to be the kind that eats another. While we don't actually do that, our stupid instincts kinda freak out - like yours did earlier. So, wolves avoid bears, foxes avoid wolves, and birds avoid foxes."

"And cats?" I asked.

She sighed. "I know pretty much nothing about them, and I've never met one in person. Not a lion, a tiger, or anything else."

Which brought up another question. "How many types of shifters are there?"

Ashley just lifted her hands and shrugged. "No idea. Wolves are the most common because we tend to have the biggest packs, which means the least difficulties in the real world. I had a friend who met a panther shifter once - or so she claimed. Rumors have snake shifters in Central America, but I have never met anyone who's seen one. So, no clue." Then she sighed, and it was much too heavy. "Am I crazy for wanting to help these guys?"

"No," I assured her. "Ash, I want to as well. There was

something so sad about them, and did you see their list? They asked for access to three trees! Just three. Not the entire nature trails. Not a safe space to run as bears. Not heavy-duty scratching posts like they have at the zoo. They asked for three trees, and it felt like they didn't think they'd be allowed more."

"Shit," she breathed.

I nodded because I understood exactly what she meant. "So, being a new wolf and all, is it even possible for the rest of the pack to get along with them?"

"I think so," she told me, "but Ian has a point about the kids. What would a three-year-old think of meeting Vic? Hell, even Scott's kinda scary in his own way."

"I actually thought he was kinda cute." And I lifted a brow, making it clear I expected her to expand on that.

Right on cue, she laughed. "It was one night, and it was with Vic, and it isn't supposed to ever be talked about." But she leaned closer, making it clear she had every intention of talking. "Although it was a very memorable night."

"So?" I asked. "You going there again? Maybe testing out his friends?"

"No." She waved that off. "You saw how Ian reacted. Now, just imagine my dad. Lane? Yeah, that would not do anyone any favors. If those guys want a chance of moving in, then I need to keep my hands off all of their big, massive... muscles."

"Oh, so bears are hung?" I teased.

"Vic is." She couldn't stop grinning. "And there aren't a lot of men in this world who can pin me down, but he sure can."

"Oh, so you have a thing for teddy bears, hm? You sure

you can't make this work? C'mon, Ash, how long has it been since you saw the same guy twice?"

"There's a reason for that," she reminded me.

"Yeah, because a decade ago, your friend and mate were assholes. But that was them! Vic isn't even a wolf. I also have a feeling that if you actually like the guy, then Ian and Henry will give him a chance."

"No," she said. "Elena, cross-species stuff? It doesn't happen. What if we could infect each other? Would that kill us? Make us some wolf-bear monster? It's just not worth it. There's a reason shifters stick with our own kind or humans. If a human gets our disease, we get fresh blood - to put it as bluntly as possible. The only downside is someone shifting, but mixing our diseases?"

"Is it even possible?" I asked.

All she could do was shrug. "No idea. That's why it's a lot better to just let that one night be one night, and not think about them that way. So, I'd really appreciate it if you didn't say anything to the guys? I don't want them to think I'm only trying to move these bears in because I slept with one!"

"Are you?" I made sure there was no judgment in the question.

Ashley let out another heavy sigh. "I honestly don't know. Vic's a great guy. He's easy to talk to, and he's not like most men I meet, you know? He doesn't stare at my tits or think I'm some conquest he can brag about later. He's... nice. Smart. Considerate, even. So, yeah, I want to help him, but I also think the bears deserve a whole lot more than they're getting."

"Me too," I agreed. "Besides, I think you nailed it when you brought up Ian's initial plans. He wanted to make

Wolf's Run into a test of sorts. To modernize shifter society, right? To bring our kind into this new digital world?"

"Our," Ashley repeated. "I kinda like hearing you say that."

"And I love saying it, but that's not the point. You brought me here to see if humans could be persuaded to accept wolves. Well, I did - eventually. Samantha and that other boy, um..."

"Theo," Ashley supplied. "The one who has a crush on Roman. Yep, Pax and Trent think it's cute, so I got cornered into asking Kim if her son might swing both ways. She doesn't think he does, which is sad because that's just too cute."

"And I'm not sure how Gabby would feel about her boyfriend cheating on her," I pointed out.

Ashley huffed like I was an idiot. "Gabby isn't going to have one boyfriend, Elena. She'll end up with a whole group, just like her mom. I mean, she's dating her beta."

Crap. She probably would. All this time, I'd been thinking that she'd be in Ian's situation, sharing her lover with Olivia and her betas, but Roman said he was both her beta and mate! If he wasn't completely straight, then it would be a lot easier for my daughter, which meant Ashley had a point.

"Well, damn," I said. "Although, I'd really rather not think about her having sex yet. I don't have that problem with you, though. So, do bears share?"

She laughed. "I'm not dating the bears, Elena. Not happening."

"But they seem lonely," I teased. "It would be the

neighborly thing to do. Just, you know, a blow job here, a little threesome there..."

"No!" she insisted, but she was laughing too hard to sound serious. "Do not even make me imagine it, because we're trying to focus on Wolf's Run, not the super-sexy trio of bears who make me think that we need a public pool for the summer."

"Mhm," I agreed. "Or just lease them a house with a hot tub like your brother has?"

"I'm never getting in that hot tub again!" she swore. "I don't even want to think about what's floating in that water now. Eww!"

"You really don't," I teased. "But, now, their hot tub... Or maybe you should get one? Just, you know, invite the guys over and see how relaxed they get?"

"I live next to my father," she reminded me. "So, no. Just no. But I kinda like how you assume those bears are going to get to move in."

I pushed to my feet. "I just called Gabby and told her to put the teens on it. She'll show up armed with information and a plan, and I'm pretty sure Ian won't expect that."

"So, you're ok with this?" Ashley asked.

I nodded. "Reading that list?" And I gestured to my belly. "It makes something in here feel weird. The same way it feels when Gabby needs me. I'm guessing that's the protective thing we get as wolves, right?"

"Sounds like it," she admitted.

"So, why am I feeling overly protective for a group of bears? Maybe because I don't know any better? Because I'm the Alpha Mate? Or could it just be because it's the right thing to do? Ash, those bears need a home. Wolf's

Run can figure out a way to make room for them. If we don't, are we actually the good guys here?"

"Then we need to figure out how to do it with the least amount of hassles," she decided. "Go forward the phones to voicemail. I'll tell Dad to pull everything he's got on bears. And for the rest of the day, you and I are going to come up with a plan. If we all have some idea of what's needed, then it'll make it that much easier to put this together."

I nodded and headed towards the door. "I'm not backing down on this, Ash."

"Which is why we're dropping everything else, Elena. If it means that much to you, then Ian is already outvoted - and not dumb enough to pull rank without knowing he'll be sleeping alone for weeks. The bears are in - we just have to figure out how."

CHAPTER 6

Trent and I were hauling brush from the culverts, clearing the winter deadfall and enjoying the almost-warm day when my phone rang. Letting out a heavy sigh, I released the handful of brush because I recognized the ringtone, but it had already rolled to voicemail before I had my gloves off and my phone out of my pocket. Seeing the name on the screen, I didn't bother to listen to the message, just called Ian back.

He answered immediately. "Hey, stop what you're doing and come home. I need my betas, because we just had something come up."

My heart slammed to a halt. "Is Elena ok?"

"She's fine," he promised, which allowed me to breathe again. "But we had some bears show up in the office today."

And my heart stopped again. At this rate, I'd die before I even ended the call. "What?!"

"Bears," Ian repeated. "Three of them, and they want to move in."

"With Elena?"

The bastard laughed. "Yeah, I was trying to avoid that part. She's fine, a little surprised, and still doing great, but it was a little tense for a bit there."

"There were bears in the office, and you think she's fine? Damn it, Ian! She was probably panicking. I've met a bear before, and *I* wanted to run. How the fuck do you think a new convert's going to react?"

"Better than I did," he told me. "Pax, she was shocked, but Ashley knew one of the guys, and that seemed to be all Elena needed to relax. I was ready to throw down, and our mate walked over and shook their hands. She's fine. I'm still recovering, but she is actually ok. The problem is that they came seeking sanctuary. They want to move into the community, and Elena wants to have a meeting about it."

"Ok, so cancel all of our plans for the weekend," I guessed, looking up to catch Trent's eye.

My best friend was hanging on every word, and from the color of his face, he was desperately waiting for me to fill in the pieces he couldn't hear. Granted, he could probably catch most of what Ian was saying over the phone. Wolf hearing and all that.

"Tonight," Ian corrected.

"What?" Trent asked, snatching the phone from my hand. "She needs to be in bed and resting," he told our Alpha.

"And I agree," Ian said, his voice muffled against the side of Trent's face. "Look, I wanted to talk about it next week, but Elena's adamant, and we all know that she'll push and fret unless we do this. So, I agreed to have dinner at our place with pretty much every wolf who has a say in this community. Dad, Gabby, Bridget, Ash, and us. Here's the kicker. Elena wants the bears there too, because she's adamant that we need to help them."

"Shit," Trent breathed. "Call Seth."

"I'm dealing with Lane," Ian said. "I need you two to get Seth and get home. Leave the rest. It's lasted this long, so what's one more day, right?"

I laughed. "Tell him we should hire the bears to clean up the brush and trail area, then we won't be so far behind."

"Heard that," Ian said. "Just get Seth? He's doing a check of the new houses on Tundra Street. Make sure he knows that Elena's ok, and then I need all of you back here to either help me hold down Lane or clean the house. New convert kind of clean, guys. Not for the guests, but because Elena's coming, and I do not want her any more stressed than she already must be."

"On it," Trent said before ending the call and passing my phone back. "Shit."

"Bears," I breathed. "And she's fine?"

"Dunno," Trent said, pulling out his own phone, "but I know who will." He pressed a few buttons and then lifted it to his ear. "Ash? Is she ok? We heard there were bears in the office."

"She's fine," Ashley promised. "She's doing amazing, and she says moving makes her feel better. She's not snappish or paranoid, either. Elena is just fine." Then she paused. "Yeah, and the bears triggered her protective urges. She wants to take care of them."

"Shit," I breathed. "I knew we shouldn't have let her go to work. Her instincts are going to be all over the place."

"This is her," Ashley said, raising her voice, which made me realize that was for me. "Guys, she's always cared about others. It's what makes her so nice, and the entire reason I thought she'd be a good human test case. Elena is a mother. Not just of her daughter, but one of those 'care for everyone she can' types. And..."

"What?" Trent demanded. "Ash, what's going on?"

"The bears are desperate," Ashley finished. "Not for a house, but for survival. It got under Elena's skin, and she's already sunk her teeth into this. You aren't going to change her mind. The bears are moving in. The only thing we have to figure out is how to do that without making more problems. And I'm supposed to invite the Kodiak bear to dinner with us."

"Fuck," Trent groaned. "A Kodiak? Not just a brown or a black, but the biggest bear shifter besides a polar bear?"

"Yeah," she said. "But there's a grizzly and a black bear too. They all might come, although I'm trying to keep it to just Vic."

This time, I was the one snatching the phone from Trent, because something about her tone made me wonder. "What did you do, Ash?" I demanded.

"I met the guy at a bar. He bought me a drink. We talked shifters. It was weeks and weeks ago, but when the video came out, he remembered that I said I worked here, and that's why they came."

"Ash..." I warned.

"Don't, Pax," she almost growled. "Do not push me, because I will push back."

Which meant she'd slept with the guy. I knew Ian's big sister well enough to know that pushing the boundaries was something she excelled at, and this was right up her alley. The woman had refused to even date since her mate and beta had run off together. Falling into another shifter's bed was the kind of risk she'd think was exciting enough to distract her.

"How long ago?" I demanded.

"End of January?" she guessed. "Well before the school shooting. Could've been middle of January. I don't know, Pax."

"So, you're ok? No side effects? Condom?"

"Pax!"

"Just answer the fucking question," I snapped.

"I'm fine," she promised. "Stop worrying about me."

"It's never going to happen," I assured her. "You're more my sister than my real siblings are, and this is definitely something you'd do. Just tell me that you're not going to die because of it?"

"If you so much as breathe a word to Ian," she warned. "Or you, Trent, because I know you're still standing right there."

"Not saying a thing," Trent promised. "And if Pax wants to talk to Elena again, he won't either."

Fuck, but he was right. I ducked my head and pushed out my concern in a heavy breath. "We'll ask the awkward questions, Ash, so Ian and Lane don't get the wrong idea, ok? Is Bridget coming?"

"Elena already invited her. And, truth be told, I think this is good for her. She looks normal, and she's been asking about her new emotions and senses, so she's not even being stupid about it. I'll handle her, ok? She doesn't get embarrassed when talking about these things to me."

"Does she know you slept with those bears?" I asked.

"One," Ashley corrected, "and she guessed the same way you did. So, suck it up, do what needs to be done, because we're being all official tonight. Seven. Your place. Be ready."

"Promise," I said, ending the call before passing Trent's phone back. "Well, I guess we need to worry about what happens when the bears end up sleeping with some woman in the pack."

Trent just nodded his head slowly. "Yeah, I can do that. Think we should tell Elena we're in on this?"

"Not until afterwards, because I'm not convinced that she won't smirk or smile at the wrong time. Trent, she should still be in bed, not making cross-shifter treaties!"

"But she's Elena," he reminded me. "She's never realized that it's ok to let someone else do for her, because no one's ever done it before."

"Which means we need to step up our game," I decided. "Her first day on her feet and she came face to face with not just one bear, but three? How the hell did she keep from screaming and running out of that office?"

"She's Elena," he said again. "Look at how she handled finding out about wolves."

"She fainted!"

"That was mostly because she couldn't watch us shift." Then he paused, his eyes flicking to the side. "I wonder if it's different now that she's shifted?"

I waved that away. "We'll worry about that later. Right now, I'm thinking she's putting on her strong face for the rest of us. Trent, those were bears. Plural. In that little lobby. As soon as she smelled them, her body would demand that she get as far away as possible, because bears break wolves."

"And she's still Elena," he countered. "Pax, you know as well as I do that fear has never stopped her. I'm willing to bet her heart was pounding and she wanted to run, but she just lifted her chin, smiled as sweetly as possible, and tried to figure it out on her own. Sounds like Ashley and Ian intervened - although I really want to know how that went down - and now Elena is completely pro-bear. And, don't you dare make her feel weak for this. Right now, she's figuring out her place as a wolf, and I'd kinda like that to be right up there with Ian and Ashley."

"You want her to be an alpha?" I asked.

He nodded. "I want her to finally have everything it takes to believe in herself. Besides, tell me you'd hate having her order us around in bed?"

Ok, he had a point. That would be pretty damned hot. It also chased off the last of my worries about her. Letting out a laugh, I slapped his arm and tilted my head back toward where we'd parked.

"C'mon. We're supposed to tell Seth about this."

Trent kicked at the brush, making it into something resembling a pile. "I kinda like your idea of hiring the bears to do this shit."

"And, if Elena's already on board with them moving in, it's one more reason to convince Ian it'll work." We started walking back toward where we'd parked.

"What if it doesn't?" Trent asked. "Not Ian, but the working part, Pax. What if this is a very bad idea? I mean, wolves and bears?"

"If Ashley can crawl into bed with one and live to talk

about it, then I think we can figure out how to live beside them."

He nodded. "Point. But is this going to push the other wolves too far? The last thing Wolf's Run needs right now is someone challenging Ian's right to lead us, and this is exactly the sort of thing that would cause a rift like that."

"We made it through Karen," I reminded him. "He kicked out the daughter of an original wolf bloodline, and the pack thanked him. I think we just need to make sure we present it properly."

"Democracy?" Trent asked.

I could only shrug, heading around the front of the truck to call back at him, "Let's not go that far. I think we can add in some democratic aspects, though. I mean, that's kinda been what we've been doing for the last few years, isn't it?"

"But wolves don't do..." He paused to climb into the driver's seat. "...Democracy like humans."

"So we'll have to figure out a wolfish way to do it," I decided. "I have a feeling our converts will be the ones to ask about that. They have both the instincts of a wolf and the memories of a human. Somewhere in all of that, there has to be the answer."

"And Elena's a convert," he reminded me, glancing over with a smile. "I bet she already has a few ideas.

I actually hoped so, because I liked the idea. Sure, I could see the problems with it, but if we could make this work? It would change everything I'd ever known about shifter society. Our pup was a converted alpha. Our mate was clearly something amazing. Our pack was living in the middle of modern society without a problem, and we'd already handled someone getting a video of a wolf in mid-shift. Those converts that most of our society laughed at had been the answer for that, so why couldn't they help us fix this?

And if they could, then that might be the biggest change of all of this. Converts would no longer be treated as lesser. Sure, they were different from natural-born wolves, but it seemed they came with their own set of advantages, and we'd already figured out how to train Seth and Gabby to embrace their new bodies. If we were lucky, this might be the next stage in shifter society, and I had every intention of making that into a good thing.

CHAPTER 7

T hat evening, Gabby and I headed over fifteen minutes early. My daughter had both her laptop and a spiral notebook filled with notes she'd made. Evidently, Olivia and Roman knew quite a bit about the other shifters, and it had given my kid a place to start. Gabby had taken that, pulled up articles about cultural diversity, and then researched various integration issues throughout history.

She'd tackled this like it was some research project for school, but with a lot more enthusiasm. Granted, she'd never put this much effort into school before, but I was not about to complain. She said she had a few ideas, and I honestly couldn't wait to hear them.

I'd taken another one of those muscle relaxers, but it hadn't quite kicked in when we reached Ian's house. I tapped at the door and walked in, making sure to give them a bit of notice, but we weren't the first to arrive. Bridget and Henry were in the living room talking to Seth and Lane. I could hear Pax and Trent in the backyard. There was no sign of Ian or Ashley, though.

"Hey," Bridget said, smiling at Gabby. "So, bears, huh?" she asked.

I nodded. "Three of them."

"Well..." She dragged the word out for emphasis. "Ash is waiting for the head bear to show up, and said she'd give him a ride over."

"And Ian?" I asked.

Seth jerked his thumb towards their den. "Still reading."

"I brought stuff too," Gabby said, partially lifting her laptop to show what she meant.

"Uh..." Seth waved her over. "Find a spot in the den. I think we're doing dinner first as a meet and greet, and then we'll get into the details after the food's gone."

"Yeah, but I have some ideas," Gabby told him.

He just beamed at her proudly. "Me too. So you're pro-bear, huh?"

"Duh," she teased before heading for the den.

The whole time, Lane was watching me. "You're ok with this?" he asked.

"They asked for three trees," I told him. "No. They asked for one, and hoped they could possibly get three. Now think about that, Lane?"

He made his way around Henry and right over to me, dropping his massive hands on my shoulders. "That feeling? It's what separates alphas and betas from the rest of the pack. It's what makes us leaders, little bunny. It's a hard thing to ignore, but if you do this, will Gabby be the one who ends up paying for it?"

"Not me!" Gabby called from the other room. "I'm pro-bear, Lane."

His eyes never left mine, but Lane's lips curled into a smile. "What about Kim's kids? What about the babies who'll smell a bear and be terrified?"

"But will they?" I asked. "If bears are always around, and a natural part of the society, would a baby really be more scared of one than of any other stranger? And, if they learn to accept bears, and lions, and foxes from an early age, wouldn't that make it even easier on all of us?"

He slowly bobbed his head. "So, you think you could balance that? The urge to take care of those little babies who are scared of the monsters and the monsters who need help?"

"I think that before I was a wolf, there were people in this world who would've called me a monster, so yes." I caught his hand. "These men need help. We're in a position to help. When I was sleeping off my first run as a wolf, you were all talking about other shifters wanting to live here, and you all sounded like it was a real possibility, so why is this a problem now?"

"Because they scared you," he told me. "That's the only reason. I will not have someone living here that makes you afraid to leave your house. Elena, you're a wolf now, and that means we can stop treating you like a human. We don't have to hide our need to step up or stand between you and anything you don't like. I don't want to lose that perfection before I've gotten the chance to enjoy it."

"And I'm not the entire pack," I reminded him.

"You are to me." He reached up to cup my face. "You're my mate, and if that means I have to step down as a beta to keep you safe, then I will. I don't want to, but I will if I have to. That's why we're trying to think this through. Not because we don't want to help, but because we don't want to ruin everything just when it's getting good."

"With me?" I asked.

It was Henry who answered. "With all of Wolf's Run, Elena. We've made it through both of you turning. We've handled the video and having a human step in to help - and that's a bigger deal than you know. Never before have wolves been saved by humans, and the girl has been made an honorary pack member."

"Why honorary?" Gabby asked, stepping back into the room. "Why can't she just be my beta?"

"She can," he assured her. "Although that's never been done before either. But she's honorary because she doesn't live here. No other reason. When she's old enough to move into the community, she'll be a full member. Right now, she's still a kid, and so are you, little pup."

Gabby rolled her eyes at him. "Whatever, old dog," she said with a smile.

Surprisingly, Henry grinned. "Go set the table, Gabby. Ashley should be here - "

He didn't even get to finish before the door opened. "I brought company!" Ashley announced.

I turned to see Vic - and only Vic - following her in. The man was dressed in a nice button-down shirt, a clean and well-fitting pair of jeans, and he looked like he'd cleaned up for this. He also paused just inside the door even as Ashley kept walking.

Lane turned and glared at the man. "You?" he asked.

"Be nice," Ashley warned him as she continued around the corner, clearly heading for the den.

"Vic," I said, heading toward him. "It's ok, you're allowed to come all the way inside."

He smiled, but then his eyes jumped up to land on the men behind me. "I'm trying very hard to be small and non-threatening, and I'm getting the feeling that it's not working."

"You aren't small," Lane told him.

"You aren't either," Vic pointed out. "What the hell kind of wolf are you?"

"A line old enough that we don't know," Lane admitted. "I also spent a couple of years living wild." He pointed at his eyes. "So, a little more yellow than most. You? Born a bear?"

"Turned as a kid. I was twelve. Dad took me hunting. We came across a massive Kodiak, and Dad decided to shoot. Bear fought for all he was worth, mauled the hell out of me, and Dad ran. The bear grabbed me by the leg, and I was too hurt to do more than cry about it. Was sure I was dead. And then he shifted into this old asshole of a man. Got a real quick lesson on what was about to happen, turned five days later on the full moon - which peaked during the day - and my family spent the entire time searching for me. Well, they found me about a day after I turned, but I was just a little too healed up. After that, they never acted the same, so I left Alaska and moved south when I was old enough."

"And the bear who turned you?" Henry asked.

Vic's eyes jumped over to him. "You have a title, sir?"

"Not anymore," Henry assured him. "Ian and Ashley are my kids."

"Ah." Vic nodded. "Well, between the age of twelve and eighteen, I would seek him out. Sometimes I found him, other times I didn't. He taught me what I needed, made it clear he didn't want me on his territory, and I used college as a reason to get the hell off his land. And, here I am."

A single laugh came from the side of the room. I looked over to find Ian standing there with his hand on Gabby's shoulder protectively. "So, a convert, huh? Kinda explains why you're so willing to live with other bears."

"Wasn't as easy to convince them," Vic admitted. "Jax took to the idea easier than Scott, truth be told, even though Scott served a few years with the Marines. But we were all crammed onto the same hillside, all trying to avoid each other, and it wasn't working so good. When the notices of bears in the area started going up, I knew it was time to leave, but they weren't as convinced. Scott took a bullet in the flank, and that changed their minds pretty quick." Then he jerked his chin at Gabby. "You got a title, Miss?"

Ian answered for her. "Next Alpha of Wolf's Run. This is my mate's pup. She turned late last year, and she's got some ideas that might help you."

Vic looked from Gabby to me. "I can see the family resemblance. So... I came alone. The guys said I'm an idiot, but Ashley gave me her word that this isn't a setup."

"It's not," I promised. "Trent? Pax? How's dinner coming?"

"Almost done," Pax assured me, making it clear that they'd also stepped in to get a glimpse of the bear.

"I feel like a spectacle," Vic admitted.

So Bridget pushed her way forward and offered her hand. "Well, I'm Dr. Bridget, the physician around here, and it's a pleasure to meet you, Victor."

"Just Vic," he corrected. "And the pleasure's all mine, Doctor."

"Relax," she told him. "Wolf's Run is a safe place, and you were invited. It's just dinner, and it's just to talk. We simply want to figure out how to make this work without causing more and bigger issues."

Which was when Ashley returned. "Table's set, looks like we have just enough room, and the only one who isn't drinking tonight is Gabby. We'll eat first, and then we dive into pack business?" She made a point of glaring at every single wolf in the house, including me. "If any of you hurt him, just know you're breaking my word. Vic is my friend."

Ashley's words were mostly for Vic, not our pack. I watched the guy's shoulders relax, so I decided to help Ashley a little. Hopefully, if both of us were on his side, then my guys would hold their tongues just enough to keep this from crashing and burning before it had a chance to become something.

"Just like me," I reminded the wolves in the room. "You all gave me a chance before I knew about any of this. So, let's give Vic the same respect." Then I gestured toward the dining room. "Shall we?"

From the corner of my eye, I caught the look Vic gave Ashley. She, however, didn't. His eyes raked across her and a wistful little smile touched his lips. It didn't take a genius to figure out that he still held a bit of a candle for my best friend, and I was going to help her out, one way or another. After all, I did owe her for pushing me at Ian.

On the way to the table, Trent and Pax broke off to head for the grill outside. Seth went for the kitchen. I wanted to help, but Lane grabbed my hand, towing me to my seat and all but forcing me to do nothing. Vic chuckled, making it clear he'd noticed. And that was when Gabby walked right up to him and inhaled deeply.

"You smell good," she said. "Cologne or bear?"

"Bear," he admitted as she made her way around to sit beside me. "You smell like evergreens, little wolf."

She grinned. "I can handle that. So, does being around so many wolves make you nervous?"

"More than you can imagine," he told her. "How old are you anyways?"

"Fifteen on Monday." And she lifted her chin, looking right in his eyes. "How old are you?"

Vic actually laughed this time. "Forty. You are definitely an alpha wolf. Didn't think that was possible for converts."

Gabby just shrugged it off. "Mom and I are special. I think it's because we have good teachers. I'm going to be the first convert to lead a pack."

"Once she learns how to defend herself," I said pointedly. "Don't get ahead of yourself, Gabby."

Vic just leaned closer. "Well, I'll stand with you if I'm allowed in. I think you've got the spunk for it, because it sounds like I'm the first bear you've ever met, and you don't seem scared of me at all."

"I'm not," she said. "See, being different doesn't necessarily make you bad. Just makes you different. Besides, it's not like we're beasts or anything."

"Truer words have never been said," he told her, flicking his eyes over to look at me. "You've got a good kid, Alpha. And I'm serious about standing with her."

"Why?" Ashley asked from behind him.

Vic turned toward her. "Because that kid has the same

look in her eye as you do, Ash. She's not scared of anything. Not bears, not humans, and not the cameras all around us. I also happen to think that the few years I had as a human have helped me survive more than my companions growing up as true-born bears. No offense or anything."

Ashley was slowly nodding. "Well, don't think that sucking up to my niece is going to get you a place in the pack."

"Wouldn't dare," he promised. "Put your hackles down, woman. I'm not here to pick a fight. I just want a real home. That's all, I swear."

Ashley flashed him a smile and turned to claim her chair. "I'm just trying to convince my family that you really aren't a problem." She turned at the sound of the back door opening. "And it looks like dinner is served."

CHAPTER 8

Dinner wasn't bad. The food was good, but the company was tense, so we betas were all being just a little more careful with what we said tonight. No promises, basically. The bear tried his hardest to be enjoyable company, but Ian, Lane, and Ashley were making it hard. Not that they did anything wrong, but Ian was acting like the Pack Alpha, Lane was acting like a fated mate, and Ashley? Well, she was acting like she had a crush on the guy. Vic just let it all slide off. It was actually rather impressive.

Unfortunately, I had no idea how to make any of this easier, so I took over refilling glasses and removing plates. Seth helped, but Pax just watched the bear intently. At one point, I had to nudge him before Vic got the wrong impression. My best friend was being just a little *too* intense for a polite dinner.

However, Gabby seemed to like the guy, and once she took over, there was nothing the rest of us could do. She started telling Vic all about her play, and then about Samantha, who was her first friend at school. Naturally, Vic recognized the girl's name - she had been on the news for a bit. It didn't take him long to figure out that Gabby and her friends had been the ones to defuse the whole situation with the video, and the man was honestly impressed.

The way to get Elena's approval was to approve of her kid. Vic seemed to, which made Lane stop glaring. Pax eventually managed to turn the conversation to inter-shifter concerns, directing his questions to Bridget, and they weren't the easy kind. Things like if we could cross infect each other if there was an accident, and such. Bridget said it wasn't likely. It seemed, like the rest of us, she'd spent the day researching.

"So," Bridget said as I cleared the last of the plates away, "this isn't exactly dinner talk, but from what I've found, our version of lycanthropy and the bear mutation of it - which is called arcanthropy - are very similar. Since we're already infected, the bear version would have no way of infecting us. Think of it as being similar to how humans used cowpox to immunize against smallpox. Same idea. Two different versions of a disease that is much too similar. Doesn't matter what version of therianthropy a person has, it automatically makes them immune to the others. Lycanthropy is simply the most prevalent."

Gabby just raised her hand. "Greek," she said.

"Literally," Bridget teased. "The first part of those words are all from Greek roots. Lycan means wolf, as an example. I don't speak Greek, but I do know the medical terms, and they came from that language. Just trust me that the shifter virus is basically the same thing in different flavors of animal bodies."

"Is there proof of that?" Ian asked.

Bridget nodded. "Yep, although it's not considered a credible source. Seems the Germans played with our kinds a bit in the Second World War. Injecting one type with the blood of another. Their records say that no one gained the ability to be more than one shifter type. Cross-infection isn't a huge worry. Now, with that said, none of these sources are peer-reviewed or even believed to be anything but historical mumbo jumbo."

"Not surprising," Henry grumbled. "But, at least it's one thing we don't have to fret about. Ok. Vic, is there going to be an issue with bears accepting wolves as the decision-makers?"

"Not really," Vic said, glancing over to Ian. "We don't have dominance like wolves, and I'm guessing you know that. We do, however, have jobs to pay the bills. That means we all say yes to a weak little human boss. Since there hasn't been a rash of animal-related murders in town, you know we're able to hold it together - and my boss is a real dick."

"What do you do?" Elena asked.

He laughed once. "Construction. Scott works with me. Jax is a bouncer at a club, so he has stupid college kids in his face all night long."

"Ok," Ian said, sounding like he hadn't expected that. "How do we get the rest of the pack to accept having a group of bears living among us?"

"My *quinceañera*," Gabby said.

"Isn't the subject," Elena told her. "This is important, Gabby."

But I could see where Gabby was going with that. "No," I said, heading back to the table. "I think she has a point. Her party is next Saturday, all day. Your parents will be here, so it's human friendly, and everyone will be on their best behavior. Have the bears come, mingle, meet people, and if it gets tense, they can just leave. It's the perfect test."

"To a *quinceañera*?" Pax asked, looking at me as if I'd lost my mind. "That's kinda like using a wedding as a meet and greet."

"Exactly," I told them. "It's formal, which means regulated. If Gabby and Ian accept the bears' presence, I'm willing to bet the rest of the pack will as well."

"So..." Vic was mulling that over. "Just come to this party and do what?"

"Wish Gabby a happy fifteenth birthday," I suggested. "No presents necessary. Have a beer, shake a few hands, and try not to smile too big at the kids? Wild guess, but most of us aren't interested in your teeth."

"Wait," Pax said, all but cutting me off. "If this does work out, then what? We just lease them a house? And if they refuse to listen to Ian's rules? Then what?"

"We get kicked out," Vic said as if that should be obvious.

"And you'd go?" Pax countered. "C'mon, Vic. You're a Kodiak, Jax is a grizzly, and Scott's a... didn't you say a black bear?"

"Yep."

"Any one of you is a tough fight for a wolf. All of you?" he asked. "Forcefully evicting you is basically impossible, and you think we should just *trust* you?"

"We have over two hundred wolves in this community," Elena pointed out.

I grunted, making it clear that wasn't necessarily useful. "Total, but almost half of those are kids."

"But isn't that enough, Trent?" Lane asked. "We have about seventy-five members of the pack who could pick a fight. Maybe another twenty-five who could if they had to, but we're talking the older members, the infirm, and kids like Gabby."

"So, civilians," Elena muttered. "But seventy-five wolves is still a lot, right?"

"More than I want to tackle," Vic assured her. "But let me counter with this. Yes, we're big. But, if this *does* work out, then you'll have all three of us to help you evict the cats or foxes when they want to move in. I've already made it clear that we're desperate. Jax and I can't be seen in our bear forms because our kind is no longer found in most of the United States. The few places where a bear shifter can survive in this country? Well, most of them either have a bigger, stronger shifter or natural bears. We've been urbanized out of existence, and this is basically our last hope."

"So we handle this like humans," Gabby said as she pushed back her chair. "Hang on, I have notes." And she hurried into the other room.

I just pointed at Vic's drink. "Another beer?"

"Sure," he agreed. "And I'm sorry, but I didn't get your name."

"Trent," I told him. "Also Elena's mate. Pax and I were Ian's first betas."

"Lane was originally tied to Ashley," Ian explained. "We picked up Seth in college. He's a convert."

"They saved my life," Seth admitted. "Then they taught me how to enjoy the benefits of being a wolf."

Vic just nodded. "And, this relationship is a public thing?" He jerked his thumb toward where Gabby had gone. "She knows you're all with her mom?"

"She does," Elena assured him. "Evidently, it's pretty normal."

"For wolves, yeah," he agreed. "Stories say that your kind are pretty accepting of most things. Homosexuality, polyamory, and such. Bears tend to be more one and done. Our women keep their own space as much as the men, and there aren't a whole lot of them around."

"Why not?" Elena asked.

He blew out a breath. "Um, the ease of finding an unrelated human? It's a lot less work than tracking down a male and then making nice when we cross paths. Same kinda goes the other way around, though. Jax said his mom was a convert. Got swept off her feet, turned, got pregnant, and then went to claim her own space. Downside of being an isolated species, I suppose. Happily ever after doesn't usually work so well for us."

I came back with a handful of beers for the table. Ian got the first, then Lane. Pax came next with Seth right after, and then I passed one to Vic. "So, you guys don't date?" I asked.

"We date," Vic assured me. "Families are a little harder. Us and a few of the cats don't really repopulate our kind so well." He looked over at Ian. "And speaking of cats, I happen to know a tiger who's also very interested in what's going on here. Single dad, has a teenage son."

"Tigers?" Ian nodded slowly. "Because bears aren't bad enough?"

"A bear can take a tiger," Vic reminded him. "I mean, it's a rough fight, but there's three of us and two of them, so we definitely have the advantage."

"Uh huh." Ian didn't seem completely convinced.

"Got it!" Gabby announced as she came back in. "Ok..." And she reclaimed her chair, setting her laptop up in front of her. "So, historically speaking, race integration has always been chaotic, right?"

"Not really the time for a history lesson," I told her, reclaiming my seat beside Pax.

"Kinda is, Trent," Gabby said. "See, that's why this is so tense. Over and over, all we've seen is the stronger group subjugating the weaker. The Spanish made slaves of the Indians. The White men enslaved the Blacks. British put the Middle East under their heel. One way or another, you start mixing cultures, and you get a pretty serious clash. So, the point is that if we want to avoid that, we need to plan for it upfront."

"How?" Vic asked her.

She shrugged. "Isn't that your job, big guy? I'm a wolf. I don't know a thing about bears, but I'm willing to bet that you don't want to be the subjugated ones, right?"

"Would prefer not to be," he agreed.

"So, we identify the problems," she said. "Look, I've got all these examples..." And she flipped through her notebook, showing dozens of pages with writing on them. "From religions to races. They all come down to your way interrupting my way, and I have more people than you. So, how do we make this work? Where are the conflicts, and how can we both meet in the middle?"

Seth made his way around the table to look over Gabby's shoulder. She tilted her computer, which let me see just enough. On the screen in front of her was a browser with at least ten tabs open. Her notebook was filled with scribbles that I didn't want to try to make out. The kid had taken this seriously, but she also had a point.

Then Seth's face lit up. "Easter," he said.

Everyone around the table turned to look at him like he'd lost his mind. "What?" Ashley asked.

"Easter," Seth said again. "It used to be a pagan holiday. Fertility, I think. Christians wanted to integrate the people - whichever people it was - so they made that day for the resurrection of Christ. The intent was to force the pagan to choose, and if they were caught worshipping the wrong god, then they were punished. Probably killed, but I'm not sure about that. But the pagans weren't that picky, so they celebrated Easter and added in a few little touches of their own. Why else do you think there's a bunny with eggs? Both are fertility symbols, and today Christians use them in their holiday."

"Meet in the middle," I said, realizing what he meant. "Nice, Seth. So, how do we do that with the full moon? Because I think that's the biggest problem."

"And," Elena said, looking at Vic, "we're not going to make you hide while we run and howl, forcing you to suffer all night."

"We just need an hour," he begged.

Gabby thumped her hand on the table. "You deserve more than that! I've only had a few moons as a wolf, and know what that feels like. My boyfriend's dad never learned his wolf form, and he hates it. Sitting there, watching us all run is almost torture for him. Why would it be fair to do that to you just because you aren't wolves?"

"Do you even run?" Ian asked.

Vic huffed. "Not the same way wolves do. We celebrate the moon, and we do hunt it, but it's more a charge, a little bit of cavorting, and a lot of milling about. We don't exactly run long distances like you do."

But Gabby's tirade had Seth looking just a little too thoughtful. "Do you play?" he asked Vic. "Games, I mean. Tag, keep away, and that sort of thing? Do bears have games like wolves do?"

"Some," Vic admitted. "The guys and I wrestle. Why?"

Gabby sucked in a breath as she whipped around to look at Seth. "Like, capture the flag?" she asked.

He held out his fist for her to bump hers against. "Knew I liked you for a reason. But yeah. As soon as the moon comes up, we want to run. So, hide and seek, capture the flag, point holds. Take some ideas from video games, and there's no reason we can't literally hunt the moon."

I could actually see where he was going with that, and it wasn't a bad idea. It also sounded like something the pack would enjoy. At least the younger wolves. A few of our older and more traditional types would hate anything but running as fast as we could and howling at the top of our lungs.

Ian was shaking his head in confusion. "What are you talking about, Seth?"

"Like, a flag," Gabby told him before Seth could say a thing. "An actual, *real* flag, Ian. No, I know! A plushie! Say, give Vic a stuffed moon, right? The bears go out and do their thing. We take off running. For the rest of the night, it's a game of keep away. Wolves can work together. Bears can too. Winner gets some prize."

Henry chuckled. "Half off rent for the month?"

And the air rushed from Vic's lungs in a rush. "That's a serious prize."

"And a very good reason to keep it all in good fun," Henry pointed out.

"I can get medals made," Elena added. "Trophy shops make them pretty cheap. Put the month and year on them so the winner will have something to remember it by. It could work, right?"

"It's worth trying," Bridget said. "Would satisfy all of our instincts. The only question I have is if we can keep the wolves from getting triggered and the bears from losing control. The last thing I want to do is patch up some kid because he took a swipe from a grizzly paw across the face."

"A test run might be a good idea," Vic admitted, "but it's the kind of thing we do anyway. We just feel the need to shift and use our bodies. Not just lie around, but actually *do* something with them."

"It's worth trying," Ian relented. "Because, in all honesty, I want this to work. I want to figure this out, and you seem like a pretty decent guy, Vic. I just have to think of my pack first. You can understand that, right?"

"I can," Vic assured him. "But I can tell you that I'm not the first person to have this idea. When that video played, my tiger friend called me. He wants a home where he can raise his son without worrying. Lev's his name, and he's also been taking care of a trio of vixens. The youngest isn't much older than Gabby. Sisters. Their parents were both killed by hunters. Years apart, but the mom was lost a couple of years back, and Lev's been looking out for them since."

"The tiger?" Ian asked.

Vic nodded. "Yep. And trust me, I know exactly how you wolves feel, because running into a pair of male tigers in the middle of nowhere? Yeah, my balls - " He stopped, glancing over at Gabby. "Sorry, kid."

"You freaked out, huh?" she asked. "Don't worry, Vic. Seth's as bad about it as you are."

"I'm getting better," Seth grumbled.

She just rolled her eyes. "You really aren't."

"Wait," Pax said, waving them all off. "So, three bears just happen to know two tigers, who are coincidentally friends with three foxes? And all of you talk on the regular? Did that start before or after you casually bumped into Ashley at a bar?"

"Before," Vic assured him. "I've known Lev a while. I've never met the foxes, but he's actually the glue here. The guy makes it a point to introduce himself to the shifter families in town, just to make things easier."

"Easier how?" I asked.

Vic paused to take a drink of his beer. "What's the next closest wolf pack to here?"

"Hidden Forest, just outside town," I told him. "Why?"

"Because that's how it makes it easier," Vic explained. "You know who's in your territory, and what to watch for. We don't have large enough groups to scare others away, so we tend to work more on an alliance system. Introduce yourself, be polite, and stay away from any mating or hunting rituals. Tends to keep us from attacking each other, because that *would* get caught on camera and uploaded to YouTube. Bear against tiger in the parking lot of Walmart. That's like clickbait."

Pax actually nodded. "He's got a point. And we don't really worry about it because we run in packs."

"Exactly," Vic said. "But three bears against a dozen wolves? We're all going to be hurting. Just makes sense for us to get the hell out of your path. More for the foxes, which are technically prey to you. Tigers? Yeah, they just climb a tree or something. I honestly dunno. But that's why wolves rule the shifter world - because packs make you safer. There's never just *one* wolf."

"Which," Elena said, "is why they want the shelter of Wolf's Run."

"And it's why my party's the perfect time to test this out," Gabby said. "Look, we'll just invite everyone. I mean, it's a party, right? So, bring the tigers and foxes. We can all meet them, and I'll make sure my betas know to - "

Ian cleared his throat, cutting her off. "Not your pack yet, pup."

"Ian!" Gabby whined.

"Ask first," he told her.

Gabby just sighed. "Can we please use my *quinceañera* to make this happen? I can't think of a better time. I mean, most of my friends can't even say *quinceañera*, let alone know what it's about, but you're all letting me celebrate my culture, and *this* is how I want to do it. I'm a Latina wolf! My *quinceañera* is my own way to be proud of my diversity, and having some other shifters there just makes *sense*." Then her teeth clamped on her lower lip and she looked at him with big eyes. "Please, Ian?"

"If Vic and his friends want to come, then they're welcome," Ian told her. "*But,* this means that you have to tell the pack." Then he looked at Vic. "Her grandparents are human, so no shifting. No talking about what we are. For the whole day, we're all playing normals, but you're welcome to bring all of your friends, regardless of species.

77

And if you start something, just know that you will be the ones exposed - not us."

"Understood, Alpha," Vic promised. "I can guarantee we'll be on our best behavior because we don't have a backup plan."

"Kinda what I thought," Ian said. "And I have a feeling we don't need to wait until next weekend to get you a house. If the pack is fine with it, then so am I. But, if you *ever* turn against us, we will chase you out and not stop. Do you understand me, Vic?"

"I do, Alpha," he promised.

Ian nodded. "Good. You're going to be my test case. You and your bear friends. I'm giving the three of you a house at the back, right next to the trails - which means there's a lot more than three trees."

Vic slowly set his beer down on the table, his eyes shining a little too much, then gently pushed it away. "And the catch?" he asked.

"Help us figure this out," Ian told him. "My mate wants to give you a chance. My pup is adamant, and she's got good instincts. I'm willing to try this, but I can't do it on my own. You're going to have to talk to us, and you'll need to make an effort to get to know the wolves."

"Anything." Vic's voice was thick with emotion. "I give you my word, Alpha." Then he swallowed hard. "And, what time can we use the trails?"

"Time? Any time you want," Ian said. "They're for the entire pack, after all."

"Excuse me," Vic whispered, pushing his chair back to head for the other room. The man was clearly struggling to keep control of his emotions.

I just looked over at my Alpha. "What made up your mind, Ian?"

He shrugged. "All of my converts think this is a great idea. Pax stopped pushing against it. You and Lane don't seem opposed. No one at this table is trying to say it's a bad idea, and this is what we've always wanted. Someone has to go first, and these bears seem honestly willing to make an effort. Now, let's just make sure this all works out."

CHAPTER 9

V ic hadn't headed toward the bathroom. He hadn't gone out back. We'd all seen the look on his face, so we'd let him go, but when he didn't come back after a couple of minutes, I excused myself to follow. It wasn't exactly hard to find the guy - he did smell like sweet grass and the dirt after it rained. My nose led me right to the front door.

Vic stood there with a hand over his mouth, staring out the little window at the side. "Hey?" I said softly as I moved closer.

He cleared his throat before turning to face me. "Sorry. I didn't mean to be rude."

"We have some chairs out back and plenty of beer," I offered.

"Probably don't need to drink much more," he told me. "I just..."

So I leaned around him to open the front door. "Fresh

air?" I offered, gesturing for him to go first. The man chuckled once, but he went. I followed, easing the door closed behind us. "Hopefully that wasn't as bad as you'd feared?"

"No," he admitted. "I honestly expected this to turn into a screaming match, which is why I agreed to come alone. I knew Ashley wouldn't let me be ambushed, and someone has to trust first, right?" Then he paused, turning to me with a look of confusion on his face. "And why are you ok with me?"

"Convert?" I guessed. "I honestly don't know. Can I tell that you're big and scary? Yep. I think the same thing about Lane, and he saved my life."

"When you ran or something?" Vic asked.

"No, when I was attacked. The alpha of another pack - well, he wasn't the alpha at the time, just another guy going to college with us. Anyways, I was a dick, and he paid me back by jumping me with a few of his wolf friends, *as wolves*. I had no idea any of this was real. I thought they were big feral dogs. And then Lane tore into them - also as a wolf."

"So, about as bad as my conversion." Vic chuckled. "Does anyone get turned without trauma?"

"Elena and Gabby." I shrugged. "Gabby found about wolves and had her boyfriend bite her. Took a bit, but Elena decided that since she's already a part of the pack then she might as well turn too. Lane's fated for her, and she asked him to bite her."

"And today was her first day back on her feet." He nodded to show he knew that much. "Impressive lady."

"More than you can imagine." I canted my head,

indicating he should follow. "So, she lives next door, right there." I pointed. "And that's the leasing office, which also doubles as the central hub of our pack. Ashley and Elena are there all day long, and they can get any of the pack leadership with a call." Then I pointed up the street toward the back of the community. "And at the very end of this road is the start of the nature trails. There are a few streets that branch off, and we have a little more room to build more houses. If everything fills up, Henry wants to buy the land behind us and make a bigger space to run, but we'd have to plant trees and let it grow up."

"Wow," Vic breathed. "And it's all surrounded by walls?"

"Yep." I gestured to the gates. "The gate guard? Yeah, it's a wolf. We can lock those down, and we have a community text group for any emergencies - like when Gabby was turning. Gates are closed and locked, cars are parked, and we come together to help. Might be a little overwhelming for a bear, though."

He moved to the end of the lawn and looked up toward where his new house would be. "I think we can cope with that, actually. I mean, isolation is no longer an option. And Ashley said you have an African Wild Dog in the pack?"

"Jesse." I just sighed. "Yeah, um, he went to Africa for some reason. Dunno if it was business or vacation. Ended up bit, turned, but couldn't stay. The guy came home thinking he could deal, but it wasn't that easy. Dogs aren't wolves, so most packs wouldn't consider him, but Henry actually made it work. He's not as fast or as aggressive as us, but he's a pretty cool guy."

For a long moment, Vic was quiet, just looking up the

road, and I let him. I could only guess what he was thinking, but the man had done a good job of playing it cool so far. There was just one last thing I wanted to get out in the open, preferably where Ian couldn't hear me.

"So," I said, dragging out the word, "about Ashley..."

"It was just a drink," he told me.

"Yeah, except it wasn't. I know that, you know that, and Ian doesn't. Neither does her dad, and I think it should stay that way."

"It was just a drink," Vic said again, turning to face me.

I lifted both hands, well aware that this man was literally twice my size. "Sure. Thing is, Ashley actually seems to like you. So, regardless of what you were doing when you shared that drink, I'm going to give you a little advice. Don't let her push you away. If you want something to happen there, you'll have to prove that you're not going anywhere. You'll need to accept that she's a natural-born wolf from the very first line of wolves to come to this country. Her family is as blue-blooded as they come, and she's never known anything but her own society."

"Kinda getting that impression," he said. "I mean, shifters who can build an entire housing community? And not slums, at that."

"Yeah, the Langdons are loaded." But that wasn't what I wanted to talk about. "Vic, she's not a one-man kind of girl. She's a wolf, and one of the strongest alphas I've ever seen. The only reason Ian is the Pack Alpha is because she didn't want it. He couldn't beat her, and he could beat anyone."

The man's eyes narrowed. "Ok?"

"Ashley is an alpha wolf without betas or a mate

because she got burned. If you want that drink to be more than a drink? You need to know that. She won't make it easy. What she lost? It breaks lesser wolves than her. For over a decade, that woman has tried to pretend she's a human. That's how we got Elena. She was Ashley's best friend, and Ash just moved her into the community and hired her for the office without asking the Alpha. Now you?"

"Is that going to be a problem?" he asked.

"No. What I'm saying is that she's used to getting her way. She hasn't met a lot of people who can make her do anything, but I have a feeling a bear probably could. I also know that my mate has the Pack Alpha wrapped around her little finger, and she's Ashley's best friend. So, if that drink happens to turn into more at some point? Tell Elena first. She'll handle the rest."

"And if I'm not opposed to that?" Vic asked.

"She'll try to sleep with your roommates," I warned him.

Vic shrugged. "Let's say I'm cool with it."

I grinned at the man. "Well, I can tell you that I just want to see her happy. Elena will kill for her though, and I will tear into you if she asks. So, don't screw her over, ok?"

"I'm honestly looking for a home," he promised. "Look, since we're being so open and honest here, I'll just lay it all out there. Ashley's beautiful. She's brilliant, determined, and pretty fucking impressive. I wouldn't kick her out of my bed. I also won't jeopardize my home for a piece of ass. It. Was. Just. A. Drink."

"I already know you're lying," I told him. "She admitted it to Pax, Trent overheard - or that could've been the other way around. Hard to be sure with those two. Elena knows, because she was smirking at you a little too much. So, keep lying. Kinda makes me respect you a little more, actually."

"You wolves are so fucked in the head," Vic said. "You bring me here to grill my ass, your Alpha just decides on a whim that he'll lease us a place, and now the smallest beta is telling me he approves of me supposedly lying? What the hell, man?"

I held up a finger. "We grilled you to see if you'd crack. We pulled in all the important members of our community to see if we could find a problem we couldn't overcome, and we seem to have solutions for all the big ones. Elena was the one who wanted to do this today, and none of us mates can manage to tell her no. She was also rooting for you, which is why Ian gave in easily. As for the lying? Well, if you're willing to risk that home for Ashley's honor? Means you deserve to live here, right?"

"Still just a drink," he said, but the vehemence was gone. "And I think I like you, Seth. You're not quite what I expected for a wolf."

"Convert," I reminded him. "I was in college when I got bit. I spent a lot of time as a human learning how to ignore differences that divide people. Recently, that's helped this pack more than we ever expected."

"Like with that video?" he asked.

I nodded. "Gabby's school was shot up. The kid who did it had somehow figured out that the students from Wolf's Run are wolves. We have no idea how. But when it happened? Yeah, Gabby snapped orders to her pack, and the wolves started handling the first aid. Her boyfriend chased off the shooter. He's the one in that video. And, in all of that mess, two humans saw him, and they worked together to convince the rest of the world that we don't exist. Why? Because Gabby didn't realize that she shouldn't trust humans. Samantha was her friend before she turned, so she didn't see a reason why the girl couldn't be one afterwards. Now? Same girl is an honorary member of the pack."

"And us?" Vic asked.

I shrugged. "I'm kinda hoping you'll decide that pack life isn't so bad. See, there's safety in numbers. Not what animal we can turn into, but in how many people you can trust to watch your back. I kept hearing you say you'd help. You'd stand with Gabby. You'd evict bigger predators that might be a problem for us. It's all pack mentality, Vic."

"For bears, we use the term friends." Then he turned and offered his hand. "So, friends, Seth?"

I slapped my palm against his. "It's a good place to start. You seem like a good guy. Didn't meet your... Pals? Roommates?"

"Sure," he said. "I've always just called them friends too."

"Well, the other bears," I said. "Just make sure they know about Lane and Elena, ok? If they so much as startle her, he can't help himself. That man could probably put the hurt on you."

"As a human, he could probably take me," Vic admitted.

I nodded. "And he's just as scary as a wolf, trust me. Just make sure the guys know that, and everything else will work out. And if you have any problems, talk to me. Not Ian - me. I can run interference for you, and it's kinda my job."

He grinned. "And never be rude to your woman and her kid. Yeah, already figured that part out." He pulled in a long breath, and then let out a contented sigh. "I just have no idea how I'm ever going to pay all of you back."

"Help us get this right," I told him. "When we screw up - and we will - then give us a second chance. When those foxes or tigers show up? Help us work with them. Man, I mean, dogs and cats, you know?"

"Tigers aren't like most cats," he assured me. "They're..."

"Big, and scary, and have lots of teeth," I teased. "No, I get it, Vic. All I'm saying is that Ian's wanted to make something like this for as long as I've known him. Now it's happening, and we all know it isn't going to be easy. Wolves will resist. Some shifter won't work well with another. Things are going to get messy, but you seem like a pretty decent guy, and you just happen to be big enough that there aren't a lot of things you'd be scared of."

He chuckled at that. "Fair point."

"So, take as much time as you need to realize that this is happening, and then come back inside and help us work out the details, ok?" I stepped back. "Welcome to Wolf's Run, Vic. It really is this nice here."

His eyes naturally went up the street one more time. "Hey, Seth?"

"Yeah?"

"What should I get that kid for her birthday bash?"

"Fuck if I know, man. I suck at this stepfather gig, but I'm pretty sure she really does want to make this place into a sanctuary for our kind. I mean, no one made her do all that research."

"She's gonna be one hell of an alpha, isn't she?" he asked.

"That's the plan. First convert to lead a pack in known history, and it's not a small pack. Now, just imagine if it's a multi-shifter thing on top of that? Almost like we might be able to survive this modern world, huh?"

"Here's hoping," Vic said softly. "If nothing else, it's a chance. One we didn't have yesterday."

CHAPTER 10

I ended up falling asleep on the couch in the den while everyone else worked out the nuances of what Vic and his friends would need. The last thing I remembered hearing was something about foxes being more like wolves. The next morning, I woke up in Lane's bed, hugging a soft coat that didn't belong to him. No, it was Ian, sleeping as a wolf. Lane was curled around me as a man.

Gabby had been sent to sleep in Ian's room, and someone had cleaned up the mess from the night before. Sadly, I'd pushed myself a little too hard and my medication was still at home. That was all it took for Lane to walk me back. When he and my daughter teamed up to send me to bed again, I didn't fight too hard. I ended up sleeping through most of Saturday, and I didn't even care.

Sunday, I was a slug all morning. Mostly because I refused to keep using the muscle relaxers. It had been long enough, and while I was tired, I no longer ached that bad. Just a little twinge when I moved certain ways. Granted, I felt a little sad that my daughter's school opened back up on her birthday. The kids had been off for two weeks because of the shooting, and the building had finally been cleared for the students to come back, so she really needed to go tomorrow.

Gabby promised she was ok with it. All of their homework had been canceled, and it sounded like everyone was out of the hospital and recovered. Physically, at least. I had a funny feeling it wouldn't be quite as easy to go back as she was pretending, but I didn't call her on it. My daughter was trying to be tough, and I could respect that.

While I focused on being lazy, Ashley came through for me. She sent me a text saying she and Bridget were at the mall and got "the goods." I knew she was talking about Gabby's present, so I told her to hold on to that until Monday at work. She agreed, letting me know she'd even wrap it for me. Her way of paying me back for helping with the bears.

Then, right around one that afternoon, Lane showed up. When he saw me sitting on the couch watching Netflix, the man smiled at me proudly and made his way over. What he didn't do was sit beside me. Instead, he squatted down right in front of me.

"How do you feel?" he asked.

"Achy," I admitted. "But good. Like I'm going to be even better tomorrow. So, are the bears all moved in?"

"Yeah..." He dropped a hand on my knee. "I was wondering if you'd help me with something? Ian stole

Gabby yesterday while you were sleeping. They made sure most of the pack knows about our new members. Well that's handled. I just thought that we should show those guys the trails, and it's a nice day."

My eyes narrowed, because he was making too big of a deal about this. "Lane, what's going on?" I asked, braced for the worst.

"I thought you might want to try shifting," he mumbled. "I have a blanket in my truck, so you won't even need to be exposed. And I figured that if you take the bears to the trails, then the rest of the pack will see they're friends of the Alpha Female, and that will put them at ease. So, a win-win situation, right?" One corner of his mouth was curling higher. "And Ian says I help you shift more than he does."

"What if I can't do it?" I asked. "I mean, change back. I had trouble the first time."

"Doesn't work like that," he promised. "You might be slow about it, or a little clumsy, and you might even pause in the mid-form, but all of that is ok."

I looked down at my slouchy clothes. "I need to change."

"Not really." He was struggling not to laugh. "The whole point is to get naked, and since you don't sound up to rolling around in bed..."

All I could do was laugh at that because he did have a point. "Ok. Do I at least get shoes? I mean, if we're stopping by Vic's new place? Wait, did Ashley get them a lease?"

"We handled it all," he promised. "You fell asleep on the couch, but the rest of us were going until three in the morning. They have a lease, a card on file for rent, their keys, and all of our phone numbers, just in case they have a problem." Then he pushed to his feet and scanned the room. When his eyes landed on my shoes, he headed that way. "You need to smell the world, right? This is going to count, and I want to make sure that your third exposure to bears is easier than the first. Put these on, and we can go."

"Gabby?" I asked, only raising my voice a bit.

"Yeah?" she asked, appearing on the stairs only a moment later.

"Lane's taking me to visit our new neighbors and then to the trails. I won't have my phone, so if you need anything, call Ian?"

"Can do," she promised. "Oh! Can I go over to Olivia's later? If you're not back by then?"

"Why?" I asked.

She chewed on her lip, making it clear she was up to something. "We're kinda writing up a covenant for *all* the species, and I wanted to surprise Ian with a finished version."

Lane chuckled at that. "I won't tell him," he promised. "It'll need to be looked at by a lawyer, though."

She nodded. "Henry said he'd finalize the wording for me."

"That's my girl," Lane said.

Something about his tone made my heart flip in my chest. He was proud of her. Honestly, completely, and without reservation proud of my daughter, and willing to let her know. Her father had never talked to her like that, and until that moment, I hadn't realized it was even missing. But seeing the way Gabby puffed up at such a simple comment proved that she needed it.

"No leaving the community without telling one of us," I decided. "Otherwise, be home by ten? If you're going to be late, call, ok?"

"Promise, and thank you, Mom!"

Then I looked at Lane. "Well, let's do this. Just... if I get stuck as a wolf, you're stuck with her. Keep that in mind."

"You won't get stuck," he promised as he turned me to the door. "Also, Gabby isn't exactly a good threat. I kinda like the kid, Elena."

Still, I was a little nervous about my first intentional shift. I could remember the way it hurt to pull my body apart and put it back together. What I wasn't sure I could do was make that happen on demand, yet I kinda wanted to. I'd run so fast that night, and I'd felt invincible. I'd never really been the kind of person who went jogging for fun, but the idea of cavorting in the trees as a wolf wasn't the same. It wasn't exercise, but play, and I really did want to try again.

But first, we stopped at the last house in the community. It was actually on the same side of the street as the nature trails, but far enough down that there wasn't a direct view from the front yard to the parking area. But, when we got closer, I saw three large pickups pulled up to the house. Two had been backed toward the garage. The last was parked on the curb and empty. Lane pulled his own truck in behind it.

I didn't even make it out before the front door of the house opened and a large Black man appeared in the door. Lane waited for me to reach his side, then dropped an arm over my shoulder, and the pair of us headed up together. The man just waited, not saying a thing, but he looked ready for the worst.

"How's the move going?" I asked when we were close enough that I didn't have to yell.

He just lifted his chin at me in that male acknowledgment gesture. "Is there a problem already?"

"Nope," Lane said, moving just before me to offer his hand. "Lane, pack beta and one of Elena's mates."

"Jax," the bear said, accepting his hand. Then he glanced back. "Guys! Company." And over to me. "Care to come in, Alpha?"

"We'd love to," Lane answered for me.

Jax stepped back, granting us access, and Lane steered me before him. Naturally, the house was filled with boxes. There was furniture as well, but the used and tired kind. Then, over all of it, was the sweet scent of bears. It was natural and nice, blending well with the woods just outside.

"Elena!" Vic said as he came around the corner. "Lane. Please tell me there isn't a problem?"

"That's what Jax said," I groaned. "No, there's nothing wrong. I just wanted to make sure everything's still ok."

"No trouble with the neighbors?" Lane asked.

The third man, Scott, joined us, moving over to lean against the wall. "We got a few stares from the house across the street, but that's about it. Why?"

"Because," Lane told them, "Ian's been making the rounds, letting everyone know that you're welcome here. And if you three have a minute, I thought we could show you the trails."

Vic jerked his thumb out towards the back of the house. "All of that?"

"Yep," Lane said. "Ok, and I want Elena to try shifting on her own, but I figure it serves double duty." He glanced over at Scott. "I'm fated for her. To wolves, that means I wouldn't do anything to risk her." Then he looked at Jax. "And she's the second in charge of this pack, so her word is as much law as Ian's. She also has no clue how to walk as a wolf, and she'll be very, very vulnerable." He paused to shove a hand over his mouth. "But Ashley's basically a sister to me, and she seems to trust you three, so I do too. Would you be interested in lending a little muscle?"

"What?" I asked, turning to look at him.

"Elena, I can't lift you as a wolf. A few of us can give you something to brace against, but you aren't a pup like Gabby. We'd make it work, but them? They can lift you. Now, it means you'll need to suck up a little pride, and you will definitely have to overcome a little fear of bears, but I have a feeling that's not bothering you anymore."

"It's not," I agreed.

He nodded. "So, let these three play the part of the Alpha Female's personal guards, and let the pack see it, little bunny. The fact that I'm the one with you? It'll be noticed, and I can't think of anything else to prove that our newest members are safe."

I chewed my lower lip, loving and hating this idea at the same time. Lane had a point, and the fact that he didn't hate these men said a lot. But the part about some strangers seeing me as a complete idiot? Yeah, that wouldn't be much fun, but it was basically just taking one for the team. In this case, that meant Ashley, since I knew she really wanted things with these guys to work out.

"Ok," I agreed. "Just don't embarrass me too much."

"Now?" Jax asked, his eyes jumping to the trees.

"It's as good a time as any," Lane assured him.

"What if there are wolves out there?" Scott wanted to know.

Lane smiled. "There are. That's why we're here. Guys, there are always wolves out there, but Vic said none of you have shifted in months." His golden eyes jumped over to Vic. "It's calling to you, isn't it?"

"More than you can guess," he admitted.

"So, I'm driving Elena over there, since she can't run on her own, and she'll be wiped when we're done. If you three want a ride..."

"Really?" Scott asked. "Just, middle of the day, run around in our bear forms?"

"Yep," Lane said.

"No catch?" Jax asked.

"None," Lane assured them. "Except that you'll have to entertain yourselves for a bit while I get Elena from a human to a wolf. But we have a few trees around, and some of them are probably big enough for you three to climb."

"And no tearing them down, right?" Vic asked.

"Preferably not the healthy ones. We only have about fifteen acres of wilderness, but there are a few that probably need to be dropped eventually. Also won't complain if you widen a few of the trails for our less agile members."

The three bears just stared at Lane like they couldn't believe it. There was something so raw about the look in their eyes, and also sad. It was obvious that all of them wanted to do this, but no one was making the first move, so I decided to do it.

"So, if you're all ready to help me out, I'd appreciate it," I said. "But I, for one, am kinda excited about this." And I turned for the front door, walking out like I was done waiting.

Yep, the bears followed.

CHAPTER 11

The bears hopped into the bed of the truck. Elena took the passenger seat, and I drove two lots down to the parking area for our nature trails. The moment my truck was stopped, the guys jumped out, and then Jax moved to the passenger door, opening it for my mate.

"Alpha," he said, offering her a hand down.

Yeah, that made my hackles rise a bit, but I ignored it. I might be a jealous and paranoid ass, but that didn't mean I had to show it. Elena smiled and accepted the hand down, but she wasn't looking at him with any interest. She wasn't being stolen away. My mate was still all mine. She was simply nice enough that everyone wanted to see her smile, and she deserved to have these guys try.

"So," Vic asked as I dug in the back seat for that blanket to shield Elena, "where do we, uh, change?"

"Right here," I told him. "Nudity isn't considered taboo

for wolves. Now..." I unfurled the blanket and looked at Elena. "You get a pass this time. One less thing to worry about, right?"

"This is going to suck, isn't it?" she asked.

"Nope." I passed her the blanket and pulled off my own shirt, aware the bears were waiting for some hint as to what was acceptable. "I'm going to be the one with my bare ass hanging out in public until you figure it out."

My shirt went through the driver's window, right onto the seat. Shoes came next. Then socks. Finally, I stripped off my pants and underwear together, and then took back the blanket. Completely naked, I headed right for the grassiest area and then crooked a finger for Elena to follow me. She did, slowly. Timidly, actually, and her cheeks were turning a little pink.

"Go ahead, guys," I told the bears. "We'll be at this a bit, I think."

"I'm cool with that," Scott said.

And the three of them immediately began stripping, tossing their clothes into the bed of my truck. Elena just turned away, which meant she ended up facing me. Struggling not to grin at the guys, I leaned in toward her ear.

"Take your time, ok? Give them a chance to be bears, and it'll save their pride. Just remember that as a wolf, those men are going to be even bigger."

Then Vic shifted. Scott moved to the grass first, but he changed mid-step, flowing from his human body to the bear without even breaking stride. The last one was Jax. I nudged Elena, letting her know it was safe to look, so she did. Together, the pair of us watched as three massive bears shook out their coats, stretched their bodies, and then slowly padded toward the trees.

Scott was the smallest, but still large for a black bear. He also didn't make it to the trees before flopping onto his side and rolling in the dry grass like a dog. Elena giggled, shoving a hand over her mouth to hide it, but Scott heard. The sound he made back was playful, but I could only describe it as a growl. Maybe a roar? One of those bear grunts, at any rate.

Then Jax found a tree. The man was dark for a grizzly, almost a chocolate color, but when he stood up to scratch his back, he revealed his lighter brown belly. Then there was Vic. His color was redder, his body was bigger, and his claws were massive. He snuffled a few times and then rushed to one of the larger trees, climbing halfway up before simply sliding back to the ground.

"They look confused," Elena said.

"Sounds like it's been a long time since they had the chance to actually enjoy themselves," I reminded her. "Now, clothes off, little bunny. I'm going to hold this blanket around you, and you're going to shift."

"Ok..."

She waited until I had the blanket wrapped around her like a cape, and then worked off her clothes. Those went in a pile by her feet. I'd carry them back to the truck before I shifted, but she didn't need to know that. Right now, I just wanted her to feel like she could do this.

"All you have to do is reach for it," I told her. "Close your eyes if that helps. It won't hurt like it did the first time. It will feel strange, but just push through it. And once you're a wolf, we'll go from there, ok?"

"Just..." She looked up at me. "Don't leave me, Lane, ok?"

"Kinda can't," I reminded her. "You can do this, bunny."

She sucked in a breath, closed her eyes, and then tried. Of course, she also failed, but I couldn't really teach her this part. It was different for everyone, and the attempt was her chance to just figure it out. I didn't even care that my butt cheeks were getting pretty chilly - let alone the other parts. The weather was nice, but it was still February!

While she focused on that, I watched the bears. Jax worked out an itch that it seemed he'd been waiting a very long time to scratch. Scott got up and shook, making a rather impressive dust cloud. Then the man did the last thing I would've expected. He charged straight at the Kodiak bear. When Vic stood up and braced for it, I actually chuckled.

The smaller bear rammed right into the chest of the larger, and the pair of them tumbled over. Vic rolled with it, pushing away Scott, but they weren't biting or clawing. Both men were actually being very careful - at least until Jax joined them. Together, he and Vic ganged up on Scott, but the little guy wasn't exactly weak. He shouldered Jax to the ground, nipped at Vic's hip, and the group of them started getting rowdy.

Elena giggled, proving she'd been distracted. "Woman," I hissed playfully. "You are supposed to be shifting."

"They look so happy," she said.

"You look like a very naked lady, and my dick's gonna get hard," I countered. "Wolf, Elena. Preferably before my balls freeze off."

She groaned but tried again. This time, something

actually happened. Her body blurred a little around the edges even while the bears kept playing. She paused for a moment and tried again, but it wasn't that much better.

So I decided to help out. "Four legs, beautiful. Fur. You're going to get shorter, and that's ok. Just reach for the body with four legs, and don't stop until you get there. Don't push, though. Reach."

She nodded once and then tried yet again, but this time it worked. Her body blurred and then began to mist. It was as if all of the particles of her being were released into a cloud that could then reform as what she wanted. No, it wasn't fast, but when she looked more wolf than woman, I pulled the blanket away, making room for her new body. It was forming, slowly but surely, and it seemed she had it figured out.

A beautiful, black wolf stood braced just before me, panting hard. "Catch your breath," I told her, daring to run my hand down her silky back. "Let me put this stuff in the truck, ok? Don't try to walk yet. Just stand there, bunny."

She huffed, the sound almost a laugh. Probably because I'd just called a wolf a bunny, but the nickname still fit. She was definitely something I wanted to eat. Maybe not as a wolf, but those details didn't matter. Grabbing her clothes, I set those in the passenger seat, but I left the blanket. Then, I looked over at the bears.

"Guys?" I asked while I still had a mouth. "Little muscle for my mate?"

And then I shifted, loping back to her side. Elena turned to watch me, but she didn't move a single foot. So I nudged her shoulder with my nose, nibbled at the fur around her neck, and then walked one pace away. When I was just out of reach, I turned around and woofed at her, hoping she'd be willing to at least try.

Instead, her ears dropped down on her head, she dipped her neck, and her eyes focused on something behind me. A little whimper of a sound came from her throat just as Jax walked around me. From down here, the man was a true monster, standing three times taller than even I did, and Elena wasn't exactly a big wolf.

But he stopped just before her and lay down. Grunting gently, the grizzly bear stretched his nose toward her, and Elena reached back. The pair of them sniffed for a moment, and then Elena's tail started to wag. Her ears immediately went up and it paused, but when she looked back, I had to laugh. The sound came out more like a sneeze, but still. My mate had completely forgotten she had a tail!

Then she tried to take a step. Our joints were completely different in this body. Our shoulders went forward instead of side to side, and they didn't rotate the same. Her wrist was now her front knee. Learning to walk as a wolf was no different than a baby figuring out how to stand, but she was smart enough to figure it out. I believed in her, and I wanted her to be willing to try this again.

One long, dark leg reached out, and she tottered. Immediately, Jax hopped up and moved to her side. Vic hurried over to the other, but neither bear touched her. They both just waited, grunting their own version of encouragement. It was enough to make Elena's mouth part and her tongue fall out. That was a smile, and my own tail wagged to see it.

Then Scott moved beside me. Slowly, clearly

demonstrating for her, he took a step, and then moved his next leg - a hind. Elena nodded her wolf head and tried to do the same. I just whuffed at her in encouragement. Clearly, these three were going to make sure she had it, and they were both large enough and slow enough that she could follow along.

Step by slow, careful step, Elena moved forward. Her tail would wag with a mind of its own, but she didn't seem to care. Me? I just watched her. She was perfection, so far as I cared. In the sunlight, her black coat shimmered with reflections of blues and golds. Not reds like most wolves, because she was just too black for that. Like Gabby, she had the pale lines under her eyes, and it contrasted with the tawny shade of her irises. She looked like a shadow come to life, and I loved it.

Her fur was a bit longer than most, and sleek. Not thick or bristly. Her body was lean, but I already knew she was fast. My mate wasn't the bulky type of canine, but I was perfectly ok with that. She looked feminine, and as elegant as a wolf as she was as a human. In my life, I'd seen hundreds of our kind, but not a single one held a candle to her, and she was actually walking!

I barked out my excitement, but it was too much. She staggered, and then everything fell apart. One leg buckled, that side went down, and my mate collapsed into a heap of her own legs. Jax just grunted at her and hooked a paw around her body. It reminded me of a man carrying a football, yet the bear was able to lift just enough for her to get her legs untangled.

Elena whuffed her appreciation and then tried again. This time, it seemed a little bit easier, yet neither Jax nor Vic were going to leave her side. Scott nudged me with his nose, then the bear looked back toward the trees, and I realized what the guys were doing. I was the goal. If she could walk all the way to me, then she could rest again, but they'd forgotten one little thing.

So I darted around her, grabbed the blanket in my teeth, and jogged back to the last bit of open ground before the roots and fallen leaves made it treacherous. There, I dropped the blanket and barked at her again. Elena's ears perked up, her bear bodyguards braced to help, but she was doing this. Step by step, my mate slowly made her way over.

At the side, Scott reared up on his hind legs and roared his approval. Her tail wagged faster, but she didn't rush herself. Each foot was placed carefully. Her balance shifted between them like it took all of her concentration, but she was doing this.

Movement caught my attention, making me look over toward the firepit. There, a pair of wolves had stopped to watch the show. In the trees there was another, keeping a healthy distance from the bears, but I'd expected that. I also wasn't going to say anything because I didn't want to distract Elena. It looked like every step was easier than the last, and she was no longer crawling. Sure, she wasn't moving quickly, but she'd almost reached the speed of a slow walk now.

Foot, foot, foot, foot. One after the other, she came right for me, starting to pant with the effort. Just as she reached the line of the blanket, I shifted to a man and grabbed it, holding it up for her to fall into.

"You did it, bunny," I told her. "Now you can change back. We got you, baby."

She fell against me, shifting back to a woman as she let

herself relax. I saw Vic turn his head. Jax closed his eyes, but Scott was bouncing with his enthusiasm, unable to see her through the other bears. The moment my mate was human again, I folded the blanket around her, hugging her as tightly as I could.

"You are an amazing wolf," I told her.

She just grabbed the overlap of blankets between her breasts and tilted her head at Scott. "I think he needs to be chased," she said, looking back at me with a smile. "I can't do it, so can you help?"

"Bear tag?" I asked, nodding. "Yep, my mate's not only beautiful, but also brave. Catch your breath, bunny. I'll catch a bear."

I changed, pausing only to lick the side of her neck, and then I was off. Sadly, bears didn't have tails to nip, so I went for the man's hip. Scott shuffled back, but when my teeth tugged at his fur, he understood. Tag, he was it. Without warning, the black bear charged forward, right at Vic. The Kodiak barreled away, but he was much too slow. Scott tackled his back, play-biting at Vic's spine, and then raced away.

Vic turned, his head swiveling between the group of us, and then he stood up showing just how big of a bear he really was. The man spread his arms wide, lifted his lips, and roared at the top of his lungs. When he slammed his front feet back to the ground, his eyes were locked on me. And then the monster charged.

I tucked my tail and spun, running as fast as I could to get around Jax, and that worked. Vic barreled into his roommate, mauling the man playfully, and then broke off. That made Jax "it," and now the game was on. Sitting on the ground, in the middle of it all, Elena just laughed, and it was the most beautiful sound I'd ever heard.

And it was just enough to allow Jax to bat me off my feet. Damn it. Now I was it again, but this game was actually a lot of fun.

CHAPTER 12

L ane dragged his ass into the house at sunset, and the man was filthy. He looked like he'd rolled around in the dirt for a few hours, but the smile on his face proved he'd had fun doing it. He also didn't stop until he was in the middle of the living room.

"Elena's in the shower," he announced. "She walked from the parking area - or almost - to the edge of the trees, and the bears helped. Then, when we were playing tag, she shifted again, wanting to join in." He paused to laugh. "And I approve of the bears. They played in slow motion for her and Scott even let her catch him. She's on top of the world right now, but Gabby goes back to school tomorrow, and no one's made dinner."

"On it," Trent said, pushing to his feet.

"And she'll need a massage," Pax added as he stood. "You coming back over, Lane?"

"Nah." He paused to look at his hands. "I had her all

day, and I need a shower. You two go spoil her." Then he looked at Seth. "Or three?"

"C'mon," Pax said, encouraging him. "I'll sleep at the foot of the bed so you have room."

"Cool," Seth said, and the three of them just headed for the front door.

I watched them, but I had a feeling there was a little more to this than Lane just sharing that easily. The door closed, but I could still hear the three of them laughing, so just waited. The fact that Lane didn't move was starting to make me nervous.

"Ok, what?" I asked.

He grinned. "I like them, Ian. Those bears? They aren't like any other bear I've met before. They're honestly friends with each other, and they respect us. Ok, and Vic is a scary motherfucker, but still. Most bears want to be left alone. They played tag with us. I even got Kim into it, which made the other wolves up at the trails relax."

"No one got hurt, right?" I asked.

Lane just shook his head. "They batted us around, but gently. Jax play-bit at my back to tag me, but never bit down. Granted, I'm covered in bear spit and mud now, but I think Gabby's idea of the games will work. Ian..." He glanced at a chair, paused for a moment, then just dropped into it. "I can't remember the last time I had that much fun."

"So, you think the pack will accept them?"

"Yeah." He leaned over his knees with a groan. "Oh, and they made me work for it. But that's the thing. When Elena took her first step? Jax and Vic shouldered her. Not touching, though. They made her do it, and Scott showed her which foot came next. I'd never even thought about that part. He moved his front right, so she did. Back left, so she did. Step by step, he led her through it, and the other two caught her or lifted her back up if she lost control. Easily, I might add."

"Uh huh." I was nodding, because Lane seemed perfectly ok with this. "So, they didn't scare her? At all?"

"Um..." He pulled in a breath. "When Jax first came close, the size was intimidating. She whimpered and submitted, but he just laid down and let her get used to him. They're amazingly gentle with us, but that's the thing." He paused again, his brow furrowing. "The way they reacted when we invited them to the trails with us? It was like a puppy who'd been kicked. Timid, Ian. Three bears, and they were waiting to be told they couldn't. Not trying to fight for the right to shift, but waiting to get the bad news."

"They asked for three trees," I told him. "Well, one, but they would prefer three. Not access to the trails. Not a schedule for them. Just three fucking trees."

"And we just gave them fifteen acres," Lane said. "Maybe I'm wrong, and maybe I'm jumping ahead, but I think those guys are going to be as loyal as any wolf we've ever met. They want a pack, Ian. They just don't know to call it that. I also think they'll fight tooth and claw to protect their wolves. Most of all, Ashley is ok with them."

"Yeah?" Because I wasn't quite following where he was going with that.

"Look, ever since she lost her betas, we both know that she's been adrift. She likes to pretend she's not a wolf. It's how she met Elena, after all. She also doesn't date. She doesn't give many people a chance. For her to speak up for these guys? The only other time she did that was for Elena, so that says a lot."

He actually had a point. My sister didn't exactly trust people. Oh, she'd entertain herself with them, but outside of these walls, she was a completely different person. A beautiful human woman who could pretend like she didn't have a whole crap-load of baggage following her around. I understood why she did it, and I wouldn't ask her to stop, but Lane had just hit the nail on the head.

That was her fantasy. She didn't bring it home. In the "real world," she was one thing, and in here she had to be something else. I didn't like that she felt that way, but she still did. It was also why she never mixed the two. Not until Elena, and now with these bears.

"So you think her instincts are reliable?" I asked. "I mean, being right with Elena doesn't mean there won't be problems with the bears."

"Nope, sure doesn't," Lane agreed. "We had a few problems with Elena too, but we worked them out. All I'm saying is that you should give the bears a chance."

"I am," I reminded him. "I agreed to the lease, in case you forgot."

Lane just nodded, dragging his tongue between his lips and teeth as he did so. "Ian..." He sighed. "Ashley doesn't bond with wolves. Not anymore. She doesn't date. All I'm saying is that she just moved in three guys that she barely knows, and they aren't wolves."

It felt like someone dumped a bucket of cold water on me. "Bears?" I asked.

He shrugged. "Bridget says it's not a problem."

"You think my sister is fucking a bear?!" I shoved to my feet before I could stop myself.

And Lane matched me. "I think they're the first men she's been willing to even think about in fourteen years, so I don't give a shit what they are! They're nice to Elena. They're respectful of the pack. Most importantly, they're fucking living with us, Ian, and you will not screw this up for her, you hear me?"

"Back off, beta," I warned him.

But Lane just smiled, and it was the cruel kind. "Pull your head out of your ass, Alpha. Who else could make Ashley feel protected instead of like a predator? Who else is strong enough for her besides a bear?" He took one step toward me, his body braced to throw down. "You will not ruin this for her."

"She's a wolf!" I snapped, refusing to give in.

"She's a broken woman, and your sister. What does it matter if she is happy with a human or a bear? You don't really have room to talk, Ian."

I knew he was right. I did, but my entire life, there had always been an unspoken understanding that we did not mingle with other shifters. We could be polite to them, but that was all. Wolves lived with wolves. Bears did their own thing. The species never mixed. No one knew if it was safe - or even possible. The cross-infection could kill us, for all we knew, and there had never been a documented case of it happening.

But no one had allowed bears into a wolf pack before either. No one had created a community of shifters in the middle of a city. No one had done half the things we were doing, and it was working out. It kept working out because I didn't want to cling to the old and stupid traditions, so why was this one thing so hard for me to accept?

"Ashley wants to be with the bears?" I asked again, losing the anger.

Lane relaxed before me. "You going to throw her out for it?"

"No, I..." I grunted, cutting myself off. "Bridget thinks it's safe. She's a good doctor, and she knows what she's talking about, right?"

"Seems to," he agreed.

So I waved him down, making it clear I didn't resent him standing up to me. Then I dropped back into my chair. "What brought this up, Lane?"

"Um, I'm not sure I should say."

Which meant something had. "Just bear with me, ok?" I asked. "I'm trying very hard to accept Gabby's diversity plan, but it's not as easy for me. I get that it makes sense to let the bears live here, but I never thought about a wolf dating them. I guess I just assumed they'd eventually bring in a human and turn her or something. Or three, I suppose, but I didn't even think that far."

"Yeah," Lane mumbled. "But those three aren't living like normal bears. They're adapting, Ian. They're learning how to share territory, and I have a feeling that's going to include their mate."

"Ashley," I realized. "Because, as an alpha, she'll need more than just one companion in her life. She'd spiral alone. Even if that's a friend, someone to work beside, and a lover. Elena helps, but she won't be enough. Plus, it's *Ashley.*"

"Bet three bears would work," he said. "Ian, I think that drink she had with Vic was a little more than a drink."

"Why wouldn't she tell me?'

He just thrust both hands toward me. "That's why. Do

you honestly care who or what she's with so long as she's happy? If she fell in love with a woman, would you get this angry?"

"No..."

"A human?" he asked.

"No, Lane, that's different."

So he sat down and clasped his hands between his knees. "Why? And think before you answer, because I'm still partly her man."

He meant her beta, and I'd always known he'd have some loyalty to her. That didn't bother me at all. I actually approved of my betas caring about my family. But those words made it clear that he felt like this was a situation where he might have to choose, and I knew that Lane would always choose one thing over all the rest: Elena.

"Shit," I breathed. "She told Elena, didn't she?"

"Or Elena guessed," Lane admitted. "I don't know, but on the way back from the trails, Elena said something about them being perfect for Ashley. Now, I know your sister well enough to make a few guesses. So, the real question is what you'll do when it comes out that your sister is fucking the bears?"

All I could do was scrub at my face, because I didn't honestly know. Nothing was my first instinct, since Lane was right. It wasn't my business who Ashley ended up with. I just wanted her to be safe, and if those bears were part of the pack, then what difference did it make? But if I was having this much trouble with the idea, then how would everyone else react? How would Dad take this?

"Dad will disown her," I realized.

"Not on my watch," Lane warned.

"Or mine," I agreed. "No, you're right. I know you're

right, and it makes perfect sense. Three men, all stronger than Ashley, who have left the rules and traditions behind that we were raised with. They really are perfect for her. Shit, and if she is actually willing to give them a chance?"

"Then we need to make sure that Henry doesn't screw this up," he finished for me.

"But how?" I asked.

Lane chuckled softly. "You use your secret weapon, Ian. Gabby. Your dad is smitten with his grandpup. If you convince Gabby that there's nothing wrong with cross-shifter mingling, then she'll all but force Henry to accept it, and Ashley will be the one winning in the end."

Just a few problems with that. "Those bears are too old for her, and it sounds like my sister's already staked her claim, so how do you propose I have Gabby bring this up?"

"Well, there's going to be a few tigers and some foxes at her *quinceañera*. Now, I'm not saying you should force Gabby to do anything, but if you tell her that they might feel alienated being around so many wolves? You know she'll do the rest. Then, you just have to make sure Henry knows that Elena will not put 'race restrictions' on who her kid dates - or takes into her pack."

"She won't," I agreed. "And even if she tried, Gabby would ignore it. So, you think I should push this, or just let it happen?"

"Talk to her," Lane decided. "To both Gabby and Elena. Make them aware of the tension between types of shifters, and explain just how new this is. They'll get it. I also think that those two know a lot more about this stuff than we do. I think this is one of those times where Elena knows best, and we need to trust her to make the right calls."

"Ok," I agreed, "but I need one thing from you."

"Anything," Lane promised.

"Make sure my sister knows that if bears make her happy, then I'm happy for her. Subtly, Lane. Make it clear she doesn't have to hide this from me, and while I may be an idiot, I will always be on her side. Head up my ass or otherwise."

"That," he promised, "I can do. And now I need to wipe her boyfriend's spit off my back." He rocked forward, onto his feet, and then sighed. "They really are pretty good guys, though. I'm glad you let them move in. I trust them with our mate."

And then he headed to his room, clearly going for a shower. But that last bit said more than any other words could. Lane trusted them with Elena. With the woman he couldn't live without. With the other half of his soul.

The least I could do was trust them with my sister.

CHAPTER 13

I headed into work on Monday with a smile on my face. It hadn't left since I'd managed to "tag" a bear yesterday. Yeah, I knew they'd made it easy on me, but I'd still managed. Then, just when I thought my great day was over, Seth, Pax, and Trent had come over to spoil me, and they'd stayed all night. And this morning, Seth had whipped up pancakes for Gabby, making sure she started her birthday by being pampered.

But the moment I was at my desk, my best friend cornered me. "So," Ashley said, giving me her best serious look. "You wolfed out without me?"

"Yeah, and with your boyfriends. Guess you should've spent the day with me instead of your other friend," I teased.

That made her smile break free. "Not my boyfriends."

"Yet," I countered. "But, you could fix that, you know."

She huffed, then crooked a finger for me to follow. I did, so Ashley headed right back to her office to proudly gesture at the pile of presents. "This is for tonight." Then she began pointing from the bottom up. "Zip-up boots for easy shifting from me. Official Wolf's Run hoodie from the guys, so the rest of the pack will see she's a part of the team. Bridget and Kim went in together to get her a pretty well-stocked Starbucks card. Heather got her a dress for her dates with Roman, and this one is yours."

"What did I get her?" I asked, because that box wasn't big.

Ashley smiled. "It's just a tiny little necklace with two wolves on it. Kinda reminded me of mom and pup, and it has the kind of slip clasp that will work if she shifts while wearing it. You know, a little memento of you both joining our pack together."

I moved to give her a side hug. "That's perfect. Thank you, Ashley."

"And you're off work as soon as she's home. The pair of you get a couple of hours to do presents, and then we're all heading up to the trails for a bitch session. Just the ladies. No boys, no bears, and no embarrassment, because your daughter really wants to see her mother as a wolf. I think that'll be the best present she ever gets."

"Thank you," I said again. "For making this happen, for shopping for me, and all of it."

"Just making sure you never want to live anywhere else," Ashley assured me. "Now go count hours, because I have a feeling it'll be slow today."

And she was right. It was. Ian stopped by at lunch to check on me. Considering I felt like I hadn't seen him in a while, it was sweet. He'd been busy with bears, and I'd been trying to recover from becoming a wolf. For just a moment, the pair of us enjoyed a little time together talking about pretty much nothing, but eventually I had to get back to work.

Soon enough, it was time. Roman honked his horn when he passed the office, making me look up. Gabby was in the passenger seat waving at me like a typical teenager, but she had a massive smile on her face. Since that was my sign, I headed into Ashley's office, picked up the pile of presents, and let her know I was leaving for the day.

"Five o'clock," she told me. "If you aren't at the trails, we'll come find you!"

"We'll be there!" I promised.

I had to use my back to open the door. Halfway home, I was sure I'd drop at least one of the packages, but I made it. Thankfully, Gabby saw me coming and opened the front door wide enough for me to make it inside without losing them either. I didn't even make it to the kitchen, stopping at the coffee table to set down my daughter's haul.

"Happy birthday," I told her. "Now, I need to change, because I've been told we have a date tonight."

"Wolf lessons!" she said proudly. "Olivia and I are going to make sure the trails are private, and you are going to get naked in public."

"Yeah, which means I need something easy to put back on." Then I pointed to the presents. "If you read the tags, you can start opening those."

"Yes!" she breathed, dropping onto the couch to grab the smallest one.

"That gets saved for last," I told her. "When I'm back. The rest you can open."

Naturally, she pulled out the biggest, making a production of shaking it. "Then you'd better hurry, Mom."

I did, trying hard not to look like it. Behind me, I could hear her ripping at the wrapping paper. As fast as I could, I found a pair of sweats, a sports bra, and the biggest t-shirt I owned. It was Lane's. My panties were the kind I wouldn't be ashamed for anyone to see - neither too revealing nor too prudish - and I picked a pair of slip-on canvas shoes so I didn't need to worry about socks. My hair got tied into a knot at the back of my neck, simply because a tie wouldn't shift with me, and then I headed back to see what Gabby thought of her haul.

Of course, she'd made her way through all of it. The boots were on the coffee table and unzipped as if she'd already tried them on. The gift card was beside them. The dress was Gabby's first little black one, and it had been folded just haphazardly enough to prove that she'd checked it out. The hoodie was lying across her lap as if she didn't want to let it go, and then there was the last little box.

"Can I open it now?" she asked.

"Yes," I told her.

Gabby tore into the side, revealing a small, white cardboard box. Her brow creased, and then she opened it. Slowly, that line went away and her mouth fell open. My daughter's eyes jumped up to me even as she lifted out the necklace.

"It's wolves," she breathed.

"You and me," I told her. "And it should be safe to shift in, right?"

She nodded, showing me how it worked. The necklace was a silver cable thick enough that it wouldn't break easily. Both ends fit through a single silver bead that could slip up and down the length, making it either a choker or a longer necklace. I was used to clasps that were a pain to get on and off, but Ashley was right. This one would stretch to fit.

"Is it ok?" I asked.

She nodded, biting her lips together. "I love it, Mom. And the guys gave me a real Wolf's Run hoodie. Look!" She proudly held that up for me to see.

I wasn't sure what made me happier, that she treasured a hoodie from my boyfriends, or that the necklace made her emotional. Either way, it felt like a win, and I owed Ashley so much for helping me pull this off.

"Guess it means you're an official part of management now, huh?" I asked.

Her tongue darted out to moisten her lips. "You know Ian wants to make me his heir, right?"

"I do," I assured her. "What do you think about that?"

"Well, I mean it's cool that he thinks I'm good enough to be the next Alpha. Especially since everyone says he's the best Pack Alpha ever. Not a jerk, you know? He's fair, and smart, and Olivia says Ian's kinda badass, even if he never really shows it." She paused, her teeth finding the corner of her lip. "But are you ok with it? I mean, if I'm his heir, then what do I call him? Just Ian still?"

"What do you want to call him?" I asked.

She shrugged. "I dunno."

Which meant she very much did know, she just didn't want to say it. So I took the spot beside her on the couch and held out my hand for the necklace. Gabby passed it over, so I enlarged the loop, pushing the bead to the ends of the cables and then held it up. Obediently, Gabby ducked her head so I could slip it over her hair, and then I pulled the two dangling ends just enough so the wolves sat in the hollow of her throat.

"You," I told her, "will always be my daughter. There isn't a single thing in this world that can change that. If you grow up, find a guy, and move to another pack one day, you will still be my daughter, Gabby. The best thing I've ever done in my entire life. And the fact that Ian thinks you're the right wolf to lead this pack next? It makes me very, very proud of you."

"Yeah?" she asked.

I nodded. "But all of that has nothing to do with what you call him. He's our Alpha. He's one of my mates. He's also a good man, and I truly believe that he cares about you because of you, not me. So what do you want to call him, Gabby?"

"Are you going to marry him?" she asked instead of answering me.

This time, I was the one shrugging. "I honestly don't know. Maybe?"

So she doubled down. "Do you love him?"

"I do," I admitted. "And I love Lane, and Seth."

"But not Pax and Trent?"

I just lifted a hand. "Close. I haven't actually had as much time with them. Not with schools being shot up and people turning into wolves." I gestured between both of us, making sure she knew I wasn't pointing blame there. "But I could. I think I'm pretty close. Why do you ask, *mija*?"

"Because they feel like what a dad should be, you know?" She paused to huff. "I mean, David's like that with Roman, and Henry's like that with Ashley. Dad was never like that with me. He always acted like I'm a pest, but Ian and his betas never do that. Not even when I *am* one. And I know I made mistakes." She risked a glance at me. "I'm also kinda not sorry, because it means we're both wolves now."

"Have you talked to Ian about this?" I asked.

She shook her head. "I was hoping that maybe you could do it for me?"

"Can't," I told her. "Gabby, this is one of those things that you need to discuss with them. Not just Ian, either. You need to ask the guys how they feel about it, and what they'd want you to call them. And don't be upset if they aren't ready to be anything but your friend, ok?"

"I was kinda thinking that maybe if you were, you know, in love with all of them, that it might be ok?" She scrunched up her nose. "Because I know it would be weird if Roman jumped to marriage when I'm still trying to figure out how I feel, you know? And I figure calling them 'Dad' when you're still working on love might be kinda the same. So, I don't want to mess things up for you, because I really do like them as your boyfriends."

"I kinda do too," I assured her. "So, then how do you want to handle this?"

"Can, maybe, you tell me when you love all of them?"

I reached over to pick at the sleeve of her new hoodie. "You going to tell me when you say those words to Roman?"

"I was kinda thinking about doing it at my party," she admitted. "I'm also really nervous about it. What if he doesn't feel the same?"

"I know," I told her. "It's scary, isn't it? Trying to decide if you're moving too fast, or not fast enough, and if he's waiting or will be horrified?"

"Yes!" She let out a sigh of relief and twisted to face me. "Is that how you feel?"

"It is," I admitted. "But I really like those two. They're great guys, and they make me feel like I'm something special to them. I just don't want to say it and them feel like they have to say it back when they aren't ready."

"Roman kinda almost said it to me," she admitted.

"How'd it feel?" I asked.

"Good. Embarrassing. Wonderful. I don't even know, but kinda scary too," she told me.

I just nodded. "Like your stomach flips over and the butterflies go crazy?"

"Yes!" she agreed. "So, I'm not messing this up?"

"Not at all," I assured her. "And I'm happy for you, Gabby. But I also want you to know that if you ever change your mind - because of him, because it just happens, or because you stop feeling like that - then that's ok too. Sometimes, people fall out of love just as fast as they fell into it, and no matter what, I will always be on your side. Even if I like the guy. Even if I say he's perfect. He will never ever be as important to me as you are, ok?"

"Ok," she agreed. "And the same with Ian and his betas. They're everything I ever wanted in a dad, but I'd rather just have you than anything else."

I just leaned in and hugged her. "Oh, I love you so much, Gabby. You've turned into the most amazing young woman, and I'm so proud."

"Yeah?"

"Definitely," I promised, leaning back to look at her. "Now, we have just enough time to eat something, and then we're supposed to meet Ashley at the trails."

She sucked in a breath. "I have to call Olivia! We get to

be the bouncers so you can wolf out. And..." She began gathering up her presents. "I get to laugh at you when you fall down. At least once, ok?"

"Deal," I told her, knowing very well that it would happen anyway. "Consider that another birthday present."

"Best birthday ever," she told me.

CHAPTER 14

At five o'clock sharp, I pulled into the parking area in front of the trails with Gabby in the seat beside me. We weren't the first ones here. Ashley, Bridget, Kim and her daughter Julia, plus Heather and her daughter Olivia, were all waiting. This was definitely a "girl fest" of the wolf kind.

"The birthday girl!" Kim called out the moment we opened the car doors. "Roman wanted to come, but I told him it was a ladies-only event."

"I told him the same thing," Gabby groaned. "Mom's not used to stripping in public."

"We'll get her used to it," Ashley promised, patting the wooden chair Trent and Pax had built for me. "This, Alpha, is your clothes holder. Julia and Olivia have already made a lap of the trails."

"I'm shifting on my own now," Julia announced proudly.

"A new thing?" I asked. "And I'm sorry I don't know that."

It was Bridget who answered. "Most wolves have their first adult shift involuntarily around thirteen. Their body kinda shorts out, they usually turn into a lycan, and then they'll either catch it or go full wolf."

Kim rubbed her daughter's shoulder. "We feel kinda strange the day it's going to happen. A little hyper, I suppose? Like we just can't settle down. I told Julia that I'd rather she stayed home and nothing happen than for it to sneak up on her at school. She called me at lunch that day, and ended up shifting just before school would've been over, at home, alone with me."

"Boys too?" I asked.

Kim nodded. "All of them. The girls, at least, can get out of school by saying it's a period thing. The boys just have to call in sick. So far, we haven't had a problem, and the older kids have been looking out for the younger."

"Now it's your turn," Ashley said. "Ok, ladies. We have two hours of sunlight left, and I'm guessing Gabby has a cake waiting at home?"

"Not until Friday," I admitted. "Someone spent last week turning into a wolf instead of buying her dress and doing other responsible things."

"We'll help however you need," Heather promised. "Olivia? Can you and Gabby start a fire? I have a feeling Elena will be shifting back to human a bit to catch her bearings. Julia? There's a blanket in the back seat of my car. That way she won't get a chill."

"Thank you," I mouthed at her.

Heather just smiled. "We're all happy to help you. Now,

clothes off!" And she pulled off her own shirt to prove it wouldn't be just me getting naked.

Not that it really helped, though. Stripping in public was just weird. Anyone driving by would see all of our naked backsides. Flabby bellies and saggy boobs would no longer have anything to hide behind. Oddly, none of the women cared, so I tried my hardest to copy them. It made me realize just how long I'd been ashamed of myself, and how stupid that really was.

I couldn't change these things, so why bother hating them? I knew that the women I compared myself to were all photoshopped until they no longer looked like themselves. And yet, I'd fallen into the same trap that I tried to keep Gabby from succumbing to. I berated myself for my age, my flaws, and anything else that wouldn't be appreciated by a man. Not by me, not by my friends, but by some generic male idea of my value to him.

So I tossed my shirt on the chair, then pushed my sweats down, and in one motion removed them with my shoes. Next was my sports bra and panties. I only tucked those into my pants so they wouldn't get blown away and lost. And then I turned toward the trees and tried to make the wolf appear.

Nothing.

So I stopped pushing for it and simply reached. In my head, it felt like forward and down, as if I was mentally stretching to walk on my hands and feet, but I didn't want my ass poking up in the air. Thankfully, that was the trick. My vision blurred, fading out for a second, and then it came back with a long nose hanging right in front of it and four short legs holding me up.

My tail started wagging when I realized that I'd done

it! That made Gabby laugh, proving that she was watching - and not shifting. A glance proved that she hadn't stripped either. Beside her, Olivia was still dressed, but Julia was bouncing around Kim, proving she'd shifted on her own.

"Ok," Gabby said. "Tonight only, I get to be your wolf mentor, Mom. So, step one? You get to learn how to walk. Bark if you understand?"

I barked.

My daughter grinned. "Good. So, take as long as you need, but you have to walk all the way over to that tree stump, go around it on the far side, and then back. Then you can shift back and rest for a moment, ok?"

I barked again, and then tried. Thankfully, Lane had given me a chance to try this yesterday, but it still wasn't easy. I moved my right front paw first, and then had to step forward with my left hind leg. Next was the left front, followed by the opposite hind, and that was just one pace. I had at least a hundred more to go!

The problem wasn't picking which leg to move. It was how they operated. My shoulders were at a whole new angle. Then there was the fact that my "feet" were really my fingertips. When I tried to crawl like this as a human, I used my elbows more than my wrists. As a wolf, all of my joints were in the wrong place. My actual knees weren't where I expected them to be on the hind legs. Instead, those were my ankles. My knees were up closer to my body, and everything felt so strange!

But doing it made it easier. Step by step, I headed toward the stump. Ashley moved to my right, and then another wolf claimed my left. Her coat was a tawny color, but her legs, tail, and all of her face was a rich brown.

That was Bridget, and I loved the way her coat looked. It was so unique, but if I had to choose, I'd pick my black shade without hesitation.

The one time I wobbled, my friends leaned in to give me something to brace against. I wagged in appreciation, so Bridget nibbled at my neck like a dog scratching another. Oddly, it kinda felt nice. Like a hand rubbing a shoulder, so supportive without being too personal. To show I understood, I did the one thing I seemed to be best at: I wagged.

But when I reached the stump, I realized that walking wasn't the hardest part of this task. Turning without falling over was! I staggered like a drunk dog, whuffing at my own inability to make my body work. Somehow, I managed to get my nose pointed in the opposite direction, and it was almost as if my legs figured out how to follow.

Nope, it wasn't pretty, but each step made me a little bit better. And when I finally reached the fire, Gabby had a blanket waiting for me to shift back. I did, wrapping myself in it, and then I dropped onto my little wooden throne.

"Oh, that's not as easy as the rest of you make it look," I groaned.

"You're doing so good, though," Gabby said. "I fell over a few times."

"When Lane brought me up here yesterday, I got a little practice," I admitted.

"Oh." Gabby looked a little bummed about that. "So you already got a wolf lesson?"

"I managed to walk five whole feet," I admitted. "And

then I was worn out. Mostly, Lane just wanted me to figure out how to shift."

"Which is why you get to change between laps," she explained. "It's how Ian taught me to do it easily. Tired, excited, or anything else. Coming back to human gets to be a habit, and turning into a wolf becomes a little smoother."

"And when you can run and jump," Olivia added, "you get to learn how to be lycan, and how to stop at that point or push past it when you're upset."

"Nice." Then I pushed out a breath. "Ok. Let's do it again before I'm worn out."

"This time," Gabby said, lifting her phone, "I'm timing you. You have to get a little faster, because if you do it slower, you don't get the break. Ready, Mom? Shift and walk!"

I tossed off the blanket and reached for my wolf body. Surprisingly, it really was a little easier. No, not perfect yet, but I didn't feel like I was fighting with myself to make this happen. And when I started walking, Kim and Heather were the wolves offering support. I stretched my strange legs as much as I could, wanting to walk faster, and then Julia trotted out ahead of me. Her little silver tail was held high, wagging behind her like a little taunt.

But when I reached the stump, something moved in the woods. On either side of me, my friends' hair stood up, and someone was growling. A second later, a large, dark shape stepped out of the trees, grunting to let us know he was there. I recognized Scott immediately, but Julia yelped in surprise.

"No!" Gabby yelled, storming over. "Man, now!"

Scott immediately shifted. "Sorry," he said, dropping

his hands before his crotch as his eyes moved to the obvious pup among us. "I didn't realize anyone was out here."

"It's bitch night," Gabby told him. "We're teaching Mom how to be a wolf, and she gets embarrassed."

Scott chuckled. "Gotcha. Am I allowed to go that way, little alpha?" He pointed back toward the trees.

"I guess..." Gabby said, enjoying her position of authority a little too much.

He grinned at her. "Good. And if I shift back, you think you might do some introductions when I'm not quite so naked?"

"Fine." Gabby waited for Scott to turn back into a black bear, and then she pointed. "The black one is my mom. The grey is Kim and the greyish tan is Heather." Then she pointed at the pup. "That's Julia, and she's never seen a bear before, I don't think."

Julia shook her head in a very human "no" gesture, so Scott took a step closer. Offering a bearish grunt, he lay down and then flopped over on his side. The gesture was an obvious invitation to come closer, because he'd just exposed his underbelly for her.

"It's ok," Gabby promised. "The bears are part of the pack now. Look..." And she walked over to pet Scott's head.

The man actually leaned into it, acting as if he enjoyed the sensation. That was all it took for Julia to come a little closer. Kim followed, giving her daughter that much more encouragement. Heather and I just waited. The cutest thing, though, was when Julia set her foot right on top of Scott's, making it clear just how much bigger his paw was than hers.

When the girl decided our local bear really wasn't a threat, she barked twice and then raced back for the fire, clearly excited about what had just happened. Kim just nuzzled the top of Scott's head and made her way back to help me. With that, the bear heaved himself back up, snuffled at us in a way that sounded like an apology, and then stepped back into the shadows. Me? I started walking again, but this time, Gabby was with us, pacing me just on the other side of Heather.

"I kinda like knowing we have bouncers out here," she said. "I mean, the bears are kinda cool, and they're all trying so hard to be nice, you know?"

I whuffed, trying my hardest to show I agreed.

Gabby laughed. "Not bad, Mom. That actually does mean something like yes. But, why do you think he came out here tonight?"

"They haven't been allowed to shift," Olivia said, lifting her voice just enough for it to carry to us. "I mean, out in the real world, you know? Bears stand out more than wolves. So, I figured they've probably been out a lot since they moved in."

I'd just reached the fire again, so I shifted back to human and reached for my blanket. "Olivia's right," I told her. "Those bears are trying very hard to stay out of our way, and this is usually the least popular time for anyone to use the trails."

"Dinner time," Heather agreed, moving to the flames to keep her bare body from getting chilled. "Kinda why we picked it - and I'm calling for a hot cocoa break."

"Yes," Olivia said, hurrying back to the car. "And then Elena has to do it again, and this time she can try to trot!"

I just groaned and dropped onto my chair. "I'm going to regret this tomorrow huh?"

"Which is why I gave you a full bottle of muscle relaxers," Bridget said the moment she was back in her human form. "And crap, it cooled down already."

"Blankets!" Olivia yelled. "We got lots, and all night to make sure our Alpha Female can put Ian to shame."

"Let's go with not falling over, girls," I told them. "This week, I want to learn how to just walk at a decent speed. Next week, we'll tackle the complex stuff, ok?" Then I looked over at Kim. "And next time we do this, make sure David knows that he's welcome to come look like an idiot with me."

"I will," she promised. "As soon as I let him know that you're not just some natural at being a wolf, I think he might even agree."

"Thank god," I grumbled. "Misery loves company, you know, and he's going to be mine!"

"And your Sisterhood is going to make sure you can run with us on the next moon," Kim promised. "Both of you!"

I just tipped my head at the sound of branches breaking in the distance. "And I have a feeling we'll even have someone willing to pick us up if we need it. Think the pack will be ok with some bears chasing the moon with us?"

Heather was pulling on her pants, and shuffled around to look at me. "I think that if our Alphas accept them then the rest of the pack will. I mean, you weren't too scared of him, were you Julia?"

"Not when he lay down," the girl admitted. "I just didn't know they'd be that big!"

"And he's the little one," I warned her. "I also got to see them play tag with Lane, and my goal is to get good enough at being a wolf so they don't have to tone it down for me."

The girl's eyes lit up. "Really? Bears play tag?"

"Ours do," I told her. "And those bears? They're our packmates, even if they are a little funny-looking."

"Which is why Wolf's Run is the best pack ever," Gabby said. "Not just the biggest, but the coolest. So, you'd better learn how to keep up, Mom."

"Cocoa first," I told her, "then we can do it all over again."

CHAPTER 15

The rest of the week became a rush of insanity. Tuesday, Ashley and I picked up Gabby after her drama rehearsal to go find a dress. My daughter was adamant that white and pink were not options. She found a red one that she loved, but I said no. It made her look closer to thirty. Just like I expected, that night, we found nothing.

But on Wednesday, Ashley doubled down, making a list of every single formal store in town. The moment my daughter was home from school, we were back out. Again, she found dresses she loved and I hated. Skintight, high slits, and more. But, just as tensions started to fray, Ashley came through for me, pulling out the most amazing golden gown.

It was made of a shimmering fabric that was just a bit brighter than Gabby's eyes. The top was mature but not indecent. The skirt was full and long, more like a proper ball gown. And the fit? It was close enough that she could've worn it off the rack, yet the older woman who owned the store insisted that she could make it better. Three hours of measuring and fitting later, and the woman promised it would be ready the next day.

Then, all that was left were the accessories. I really should've done this sooner. I knew that waiting till the last minute was a bad idea, but we'd only decided to actually have her *quinceañera* right before she turned, and then the winter holidays had been upon us. Since then, it felt like we hadn't stopped. I had no idea where the time had gone, but I could feel my hair turning greyer with each new task I remembered I hadn't done yet.

But it all came together just in time. Pax had found a DJ for the music. Ian and Lane handled decorating the community center. Heather and Kim hand delivered the pack's invitations. I had a hotel set up for my parents, but they showed up at the community gates just as I got off work. I was locking up the office when the wolf at the gate let out a sharp whistle.

"Elena?" he yelled. "You expecting company?"

I looked over to see a rental car, and my mother waving in the passenger seat. "That's my parents," I called back. "Let them in, would ya?"

The man activated the gate and then leaned closer to say something. I'd barely made it to the curb before my father pulled the car up beside me and rolled down Mom's window. Leaning in, I pointed right at my house.

"I'm the one in the very corner. Feel free to park in the drive and I'll be there by the time you're out, Papa."

I would've climbed in, but of course they'd picked the

two door model, and I had no interest in wedging myself into the car for that short of a walk. My father made sure he had the right place, and then pulled away. Sure enough, I'd just stepped into my yard by the time they had the car parked, turned off, and were getting out.

"Nice place," my father said.

"Comes with the job," I admitted, "but I like it here. The school is really good - "

"There was a shooting!" my mother hissed, slamming the door to show what she felt about that.

I just sighed. "There was, but Gabby's fine, no one was killed, and the school had proper protections in place to make sure it wasn't nearly as bad as it could've been. Gabby actually just went back this week, and she said it's not as bad as she expected. Even the kids who did get shot have all completely recovered."

"Huh." My mother didn't sound impressed, but I hadn't really expected her to be.

But I led them inside. My father nodded as he looked around, clearly approving of the place. My mother glared, eyeing my furniture and decor tastes. Thankfully, just before she could open her mouth to tell me her opinion, Gabby realized we had company and rushed down the stairs.

"*Abuela!*" she squealed. "*Abuelo!*"

"Gabriella," my mother crooned, hugging her so tightly. "Look at you, all grown up."

"Just wait until tomorrow," Gabby said.

My father just lifted his chin toward me. "Is it going to be a problem getting in tomorrow too?"

"No," I assured him. "You just weren't on the list for today. I honestly wasn't sure when your flight was getting in. And if you'd like, I can show you the building."

"Not a church?" my mother asked.

"No," Gabby said, taking that out of my hands. "I'm not doing Mass, *Abuela*. No *mariachis,* either. I gave Mom a list of the traditions I want, and she said that since it's my big day, I can modernize it however I want."

"And it's pretty modern," I warned my mother. "She does have a court, but not a big one, and that was her call."

"Because you keep moving her around," my mother snapped.

"Maria," my father warned. "We moved around plenty when Elena was growing up. She's doing a good job."

My mother simply huffed. "Divorced. Will Gerardo be there for her dance, at least?"

Gabby stepped in front of me. "He's not coming. I even asked, and he said he had to work, so don't you blame Mom for that, *Abuela*."

"Not..." She looked at me.

I just shook my head. "He's not. I was hoping that you'd step in for a few things, Papa?"

"I..." Gabby looked at me. "Um, I kinda have someone to dance with. I asked yesterday, and um... it's going to be a surprise, ok?"

All I could do was nod. "Will I approve, Gabby?"

"Yep." Then she grinned. "It's going to be perfect. Promise."

I sincerely hoped so. Thankfully, Gabby changed the topic to the aspects she wanted her grandparents to be involved in. A few of them, I knew about. My mother had picked out Gabby's tiara. My father would help her cut the cake. We were just going through the last of the details when my back door opened. I turned, realizing that this might be a little hard to explain, just as Pax walked into the living room.

"Elena?" he asked.

My mother's eyebrows jumped up into her hairline. "And you are?" she asked.

"Pax, I'd like you to meet my parents," I told him. "Maria and Manuel Flores."

"Paxton Romero," he said, heading over with his hand out to my father. "I'm Elena's neighbor and got conscripted for the big event. Which..." He quickly shook my father's hand, smiled at my mother, then looked back to me. "I turned the entire arrangement sideways so Gabby will be able to make an entrance. We still have enough time to turn it back, though."

"Which way?" I asked.

"The main area will be in front of the large windows to the south. We've got the flowers being set up - "

"Flowers?" I asked.

"Uh..." He chuckled. "Yeah. Ashley may have gone overboard. But look, this puts the yard door at the front, so Gabby and her court will have the best entrance possible." He turned to her. "And you're to text me if any of those boys have problems, right? Ties, formalities, anything."

"Promise," she said, "but David's helping too."

"David?" my father asked.

"Her boyfriend's father," I explained. "They live here in the community too."

"Oh." He seemed honestly impressed. "Well, you'd better introduce me to this young man tomorrow, Gabriella."

"I will," she assured him.

But Pax tilted his head toward the back door. "Can I borrow you for a moment, Elena? There are a few of those surprise things I wanted to check on."

"Sure..." Although we didn't really have any surprise things.

I still excused myself and followed him out on the back porch. Pax blew out a breath as soon as the door was closed, yet he listened for a moment longer before he decided it was finally safe to talk.

"Vic invited his friends. Lev's Russian, evidently. His son is about Roman's age, and will be there as well. I gave them the basics of the event, let him know that a suit was appropriate, and that this was merely a cover - but also the Alpha Mate's pup's birthday. He's bringing the foxes. Three young ladies. Are you going to be able to sneak in a talk with them at some point?"

"I'll make sure of it," I told him. "And they know it's a human mingler, right?"

He chuckled. "Kinda like that term, actually. But yes, I told them. I also have Ashley standing in as your beta of sorts. Second? I don't even know what you want to call it, but made it clear that she's your assistant in running the pack. Evidently, that made perfect sense to a tiger, and the foxes are just excited to be considered." He ducked his head and shook it. "Those girls..."

"You talked to them too?"

"Yep." And he dragged a hand across his face. "Sheridan's the oldest. Twenty-three, basically raising her younger sisters. Let's just say that they're definitely foxes. The girl is just a bit higher strung than I'm used to. Although I'm not sure that's the right word. She's smart, she's got a sense of humor, and while she's just as desperate as the bears, she doesn't have that melancholy feeling about her. She's one of those people who laughs easily. I think they'll be a good fit, but they're not moving in unless we take the tigers."

"An ultimatum?" I asked.

"Not exactly," he admitted. "It's more that Lev's basically been looking out for them, and Sheridan's not willing to live someplace her pseudo-father isn't welcome. She says she's not sure she could hack it on her own with both of her sisters."

"Sounds rather packish," I pointed out.

Pax just smiled. "Kinda what I thought. Vic says this Lev guy has been urbanized for a while, so he thinks it'll work."

"And how is Vic doing anyway?" I asked.

Pax sighed. "Good. Better than I would've guessed. Those three have been on the trails every chance they can get. They've also been cleaning up the place. We have a tree down across the creek now, and one big enough to use as a wolf bridge. They made sure there's a way down and up along various spots on the creek, and it seems Scott's taken to removing the poison ivy-sumac-oak stuff. I didn't even know it's there, but he says he's mostly immune to it, and didn't want someone getting a rash."

"I kinda like them," I admitted. "They seem like good guys."

"They really do," he agreed. "But Lane kinda made it clear to Ian that Ashley's... Um... Interested?"

I narrowed my eyes, trying to figure out how much he knew. "And?"

"Elena, it's not done in our circles. There's always been

the fear of cross-contamination, and the chance that it could be fatal? It was always thought to be safer to stay away. Now, I happen to trust Bridget, and medical science has come a long way in a short time. More for this than we want to admit. But there's still that cultural problem. For so long it was off limits."

"And?" I insisted.

"Ian was shocked, but he just wants Ashley to find someone she can be happy with. He said that if it's them, then he'll fight for her right to do whatever she wants. Doesn't mean it'll be easy. Also doesn't mean Henry will approve. I know for a fact that my parents would lose their minds, but they're in Cheryl's pack now - thank God."

"What about you and Trent?" I asked.

Pax just shrugged. "I kinda gave up the old traditions about the time Ian took Seth as his beta. Doesn't mean I don't have knee-jerk reactions, but I honestly don't want to have them. So, I'm all Team Ashley on this. I was kinda hoping you could let her know, though. You know, so she's prepared? All five of us know - or have guessed - that her little drink wasn't just a drink. Seth says that Vic refused to admit anything else, but he's pretty sure more happened."

"Not betraying her trust," I told him.

Pax just leaned closer. "You kinda just did. If she hadn't gone there, you would've just said that." Then he kissed my forehead. "Now, go have fun with your parents. Sorry about barging in. Just tell them I was on Gabby duty until you got off work."

"I intend to," I said. "And turning everything was a good idea. Thanks, Pax."

"Gotta take care of our girl," he told me as he left. "Early morning, honey. We're staying home tonight so you can get some sleep."

"Then have a good night, Pax," I called after him before heading back inside my house.

And, just like I'd guessed, my mother immediately had questions. "Why did that man walk into your house without knocking?"

I gestured to Gabby. "I asked him to check up on her. Pax works in the community. He and his roommates drive around all day handling things like stuck drains and what not. So, they check in to make sure my darling little daughter isn't breaking her rules. He just didn't know I was already out of the office. I'm usually a little later than this."

"Mom won't let me play certain video games," Gabby grumbled, supporting the story.

But it worked. My mother smiled at me proudly. "Well, he seems to be a very nice young man. I'm glad you have some friends in the neighborhood, Elena. Looks like you've actually done very well for yourself."

I almost didn't know what to say to that. My mother was the kind who always pushed me to do better. For her to give me a compliment like that? It meant she was very impressed. I just hoped I didn't ruin it when I made dinner for them. Or, I could simply take them out to eat. Yes. That would be much safer, and if I paid for the entire family, it sure wouldn't hurt.

"So I was thinking," I said. "There's this nice little restaurant down the street. Can Gabby and I take you two to dinner? Give you a chance to just sit down and relax without needing to worry about anything." I looked at my father. "My treat, Papa."

He pushed to his feet. "Sounds great. I'm starving."

Which meant my mother had to accept by default. Yep, I had this. I could do this. If I could face down three bears, then I could survive a weekend with my parents.

CHAPTER 16

Saturday morning started early. I got up, did my hair into an elegant updo, painted my face, and then headed upstairs to help my daughter. Together, we pinned, curled, and fastened her hair just the way she wanted it. Then, the two of us got to work on her face. I nixed the red lipstick she wanted in exchange for a softer peach color. She added a little gold glitter to her eyes.

But she refused to remove the wolf necklace. I'd found an elegant set of earrings to complement her dress, and I'd tried to get her to wear a nicer necklace, but she was adamant that this one was perfect. Soon enough, my daughter was ready, but I couldn't figure out how to head over and meet people while simultaneously being available to make sure Gabby was ready for her big entrance.

Thankfully, Trent and Pax came to my rescue. The pair banged on the front door, warning us they were here before simply walking in. "Elena?" Pax called up the stairs.

"Hey," I said, looking down at them over the banister.

Both men wore suits. Both of their ties were in the perfect turquoise and gold colors to match Gabby's big day. The patterns were different, but they matched Gabby, and that was all that mattered. Not to mention the fact that these men looked good. There was just something about a guy who could grunge up so good and then clean up so nicely.

"Ian's waiting to give you a ride," Trent told me. A little smile curled his lips because he knew I'd just checked him out. "We're here to escort the princess for the day."

"Roman?" Gabby asked.

"Making sure Theo is presentable," Trent assured her. "They're going to meet us up at the community center. Kim said there was a slight fashion mishap, but they're handling it."

"Sam and Olivia?" she asked.

"With Heather," Pax promised. "So, you've got fifteen minutes, Gabby, then we need to meet them over there for the final check. Your mother, however, has to play Alpha because you invited a lot of friends for this."

"And my parents," I groaned.

"Go," Pax said. "We'll make sure Gabby's fine, and I'll call Ian if there's a problem." His eyes raked over me. "Since I have no idea where you'd hide a phone in that dress."

"Pax!" Gabby groaned. "Not in front of me!"

"What?" he asked. "It doesn't have pockets!"

"And you stared at her boobs for too long," Trent pointed out. "Go, Elena. We really do have this."

So I went. Sitting in my driveway was Trent's truck, but Ian was behind the wheel. His SUV was parked beside it, though, which made me a little confused. Still, I hurried to the passenger side and climbed in.

"You traded trucks?" I asked.

"Figured my SUV has more room in the back seat for Gabby's dress," he explained. "And you look amazing."

"I'm really enjoying the suits," I admitted. But as he backed out of the driveway, I realized there was something else he needed to know. "I didn't exactly tell my parents about us."

"Does that mean I'm just the friend?" he asked.

I shook my head. "No, um... " I paused to lick my lips. "The truth is that I was hoping a public situation might limit my mother's antics."

"Elena, I can handle it." He glanced over. "Promise. It's just a workplace romance. I also happen to be serious about you, and I've had more than enough people yell at me in my life that I'm not scared of it. I just want to know how you prefer to handle this."

"No, I want to tell them," I promised. "I actually hate that I can't say anything about the betas, but I want to at least tell them about you."

"Then let me handle it," he said.

Unfortunately, that didn't stop my nerves from screaming at me. I knew that something would go catastrophically wrong today. It was impossible to make an event like this truly perfect, yet I knew we'd handle it. Ian, Trent, Pax, Lane, and Seth always found a way to step in just when I needed them. Plus, the Sisterhood of Being Too Old for That Shit had my back. I wasn't doing this alone, so we'd make it perfect for Gabby.

We arrived to park right in front. There were temporary signs posted in front of the best parking spaces. One of them said, "Mother." Another said, "*Abuelos*." The last one, however, was the cutest: "*Princesa*." That was for Gabby, and I had a feeling she'd love it. The only problem was that my parents had managed to beat us here.

Ian opened my door and then offered his arm, so I let him escort me inside, but I hadn't yet seen the actual room. The guys had promised that they'd handle it, and I'd simply believed them. And they definitely had. Our community center looked like it had been turned into a wedding reception. Tables were placed around the edge of the massive room. White tablecloths were accented with turquoise and gold. From the flowers to the napkins, everything just worked, and it was gorgeous.

"Wow," I breathed. "Ian..."

"That wasn't just me," he admitted, gesturing to where Ashley was talking to three very large men in suits. "Ash!"

"Elena!" she called, seeing me. "Are you losing your mind?"

"Close," I admitted, letting go of Ian to give her a hug. "Pax and Trent are helping me be in two places at once."

Then Vic stepped up behind her and offered his hand. "Elena," he greeted me. "You look beautiful."

Ian's eyes narrowed. "Mhm," he said, the sound an obvious warning.

"So far, I've seen her in sweats more than dresses," Vic reminded him. "Nothing inappropriate, sir."

Jax chuckled behind him. "Already in trouble, Vic?"

"Just trying to be nice," Vic promised. "And I think I'm going to go back in my corner."

"You're fine," Ian assured him. "I'm just giving you a hard time. Have your friends shown up yet?"

"Not yet," Vic said. "I told them to come later so the family thing wouldn't get awkward."

"Well, let me know when they do," Ian said. "And now, I get to meet my girlfriend's parents." He lifted a brow and looked at the guys. "If you see my, um, roommates? Let them know I might not make it through the day."

Vic chuckled. "Don't envy you at all. Meeting the parents is always the worst. Good luck."

Then Ian offered his arm again. I took it, but this time I was the one leading us around the room. Soon enough, I spotted my parents at the side, huddled together because they didn't know anyone else. I pushed out a tense breath, lifted my chin, and decided that I might as well get this over with.

"Mama," I said when we were close enough. "Papa. I'd like to introduce you both to Ian, my boyfriend."

Surprise took over my father's face. "Boyfriend?"

"Yes, sir," Ian said, offering his hand. "My sister and Elena have been best friends for a while. When she started working here - "

"You work here too?" my mother asked.

Ian ducked his head and chuckled. "Technically, yes."

"Technically?" my mother asked, an accusatory note in her voice. "And what exactly does that mean, young man?"

"It means that I don't really get paid for it because my family owns Wolf's Run, Mrs. Flores. So, yes, I work." He let go of me to offer his hand to my father. "Mr. Flores, it's a pleasure to finally meet you."

"How old are you, boy?" my father asked.

"Thirty," Ian admitted. "I know, I'm younger than your daughter. It's the first thing everyone says, including her."

"And Gabriella?" he asked. "You do realize that you don't get one without the other."

Ian's lips curled into a smile. "Trust me, Elena made that very clear the first two times she turned me down. I happen to like that little girl, though. Well, usually. She's a handful, but she's also amazing."

My mother just turned her glare on me. "Why didn't you mention a boyfriend last night?"

"Because we were discussing Gabby's *quinceañera* and catching up." Then I sighed. "I also knew that you'd hate him because he's not Hispanic and younger than me."

"Well..." My mother plastered on a smile and looked up at Ian. "Guess it's really not my place to have an opinion."

"Sure it is," Ian told her. "Doesn't mean I'm going away, though. Hate to break it to you both, but I'm in this for the long haul. Now, can I introduce the two of you to a few of our friends?" And he gestured to the side where his father was talking to some other pack members. "This is a very close community, and Gabby was adamant that she wanted all of her friends here."

He caught my eye as he guided my mother away, but my father hung behind. "A younger man?" he asked.

I just sighed. "Yes, Papa. Ian's great, though."

"Rich," he corrected.

"It's really more capital and less cash," I assured him. "But I'm not dating him for his money. He and his sister have been running this business since their father was in a car accident. Henry had a long recovery, so they took over and just never stopped. The Langdons are closer than we ever were, and they've been great for Gabby."

"What about you?" my father asked. "Elena, all I want is for you to be happy."

"I actually am," I promised. "Ashley's been my closest friend for years, and Ian? He's so much like her. We clicked. The fact that his roommates - like the guy who stopped over yesterday - are basically Gabby's uncles? Trent's been helping her with drama, Pax makes sure she's not in trouble, Lane steps in to threaten her boyfriend when I'm not around, and Seth helps with her homework. The guys are great with her, Dad."

"Guys," he said.

Which was when I realized I'd slipped up. "Yeah. Pax, Trent, and Lane were all basically raised by Henry. Lane's parents were killed when he was a boy. Pax and Trent had very absentee parents, but I guess they're like second cousins or something? So they're basically Ian's brothers. Seth was a college friend who kinda joined the family through attrition, it sounds like. And when I showed up, Henry decided that since I'm Ashley's best friend, I got to be included as well. He calls Gabby his granddaughter by default, since none of his children have given him any."

"And when Ian wants kids?" my father asked.

"Can't have them." The voice that answered didn't belong to Ian, and it startled me enough to make me spin around. Ashley just rubbed my shoulder, making it clear I could relax. "My brother can't have kids," she explained. "He always wanted them, but he found out in his twenties that it just wasn't going to happen. Ended up in a very nasty breakup, and he was single for a long time after that."

"Ashley," I said, "I'd like you to meet my father, Manuel

Flores. Papa, this is my best friend in the world, Ashley Langdon."

"Ian's big sister," she told him as she offered his hand. "A pleasure, and yep, we're claiming Gabby. I call her my niece."

"I'm just worried about my own little girl," my father explained. "Your brother is quite a bit younger than her."

"Only physically," Ashley assured him. "Ian was that kid who graduated high school early and blew through college. He's a go-getter, and he takes family very seriously. We were raised that there's nothing more important. I'm just waiting for the day that I can finally call Elena my real sister because she marries into this mess." She grinned. "But let me show you the drinks. We have a full bar with both alcoholic and non-alcoholic versions. It's right - "

The music suddenly went quiet and a door at the back of the room opened. The light from outside worked as a natural spotlight, showcasing the two girls and two boys who walked in first. Samantha was escorted by Theo. Behind them came Xander and Olivia. Then, at the back, Roman led my daughter in looking like the proudest boy in the entire world.

And in that gold dress, she really did look like a little princess.

CHAPTER 17

I had no clue about half of these traditions for a *quinceañera*. In truth, I was completely and totally faking this, but it was important to Elena and Gabby, so that made it important to me. But when a chair was pulled to the front of the room for Gabby to sit down, I couldn't help but think that my pup looked so grown up and beautiful. The smile on her face was the best part, though.

She'd wanted a fairytale, and we'd done everything to give it to her. That gold dress shimmered like it was made of metal. The flowers around the room let off the sweetest scent. Her friends all matched, setting them apart, and my little heiress had no problem being the center of attention.

Her grandparents came first. Maria stepped in to place a sparkling tiara on her head, securing it so it would last all night. Manuel passed her a little baton and what looked to be a small china doll dressed almost the exact same as Gabby. The girl beamed at her grandparents, said a few things that were lost in the murmuring of the crowd, and then the pair stepped back.

Next, it was Elena who walked forward. While Gabby sat there with the little doll in her lap and the baton - no, that was a scepter - in the crook of her arm, Elena knelt. Slowly, my mate worked off her daughter's shoes and replaced the flats with heels. At one point, Gabby had to dab at her eyes, and I had a feeling Elena wasn't much better.

Pax had explained this part to me, though. Usually, it was the girl's father who removed her childish slippers and gave her the heels of a woman. The whole thing was symbolic, so I thought it even more fitting that Elena was the one to guide Gabby into adulthood. Sure, she was still a child to me, but she no longer looked like one. Somewhere in the last few months, our little girl had turned into a pretty amazing young lady.

Then Gabby caught Elena's hand and said one last thing. I caught a look of confusion on my mate's face, but she just nodded and stepped back. That was when the music began to play, and it meant it was my turn. Just like at a wedding, the father-daughter dance was a very big deal, and my little girl no longer had a father. That she'd asked me, of all people, to stand in?

With everyone watching, I walked straight through the crowd and bowed before her like the perfect gentleman, offering her my hand. She placed hers in it and the first chords to a lovely symphonic waltz began to play. I paused to kiss her knuckles, and then lifted her from the chair. The smile on Gabby's face proved that I'd just nailed it.

"You know how to follow?" I asked.

"I know how to waltz," she teased. "Do you?"

"I've been to a few formal weddings," I said as I clasped her waist and moved into position.

Then I stepped, and my pup followed perfectly. No, she wasn't the best dancer, but neither was I. Her dress, however, made up for it. With everyone watching, I swept her around the small dance floor, making her skirts swirl like something from Beauty and the Beast. When I snuck in a little spin, she giggled loud enough for everyone to hear.

"Where did you learn to dance?" I asked when she was against me again.

"Dad used to do these fancy things for work, and he thought it was cute." Then the little imp decided to send me out in a spin.

I went with it, and the crowd of watchers laughed, but Gabby's was the loudest. As the pair of us made a production out of having fun, I caught a glimpse of Elena standing with her parents. She had one hand pressed to her lips and her eyes were sparkling just a little too brightly. It actually was a good look for her.

"I think we're going to make your mom's mascara run," I warned Gabby.

"Probably," she agreed, "but you really are the best dad I've ever had, Ian. My real one never cared, and I know you don't just like me because of my mom. I..." She bit her lips together and moved with me through the corner. "That's why I wanted it to be you, because you are my dad in a way."

"As much as I can be," I promised her. "No matter what ever happens between Elena and me, I still want you as my heir. Gabby, you're an amazing girl. You're going to grow up and become a miraculous woman, and any time you need a father figure, I will be there. For broken hearts, for chasing off boys - or mean girls. I don't care." And I leaned in to lower my voice. "You're my pup in spirit if not truth, ok?"

"Maybe your daughter too?" she whispered.

"To me, it's the exact same thing." I squeezed the hand I was holding. "You're mine, Gabby, and I take good care of those I care about."

She didn't care about the music. Gabby just stopped and wrapped her arms around my waist, hugging me as hard as she could. I pulled that girl tight against my chest and hugged back, daring to kiss the top of her head just in front of her tiara just as the song came to a close.

"Makeup ok?" I asked her.

She sniffed but nodded, looking up at me to prove it. "I think so?"

I wiped the corner of her eye, where just a bit was threatening to smudge. "Beautiful. And now it's time for your little court." So I bent and kissed her hand again, and then sent her off towards Roman.

Me? I walked off the dance floor and right to Elena. My betas were there, along with Ashley. That made me check to see where the bears had ended up. I was almost to Elena when I saw them talking to a man in the corner. I didn't recognize him, but the teen boy at his side made me think that our tigers had just arrived.

"She asked you to dance with her?" Elena asked, not caring about anything else.

I nodded. "Surprise? I mean, I wasn't about to say no."

She just took my hands. "Thank you, Ian. It really does mean a lot to her. And to me."

"And to me," Manuel said. "Thank you, son. This is a big day for that girl."

"I'm learning," I assured him. "I just can't believe she's so grown up already. It feels like just a few months ago she was a bratty little kid sulking because she had to move in next door."

That actually made Maria chuckle. "And they don't stop growing up," she warned me. "I hope you know what you're in for, young man."

"I do," I promised. "Today, I get to have the two most amazing ladies in the world on my arms."

"Yeah..." Ashley said, pushing her way in. "Hate to break up your moment, Ian, but we're running low on wine."

Elena turned. "Oh, I think we - "

"We got it," Ashley promised. "Be a mom for a day and let us handle the details. Lane? I need muscles."

Which meant that this had nothing at all to do with the wine. Considering that I'd already seen the tiger, I was honestly impressed with my sister's subtlety. Still, I dared to kiss Elena's cheek before letting Ashley tow me toward the door. Just as we reached them, she jerked her head at Vic but didn't stop walking until we were outside. Lane followed a second later.

"Foxes aren't here yet," he told me just as the bears stepped out of the doors.

"Ian," Vic greeted me. "This is my friend Lev and his son Nikolai."

"A pleasure," Lev said, offering his hand.

I accepted, aware of the musky scent of this man. It wasn't strong, but just unique enough to be noticeable. "I hear you're looking for a place to call home."

He let go of me and pulled his son beside him, clasping the boy on the shoulder. "This is my boy. I want him to go to school and get his diploma. To do that, we need a home, and there aren't a lot of places for people like us. Vic says you are reasonable, so what do we have to do to prove ourselves?"

"My main concern is whether or not the community will accept you, and how the two of you will deal with our method of leadership. You see, the community of Wolf's Run works together, and I'm the one who makes the rules. They will apply to you."

He nodded, glancing over at Ashley. "His mate, I presume?"

"Sister, actually," she told him. "The Alpha Female is my best friend, and this is her daughter's big day. I stand in for her when she's not available."

Lev's head twitched, tilting to the side, and he looked back at me. "The Spanish woman?"

"Latina, but yes," I assured him.

"She is not an alpha," he pointed out.

Vic chuckled. "Lev, she just turned last week. And that young lady in the gold dress in there? She's the next in line."

Lev glanced at his son. "Which means you treat her with respect, Nik."

"Dad," the boy groaned.

I lifted a hand. "We're not that stuffy, I promise. Gabby can also take care of herself. All I'm saying is - "

"Lev!" A young girl squealed as she jogged toward us, her heels clicking loudly on the concrete sidewalk. "You're in a suit!"

"Ridley," Lev groaned. "Sweetheart, a little decorum.

This is Ian Langdon and his sister." And he gave her a pointed look.

The girl - who was clearly one of the foxes, even if her hair was as black as Elena's wolf coat, sucked in a breath. "Oh! I'm so sorry, sir. I... We..."

"You're fine," I assured her.

"Ridley," a redhead hissed when she got close enough. "Manners. Public." Then she looked from me to Ashley and over to Lane. "Alpha?"

"Him," Nik said, flicking a finger at me.

The youngest girl, who had impressively dark red hair, grabbed his wrist, pulling it back to his side. "We're being good," she breathed at him.

And that was the moment I decided I liked this group. Sheridan was the older redhead, I knew that much, and she was trying so hard to not act like the typical fox. Her sisters, however, weren't quite managing. Ridley was the worst, but there was something impish about the youngest that reminded me a bit of Gabby.

"So," I said, "we're looking at two houses, right? Three bedrooms for each of you, since that's the smallest we have?"

"Uh..." Lev glanced at the girls. "Sir, I was thinking that maybe a five, and we could all - "

"I don't have a job," Sheridan said quickly, cutting him off. "I'm trying, but we haven't been here long, and I don't have much I know how to do, so - "

"It's fine," Ashley said, stepping forward to calm the girl down. "We don't bite. If we tried, I think the bear might bite us."

And Sheridan let out a heavy sigh. "I'm sorry, I just don't want to lie to you, and Lev said that we could stay with him until I can get work to support my sisters, and Ridley's supposed to be applying to college, but Zaria's just a sophomore in high school."

"I'll take care of them," Lev assured me.

I just lifted a hand. "This is your first lesson, sir. We are a pack. That's why I wanted all of you to come today. If you want to live among wolves, then you have to understand that one very simple thing. We're a pack, and that means we work to take care of each other. Just like Vic and his friends helping my mate learn to use her new feet."

"Yes, sir," Lev promised. "I've kinda been getting a crash course from the girls, but I'm not going to leave them alone, you see. I don't really know what wolves need, or what we can do, but my boy and I are more than willing to help out."

"There really aren't a lot of other options for us," Vic told me. "Don't know of another skulk in this state, and well, Lev and us? We kinda stand out." Then he looked at Lev. "But they have acres and acres of just trees and trails back there. Big trees that I can actually climb."

"In, like..." Lev looked over to me. "Would we be allowed to..."

There was that desperation again. I watched as the teen boy swallowed, clearly refusing to meet my eyes, and I knew it wasn't just the bears who'd had trouble shifting. The girls looked excited at the idea, but not quite as desperate, and yet the fact that this tiger was treating them like his own family? It said more than the man knew.

"Vic? Would you take them inside and show them

around?" I asked, lifting a finger to let Lev know I wasn't done with him.

"Sure," Vic said, "but I'm sending Jax out instead."

"That's fine," I promised.

Then we all waited until the three foxes and Lev's son were gone. Thankfully, this tiger wasn't bracing for a fight. He simply waited with me, looking nothing but curious. As soon as the door closed, giving us some semblance of privacy again, I asked the one question that would make or break this deal.

"Why are you taking care of three foxes?"

Lev simply smiled. "When I was a young, dumb cat, I got myself boxed in by humans. Couldn't shift, or I'd have to explain the naked man. Can't exactly bust out as a tiger when the group were all hunters. So, I did the next best thing. I tried to hide, but they just kept on coming. Then this sly little fox showed up, shifted into a man - yes, a man - and tossed a bunch of clothes on the ground. Not my clothes. Just clothes I'd never seen before. I shifted and he kissed me just as those hunters stepped into view."

Lane ducked his head and laughed. "And they didn't shoot you?"

"Nope," Lev said. "Thought they'd walked in on some pretty kinky stuff, blushed as bad as I was, and hurried off the other way. Well, that fox was their dad. Said he figured it would explain my lack of clothes, and yeah, it kinda did. We became friends, meeting up for drinks after that. About once a year, give or take. Well, he found himself a little vixen, invited me to the wedding, and they had those three girls. When the hunters got him, I swore I'd take care of his family. His wife died about two years ago now, shot by some farmer, so I convinced the girls to come here. Heard about Wolf's Run, and I was kinda hoping to get them and my son the chance to grow up in a way their parents never could."

"Where's Nik's mom?" Ashley asked.

Lev just pushed a hand across his mouth. "California, eight years ago. Tiger escaped an exotic breeding facility. Got shot making a run for it." He tried to force a smile but failed. "They used helicopters to track her. She couldn't shift. She couldn't get away. They fucking shot her on the evening news, and my boy saw it."

I closed my eyes and just clenched my jaw. It was a story I'd heard too many times. Hit by a car. Shot by a hunter. Caught in a trap. Over and over, our kind always ended up having to make the hardest of choices. If we exposed ourselves we might live, but it would endanger everyone else like us. Our friends, our families, and our loved ones.

"We'll find a way to make this work," I decided. "I don't know how, Lev, and if you turn on my pack, we will make you regret it, but my little girl? That young lady who's birthday we're celebrating? She says that diversity can make us stronger, and I'm fucking tired of hearing about us dying. The world is changing, so we need to change with it. I honestly think this has to be the first step."

"We won't be perfect," Lev told me, "but we sure will try. You just point me at who I need to impress, and I will be the nicest house cat you've ever seen."

"I'd kinda prefer a tiger," I assured him. "Just try not to scare the kids?"

"I'm good with kids," he promised. "It's usually the men who don't like me so much." And he looked over at Lane.

"Kinda like you. You smell more like wolf than all the rest."

"Raised by wolves," Lane assured him. "I'm also friends with bears, so sounds like we have common ground."

"I just want to make sure my son doesn't need to run," Lev told us. "If you want me to jump through burning hoops? I can do that. Don't even care about my pride anymore. I just want to know that my boy and those three girls can one day get old. Everything else is just gonna be me learning how to make that happen."

"Then welcome to Wolf's Run," I told him. "Looks like we're winging this now."

CHAPTER 18

I watched Ian and Ashley sneak outside with the bear, his friend, and the teen boy. I noticed when the foxes arrived out front. Now, Gabby was giving a little speech, which was actually rather cute. The whole group had made their way in while she talked - mostly in smaller groups - and my eyes were tracking the new predators mingling among my pack. Since I couldn't be Elena's boyfriend today, and I wasn't really needed for most of this celebration, I decided to keep my eye on the newbies.

"Hey, Seth?" Trent asked, grabbing my arm to catch my attention.

"Foxes are here," I whispered.

He just tipped his head the opposite direction. "Tiger. Kinda more worried about him than the girls. Lane's watching the dad."

"How about I pace the boy and you get Heather and Kim to meet the girls?" I suggested.

"I can keep an eye on the boy," Trent scoffed.

I just gave him a pointed look. "You have to play nice today. Pax has to step in when Ian can't. Elena's going to need help, and I'm not boyfriend material. So, let me do this, and the rest of you make sure Gabby's big day is everything she wants."

Trent patted my shoulder. "Can do. I'll also make sure she knows."

"She knows," I assured him, because I'd already caught Elena looking at me a few times.

She wanted to say something. She'd managed to brush her fingers across my hand or arm at least three times now, but we were both aware of her parents hovering at her side. If they had a problem with Ian, there was no way they'd accept a guy like me dating her, and that wasn't a fight any of us wanted to have today.

I would, though. If I had to fight to be with my mate? Yeah, I would throw down in a serious way. Damn, but that woman made me feel wonderfully stupid. Just thinking about her curling up against me put a little smile on my lips as I slipped through the crowd, trying to see where the young tiger was going.

Naturally, to the bar. I strained my ears to listen, only to hear the boy ask for a Coke instead of a beer. Granted, his father was around here somewhere, and that would probably put a bit of a damper on things. Then Roman, of all people, noticed him.

"Hey," Roman said, moving to the guy's side. "I'm Roman, with the birthday girl. Haven't seen you around."

"Nikolai," the kid responded. "Kinda here by invitation." Then he closed his eyes and inhaled. "You live here, right?"

Roman just smiled. "Yep. Gonna guess you're a cat man, huh?"

"Definitely," Nikolai agreed. "You're more of a dog kinda guy, huh?"

"Oh yeah," Roman said around a laugh. "Tenth grade?"

"Yep," Nikolai said. "You?"

"Same. Gabby's in the ninth. The blonde beside her and the Black girl are too." Then Roman jerked his thumb that way. "I can introduce you if you want."

Nikolai's green and yellow eyes just narrowed. "You related to someone special or something?"

"My girlfriend is," Roman explained. "She's also pushing for a little diversity. Kinda why she has a human as her beta. C'mon, let me introduce you. Promise, we don't bite unless you do."

"Sure," Nikolai decided, letting Roman lead him deeper into the crowd.

I had to admit, I was a little impressed with the kid. Sure, tigers were supposed to be isolationists and all that, but this was still a room filled with wolves, and he had to be able to tell. Between all the amber eyes and the smell of us all around, there was no way Nikolai had missed that, but he was still willing to follow a strange teenager deeper into this mess.

It kinda made me realize just how desperate these people must be. And if we'd already found this many without even trying, how many more were out there, too scared to even ask? As I made my way around the crowd, making sure I wasn't acting too stalkerish, I thought about that. We had about eight more houses without tenants. There was another block ready to build, and that would give us another dozen.

And then there was the land behind us. If Henry purchased the abandoned apartment complex at the side, we could effectively double the available space for housing. Granted, that was a multi-million dollar investment, but I was starting to get the feeling that it just might pay off. Not that it would happen fast, but it was definitely something we needed to think about.

When I reached the kids again after coming around from the other side, I found Nikolai being introduced to Gabby's betas. Samantha smiled at him like it was no big deal. Then again, had anyone told her what he really was? Probably not. Olivia was clutching Xander's hand, making it clear she was taken, but that wasn't who the boy was looking at.

Nope, Nikolai's eyes kept making their way back to Theo. The same boy who'd made a mess of things by releasing a video, but there was no way for the tiger to know that. Samantha had taken public credit for it. So far as the rest of the world knew, Theo hadn't been involved at all. The rest of us were aware that he'd made a stupid and innocent mistake because he happened to have a crush on Roman. One that wasn't exactly reciprocated. But from the way Theo was blushing, maybe things weren't going to turn out so bad after all.

"Champagne?" Pax asked as he fell in at my side, all but pushing a glass on me.

"Beer?" I asked.

"Not at this event," Pax said, making it clear I would take it. "So, anything of note?"

I paused to taste the bubbly, surprised to find that it wasn't as bad as I'd feared. "Remember how you thought the whole Theo and Roman thing was cute?"

"Mhm," Pax mumbled.

I just tilted my glass toward the kids. "What do you think of that?"

Roman patted Nikolai's shoulder like they were old friends and then moved around him to say something to Xander. That effectively pushed Nikolai right beside Theo, and the human ducked his head to smile at the ground. Nikolai just offered his hand and introduced himself as gracefully as any man could hope to.

"Nikolai," he said. "I got invited and don't really know anyone here at all."

"Theo," the other boy told him, blushing just a little too much. "Um, I came with Samantha. I mean, no. I didn't..." And he sighed. "She needed a guy to dance with, and since I kinda owe her one..."

"So, not your girlfriend?" Nikolai asked.

"Oh, god no," Theo said, and then clamped his mouth shut quickly. "Yeah, I'm not really into that."

Nikolai just smiled a little more. "I see."

Pax chuckled beside me. "Go, Theo," he mumbled. "Think he'd be as friendly if he knew the kid's basically an honorary member?"

"I'm not so sure that boy cares - either of them." I flashed a grin at Pax. "C'mon, you remember being their age. It was more about quantity than quality, am I right?"

"Karen," Pax reminded me. "We had her, and her, and pretty much nothing else until we got into college. So, not really the best example here, Seth."

"Point," I admitted. "How are the girls doing with the crowd?"

Pax subtly pointed to the other side of the room. "Heather's showing them around and..." He paused to laugh. "Looks like they're a hit, but I'm not really that surprised. The girls are a little intimidated by us, but the more people who are nice to them, the more they're opening up."

"Kinda like a wolf surrounded by bears, huh?" I pointed out, making the comparison to being surrounded by much larger predators.

Because wolves could do a number on a fox. Granted, that made it easier for the rest of the pack to accept the girls. They weren't really threats the same way as the bears. Then again, I saw Vic and Scott talking to a few people, and that seemed to be working out. Granted, not everyone was happy about our latest members, but most showed that by avoiding them, not snarling.

I was busy watching the visiting shifters when Gabby suddenly appeared before me. "You have to dance with me," she said, stealing the glass from my hand so she could pass it to Pax. "And you're next."

"I don't really dance," I told her.

Gabby didn't seem to care. She just grabbed my wrist and tugged. "I danced with Ian, Mom, my *abuelo*, Trent, and now it's your turn."

Thankfully, we weren't the only ones on the dance floor. Quite a few couples had moved in, which made me feel a little less obvious, but I still sucked at this formal event stuff. But if Gabby wanted me to dance with her, then that was what I'd do.

"Ok," I said, holding my hands out, "but you're leading."

"Deal." She put one hand in mine, placed my other on her waist, and then stepped. "So you know," she told me while guiding me around, "Mom thinks it's adorable when you guys are nice to me. Kinda gives you brownie points and all that."

"Believe it or not, I don't need brownie points with your mother. I'm doing fine, thanks."

"Mhm, she told me." And Gabby smirked like she knew just a little too much.

All I could do at this point was give in. "Do I want to know?"

"We were talking about relationship stuff," she admitted, "and I need some serious advice from a guy."

"I'm a guy," I agreed.

"Seth..." She huffed, never missing a step. "How do I tell Roman that I don't just like him?"

"You mean love?" I shrugged. "I kinda prefer the blurting it out method. I also suggest you brace for it not to be said back, but that's actually ok."

"No, it's not," she insisted. "If I say those words and he doesn't feel the same?"

"So?" I countered. "I kinda fell for your mom before she fell for me. Granted, I also didn't get to say it right away because someone's school got shot up, and then there was a video, and a bunch of other stuff happened, but it didn't change anything. I felt that way, she deserved to know, and she got there."

Gabby glanced over her shoulder, checking on Roman and her friends. "So, how do I let him know that?"

I leaned in a bit. "You say, 'Roman, I think I'm in love with you, and I just want you to know that. If you're not there yet, that's ok, but I am, and it's only fair for you to know.'"

"Oh, that's good," she agreed. "And if he says it's not like that?"

"He won't," I promised.

"But if he does, Seth?" she begged.

I dipped my head to make her look at me. "Gabby, he won't. Now, maybe this is news to you, but a guy doesn't risk exposing his entire species and take the chance of getting killed for just anyone. He does that for a girl he's in love with. Trust me on this. Maybe he hasn't realized that connection, but it's still there."

"Yeah?"

I nodded. "Yeah. We're pretty simple, Gabby. We like pretty girls who like us back. We go stupid over strong women who can keep up and don't need us to do everything for them. And give us one who is as sweet and smart as you can be sometimes?" I let go of her waist to tap her nose. "Look, I don't care if he's your beta, your mate, or both. I don't care if your little group breaks all the rules and makes new ones. In fact, I kinda think you should. I think that you need to be true to yourself first, and if that means telling him how you feel, then I'm here to help however you need."

She bit her lower lip. "You sure about that?"

"Why...?" Because that sounded like she had a plan.

"After the party, my grandparents want to take me out. Just them. That means I'll get home late, and the last time I tried to get Roman to come over at night, we got in trouble. So... I kinda want to do it tonight so that it's the most perfect day ever."

I just hung my head, right as the song ended. Taking the reprieve, I let her go and offered my arm instead, guiding her back towards where Pax stood holding both of our glasses. Unfortunately, Gabby was still watching me, making it clear she wouldn't let this go.

"We're making plans," I assured her just as we reached Pax. "Hey, man?" I asked. "Our girl needs a little help. You in?"

"Sure?" He gave me a wary look.

"I've just agreed to chaperone date night with her and Roman. I think they're going to use our hot tub. You and Trent need to keep Elena out of it, because Gabby has a big moment with her boyfriend tonight."

Pax's eyes narrowed. "Yeah, no."

"Not sex," I groaned. "Words, Pax. Important ones."

A smile took over his face and he looked over to Gabby. "So, that's how it is, huh? Ok." And he turned toward her. "I'll get Trent and Ian at your house, and we'll distract your mom."

"Eww," she said.

"Says the girl talking about making out in my hot tub," he teased. "No judging, kiddo. But that means you'll have Lane and Seth in the living room, right on the other side of the windows."

"I'm not going there," Gabby insisted. "I just want, you know, to not have Ian or Mom listening in."

So Pax looked at me. "You cool with her spending the night?"

"Yeah?" Even though that was kinda weird.

"Ok," Pax said. "So, you're crashing at our place with Lane and Seth. You can use Ian's room again. Get your stuff together before you leave with your *abuelos,* and we'll make sure it gets there. Then, Seth and Lane will be chaperones, so Kim will let Roman stay out late. I'll take the heat from your mom, but you, young lady, have to promise me one thing."

"What's that?" she asked.

And he offered his hand. "That you'll dance with me."

Instead, Gabby threw her arms around his neck and hugged him. "Thank you, Pax. I knew you'd understand."

He just hugged her back. "I do, Gabby. Kinda working up to having the same kind of date myself. Besides, this is what your betas are for."

She let go of him and wrapped her arms around my waist. "I love you guys, you know that? Thank you, Seth. For all the advice. And you, Pax, for the plan."

"And you still owe me a dance," Pax told her. "Seth? Cats on the move." And he stole our pup away, grinning just a little too much.

Damn, I could get used to this. Not the tigers and bear stuff, but the family stuff. Ian was right. I'd always assumed kids would be a mess and that I'd suck as a father figure, but right about now, I felt like I had this. I might even work up to being a good influence. Then again, I wouldn't put money on that.

But my little girl was in love. I was in love. My pack was growing, and all was right with the world. Hell, even the champagne was pretty good, and I had the rest of Pax's glass to finish too.

CHAPTER 19

The cats were friendly. The bears took the focus off them, and the foxes seemed to get along with everyone. I noticed, but I was too busy with everything else to be as social as I wanted. I still watched as every one of my guys made a point of dancing with Gabby. Seth was wonderfully awkward, allowing her to lead. Trent, Pax, and Ian all had grace and danced as if they were used to doing it.

Then there was Lane. Gabby didn't even try to dance properly with him. She just got into the right position and the pair of them kinda shuffled. I could see their mouths moving, proving the pair were talking about something. At one point, Lane nodded and my daughter tossed her arms around his waist. Lane just beamed at her like she was the most adorable thing he'd ever seen.

When that was done, she stole one more dance with her boyfriend, and then we started closing everything up. Gabby made another little speech, thanking everyone for coming out, reminding them not to drive if they'd had too much to drink, and thanking her friends for helping her celebrate. Not long after, people began to disperse.

"Elena?" a man asked, stepping around my father. It was the tiger, and for a split second, I couldn't recall his name.

"Lev, right?" I asked.

"Not a friend of yours?" my father asked.

Lev just smiled. "My son knows the young lady. I'm pretty much out of my depth."

But Dad was eyeing him. "Is that a Russian accent?"

"It is," Lev admitted. "Moved to the country for college, managed to stay." Then he looked at me. "Can I borrow you for a moment?"

"Sure," I said. "I'll be right back, Papa. Make sure Mama doesn't embarrass Gabby?"

"Promise," my father said as I walked away with Lev.

As soon as we were out of earshot, the man leaned a little closer. "I spoke with Ian and Lane. They said we get a chance, and I'm supposed to see you Monday for a lease and the official parts. I, um..." He paused to scrub at his mouth. "The girls. Ian said that he was willing to give them their own house, but they can't afford it yet. I know they'd like it, but we don't want to ask for too much. Well, I don't. The kids? I mean, Sheridan's still a kid to me, and they don't know how far out on a limb you all are going for us. But..." He looked incredibly uncomfortable.

"Just ask," I told him.

"Is there any way their place can be close to mine? I just want to make sure that if anything happens, I'm close enough to keep them safe."

"I'll make sure of it," I promised, offering him a gentle

smile. "And thank you for coming, for putting up with this insanity, and everything else."

He just nodded. "It's kinda nice. I'm not really the most social man in the world, but I'm guessing you know that. My son, though? He made some friends, and he said he wants to go to school some place where he could be with others like him."

Which was when it hit me. These were all families of one kind or another. The tiger had a son and had all but adopted the foxes as his daughters. The bears treated each other like brothers. The pack? What were we if not one very large and somewhat dysfunctional family?

And that was the tie that would bind all of us together. Regardless of species, or type, or however they differentiated shifters, we were all trying our hardest to take care of our families, and wolves had a bit of an advantage there. Was it really such an insane idea to allow these other shifters to benefit from that? The diversity would only make us stronger, right?

"You know," I told Lev, "sometimes, I think that our kids accept things a lot easier than we do. I kinda feel like we might learn a thing or two from them. I'm sure Gabby will be happy to introduce him to a few people."

"She seems like a very good kid," he told me. "Her eyes are a little darker than I expected, but so far as I care, that's a good thing. Now I'll get out of your hair. Thank you again for inviting us, ma'am."

He bobbed his head and stepped back, fading into the crowd as easily as he would a forest, I suspected. The strange thing was that I wasn't scared of him. Not even a bit. The bears had shocked me when we first met, but the tiger? Oh, I would probably have a mild-freakout when I saw him in his other form, but as a man, he just seemed like a struggling single dad. That was something I could relate to.

But I wasn't done yet. With the guests leaving, I needed to thank them all for coming. So many had brought presents, and Gabby had managed quite the haul. Considering that most of these people had never even heard of a *quinceañera* before this? I wanted to make sure they all knew we weren't taking it for granted.

I was standing beside the door shaking hands and thanking people when my darling daughter showed up with her entourage. "Mom!" she said, all but pushing into the line. "Hey, I wanted you to meet my friends. I didn't really get the chance to introduce you earlier." And she glanced at my parents pointedly.

"It's ok," I assured her. "It was a little hectic at first."

"This," she said, "is Nikolai. He's in Roman's grade." The boy smiled and nodded, looking only slightly awkward. "And this," Gabby went on, "is Zaria. She's a sophomore too. That's her sister Ridley, who graduated last year. And the redhead is Sheridan, their oldest sister. I've already decided that Zaria and Nikolai are going to end up hanging out with us."

I just nodded. "Sounds like you have it all figured out. But, you still have a date with your grandparents tonight."

"Yeah, my *abuelos* are taking me out for dessert!" And she gestured to the door. "Let me walk them out and I'll be right back, Mom!"

It took her a while, though. Ian found me not long after that and proceeded to help thank everyone. Ashley and Henry made it clear that they'd handle cleaning everything up. The entire Sisterhood promised they'd pitch in with gathering up Gabby's presents, but Ian said they could drop them off tomorrow, and the little smile he flashed me made it clear he had plans for tonight.

Then, after what felt like the longest day of my life, it was all finally over. We headed back to my place, Gabby headed upstairs to change out of her dress, and then came back down with a backpack that she left beside the door. I noticed, but didn't want to say anything. Not until my daughter - still wearing her tiara, even if she was in jeans now - and my parents left for their big evening out.

And then I sighed and flopped back into the nearest chair. "Oh my goodness, that was a long day," I groaned.

"About to get longer," Ian said as he pulled out his phone. "Evidently, your darling daughter asked Seth for a little help, and he's now conspiring with her."

"Uh..." That sounded almost nefarious. "What are they doing?"

Ian quickly typed out a message and then put his phone back into his pocket. "It seems that she wanted to do something special when she tells her boyfriend how she feels." He pushed his hands into his pockets, still standing before me. "So, Lane and Seth have offered to hang out in the living room while Gabby and Roman have a hot tub date. Since it's her big day, we made a guess that she'd be allowed to stay out late so long as she's mostly supervised, and then she can just crash in my room for the night. The guys will make sure that Roman leaves."

"And those two will hear if anything gets out of hand, so they don't even have to watch," I realized. "Ok, that's actually kinda cute."

"Yeah, well, we were going on the theory that you keep saying you wanted her to make her own decisions, but guessed that you'd prefer they aren't completely turned loose. Elena, is this ok? We can cancel it."

"No," I decided, "it's actually perfect for her. And the fact that she asked? That's huge, Ian. Girls her age do not talk about this stuff with adults."

"She talked to Seth," he reminded me.

"He's still an adult," I pointed out. "Ok, so he seems a lot more approachable than her mother, but that's a good thing, don't you see? And she's already talked to me about wanting to tell him, so I think this is the best way to let her spread her wings a little without removing her safety net."

But he still didn't move. "Are you ok with me taking that dance with her?"

"Yes," I said, making it clear there were no "buts" about to follow.

He nodded. "Because I'm trying very hard to not overstep my bounds with her..." He paused to push out a breath. "Elena, I love that kid. I know she's not mine, and I know I don't have any right to claim her like that, but I still adore her. I want to start letting the pack know that she's my heir, but it could cause a few scuffles among the kids her age. Dominance, you know, but I honestly believe she can handle it."

"I'm ok with that," I assured him.

And yet he still looked nervous. "When we were dancing, she told me she sees me like a dad." He paused to bite his lips. "And I kinda told her that no matter what, even if things don't work out between you and me, that I will always be her dad when she needs one. I will, too. I just... I want you to know that it happened."

"Are you ok with sharing?" I asked, easing myself back to my feet.

His eyes slid down my body. "Thought I already proved that."

"Her, you lug," I laughed. "Because Gabby told me that she thinks of all of you that way. Her five dads, and she doesn't want to mess up my relationship with any of you by jumping the gun."

"Trent and Pax," he realized.

I nodded. "I'm close, Ian. I really like them, I just..."

He caught my hand and pulled me up against his chest. "Well, they're actually on their way over. I figure I can always go help Seth and Lane - " He paused as the back door opened. "Babysit," he finished.

"Mm..." I tossed my arms around his neck. "Or maybe you should help me celebrate the fact that we survived all of this today. Cats, bears, foxes. I mean, all we need now is a lion, right?"

"Oh," Trent groaned as he walked into the room. "No. Just no. Lions come in prides, and that's a lot of cats."

Pax chuckled. "Lions, tigers, and bears, Trent."

"I know," Trent said. "I'm just saying - " He grunted. "Never mind."

Seth chuckled softly. "I'm just going to sneak through here quietly, grab Gabby's stuff like I promised, and vanish." But after he picked up the bag, he turned back to face me. "You are ok with this, right? She wants to say the big L word, and I kinda gave her a few pointers on that."

"You?" Trent teased.

Seth just pointed at himself with both hands. "Me. Keep up, Trent. I managed to not screw it up at least once." Then he headed over to where Ian still held me against his chest.

Without asking, and acting like he didn't care at all, Seth leaned in and pressed a kiss to my mouth. "Love you, Elena."

"Love you too, Seth," I said.

Ian just chuckled. "And I think Seth just showed you up, Trent."

"I told you," Pax teased, "don't pick on him. Seth's a romantic at heart."

As he walked backwards for the door, Seth just pressed his hands over his heart. "Complete romantic. And if that boy doesn't tell her he loves her back, I'm chasing his ass back to his house on my own. You three have good, clean, wholesome fun while I'm pretending to be all grown up and shit."

"Night, Seth," Ian called after him, and then he chuckled. "And this is the perfect ending to a good day."

"Almost," Pax told him, reaching out to me with his palm up. "I think our mate deserves to get out of those heels and slip off that dress. Preferably while we're watching."

I placed my hand in his and let him steal me from Ian's arm. "Oh yes, I think that's a brilliant idea. Going to help, Trent?"

"Oh, yeah," Trent said. "He can deal with the shoes. I'm taking you out of that dress. Ian, lock the front door, just in case."

CHAPTER 20

We tumbled into my room with Pax kissing my lips and Trent pressed close against my back, sucking at the side of my neck. The men were still in their suits - all three of them - and I was trying to take off Pax's tie without lifting my lips from his. That was when Trent's hand found the zipper on the back of my dress. Slowly, he pushed it down, kissing every inch of skin he exposed along the way.

Ian came into the room last, closing and locking the door behind him. Then, he simply walked over to the table beside my bed and pulled open the drawer. I paused for a moment, aware that we hadn't used condoms in a while, but that wasn't what he was looking for. Evidently, my mates had been in here just a bit too much, because Ian reached all the way to the back and pulled out my vibrator.

That got tossed onto the bed, but it clearly wasn't what he was looking for. His hand made another pass through the drawer, and then he found it. Glancing back, he held up a little bottle of lube that I kept for, you know, emergencies. Pax just chuckled at the sight.

"Seems our woman is rather prepared." And then he kissed me again.

"She's still wearing her shoes," Ian pointed out, moving around the foot of the bed to claim the chair in front of my makeup table.

That, he pulled out and turned around. Before he sat down to watch, he made a point of unbuttoning his suit coat and spreading it open. Pax's mouth moved to my throat. Trent's was midway down my spine. My eyes were locked on Ian as he stepped over the chair and sat, crossing his arms over the back to enjoy his own personal show.

And I loved it. I could feel my nipples getting hard from nothing more than the feel of his eyes, but Pax was still moving lower. His mouth brushed my clavicle, I felt the heat of his breath through my dress, and then he kissed my stomach as he sank to his knees. And there, under Ian's command, he lifted my right leg and carefully removed my shoe, tossing it well out of the way.

"Kiss that while you're there," Ian told him.

Immediately, Pax's lips found the spot just above my knee, and then he placed my foot back on the ground. That forced my other leg to bend, compensating for the heel on that side. With a flick of his finger, Ian made it clear that should go as well. Pax barely had the second shoe off before Trent finally got the zipper all the way down.

"Slowly," Ian said. "I want to watch that dress slide across her body."

Trent obeyed, slipping the sleeves down my shoulders and guiding the whole thing toward the floor. I felt every brush of the fabric against my skin, but my eyes didn't leave the Alpha, and his hung on me. There was something so amazingly intimate about it. This man was truly in control, and I'd told him that I liked seeing it. Now, it seemed, he wasn't going to hold back.

"Bra," Ian commanded. "Pax, panties. Hands only."

Pax groaned, but he hooked his fingers in the straps over my hips. Trent released the clasp behind my back. I felt the cups sag, but then he was working the straps down my arms. It was hard to keep track of what I needed to move next, but the guys made sure I didn't have to worry. Arm, arm, leg, and then my other leg, and I was standing before the three of them completely bare.

"Hold her," Ian ordered. "And now you can play with that, Pax."

Trent's arm immediately wrapped around my waist just as Pax leaned in to kiss the lips of my pussy. Then his tongue flicked across me, even as he guided one leg up and over his shoulder. That gave him more access, and the man shoved his face closer, sliding his tongue right between my folds, seeking my clit by feel.

I moaned when he found it, letting my head fall back against Trent's chest. My hips twitched on their own, wanting to pump into the sensation of that tongue, and Trent murmured his appreciation against my ear. Yeah, that was sexy. I could feel the stiff fabric of his suit and the hard ridge pressing against my ass. I wanted to grind into him. I wanted to buck against Pax's mouth. Sadly, the position they had me in meant I could do neither.

"Let me play, Alpha," Trent said, refusing to plead.

"Not yet," Ian told him. "No, you can hold her arms out of my way, though."

Trent growled in frustration, but he hooked his arms in mine, pulling my elbows back to thrust my chest forward. If he wasn't holding me up, I probably would've fallen over, but Pax didn't seem to care at all. He just kept licking and sucking, driving me ever higher, and I wasn't fighting it. His mouth felt amazing. Knowing I was being watched only made it better.

But then Ian pushed himself out of his chair and headed for the bed. My heart raced in anticipation, but he simply picked up the vibrator and bottle of lube. Turning to watch me, he made a point of drizzling the clear liquid across the silicone toy. When he began spreading the lube around, Ian's hand stroked my toy as if it was himself. The corner of his mouth curled higher, then he fisted the vibrator again.

Pax paused when Ian stepped beside him, then shuffled over, spreading me even wider when he refused to let me pull my leg from his shoulder. Then Ian knelt beside him. Both of those men on their knees before me, their suits almost matching, and both of them were completely focused on my body. While Pax continued to lick and tease, Ian lifted my vibrator and gently eased it into my body.

Then he turned it on. I jerked, feeling the rush of pleasure, and Trent just held me pinned against his chest. Ian and Pax were leaning around each other, both struggling to fit, but neither seemed to care at all. They wanted me too much to worry about anything else.

When Ian began to pump the toy into my body, I knew I wouldn't last. I fought to hold in my moans, but I was losing. The first gasp broke free. Next, my hips began to tremble, and it wasn't just the touches. It was the sight of them. The knowledge that all three of these men were mine, and they cared about nothing else right now except me. I let my eyes close and gave up trying to be quiet.

The first moan burst from my lips and Trent pressed his head beside mine. "Oh, that's my girl. Take it, Elena."

Ian tilted the vibrator inside me just as Pax sucked, and the next sound that came out was almost a scream. I tensed the leg over Pax's shoulder, bucking my hips with the rhythm of these men, and knew I was going to come so hard. I could feel Trent's breath against my cheek. Pax reached up to hold my hip, controlling the way my body was struggling to help, and Ian began to thrust just a little faster.

That was all it took. I came, unable to wrap my fingers in anything because of how I was held. I couldn't kiss or cling to them. I simply lost control and shuddered as the pleasure took over my body, leaving me completely and totally at their mercy.

"Fuck," Trent groaned, shoving his hips against my back as he took my weight.

I could feel his hardness. I could hear him panting, and it matched the sound of my own breath as I tried to recover, even as Ian removed the vibrator from my body, turned it off, and rocked back on his heels.

"Open your eyes," he said. When I did, I found Ian standing right before me. His eyes slid down to my throat, hanging on my pulse, then back to meet mine. "Think you can handle both of them, Elena? At the same time?"

"Yes," I panted.

He smiled. "I'm going to let Trent have your ass if you don't stop me."

The man in question ground himself against me one more time. Clearly, he liked that idea, but so did I, so I nodded. "I'm not stopping you."

"Then take his suit off."

Ian just turned and headed for his chair again. Pax moved my leg back to the floor, but when I turned to face Trent, I felt his hands on my hips, making sure I didn't stumble. My hands went for Trent's tie first, but I felt Pax stand behind me. Once again, I was caught between them, and it was starting to become one of my favorite places.

"No, Pax," Ian said, "leave it. She'll want the show."

Pax growled, but whatever he'd been doing, he stopped. Trent's eyes jumped over my shoulder just as I tossed his tie away, and he smiled. But I no longer had any patience left. I quickly released the buttons of his coat, then went for the ones on his shirt. Once his chest was exposed, I pushed everything off, shoving his shirt and coat down his arms without caring where it landed. Then I reached for his belt.

"Pax, hold her," Ian commanded.

Arms wrapped around my waist and Pax immediately began kissing my neck. That gave Trent just enough room to kick off his shoes, then he opened his pants. I could see his dick straining against the fabric, but he took his time about exposing himself. Then he simply bent, pushing his pants, underwear, and socks off together.

"Here," Ian said.

I glanced over just in time to see him toss that bottle of lube at Trent. The man caught it and moved to the bed. Pax turned me so I could watch as Trent moved to sit in the center, using my headboard and pillows as his backrest, and then he began to work a very large handful of lube across his hard dick. And then Pax simply let me go.

I didn't wait for "permission" from Ian. I simply crawled across the bed to kiss Trent. His hand found the side of my face and he leaned into it, allowing his tongue to explore my mouth. Behind me, Ian purred as if he was enjoying this, but Pax said absolutely nothing. Damn, but I was ready to go again.

"Turn around," Trent breathed against my lips. "Reverse cowgirl, baby. Promise, I'm going to be very gentle with you."

I moved to straddle Trent's waist, facing Ian. The hands on my hips, guiding me where he wanted, belonged to Trent, but Ian's eyes were what I felt most. His gaze dropped to the junction of my legs, then down to where Trent's erection stood waiting. Then I felt a cold, slick hand slide down my seam, pausing to play with the pucker of my ass.

Ian stood, still straddling that chair, and made a production of removing his tie. That was tossed to the side, and then he released the button at his throat. But when he looked over at Trent, Ian had to reach down and adjust himself. His hand slid all the way down his length, but a tilt of his head gave Pax the permission he needed to join in.

While Pax removed his coat, Trent's thumb pressed against my ass. As he loosened his tie, Trent pressed in, easing my ass open. Pax's shirt earned me a little more as Trent pumped and teased. But the moment Pax began to focus on his belt, Trent removed his hand and something else pressed against me. My eyes hung on the man slowly revealing his delicious body, but I could feel the pressure, the stretching, the excessive amount of lube making my body accept this a little easier.

"Breathe," Trent whispered. "I'm not going to hurt you. Relax and breathe."

Pax opened his pants and shoved everything low enough to grab himself. I breathed, and he stroked, allowing me to watch as the head of his dick strained against his grip - and then Trent was in. I gasped in surprise even as he lowered me down, filling my ass completely.

"Fuck, that's good," Trent whispered.

"Go," Ian told Pax.

That was all he needed to strip off the rest of his clothes without grace. The moment Pax was bare, he crawled onto the bed, heading right toward me. "Legs," he told Trent.

Trent spread a little wider, making room for his partner and exposing me completely. I could feel the cock in my ass, throbbing in excitement, but he didn't thrust. Trent simply held me in place, even as Pax moved in to kiss me harder than he ever had before, pushing me back, forcing me to lean until my shoulders found Trent's chest.

"God, you're gorgeous," Pax breathed, dragging himself down my belly as he moved into place.

One of his legs was braced between Trent's thigh and mine. Pax pressed his other knee right between all of us, and then he reached down to angle himself, and I felt his dick slide across my folds until he was right there. When he kissed me again, Trent pulled me back a little more, and Pax leaned in. I felt his dick enter my body, stretching me slowly, and I moaned against his mouth.

I'd never felt anything like this in my life. Both of these men. Both inside me. I could feel Pax grinding against Trent's hardness as he made his way in, and Trent throbbed in anticipation. I could barely think to keep kissing Pax. All I could do was grab at his back, my other arm reaching for Trent, seeking some way to keep my mental balance.

Then they began to move. Every time Pax pumped into me, Trent retreated, and it did the most amazing things to my body. Slowly, they eased me into it, moving just a little faster, pushing a little deeper with each rock of our bodies. I just closed my eyes and let it happen. I didn't care that they weren't playing with my breasts. I could barely keep up with Pax's mouth on mine. Then Trent's lips found my shoulder, sucking at the skin even as the three of us rocked together.

It all felt so good. I'd read about this, but I'd never imagined how it would really feel. These men were so close, not caring if they touched each other in their quest to get to me. They groaned, grinding against each other inside my body and clearly loving it. I whimpered, unable to worry about how loud I got, because I didn't want this to stop. I even forgot that Ian was still in the room - until he tossed his suit coat beside the bed.

My eyes jumped open, but he noticed. "Oh, don't mind me," he said, hurrying to get his shirt off.

"She feels so good," Trent groaned, sounding like a warning.

"Not yet," Ian told him. "You're pleasing her, remember?" Then he lost his pants.

Ian made his way onto the bed, pushing right between both of these men. His hands found my breasts, but I wanted something else. While Trent and Pax both worked my body higher, I reached down to wrap my fingers around Ian's dick. As if that was all he needed, Ian arched his back, leaning his hips even closer, and I twisted to get that length in my mouth.

"Oh, suck it, honey," Pax groaned, thrusting into me a little harder.

I felt Trent's legs shift, the man bracing his feet on the mattress, and then he began to lift his hips up, driving himself into my ass. Long, deep strokes, paired to match the way Pax was pounding himself into me, and I groaned around Ian's dick. This felt like a dream. All three of these gorgeous men, each one losing himself in my body, all at the same time.

It felt so good, so wonderfully wicked and sensual. They made me feel powerful and seductive, beautiful and daring, all at once. This was the woman I'd always dreamed of being. Not the one too scared to try something new. Not the maid or wife or even the mother. No, caught between all of them, being pleased by my mates, I realized that I'd finally become the one thing I'd always wanted.

I was the Alpha Female. Their mate and lover. It didn't matter if I was weak or strong. No one here would judge me on that. All my men wanted was me, however I was willing to be with them, and it was the most amazing thing I'd ever imagined. It felt good. So many hands, mouths, and each one of them driving me just a little higher, until I couldn't take anymore.

I came so hard, struggling to keep working Ian, but he

took over. His hand found the side of my face and he pumped into my mouth as the waves of pleasure washed over me. Trent groaned, grabbing my hips to lock me against him. Pax thrust, taking over, riding my orgasm and doing his best to prolong it, and then Ian gasped. Warmth flooded my mouth just as Pax lost control, spilling himself into me with a deep growl of pleasure, and still my body tingled, that intense climax taking its time to fade.

"Swallow," Ian told me as he pulled himself from my lips.

I did, looking up to find his golden eyes soft and tender. Then Pax leaned back, slipping free of my body. Trent simply lifted me higher to extract himself, and then he guided me down to the bed beside him, refusing to let go of my waist. Instead, he snuggled closer to kiss the back of my neck.

"I'll get us something to clean up," Ian assured them. "You two just cuddle with her."

As Ian headed into the bathroom, Pax flopped down in front of me. "So," he asked, "is that ever going to happen again?"

"A lot," I promised.

He smiled. "I meant the butt stuff, honey."

"Mm." I caught his waist, tugging him closer so I could press my face into his chest. "Me too. Trent's pretty good with that."

That earned me a chuckle against my neck. "Pax did most of the work, beautiful."

"Mhm," I agreed. "He's pretty good at that, too. I think next time, Pax should get my ass, Trent should let me suck him off..."

Pax turned, looking toward the end of the bed. "Make him do a little work, huh?"

Ian was walking back from the bathroom, clearly listening to us, so I nodded. "Yeah. See what happens when he's not the one calling the shots."

His steps faltered and Ian bit back a groan. "That..." He sighed, held up a damp cloth, then tossed it to Pax. "Yeah, the idea of a woman willing to tell me what to do? Hot, Elena. You decide you want to be the alpha bitch, go right ahead."

"Guess Ashley's not the only one who thinks dominance is sexy, huh?" I teased, realizing that maybe Ian had the same problem she did.

And while he'd never tried to hide that his sister was stronger than him, she was still his sister. That meant finding a woman who wouldn't submit before him had to be nearly impossible. Now that I was a wolf, I was finally figuring out just how impressive these Langdons really were.

"We," Ian said, "do not talk about my sister when I'm thinking about sex. You hear me, mate?"

I just grinned. "So, I guess that means I shouldn't mention how I got all my best moves from her?"

But he was grinning. "Not talking about it, Elena."

"Maybe I'll ask her for advice on how to tie you down, and then these two will give you a show where you can't help. Oh, I bet she has a gag somewhere to keep you from barking orders."

A muffled laugh came from behind me. Pax shoved a hand over his own mouth, but his eyes were sparkling. Then Ian crawled onto the bed, right across my body, not caring at all that his betas were still pressed against my side. When he was above me, he leaned down, brushing his lips across mine.

"This is why I love you, Elena. So strong, so amazing, so incredibly beautiful, and not a single mean bone in your body."

I just cupped the side of his face, pulling his lips back toward mine. "I love you too, Ian."

And I kissed him, aware that both Trent and Pax were right there, and those three words also kinda applied to them. Soon, I'd be able to say them. Hopefully, very soon, because I really liked this. It was everything I'd ever dreamed of, and so much more.

CHAPTER 21

I'd just made it out of the shower when Gabby got back. The guys were all helping me with dinner, and of course my parents decided to come in for one last little chat. My father looked from Ian to Trent to Pax, weighing each of them, but he didn't say a thing. My mother was simply impressed that I had a little help.

Gabby decided to make my life a little easier and thanked Trent and Pax for coming over like they'd promised to help her rehearse for her play. Pax rolled with it, telling her she owed him big time for being Alice again. Ian told me to go sit down and he'd handle dinner for the two of us. Then, just to keep the ploy going, Gabby took Trent and Pax into the dining room, and the three of them began calling out lines. Gabby laughed loudly at how bad Pax was as Alice.

I was tense the whole time, all too aware of the aches in my body and what we'd been doing while they were away. But one glass of wine was all it took to make my mother sleepy. Dad said he was taking her back to the hotel. We all said our goodbyes, and then it was safe again. But as soon as Ian told Gabby she was free and clear, my kid bailed, leaving the rest of us alone for a wonderfully relaxing evening.

The rest of the weekend was amazing. That night, Gabby got to tell Roman she loved him. He said it back, and she was on cloud nine. According to Lane, the two of them were in the hot tub kissing until about two in the morning. After that, they moved to the den, and then spent a little longer actually talking. At four, Seth decided it was late enough and sent Roman home. He said Gabby hugged him so hard before heading upstairs to pass out.

And Sunday, the group of us lounged around their place - Gabby included. She gave all of us a play by play of her big night. I, however, did not. Still, Pax made a point of sitting with me and holding my hand a little too much. Trent stole a few extra kisses. I noticed, and from the way my daughter was grinning, she did too.

Monday came much too soon, but I had wolf lessons again that evening. I also was expecting at least one tiger to show up in the office at some point during the day. Evidently, Lev was not a morning person, because it was just after two when he finally sauntered into the lobby with a smile on his face, acting like he was completely comfortable in a place that had to reek of so many wolves.

"Alpha," he greeted me.

"Hi, Lev," I said, grabbing the clipboard I'd already prepared for him. "Thanks for coming this weekend. Gabby had good things to say about your son." And I waved him over. "But I have a question for you."

He moved to the side of my desk. "Ok?"

I set the map of the community between us. "We have a pair of empty houses here. The rest of this street is packed with wolves. The bears live here..." And I tapped their house. "This is our nature trail area, but..." I made a circle on the other side of the map, right around the land that Henry had been thinking about buying for far too long. "We might be expanding here, and I wasn't sure if we should look into putting the non-wolf shifters together. Would that make you all feel better or more isolated?"

The man looked at me with a critical eye. "So, you're newly shifted, and that *quinceañera* makes me think you were raised as a minority, right?"

"I was," I admitted. "Grew up speaking Spanish at home until I was in middle school. Gabby and I use English as our primary language, though."

"Yeah, but you know what it's like to be the odd one out. Kinda didn't expect that." He looked back to the map. "In truth, I don't think it matters if you put the not-wolves beside each other or not. Tigers and bears don't usually talk, you know."

"But you know Vic..." So I'd kinda assumed it was normal for shifters outside a pack to be friendly.

Lev just shrugged. "Doesn't mean I want to live beside him. Sure, we've had a few beers when we're in the same place. Doesn't mean we're having family cookouts. Elena, those bears could crush me, and my son? They'd kill him without trying. I take care of the fox girls because I owed their dad a big one, but most large cats would want nothing to do with them. You wolves? You're like the middle ground. You're not so big that you make us nervous to be around, but there's so damned many of you that we know better than to start shit."

"So spread out," I decided. "Well, these are the only two three-bedroom homes I still have side by side. This one's on the corner, but it's a quick shot to the trails, and there's also a drainage culvert right here that will let you slip into the woods next door. For the girls, I mean. Can't really risk a tiger wandering around the city, I'm sure."

He chuckled. "No, but how safe is it out there?"

I groaned. "I don't like my daughter playing outside like that, but it's natural enough that no one would think anything of it. This apartment complex was condemned, so it's empty, and everything else is a business. No farmers to start shooting. Just watch out for animal control or the police, and it should - in theory - be safe enough. Or so I've been told."

"I'll just make sure the girls stick to the trails," he said, pausing when Ashley's door opened.

"Lev," she said, walking forward with her hand outstretched. "I'm glad you actually came back. You decide how we're handling the non-wolves, Alpha?"

"Mingling," I told her. "If we want everyone to act like one pack, then we need to treat them as if the animal they turn into doesn't matter. Lev said they don't have some common bond, and that was basically my final decision. I am trying to make sure that none of our smaller and more vulnerable shifters end up living in a corner, though."

"You have more than just us?" Lev asked.

"We're planning for it," I admitted. "But no, right now it's just the three groups of you."

"Go ahead and tell him," Ashley encouraged.

I nodded. "Wolf's Run was made to be something new. Something better, to deal with the changing world that's made it harder for shifters to go unnoticed. Until Vic stopped in recently, we'd never thought about the other kinds of shifters. I didn't even know about half of this. But, with that said, we do have an advantage. Wolves are stronger because we live in a pack. Why can't we use that to make a type of sanctuary for all of us and stop the segregation and shifter-racism that seems to have made life harder for all of us?"

"Like, a shifter haven?" he asked.

I nodded again. "Yeah, but the caveat is that this is still a pack. It's still a community where we all have to work together to keep our secret. You show tendencies of that by caring for those foxes. Vic lives with other bears. You and he seem to know each other. That makes us think that you can work within our society. And never forget that it is *ours*. This place is owned by wolves and run by wolves - but we want you to help us make it friendly for everyone. Diversity will only make us stronger, right?"

"Says the woman who grew up human." He chuckled. "I actually like that, though. So, if my boy starts dating your girl, you gonna change your mind?"

"No," I assured him. "You might, though. I'm pretty sure Gabby can handle one tiger. Maybe even two with her betas. I also think that she's the one who's pushed the hardest for this. The next generation, and all that."

Lev bobbed his head in agreement. "I like this idea. Just..." He looked back to Ashley. "Maybe you ladies can help keep the Alpha from losing his temper when we don't immediately jump every time he asks? Tigers don't have that instinct. Bears don't either. We'll try, but we will never be wolves."

"Ian's not like most Alphas," Ashley assured him. "He thinks there's a very big difference between leading and terrorizing." Then she held up a finger. "Also, I wanted to talk to you about Sheridan. She still needs a job, right?"

"She does," he agreed. "She hasn't done much, though. The girl has basically worked at minimum wage jobs all her life, just trying to make ends meet."

"This is an entry level position," Ashley said as she headed around my desk and pulled out an employment application. "It's night shift work, though, but we need a gate guard."

"Like..." Lev pointed back at the front gate.

Ashley nodded. "Yep. Seven pm to seven am, Friday, Saturday, and Sunday. Full time, salaried, and it would give her time to go to college or worry about her sisters during the day. She can study in the booth, we have wifi there, and no one even cares if she naps, so long as she wakes for cars or people trying to get in."

His brows went up. "That's pretty nice for a girl her age. You think the wolves will mind?"

"I think," I said, breaking in, "that the wolves will get used to it. Both Ian and I are giving all of you our protection. Just don't make us regret it." But I couldn't stop smiling as I tried to make that sound something like a threat.

Lev just chuckled at me. "You're too nice to be an Alpha, but I'm not complaining. I'm pretty sure Sheri will jump on the job. I'd rather the others made it through school, though. Ridley's a smart one. She'll get into college if she can get the funds for it. Zaria's going to be the same. Hell, Sheri too, but she had to step up too young, you know? I just..." He looked down at me. "They aren't my kids, but they might as well be. You wolves get that, right?"

"We do," I assured him. "I'm also waiving rent for Sheridan if she takes the job. House is a perk of the job."

"But," Ashley added, "she'll only make fifteen dollars an hour."

"With free rent?" Lev let out a relieved sigh. "No, that's more than enough. She'll be able to afford the bills, and I'll help with everything else. No, that makes all of this easier. Thank you, Alpha. Thank you..." He looked at Ashley. "Beta?"

"No," I said, but Ashley didn't let me finish.

"I'm her beta," she agreed. "Although that's usually only a position for the pack leader, not his mate."

Lev reached for a pen. "Kinda feels to me like Ian makes the big decision, but Elena handles the personal stuff. Almost like two different departments. Just figured she had her own team."

"I do," I assured him. "We call ourselves the Sisterhood of Being Too Old for That Shit."

"Love it," he laughed. "You ever need an old man to join you..."

"You aren't old," Ashley countered.

"Darling, I'm forty-five. Gotta have a decade on you both."

"Thirty-eight," Ashley admitted, "so close, but Elena's forty. So not as much as you'd think."

Lev took a step back and let out a low whistle. "Seems like being a wolf is good for the female population. And I don't mean any disrespect by that, ladies. Just saying that you both are rather impressive women. Now, I'm going to fill out my application and as much of Sheridan's as I can. I'll get her to drop off the rest and the job form tomorrow, if that's ok?"

"It's perfect," I told him. "Glad to have you as part of the pack, Lev."

"Still feels weird to think that I'm becoming a groupie," he joked. "Oh! One last question. Exposure?"

Ashley handled that. "Our doctor says that we're all infected with therianthropy, just different mutations. So, we can't catch yours, you can't catch ours, and we're fine. We all have the same thing, just a slightly different symptom."

"Which beast we become," he realized. "Well, that makes this even nicer. So, I won't find myself losing my claws any time soon, and no need to panic if my boy kisses a wolf." He claimed a seat and began writing. "Because he will. All weekend long he yammered on about finally having friends who could understand him."

"He's just going to have to get used to calling himself a wolf at school, though," I warned. "That's how the kids refer to themselves, and after that boy went crazy? I think adding 'tiger' to that might cause a few too many questions."

"We can be wolves," Lev promised. "Just really big, really stripey ones."

He smiled, but in my head I added in, *with very big teeth and claws. Dangerously big.* I just hoped this didn't backfire on us.

CHAPTER 22

Monday, after work, the Sisterhood met me for wolf lessons again. This time, David agreed to join us, so I'd asked the guys to let us ladies handle it. I got the impression that he'd be a little less embarrassed for his first try if he didn't have the pack leadership watching him fumble. Reluctantly, my mates had agreed.

Luckily, the weather was slowly but surely getting warmer. While the sun was still out, it actually wasn't too bad. That made stripping to shift a little easier, even if still embarrassing. The ladies didn't have that problem, but it seemed that David wasn't much better than me. The pair of us made a point of not looking at each other, and then we changed into wolves.

Kim's husband was actually a rather striking wolf, too. Like his wife, his coat was in the typical grey and white pattern, but his grey areas were much darker, more what I'd call blue. It looked like he had a dark undercoat across his back and tail, mixed with a scattering of white and silver hairs. The patch on his head was stark, with a very distinct line between the dark and white areas. In other words, he was a good looking wolf, even if he still had a bit of a belly and not as much muscles as most of the other males.

Then, we struggled to walk. I was doing pretty good at that now. I still turned like a whale, but I could get where I wanted. David, on the other hand, needed Ashley and Kim to brace him. Then, on impulse, I did the same thing for him that Scott had done for me. Letting out a bark to make him look, I pointedly moved one foot, then the next, waiting for him to copy me.

It helped. Step by slow, ponderous step, he found the rhythm, and that led to his balance. By the time we called it a night, he made a lap from the fire pit to the tree stump all on his own, and the man's tail was wagging so hard it made a circle.

On Tuesday, the guys joined us. That made David struggle a little more, but Lane and Ashley moved in to hold him up. There was no judgment, just genuine offers to help. I decided to try trotting, which resulted in my nose spending a bit of time in the dirt, but Pax and Trent kept encouraging me to try again, then again until I actually got it.

The problem was keeping track of my hind feet. Now that I could make them all move when I wanted - and where - I had to think about what I was going to step on. Twigs hurt my little uncalloused paws. Rocks were worse. Branches could catch my toes, sending me down, but the faster I went, the easier it was to turn and weave. I even tried out a little jump - and managed to land on three of my four feet like I intended.

That night, Lane came over to give me a massage. I got a little lesson in how our two forms were connected, so injuries in one transferred to a corresponding problem in the other, and that included muscle aches. Strength in one form helped the other as well. It was why my mates were all so very fit. The gym in their garage was mostly for strength, but the stamina came from chasing the moon every month. As the pack leadership, the guys needed both: enough strength to win a fight and enough stamina to keep going on to the next problem.

But I was starting to feel like I might not be a failure as a wolf. Watching David slowly but surely improve also made me feel good, but in a different way. The man was my friend, and he'd spent years wishing he could keep up with his wife and kids. Now, we were making that possible. It made me feel the same way as I had watching Gabby give her speeches at her *quinceañera*, or even when she was dancing with Ian.

I felt proud, but not for myself. Maybe maternal was a better word? Although that didn't really fit with helping out my friend's husband. Nurturing was the best I had, but it wasn't quite right. This wasn't about feeding and cleaning. It was the joy of knowing I'd helped someone else succeed, even if it was in a very small way. Still, I'd done my tiny little part to make the pack stronger.

Wednesday started out by Ashley interviewing Sheridan for the job working our main gate. She and Lev had turned in their applications the day before. They were all approved and I had keys for them both. The only question was going to be if Sheridan and the foxes were getting a free house or if I'd need to set up a payment plan for her.

I tried not to eavesdrop, but with my new hearing, it was pretty easy to listen in. So far, it sounded like everything was going pretty well, and Ashley was laughing with the girl easily. I was just starting to hope that this would really end up a good match when my phone rang, forcing me to get back to work.

"Wolf's Run, Elena speaking," I answered.

A cruel chuckle sounded on the other end, but it was a voice I knew too well - Karen's. "Well hello, Elena. Guess this means Ian hasn't gotten tired of your human ass yet. You fucking him now?"

"What do you want, Karen?" I asked, seriously considering hanging up on her.

"Just figured you should know that we've had two pack members shot and killed because of Wolf's Run."

The woman didn't honestly seem upset about it, though. Pissed, sure, but that seemed to be her default emotion. For me, thinking of our pack members dying was the sort of thing that would make me honestly sad, yet there was no quavering in her voice at all. If anything, it made me hate her more than I had before. It was almost like she thought every other wolf in the world existed simply for her convenience, and them getting killed had somehow put her out.

"And how is that our fault?" Because, I couldn't begin to figure out how she was blaming us for it. Besides, Karen loved to throw blame around, and I wouldn't honestly be surprised if this was all just a bunch of lies to make herself feel good.

"After everyone started talking about werewolves on

the news," she snarled, "hunters decided that shooting us was a whole lot more fun. We lost two. Dry Creek Pack lost one. All of a sudden humans are noticing the wolves running across fields, roads, and pastures, and they're pulling out guns. Your kids did this to us. They made people think about what's running around at night, and I'm going to make sure you pay for it."

"You got yourself kicked out," I reminded her. "That's why you don't have safe walls to hide behind. And none of us asked that kid to shoot up the school or lose his mind. Blame someone else, Karen."

"But he knew about wolves, and that means those kids let it slip."

She had a point, and a good one. The problem was that she was wrong. The kids hadn't shifted where he could see. Mason had simply overheard something and latched onto it. The simple fact that we all had amber-colored eyes only helped to confirm it. That the kids called themselves wolves probably didn't help, but proof? There was none.

"And werewolves don't exist," I told her, repeating what Gabby had said so many times. "The whole world knows that boy is insane. It has nothing to do with us."

"No? Not even that video?" she countered.

"The one a girl made using special effects?" I scoffed. "Keep trying. We kept a bad situation from getting worse. We made sure to take care of our community - which is what you should be worrying about instead of trying to blame everyone else. Playing the victim doesn't suit you. It's a hard world, so suck it up and learn how to survive without your daddy covering for you all the time."

And then I slammed the phone down, ending the call.

"Elena?" Ashley asked, proving that both she and Sheridan were standing at the corner of the hall, looking at me with concern.

I just let out a heavy sigh. "Karen."

"Shit," Ashley breathed.

"Who?" Sheridan asked.

"Former pack member," Ashley explained. "Her father became my father's beta, all but raising Ian as a second dad. I was older, but he was always a family friend. The girl tried to force Ian to choose her as his mate after he'd already claimed Elena publicly, and she wouldn't back down. She went full lycan once - in the community, thankfully - and tried to attack Elena while she was still human. So Ian threw her out of the pack."

"Oh," Sheridan breathed. "Do you think she'll try to come back?"

"No," I said, waving that off. "She just wanted to let us know that Hidden Forest and some other pack - um, Dry Creek, I think - have had hunters shooting at them. A few wolves were killed."

"No," Sheridan breathed, sounding mortified.

"It happens," Ashley told her gently. "That's why we built this community, actually. My father got hit by a car trying to get another wolf out of the way. He managed, but we weren't sure if he was going to make it. Got him to shift and to a hospital, but it was a lot of fun explaining how the injuries had happened." She rubbed the girl's shoulder. "Thankfully, we have our own doctor now, and she handles a lot of that."

Sheridan just nodded. "I was told. Um, how will I tell our wolves apart from the ones that aren't ours? I mean, if

I get the job, and if I'm responsible for letting people in, and all that."

"You've got the job," Ashley assured her. "I'll have Mitch sharing the shift with you at first. He'll give you all the tricks and show you how the emergency precautions work. Things like locking the gates when we have someone about to turn and the secondary blockades in case the gates ever fail. Like I said, this place was built to keep us safe, and so far it seems to be working."

"Which means," I added, holding up a set of keys, "these are for you. And if you're going to see Lev, can you give him his set?"

The little fox pressed a hand to her lips, looking between the pair of us. "We get our own place, and my job really covers it?"

"It does," I assured her. "Just let me know when you're done moving in and I'll get you on the work schedule. I figure, what, about a week to move and unpack?"

"Sounds about right," Ashley said. "Might be more since she has to transfer the youngest to a new school."

I nodded. "Yeah, I was lucky and moved in before the semester started. But we'll have Gabby introduce her to a few people."

"She knows Nik," Sheridan said. "Lev's son. He kinda intimidates her a bit, though."

"Tiger and a fox?" Ashley nodded like that only made sense. "Don't worry, Gabby will make sure she has some friends who won't set off her instincts. Maybe even our honorary pack members."

"Honorary?" Sheridan asked.

"Human teens," I explained. "They found out about us in the school shooting, and helped cover it all up. They're not allowed to turn until they're over eighteen because life without a pack would be too hard. After that, it's their decision, but as soon as they can move in, the kids are going to become full pack members, regardless of if they can shift or not."

Sheridan just smiled. "I actually like that. It sounds so... fair, I guess? Makes me think that we're not just some charity case."

"You're not," Ashley promised. "Foxes are quick and cunning. It's why I thought of you for the gate. Rumor has it that pulling one over on your kind isn't as easy as we wish."

The girl ducked her head and laughed softly. "Um, I think that's a stereotype, but I'll do my best. Thank you, Alpha." And she turned to Ashley. "Thank you, beta."

"And that's going to stick," Ashley said.

"Ash..." I groaned.

She just waved me down. "I have no problem being your beta, Elena. I actually prefer it to just being Ian's big sister. Also means that people might stop asking me when I'm going to start my own pack." She winked playfully at Sheridan. "Won't happen. Not leaving my family for anything, and I have no interest in leading."

Sheridan was smiling a little too much. "I might have to tell Vic that. Seems he has a thing for this woman, but he said he wasn't sure how long she'd be sticking around."

I pointed at Sheridan. "She needs to start coming on Thursdays."

"What's on Thursdays?" she asked.

"Wine and girl gossip at my house," Ashley told her. "But, showing up means you've joined the Sisterhood. I mean, we might have to change the name, because right now we're the Sisterhood of Being Too Old for That Shit."

"Don't change it," Sheridan said, "because most days I feel like that. Especially with my little sisters. But if you're serious, I'd love to. I..." Her smile faltered for a split second. "I don't really have a lot of friends. Kinda hard, you know, being what we are."

"And now you have a whole pack," Ashley said. "Welcome to the Sisterhood, little fox, and to Wolf's Run."

CHAPTER 23

Pretty much every evening, the guys and I headed up to the trails to help our mate learn to be a better wolf - and she was learning so fast. Maybe she wasn't as agile and adaptable as her daughter, but not even Seth had adjusted as quickly as she was. Granted, I also hadn't wanted to pin Seth between myself and my best friend, so that may have had something to do with it.

With Elena, however, this was becoming one of my favorite things. Pressing her against Trent on the trails, in the bedroom, and any other time she'd let us get away with it was quickly becoming an addiction. It was like I couldn't get enough of the feel of her, the smell of her hair, or the taste of her lips on mine. I'd tried to tell myself it was all about enjoying her body, but I knew that was a lie.

It was all of her. I loved watching Elena master something new. It didn't matter if that was moving from a trot to a lope or seducing us at night. Even something as simple as hearing her laugh when she picked up on a joke drew me in a little more. The only downside to this entire situation was having to share. Not that I begrudged my friends the chance to be with her - they deserved that, and so did she. It was simply that I kept finding myself turning to include her and she wasn't there.

Ian claimed his rights as the Alpha as often as he could. Yes, he was still fair about it, but hearing about her from him the next day? It just wasn't the same. And I knew that Lane needed to be close to her. That man literally lived for her now. Oh, he tried to play it off as no big deal, but I'd known him long enough to know better. If anything, he was worse than me.

Never mind Seth! He'd sworn that he wouldn't have a problem sharing a mate when he'd become Ian's beta so long ago. I was pretty sure that none of us had expected him to fall for an older woman - and to do it so completely. The simple fact that he was trying so hard to become a father figure for Gabby? It spoke volumes. It also made me respect the guy that much more.

Then there was Trent. Thursday night, while Lane and Ian spent the night with Elena, the pair of us retreated to my room to watch a movie. Seth was watching one of his shows downstairs, so we let him have the larger screen. The problem was that Trent and I never even managed to start one. Instead, we ended up sitting on the bed staring at the selection screen, and talking all about her. About how easily she accepted the pair of us with her. About how she never tried to convince us to be with her alone. About how she made us both feel like we were the most important man in her life, even though we knew she did the exact same to all the others.

"We need a date," Trent told me, flicking down on the remote without really caring about what he was flipping through. "Me, you, and her. It doesn't feel official until we have an actual date, you know?"

"Feels pretty official to me," I countered. "Trent, I'm completely obsessed with her."

"Then fuck her on your own."

The fact that his eyes never left the screen made me grumble a warning. His lips just curled, daring me to follow through on that, but we both knew I wouldn't. He was just pushing my buttons, but the problem was that it kept working.

"I'm not fucking her," I told him.

"No? More for me." This time, he glanced at me, but only for a second.

I just sighed. "I'm sleeping with her, ok? Fucking sounds... I dunno, like what we did with Karen."

"Making love?" he offered.

Yeah, that was the issue. That one word was a very heavy one. It also felt right. It felt like this crazy feeling that hung in my chest when she wasn't around, making me smile like a boy when she was. Yet there was only one simple problem with that word.

"Doesn't feel right to say that until you're ready," I mumbled.

He gave up on the TV and turned it off. "I want a date with her," he said again, but this time I could tell he was completely serious. "Just the three of us, and not here. Not trying to juggle the pack, our kid, or any of that. I want at least an hour of the three of us alone, dressed, and talking before I'll say I'm there."

"Why?" I asked. "You can't tell me you don't feel something for her."

"I do," he insisted. "But I also feel my dick getting hard and my responsibilities. I like her, Pax. A lot. I like that woman enough that I do not want to toss out that word like it means nothing. I want a fucking date, and that means you need to agree to it."

I reached up to rub at both of my eyes with one hand. "I agree. I will definitely go, so you can stop worrying. I just... They're all there. Hearing her tell Ian that she loved him? Man, I fucking want that too."

"Yeah, but do you just want the empty words, or do you want to know you can believe it?" he countered. "Because I know you well enough. You'll profess your feelings, she'll say she feels the same, and you'll spend the next month trying to figure out if she meant it or was just being nice. You'll talk yourself in circles, overthinking what exactly it means to love Ian's mate and how this is supposed to work for us." He let his head flop over so he could see me. "I know because I'll do the exact same. That's why I want a date before I'll say it."

"And then?" I asked.

He shrugged. "Then we'll worry about the next step."

My eyes narrowed. "What step comes after loving someone? She already said she's not having more kids."

He grunted like I was a complete idiot. "Marriage, Pax. First comes love, then comes marriage. Pretty sure you know the rhyme. And if you don't think that's where Ian's going with this, you're a damned moron. He's already asked me once where we're at. Seth's made it clear that he's all in. We know Lane's there. Ian was wondering if we're on this ride or just kinda spectating - and he's honestly fine either way."

"I'm on this ride," I assured him.

Trent just nodded. "Yeah, that's what I told him. Let him know that we're right there, but it's a little more complicated when working as a pair. He said he understood; he just didn't want us to feel pressured."

I reached for the remote, turning the TV back on. "You think he'd cut us if we couldn't love her?"

"No," Trent assured me. "I also think he'd be fine with us fucking her, so long as she's into it. Look, all he wants is for us to be honest. If you need more time with her, just tell him that. He'll make Lane back off, or tell the big guy to expect us to crash his party. And if that's what you want, I'm there. I just know that what we really need is a little time alone with her where the pack isn't in the middle of one crisis or another. Just an hour or two so we can be sure the conversation won't run dry, the looks won't get awkward, and that this isn't all because she's absolutely amazing in bed."

"Yeah," I decided. "You're right." Then I sighed. "I need to stop over at the office more. Find reasons to just be with her. We aren't Ian's only betas, so there's nothing wrong with taking a few minutes off, right?"

"Exactly," Trent agreed. "I'm right there with you." He snatched the remote from my hand and changed to view only the romance movies. "What do you say about stopping in to have lunch with her tomorrow?"

"Oh," I said when the selection lit up a movie that didn't look completely boring. "That one. And lunch sounds good. Maybe we can even ask her to dinner? I know a pretty nice steakhouse."

"For a date?" Trent asked. "No, we should go nicer. Like, I dunno, seafood?"

I groaned. "Too normal. Besides, she's a wolf who's building her muscles. She'll be craving red meat. So long as it's not Mexican, I don't care, because I do not want her to think we're complaining about her cooking."

"Italian?" he suggested.

"Protein, Trent," I said again. "Hell, Lane would probably have an idea."

Then we both looked at each other as the same idea hit us both. "Ashley," we said in unison.

And Trent pressed play, because that woman would definitely know not only where Elena would like to go, but what places would be nice enough. One item off the list. Next up, a little relaxation where I could think about my woman, sit beside my best friend, and not get laughed at for being just a bit of a sap and sniffling at the sad part of the movie.

But even the best laid plans had a way of getting thwarted lately. Trent and I showed up to the office the next day to see Seth's little truck parked out front, along with a beat-up old half ton. The two of us shared a look as we headed inside, and the moment I opened the door, I knew our happy little moment had just been postponed.

Even from the back, I recognized the Alpha of the Hidden Forest pack. Then there was Elena, standing at the corner of her desk. Ashley was just behind her, and Seth was braced before her protectively. Damon stood at least four inches taller than Seth, but the beta was not about to back down. Not with his mate behind him.

"You act like you were born to these people," Damon snarled.

Seth just narrowed his eyes. "No, they just picked me up after you slung me aside."

"What?" Elena asked.

Ashley grabbed her arm before our mate could storm into the man's face. "Leave it," she hissed.

But that was all I needed to hear. "Why are you in our territory, Damon?" I asked.

He turned, but it wasn't fast. The man who'd constantly chased our social circles looked first at Trent and then to me. I watched as his jaw clenched in anger, but he was now outnumbered, and the fool didn't realize that the most dangerous beast here wasn't one of Ian's betas.

"Well, well," he drawled, doing his best to sound smug. "Looks like the spoiled brat sent his puppies to do his work again."

"Yeah, we actually came for the women," I taunted. "You know, because our pack actually has a few. But wait, you ended up with Karen, right? Our reject? How's that working out for you anyway?"

"Oh, I mated her," he told me. "She said it was nice to finally find a man with a real dick."

Elena scoffed and muttered something under her breath in Spanish about caverns. I had to shoot her a warning look because the last thing I wanted to do was laugh in this guy's face.

"Why are you here again?" I asked, stepping aside so the path to the door was clear and he knew he could leave.

Trent matched me on the other side, and the pair of us moved around him to join up with Seth, forming a line between the strange male and our mate. The problem was that Elena knew no fear. I saw Ashley try to tug her back again, but she wasn't about to budge. No, she looked like she was ready to lay into the man herself, and I knew she would if things went south.

"I came for reparations," Damon said. "Wolf's Run caused two of mine to get shot by humans."

"Can't make humans do much," I countered.

"Should find better places to run," Trent added.

"Two families!" Damon snapped. "Two. One man had a kid, and now what? Your pack is the one who risked mingling with humans. Your pack is the one who got caught on tape. It was your pack that suddenly made people take a second look at the wolves that had been there all along, and now my pack is dying!"

"Then protect your pack better!" Elena yelled, yanking her arm away from Ashley.

But Damon just pointed at Seth. "First you take my convert. Now you're getting my natural-borns killed. Wolf's Run owes Hidden Forest, and we will collect. One way or another, I'll make damned sure that all of you pay for this. I just figured a check would be easier than claiming the entire pack."

"What convert?" Elena asked, glancing over at Seth.

He grumbled under his breath. "Yeah, that guy who bit me?" And he tipped his head at Damon. "Told you it was some dick. Didn't approve then of how he treated women, and from the sounds of it, I still don't. Too bad for him, his plan backfired. I'm not dead, I'm his least favorite person's beta now."

"Shit," Damon laughed. "If you think a convert can keep up with a real wolf, boy, it says nothing good about this pack. Maybe I should just drop Ian already and weed out the weak ones before you all get any more real wolves killed. Can't say I'd mind being the king of this castle."

And then Elena did the last thing I'd ever have expected in my life. A litany of Spanish profanity began to fall from her lips and she bent over, grabbed the high heel from her foot and stormed at Damon like she was holding a dagger.

"Out!" she finally said. "Get out of my lobby, out of my community, and away from my mate. You hear me, little boy? Go back to where you came from or I will use this on you, and you do not wanna see what happens when a Latina mama resorts to her shoe!"

Damon's eyes went wide and he stepped back. From the look on his face, he had to be convinced that Elena was diseased, but I understood a little too well. My own mother had whacked me with a flip flop a few times, and my grandmother - the convert - was even worse. And yet, for some reason, I'd assumed that Elena was far too cultured to do anything like that.

But damn if it didn't look good on her. She didn't have to snarl or snap. There was no threat to shift and go after him as a wolf. Nope, she simply stormed at him, limping due to the difference in height, and kept ranting at the top of her lungs.

"You do not come into my house and treat me like that, and if you ever talk to my guys that way again I will wash your mouth out with soap. Do you hear me, pup? I will show you what it means when you mess with Wolf's Run."

"Fuck me," Damon breathed, spinning to push the door open and rush outside before the crazy woman could even touch him.

But the moment he was outside the office, Elena

stopped and nodded like she'd just accomplished something great. Then, as calmly as I'd ever seen her, she bent back over and put her shoe back on.

"What the actual fuck was that?" Trent asked.

"Amazing," I told him. "That, Trent, was the modern version of a *chancla*. Although you were supposed to throw it, Elena."

"Do you have any idea how much these shoes cost?" she asked. "If it had been a flip flop, I would've." Then she gestured to the door. "But it worked, didn't it?"

"Yeah," Seth breathed. "Holy shit. I think that is going to go down in pack history. Alpha male chased from the Wolf's Run territory by a newly-converted wolf with her shoe." And he turned to smile at her. "You, my dear, are my new hero."

She just caught his hand. "He turned you?"

"Yeah," Trent said, moving closer to clasp Seth's shoulder. "Damon always wanted to be like Ian, and he keeps failing. The fact that we interrupted his revenge? Because I don't think *turning* Seth was his plan."

"He wanted to kill me," Seth admitted.

Elena's lip tensed, the first sign of a human snarl, and her eyes jumped back to the door. "He'd better hope I never see him again."

I just moved to cup the side of her face. "Honey, leave fighting for us. Throw the shoes if you want, but that man? He's a Pack Alpha, Elena. You can't win against him."

She just lifted her chin. "Watch me, Pax. I'm starting to figure out that if I try hard enough, I really can do anything."

"Not this time, beautiful. You're still learning to run. Let us be the tough ones for just a little longer, ok?"

Her tongue darted out to moisten her lips, and her eyes flicked between all three of us, and then she finally nodded. "Ok," she agreed. "But just for a little longer, because if he comes after Gabby, there's not a damned thing in this world that will keep me from tearing him apart."

"And we'll be right beside you," I promised.

CHAPTER 24

I honestly had no idea what had come over me. Using a shoe on the Alpha of another pack? The moment I'd heard he's attacked my mate - even if it had been so long ago - just made something inside me snap. I was supposed to protect these men, just like they wanted to protect me. Ashley said it had been my wolf instincts taking over, but when Ian heard about it after my last wolf lesson for the week, he had another theory.

"She's part bear," he joked, dropping into one of the camp chairs around the fire. "I mean, that's what they say about mama bears, right, Vic?"

Vic grunted as if he'd heard the joke a few too many times. "Wouldn't know, Ian. My mom was human, and I've never actually seen a female bear."

"Oh, you don't want to," Scott joked. "You've heard those jokes about dwarf women, right?"

"Little people?" Bridget asked.

"No, like the opposite of elves," Scott told her. "Can't

tell the men from the women because they all have beards."

"He's joking," Jax said, but he turned to Lev. "What about tigers?"

"Please," Lev said. "Cats. C'mon, we're all sexy."

The group of us laughed on cue, but this was nice. There was a fire going in the fire pit. Lane had brought beer for the guys. Ashley had found a collection of flavored drinks for the women, and the weather was actually nice enough that none of us were shivering. I sat on my wooden throne, completely exhausted but happy about how I'd done.

Then there was David. After one week of wolf lessons, the man was now walking around the area on his own, and he'd even trotted a few steps. Granted, the two of us also felt like we'd just entered some kind of intense training regimen, and I was pretty sure that every single muscle I owned hurt in one way or another.

"Someone pass me a drink?" I begged. "Please don't make me lean forward."

"Abs sore?" Bridget asked.

"Everything," David moaned.

So she looked at Kim. "Stop by my place on your way home, and I'll get some muscle relaxers for him. Sorry, David, no fun side effects. Just a little help with the tension of getting all wolfed out." Then she looked at me. "You out yet?"

"Not even close," I assured her.

"Shit," Jax said, "you wolves are pampered."

"Tell me about it," Lev agreed. "I mean, I thought the walls were nice, but the houses are gorgeous, there's a doctor, and an entire pack of feral kids."

"And," I told him, "I'm pretty sure that your son is at my house. I think Gabby's enjoying this mixed pack thing a little too much. She's adamant that she's going to write up a multi-species covenant for the pack."

"She's a good kid," Vic said. "You know she came by my place last week to ask if there was anything we bears needed?"

"No," I groaned. "Oh, please tell me it wasn't awkward?"

"It was cute," he promised, looking over at Ian. "She told me she was assisting the Alpha, and wanted to make sure that we were happy here. I half expected her to hand me an order form for one of those school fundraiser things. You know, candles or candies, or such."

"That girl's going to be the best Alpha this pack has ever seen," Ian said. "If she hadn't turned, I'd say she'd end up the President. Pretty sure there's nothing in the world that stops Gabby when she sets her mind to it. Well, except Elena."

"Not even me," I admitted. "Hell, look at how she became a wolf."

"Shit," David said. "Pretty sure Roman realized how big of a mistake that was when you stared him down as a human. Swear his tail was stuck between his legs for the next month."

"Serves him right," Kim said. "I'm still pissed about it." But she smiled at me. "Not that I regret either of you turning, but the mess he made of that?"

"I wouldn't have believed it if it didn't happen," I admitted. "Took Lane shifting in front of me, and I still wasn't sure."

Lev chuckled. "And now look at you. You're a good

Alpha Mate, Elena. The kind who takes care of - " He paused when his phone began ringing in his jacket pocket. From the look on his face, it was a ringtone he recognized. Lev answered quickly, "Yeah?" Then a long pause. "Elena? Yeah, she's right here. Ok, yeah." He looked up at me. "Gabby's been trying to call you."

"Crap," I breathed, leaning forward to get up.

But Lane beat me. "Where's your phone?" he asked.

"Front seat of my car," I told him.

Lane jogged over, leaned through the window, and came back carrying it. "You silenced it, little bunny."

"Because I didn't have hands." As soon as he handed it to me, I saw the notification for seven missed calls. I pressed the first one and called Gabby right back. "Hey," I said when she answered. "Please tell me no one's dying?"

"Physically, no," she said, sounding much too serious. "Mom, you remember Theo? The guy with the video? Yeah, um... Sam's bringing him over. I just called the front gate and told them to let her in."

"What's going on?" I asked.

Gabby pulled in a breath, and the trembling sound made me realize that this wasn't just some silly teenaged thing. "Mom, he got kicked out. He said his dad was asking when he was going to get a girlfriend, and they've been kinda pressuring him, so he told them he's gay. And it kinda sounds like his father said he couldn't live there. Theo packed his things into his car and made it to Sam's before losing it, and now she's bringing him here because I told her to."

"Oh, no," I breathed. "Yeah, we'll take care of him, *mija*. Who's there with you?"

"Roman, Olivia, Nik, and Xander. Mom, what are we going to do? It's not his fault he's gay!"

"No, it's not," I promised. "When he gets there, you just make sure he knows his pack will take care of him, and we'll figure out how to get Sam home, ok?"

"Ok. You coming back soon?" she asked.

"Very," I assured her, and ended the call.

But every parent in the group was watching me. "What's going on?" Kim asked.

"Theo came out to his parents, and it sounds like they kicked him out," I said.

Vic huffed in a way that did not sound happy. Seth mumbled something that I was pretty sure I shouldn't ask him to repeat. Trent and Pax moved to start putting out the fire. Ian grabbed his phone and started searching for something. Lev just shook his head as if that was the stupidest thing he'd ever heard.

Then Heather leaned closer. "Where are we putting him?"

"I have a spare room," I told her.

"So do I," she countered. "You also have a circus of men coming through, and that boy is still human." Then she pointed at Kim. "Her son is his crush, so that's out."

"I could - " Lev tried.

"No," David said. "You're already taking care of those foxes. The last thing you need is another teenager to chase around."

"We don't have room," Vic said, "and none of us know how to be parents, but we'll help."

"I got this," Heather said. "He's one of Olivia's friends, and he has no interest in girls, plus I'm not at all opposed to a little interference between her and Xander."

"Yeah," Kim agreed, "even Roman said they're getting a little out of control."

"And not just sexually," Heather admitted. "Xander likes the idea of a beta who's his mate. Says that if Gabby can do it, then he can too. And he's made a few comments about how Olivia would be better with him than Gabby."

"Gabby would destroy him," Pax said.

Heather just shrugged. "I agree, but Xander's never been rolled by a wolf his own age. Just make sure that girl can do it, Pax, because he seriously needs it."

So I pushed myself to my feet. "Ok. Are you sure about this, Heather? I have no problem putting him up for the night."

"No, I'm sure," she promised. "Let me head home and make sure there's clean sheets on his bed. If he needs a little reassurance from his friends, then give him time."

"And tell Roman," Kim decided, "to take Samantha home when she's ready."

"Ok," I said. "I'll text all of you to let you know what's going on."

"Have my number?" Lev asked. "If Nikolai can help, put him to work."

I got his number and entered it into my phone, then took one last look around the area. "Am I forgetting anything?"

"Just go," Ian said. "Seth, ride with her. If they need anything, make it happen. If we need to talk to his parents tomorrow, we can do that. If this is a done deal?"

"I'll make sure he knows the pack won't leave him," Seth promised. "I'll text with an update."

And then we left. I was sure I'd forgotten to do something, but they'd all handle it. I knew they would. I just felt a little dumbfounded at the idea of a parent rejecting their child over who they loved. It wasn't like they got to choose. Besides, it didn't take a genius to figure out that Theo wasn't exactly attracted to women.

"Were they pushing him to try to make him straight?" I asked, the question mostly rhetorical.

Seth just reached over to rub my leg. "Or hoping? No way to know, Elena. Some people think it's wrong, and most wolves don't understand."

"Like race?" I asked.

He made a face proving that wasn't quite right. "Wolves tend to be more open-minded about some things. Group love, as an example, or homosexuality, gender fluidity, and things like that. The pack is already so close that guys like Trent and Pax? They're completely straight, but they never learned the same hang-ups as most human guys. Hell, the same ones I did."

"You seem pretty open-minded now," I pointed out, just as I got close enough to realize there was a new car in my drive.

"I'm a wolf now," he reminded me. "But I promise that before I turned, I would've thought that laying naked in a bed beside a man was pretty gay. I also would've assumed that meant I was less of a man. Now, I happen to know that there are some very big and very tough gay wolves in the world, and they'd roll my ass for thinking that way. Theo's car?"

"I'm guessing," I said as I pulled in beside it. "Gabby sounded pretty upset, and I'm going to guess this kid's a wreck." I opened my door. "You sure you're ready for this?"

He climbed out and spoke to me over the roof. "I got

picked because I'm the convert. This kid's human, and someone has to translate our easy acceptance so he doesn't think it's a trick." Seth pointed at himself. "That's me, the human whisperer."

"Good, and Heather's really ok with getting a new kid dumped on her like this?"

He jogged to catch up with me. "She's as much a mother as you are, so I'm guessing yes. She's also been a member of Wolf's Run since she was born, and we owe this kid for speaking up when staying quiet about that video would've been easier. We'll make sure he's taken care of one way or another." He reached for the front door and paused. "I swear, Elena. He's one of our pups now. We'll protect him."

Those words were exactly what I needed to believe that this had really been sorted out that easily. Nodding was all it took for Seth to open the door, and I walked in. The living room was empty, but I could hear the kids talking upstairs - and there were a lot of them. At least three were talking at the same time. I was pretty sure they had no idea we'd made it home yet, but I also didn't want to interrupt.

So, tossing my jacket on the couch, I waved for Seth to do what he needed and made my way up the stairs. Not surprisingly, Seth followed. As I got closer to the top, the voices began to separate, finally letting me make out what the kids were saying.

"He said no son of his would be a queer," Theo was mumbled, his voice tense as if he was about to cry.

"It's ok," another boy soothed, and I could only guess that was Nikolai.

"Mom will let you crash with me," Roman assured him.

"We'll figure out the rest tomorrow, man. I told you, I've got your back."

"We all do," Gabby said.

I rounded the corner just in time to see Nikolai caressing Theo's face. "And my dad will help too. This is a good place, Theo. I've only been here a few days, and I can already tell that."

"But what happens when they find out I'm gay too?" he asked.

I just tapped at the door frame, letting them know I was there. Theo jumped, but the rest simply looked up from where the entire group sat in the middle of the floor in Gabby's room. My daughter smiled in relief, but Theo looked like all of the blood had just drained from his body.

"You already told me you were gay," I said. "I didn't care then, and I don't care now. You're part of the pack, Theo, and we take care of each other." Then I looked over at Olivia. "Your mom's making up a room. Sounds like you got a new brother for as long as he wants to stay."

Gabby huffed. "Why not us?"

"I offered," I assured her, "but I was outvoted. Kim said she'll make room if there's no other option..." And I looked at Roman.

He chuckled. "But she knows you're into me, Theo. Means no sharing the same room."

Then Seth moved to my side, wrapping his arm around my waist. "And that thing about 'no turning until he lives here' means on his own, *after* he's eighteen. If any of you even think about biting him..." He looked at Nikolai. "Regardless of species." Then at Gabby. "The Alpha will deal with you himself."

"And when he's done, I will," I promised the kids. "Theo, you and Samantha are packmates. Being human doesn't change that. Being young doesn't change that. Being gay or straight or anything else doesn't change that. You helped us, now let us help you. Heather's made sure you have a home. Your friends will make sure that you're ok. Seth and I are going to go downstairs to fix some dinner to make sure that you're also fed. Have a taste for anything?"

"She makes the best tacos," Gabby told him.

The boy just smiled. "Anything's fine. Thank you..." He paused to swallow, then mumbled, "Alpha."

"You're welcome, Theo. And the rest of you? Text your parents that you're all ok, but you can stay as long as Theo needs."

"Roman," Seth said, "you're supposed to give Sam a ride home."

"I kinda told my parents I was spending the night," Sam admitted.

"Then tomorrow," I told her. "Kinda sounds like Gabby needs her betas." I leaned my head a bit and looked at Theo. "If you need to talk, I'm always available, ok?"

"Thank you, Elena - I mean, Alpha."

"Either one works," I assured him. "You're fine, Theo. I'm so sorry this happened to you, and I promise that your pack just wants to help."

He bit his lips together and nodded. "You are. That's why I came here, because Gabby always said wolves take care of each other. I just..." His voice cracked.

"Shh," Nikolai breathed, pulling the guy against him. "It's ok. We got you, Theo."

I caught Gabby's eye, nodded to make sure she knew

she was doing the right thing, and turned to go back downstairs. She had this. My little girl wasn't even out of high school, and she was already handling a crisis like she was made for it. But, when I was almost to the living room, I realized something else.

I was doing the same thing. I was truly the Alpha Female, and it actually felt pretty good.

CHAPTER 25

Elena and Seth took off. Heather left only a moment later to get her house ready. The rest of us started cleaning up the area, putting away the camp chairs, and making sure all the bottles and trash got picked up. There was a tension in the air, though. Something I just couldn't quite put my finger on. A glance at Pax proved that he felt it too.

"Ok, what?" I asked, standing up to look at our group of friends. "The kid isn't hurt - "

"Physically," David mumbled.

Granted, he had a point, but that wasn't it. "Right. But he has a place to stay, a pack to lean on, and we already know he's not a bad kid, so why does everyone feel so tense?"

It was Scott who answered. "This is the same kid who leaked the first video, right? Trent, are you sure he's not going to do it again?"

And there it was. Yes, their concerns made sense, but

what other option did we have? Then Lev sighed. "I'm more worried about his parents demanding to know where he's living, and us having to explain why we took the kid in."

"That's easy," Pax said. "Theo's friends with Olivia. It makes sense for him to seek out his friends. Heather has both the means and the space for him."

"And not that human girl?" Lev countered. "Doesn't she live closer?"

"Stricter parents," I said. "Don't know if that's true, but if it's the line we go with, it'll work. Not everyone would be ok with a boy moving in with their daughter."

"But he's gay," Jax said. "I mean, Kim has a point, especially if this kid has a thing for her son."

"And now he knows that Roman's straight," I pointed out.

"Doesn't really stop a man from looking," Jax countered. "Even at that age. Hell, half the time I'm into a woman, she's not interested, so what's the difference?"

"That," Kim told me, "and I'm not completely convinced that Roman isn't flattered. There are more options than simply gay and straight, and my son is a wolf."

Vic made a sound, almost a grunt, as if that surprised him. "But he's with Gabby."

"Yeah," Ian drawled. "Roman's her beta. He says he's also her mate, but he feels the pull to be her beta first. That means he's not going to stop her from finding another guy. Pretty sure Gabby's only into boys. Not convinced that Olivia wouldn't consider girls, though."

"Nikolai likes the ladies," Lev told us. "A little too

much, if I'm honest. Boy's going to make me a grandfather before he's eighteen at this rate."

"Xander?" I asked.

Pax shook his head. "Theo's basically one of Gabby's betas now. Not officially, but he's hovering like one."

"She may have asked already," Lane said. "She wouldn't tell us until it's official."

Pax dipped his head as if that just proved his point. "So, putting her beta with Xander? It's all but undermining her budding authority. That's even assuming Theo would feel comfortable enough for that option. Wouldn't shock me at all if Xander's already threatened him a few times just to assert his dominance."

"Kid needs a kick in the ass," I grumbled.

"And none of that," Scott said, "means the boy won't make another video. He doesn't even need to record us shifting. Just catching bears, wolves, and tigers together? Animal control will come out here to look into the exotic animals on the loose."

"And after the first video," Vic added, "the whole thing would start up all over again."

"Pretty sure the kid wouldn't do that," I assured them. "Guys, you've never seen this guy. He was mortified when that video got out. He doesn't exactly have a lot of friends, and he's basically obsessed with Roman. Completely puppy love, and Roman's taking him under his wing."

"It's cute," Pax told them. "Seriously cute."

Ian just waved us all down. "I'll talk to him. Gabby probably already has, but I'll make a few things very clear. Besides, our mate probably needs a little help if she's got a house filled with emotional teens."

"I'll get the rest of this," Lev offered. "You four go play the hero."

"We'll help," Vic assured him.

Bridget just gestured to her car. "Kim, if you and David stop by my place, I'll get those pills to help with the aches."

"And you're doing good," Vic said. "Learning faster than I did. Don't worry, the aches only last for a couple of weeks."

"Thanks, guys," David said. "I'm just thrilled that I can finally walk. I still feel like a drunk wolf, but at least I now feel like a wolf."

There was a round of "good nights" and then we all headed to our cars, leaving the three bears and Lev behind to handle the last of the mess. I climbed into my truck, and Pax joined me. Ian and Lane took his SUV. We waited for Kim and Bridget to leave first, but I pulled out before Ashley could.

"This just killed our chance for a date this weekend," I told Pax.

He huffed as if that should've been obvious. "Damon earlier, the boy this evening. Starting to feel like the universe is trying to tell me something."

"Don't say that," I warned. "Shit, every time we get things going the right way with her, it's like something pops up to ruin it."

"So what's Plan B?" Pax asked. "Seriously, Trent. You're so hung up on this idea of a date, but we're running the largest pack of shifters I've ever heard of. The reality is that we might not get a day off. Between Ian and Elena, the pack is always going to come first, so how do you get your proof that this is real if you're basing it on some bullshit night in town?"

I could only shrug. "I just want..."

"What?" he demanded when I let that trail off.

"I want to prove to her that we're as good as Ian and Lane, ok?"

For a long moment, Pax said nothing. The whole time, Elena's house kept getting closer, and I knew this conversation was coming to an end. Then, just as I pulled my truck into our driveway, he looked over at me.

"Then we prove it," he decided. "We do the same shit they are. You put in more time with Gabby. I'll help with the house. The things we're good at that we know she needs. We make it clear to her that we're a benefit, not something else for her to take care of. The handle to her bathtub faucet is sticky and leaks if not turned off all the way. The carpet's coming up on the stairs. These are things we can do for her, Trent, so let's do them."

"That's not a relationship, you moron," I said. "Pax, that's being her handyman. I'm talking about emotions. About showing her that we actually do care. How the fuck do we make that clear?"

He just opened his door and stepped out. "How did Seth? How did Lane? How did Ian? They took care of her, Trent. They held her, they made her feel beautiful, and they did things without needing to be asked. Know how I know?" He waited until I was out of the car and standing. "I asked Lane."

"And he told you that?" Not what I was expecting.

Pax nodded. "He said he just wants to see her happy, and we make her feel beautiful. I figure that means we're not doing half bad, right?"

"So now we make her feel important," I decided.

"Strong, competent, beautiful, sure. But most of all, we need to make it clear that our mate is important to us."

"Wanna crash at her place tonight?" he asked.

I just laughed. "Duh."

He nodded, still thinking. "Breakfast in the morning for the kids, since I'm sure a few will still be here. Let her sleep in, and play the middle man so she can relax for a bit?"

"Sounds like a plan," I agreed just as Ian pulled in beside us. "Hey, if she's taking company tonight, it's our turn," I said as soon as the first door opened.

"Works for me," Ian said. "Means I can make sure Heather's honestly ok with this arrangement. I'll drag Ashley into it, just so none of them feel like I'm ordering them around."

"I'll help Ian," Lane offered. "Dunno if Seth's already invited himself, though."

"I'll sleep as a wolf if I have to," Pax said. "We'll make it work."

As a group, we headed around to the back to enter her house. The scent of Elena's tacos hit me immediately, making my stomach growl. I glanced over, caught Pax's eye, and made a straight line for the kitchen. Lane paused to strip off his muddy boots. Ian headed for the living room. Pax followed behind him.

"How do we help?" I asked the moment I saw Elena.

She was standing over the stove, stirring the ground beef. Beside her, Seth was chopping tomatoes. A stack of paper plates had been placed on the counter, but it looked like she was preparing to feed an army.

"Um..." Elena turned to smile at me. "Someone needs to clean off the table. We're probably going to need some more soda for the herd I have. And, um..." She flashed me a weak smile. "Can you check on them? Last I saw, Theo looked like he was about to cry and Nikolai was consoling him. For all I know, Gabby might need a little help managing that troupe so Theo's not overwhelmed. She and Sam trust you, Trent."

"Then I'm on it," I promised, heading for the stairs.

On the way, I told Pax what else she needed, but he was already on it. Ian said he'd get the sodas. Lane didn't ask, just moved to take over the table. As I jogged up the stairs, I saw my best friend flop his arms in frustration, because all of the tasks had just been assigned.

"Help Seth," I hissed at him. "She's not done cooking."

He lifted his thumb and went to do that, so I kept going, reaching the top of the stairs in time to hear Gabby's voice.

"What if you leaving makes them realize that this isn't a joke?" she asked.

"No," Theo mumbled. "You didn't see my dad, Gabs. He was livid."

"Your mom's cool," Nikolai said, his voice deep enough to sound like a tiger's purr. "And you're a girl."

"That has nothing to do with it," Olivia snapped.

"Kinda does," Nikolai countered, making my feet pause as I listened in. "Sure, some parents have an issue with it because it's a sin, or wrong, or things like that. But for girls? It's just about who you love. For guys? If we aren't big, strong, and tough, then we're failures. If we like guys, then clearly we're sissies. Doesn't mean it's true, but that's how it works, and there's no going back once it's out, ok?"

I made a point of clearing my throat just before I rounded the corner. Through the open door, I watched as the group of kids all flinched, turning to see who'd just walked in on the somewhat sensitive subject. I paused at the doorway and scanned them until I found Nikolai. He was sitting with Theo, his arms wrapped around the boy in a clearly romantic sort of way.

"So, I'm guessing this means I should pretend I didn't just hear any of that, huh?" I asked.

Nikolai's jaw clenched. "Thought wolves would make more noise."

"The herd downstairs does kinda drown it out," Olivia countered. "Nik, Trent's cool."

"He's not out," Gabby said, cutting straight to the chase. "Theo isn't really either. Well, I mean, except to us. So, it'd be better if you didn't say anything."

"I'll have to tell the tribe downstairs to ignore it too," I told her. "They all know about Theo."

"But not Nik!" Gabby hissed.

"They will," I countered. "Gabby, you know as well as I do that what one of us knows, the rest find out quickly. It's why we work so well with Ian. And your mom? She's not an idiot." I glanced over at Nikolai. "She also talks to Lev quite a bit."

"My mom's not stupid either," Olivia said. "If Theo's moving in with me..."

Nikolai glanced at her, a little smile curling one side of his mouth. "We're all just hanging out, though."

Olivia rolled her eyes. "Uh huh. Because you're so subtle about hitting on him, Nik." And she flopped both arms at him, gesturing to the way he sat with Theo.

"I kinda want to come out," Theo said. "I mean, I got kicked out. What more do I have to lose?"

"You're mostly out already," I told him. "And wolves won't care."

"Mom won't say anything if I ask her not to," Olivia told Nikolai. "I mean, she won't let you spend the night or anything, but she won't tell your dad."

"I..." Nikolai looked up at me. "Dad wouldn't understand."

Which didn't fit what I'd seen of Lev so far, but I knew what it was like to be scared of the unknown, so I just nodded. "It's not our place to tell him, and you're right, he doesn't seem to have a clue. He thinks you like girls."

"I kinda do," Nik admitted. "I just..." He looked at Theo, then right back to me. "Please don't say anything? We just moved here, and I don't want him moving us out because he thinks this place changed me." He looked at his new friends desperately. "You all just make me feel like it doesn't matter what I am."

"Hey," I said, walking into the room. "Sam, Theo, Nikolai? I know you three are new to our ways, so let me make this very simple. At any time, for any reason, you can talk to your Pack Alpha. As Ian's beta, I'm nothing more than an extension of him. Talking to one of us is the same as talking to all of us. Our responsibility to you is to protect you and help you in any way we can, for the good of the pack. It's not to out you, to hold you back, or anything else. It's to guide you toward the best decision. At any time, you can talk to any of us, and that includes the Alpha Female."

"My mom," Gabby told them.

I nodded. "So, if you're not ready to tell your parents, the other members of the pack, or anyone else, we won't make you. We're also here to listen, stand with you, or anything else you need, ok?"

"Kinda like a priest?" Samantha asked. "You know, confession and advice with a side of moral support?"

I chuckled at that. "Well, I promise I don't feel like a priest, but yeah. It's a lot like that. Now, dinner's almost done. Come down when you're ready. I'll handle the gaggle of adults who already know too much. Your secret will be safe with us so long as it doesn't endanger the rest of the pack."

"Thank you," Nikolai breathed, and beside him, Theo nodded in agreement.

CHAPTER 26

The kids ended up staying pretty late. Well past midnight, at any rate. I didn't last that long, but Trent and Pax promised they'd keep an ear out for them even as the pair fell into bed with me. Seth gave me a long kiss and said he should probably help Ian. After that, I remembered nothing until I woke to the smell of bacon the next morning.

Everyone except Samantha had gone back home. Still, Trent and Pax were up and making breakfast for their girls. I staggered into the kitchen and was handed a fresh cup of coffee, then told to sit down until at least half of it was in me. After I started sipping, I got the update. Theo's parents started blowing up his phone sometime around midnight, wanting to know where the hell he was. From there, things had gotten tense, but it had been handled. Olivia and Nikolai ended up taking Theo to his new home around two. Roman and Xander left not long after. Sam and Gabby, however, had stayed up even longer giggling, and they weren't any better now.

"So," Gabby said, "When Theo's dad told him to get his ass home or else? Theo took a selfie kissing Nik, and sent that as his answer. His dad kinda lost it."

"Gabby," I said, not wanting her to make light of what the boy was going through.

"Mom, really?" she shot back. "The man is pissed off because Theo's gay. He said they'd get him 'help.' As if it's something he can just fix! No. So, Nik kissed him, Theo took the pic, sent it, and I'm pretty sure they're a couple now."

I just nodded, knowing I wouldn't win this. "And Lev doesn't know that Nikolai likes boys, right?"

"He's bi, Mom," she said. "So, no, he didn't tell his dad. He kinda doesn't want to mess things up now that they've just moved in, especially since the foxes are getting the last of their stuff this weekend."

"Today, right?" Samantha asked.

Gabby nodded. "Zaria goes to school with us on Monday. So, if you're in one of her classes, make sure she's ok?"

"Promise," Samantha said.

Pax put a plate of food on the counter in front of me. "Which one of this crowd are you with, Sam?"

"Uh..." She looked at Gabby desperately. "None of them?"

"Sam doesn't want to date," Gabby said. "She doesn't have to, either."

"I was just trying to count heads," Pax assured her. "Do you identify as asexual, demisexual, or just not into that much hair?" And he waved the girls to get their food.

"Lame?" Sam offered as she headed into the kitchen. "I don't know, Pax."

"Well, you're not lame," Trent told her. "The rest? You'll figure it out, and we don't actually care."

"In truth," Pax said, "I'm mostly worried that adding another girl - like that fox - to your little group of friends might strain it. Especially if Theo and Nikolai are together. Jealousy can tear apart a beta group, Gabby. It's why we don't date."

"Not putting those rules on my betas," she told him. "I mean, I like that you guys are with my mom and all, but it's not fair. Betas are people too. Who they love doesn't change anything about how they help me."

"Until you decide that you want to add another guy to your little harem," Pax teased. "I give you a few more years before you start thinking that way. And Sam? You can tell your alpha no. You might have to stand your ground, but that's part of our job too. We're the sounding board, and being yes-men helps no one."

"I'm actually pretty good at that," Sam assured him.

I watched the whole thing, kinda impressed with how easily those guys were teaching Gabby to be a fair alpha to her pack. I had a feeling Ian was a little more blunt about it, but they'd clearly made their point. I also thought Gabby was right. Her betas were people - kids, actually. They wanted to fall in love, change the world, and help their friends. I couldn't wrap my mind around any of that being a problem.

But after breakfast, the girls headed back upstairs. Then a little more giggling happened. While I was stuck keeping an eye on them, I decided to get a little house cleaning done, but there was just one problem. The guys had been over enough that I really had nothing left to do. I put the last load of laundry on to wash - the stuff I'd been wearing to my wolf lessons - and accepted that having five boyfriends might be a lot nicer than I'd expected.

It was early afternoon when Gabby came bounding downstairs with a grin on her face. "Hey, Mom? Do you mind being the hookup spot for my friends?"

I had to do a double take. "What?!"

That made Samantha laugh, proving she was on her way down as well. "Olivia and Theo are coming over. Theo wants to see Nik. Gabby wants to make sure everything's still good, and then Roman and Xander are coming over."

"And Xander wants to take Olivia out to do something today," Gabby continued. "So, that means Theo's kinda on his own, and he said he doesn't really feel comfortable with staying at Heather's alone, so I said he could come here. Which was when Nik said he'd show up. I just figured that the guys want to, you know, have some time to get to know each other better."

Yep, that was not covered in Parenting 101. Nor in my recent Raising a Wolf course. I was pretty sure that it fell under something more closely called Having an Alpha Daughter, and I needed to call in Ashley for a little backup. But at the same time, I already knew my answer. It was the only one that made sense.

"Sure, Gabby. Your friends can hang out. Just, if the boys are going to be upstairs, keep the door open, ok?"

"They aren't into me, Mom," she groaned.

"I mostly meant because they're into each other," I reminded her. "And that means your friends need to keep it a little PG in this house, young lady. This is not, no matter how funny you think it is, the local 'hookup' spot."

"Keep the shifting outside," Trent said. Then he looked at me. "You need a little backup if the teen pack is showing up?"

"No, I'm fine," I assured him. "I have a feeling that all of you have more to do than constantly cleaning my house."

Pax made his way over and claimed the spot on the other side of me. "Just looking for excuses to stay longer." Then his head tilted. "Gabby, your friends are here!"

The strange thing was that I heard the car too. It sounded kinda sad, and didn't exactly run smoothly, so I figured that had to be Theo's. A few minutes later, there was a knock at the door, and the girls scrambled to get it. On the other side were Theo and Olivia. She all but pushed the shy boy inside. A few minutes later, Nikolai showed up. Thankfully, the whole group moved out back.

"Hey," Trent said the moment we were finally alone. "I have a question for you."

"Ok?" I asked, just as another car pulled up in front of my house. This one, however, I knew. "Hang on. That's Roman," I told him.

I got up, heading for the door, but didn't miss Pax letting out a heavy sigh behind me. Clearly, that question was an important one, and it made my guts tense a little as my mind spun through the millions of things that could be going wrong. There was nothing like the phrase "we need to talk" to make someone paranoid. "I have a question," was only minorly better.

But I opened the door to see Roman and Xander getting out of Roman's car. "Guys!" I yelled. "Everyone else is around back."

"Thanks, Alpha!" Roman called back, pointing toward the side gate so Xander would head that way.

As I shut the door again, I braced for the worst. "Please tell me this is nothing bad?"

"Nothing bad," Pax promised, patting the seat for me to join them again.

I did, and Trent immediately took my hand. Yep, this felt serious. My pulse picked up, and I looked from one side to the other, trying to get some hint, but neither man was talking. Pax tipped his head at Trent. Trent licked his lips like he was nervous. I could tell that whatever came next was going to be important, but I couldn't tell if it was good or bad.

"Elena," Trent finally said, "I know it's been crazy lately. Look, yesterday we came to the office thinking it would be a nice surprise, and Damon was there. I mean, watching you with the shoe was amazing."

"It was perfect," Pax agreed.

"But there's something I honestly wanted to ask. And, I know we've talked about it, but - "

"What the hell!" The scream came from the backyard and had all three of us on our feet in an instant.

Then a growl followed. "Oh, no," someone else said. I was pretty sure that was Roman.

"Think hard," Gabby warned even as I hurried through the house to get to the back door. "You don't want to do this, Xander."

"Elena," Pax hissed, catching me just before I reached the door. "She has to do this."

"What 'this'?" I demanded.

But I could see. Through the paned window, I had a perfect view of Xander as a wolf, pacing back and forth before Gabby with his hair up. My daughter was pulling off her clothes just as fast as she could, but clearly it wasn't fast enough. Xander darted in, and that was more than I could take.

I pulled out of Pax's arms, yanked open the door, and rushed onto the porch just in time to see Roman kick his best friend in the gut. Xander turned on him, growling so low I could feel it more than hear it. When he took a step closer and snapped, I knew this wasn't just a minor squabble.

Then Nikolai shifted and moved between the wolf and Roman. The kid was honestly a tiger. There was a big difference between knowing that in theory and seeing a cat that size snarl at a wolf. Xander looked like a Chihuahua beside the beast! Yet Trent caught my arm, holding me in place just as Gabby got her bra off. My daughter immediately shifted, and then the pair of wolves began to circle each other.

"It's a wolf thing," Theo told the tiger. "Nik, don't get in the way."

"Win, Gabby," Olivia breathed. "No matter what he says, I'm your beta."

"Dominance," Trent whispered beside my ear. "Both Xander and Gabby are alphas. They didn't get to grow up together - "

"They're *kids,*" I snapped. "They haven't grown up yet!"

Pax just moved before me, catching my face. "They're teenagers and learning to be adults. Most wolves settle this by the time they're in middle school. Gabby turned. She's been gathering her betas. This was bound to happen, Elena, and you have to let them sort it out, or it's just going to keep happening."

"But - "

"No," Pax said, forcing my face to his. "No buts. This is what it means to be a wolf. *This* is the downside. I give you my word that if it goes too far, Trent and I will break it up ourselves, but they need to - " The first snarls broke out, cutting him off. "Finish this," he said even as he turned to watch.

Xander had rushed in, catching the hair at the side of Gabby's neck, but she was quick and agile. My daughter bent, yanking the back of his head until Xander had to let go, and then Gabby was on him. Xander rolled, strong enough to push her off, but Gabby didn't care. As the wolves snarled, snapped, and rolled on the ground, Nikolai paced just out of reach, his eerie yellow and green tiger eyes constricted to mere slits.

Theo had a hand over his mouth. Samantha held Olivia's shoulders from behind, almost like she was supporting her friend more than holding her back. Then there was Roman. Both of his fists were clenched at his sides and he looked angrier than I'd ever seen him before. He looked the exact same way I felt, and neither of us could do anything.

That was when the guys arrived. Seth hopped over the privacy fence between our houses. Lane shoved through the gate with Ian right on his heels. He looked over, saw me, and then headed right toward the kids. What he didn't do was stop the fight. Instead, Ian grabbed Roman and pulled him back. Seth pointed at the girls, making it clear they should give the wolves room. Lane? He just pulled off his shirt, kicked off his shoes, and stood there waiting.

"Now it's witnessed," Trent explained. "Xander can't

call the kids liars. Whatever happens here is what will be accepted by the rest of the pack."

"C'mon, Gabby," Pax breathed. "You can do this. Use your shoulder, girl. I showed you how."

But she wasn't. The smaller, darker wolf was darting and dodging, making Xander rush in only to find that she'd already moved. Considering that the boy was significantly bigger than her, I didn't blame her for keeping a little distance. No, wait. That wasn't what she was doing at all.

"She's wearing him down," I realized. "He's too big."

"And she's quick," Trent agreed. "I guess Seth's lessons paid off after all."

"And Xander's getting over-confident," Pax realized. "She's pulling him off guard!"

Because now that she had more room to work, Gabby didn't stay in one place. She reminded me of those bullfighters who ducked and dodged around the larger animal, forcing it to keep spinning back on itself. But each time Gabby slipped around Xander, she snuck in a bite, almost as if she was proving it had been intentional. She wasn't running from him. She was controlling him, and my daughter was so much more impressive than I'd realized.

At the side, Nikolai rubbed his body against Theo. The tiger's back was even with the boy's waist, and Theo wasn't a short kid. He also didn't seem to know what to do, so Nikolai rubbed his head against him like a house cat, making it clear he wasn't going to hurt him. Without taking his eyes off the wolf fight just feet away, Theo finally reached down, resting his palm on the back of Nikolai's head.

Which was when Gabby finally made her move. She feinted one way then dodged the other, coming back at Xander low enough to get her shoulder in there. The pair collided and Gabby heaved, knocking Xander on his side - then she was on him. Her muzzle locked on Xander's neck and she thrashed like a dog playing tug-o-war, shaking him hard.

I gasped, terrified that my daughter was about to kill the boy.

Xander still tried to bite back, but he couldn't turn that far with her holding his neck. No, his fur, I realized. She had a good lock on him, but she hadn't even broken his skin. Instead, she simply pinned him, growling as she waited for him to give in. Twice more, Xander tried to bite at her, and then he just stopped.

Gabby still didn't let go. I could see both wolves breathing heavily, but my daughter wasn't going to make this easy on the boy. I had no idea what he'd done to start this, but Gabby was clearly going to finish it. Finally, Xander relaxed completely and whimpered, declaring his submission.

"Let him up," Ian said.

Gabby let go, stepped back, and shifted into a human all in a single move. "Olivia is mine," she told him. "You do not own her. She is not a possession for you to show off or order around. That is my beta, Xander, and you'll respect her, or you'll get the hell out of her life, you hear me?"

"We're done," Olivia told him. "I told you that she's my alpha. So, you want me to choose, Xander? Fine! I choose her."

Xander shifted back to human while still lying on the ground. "Olivia, you don't mean that."

"Oh, you watch me. There are a whole lot more wolves in this pack - and tigers, and bears, and we all know there will be more." She bent, grabbed something from the ground, and then threw it at him. That was Xander's clothes. "And now she's your alpha too. When you figure your shit out, then we can talk."

"Go home," Roman told him.

"Or I'll make you," Lane added.

"I was supposed to be the next Alpha of Wolf's Run," Xander hissed at Gabby. "But no, you had to turn, didn't you?"

"I did," she said, sounding much too calm. "I also don't hate you, but Ian's worked hard to prove that leading isn't the same as ruling, and you can't seem to figure that out. So try that shit again, and I will throw you down again and again until you either leave or learn. I honestly hope it's the second."

Xander pulled on his pants, but paused when she said that. "Then teach me."

"First," she said, "you have to *listen*. Go home, Xander."

He just nodded. "Yes, alpha." And then the boy actually left.

CHAPTER 27

"Roman, take Samantha home," I ordered before flicking a finger at Gabby. "Get dressed, pup. Nikolai..."

I turned, intending to tell the tiger to shift as well, then realized just how big he was. Holy shit, and he was just a juvenile? No wonder Lev hadn't wanted to shift with us. I'd have to talk him into it, though, because that would take a little getting used to.

"Shift, get dressed, and go home. Yours, his, doesn't matter," I finished.

"You two can come to my place," Olivia said, "because I have a feeling I'm getting kicked out next, right, Alpha?"

I smiled at her. "You are, pup. I need to talk to my heir."

A grin split Olivia's face. "So it's official now?"

"She just proved herself, so I think so," I decided. "And you can start helping me think of how we're going to announce this."

"Congrats, Gabby," Olivia said as she headed toward Nikolai. "Can I..." And she reached her hand out.

Nikolai shoved his head into her palm without hesitation. Olivia's mouth fell open in awe, and then she scratched the top of his head the same way we did with each other. To me, it felt a lot like a miniature massage. A similar experience to someone quickly rubbing the back of my neck, and it was kinda nice. Just a little gesture of closeness. From the way the tiger's eyes closed, it seemed that was a universal thing.

"Human," I reminded the boy.

He stepped back and shifted, not caring that he was naked at all. Clearly, the boy was a natural-born. Converts tended to be a little more aware of showing themselves in front of others. I'd thought he was, but Lev hadn't exactly clarified, and after the changes in Wolf's Run recently, I was trying very hard not to jump to conclusions.

Beside me, Lane was putting his shoes back on. Seth headed onto the back porch to check on Elena. I wanted to go with him, but she didn't need me right now and Gabby did. So, once the girl was completely clothed, I headed straight to her and hugged her fiercely.

"I'm so proud of you," I whispered into her hair.

She wrapped her arms around my back. "Yeah?"

"Very much." Then I leaned back to see her smiling face. "You used your strengths, kept your wits, and you weren't cruel." Then I ducked my head a bit. "What started that, Gabby? Did he challenge you, or did you challenge him?"

"He told me Olivia was his beta," she said, pausing to wave as her friends headed toward the front yard. "Text me!" she told them.

"Promise!" Olivia called back.

"And then?" I asked, reminding her she hadn't finished.

"Um, Olivia said no, but he said yes. They were supposed to go out today, but she told him to leave and that she wasn't going anywhere with him if he was going to be a dick, so he said she had to. His beta had to obey him was what he meant. I said she's my beta, not his, and then he challenged me. He said he was the alpha here, I said he wasn't, and he said we should settle it. And then he just shifted." She sighed. "And I would like to add that women's clothes take way too long to get off. Especially the cute ones."

I couldn't help it; I laughed. "A few extra pieces too, like your bra. How'd Nikolai end up shifted?"

Gabby bit her lip. "How many betas can I have, Ian?"

I just turned her toward the back porch. "Yep, this is going to be a long talk. Go tell your Mom that you're ok." And then I raised my voice to the guys. "Lane, can you text Dad and reschedule for me? Guys, we have a new little alpha who needs some advice. I think it's time for a family chat."

Gabby turned back to me with a smile. "Family, huh?"

"Sorry, kid, I'm keeping you," I told her. "Living room, everyone. And yeah, I need a coffee."

Trent turned Elena toward the house, and I could see him leaned close to her ear. Most likely, he was filling her in on all of the important things. Gabby hugged her mom on the other side, promising that she was fine. Might have a bruise on her butt, but only because she'd landed on it. Seth and Pax followed, but Lane caught me at the back door just before I could go inside.

"Is it settled?" he asked.

I nodded. "I have a feeling Xander's going to sulk for about a week, then he'll come crawling back to Olivia. She's made it clear that she's already bound to Gabby - and I don't doubt at all that she is. I figure that in about a month, Xander will truly submit to her and be dragged back into the group."

"He and Roman would be strong betas for her," Lane pointed out. "Not necessarily easy ones, though. And the relationships? That's going to get complicated."

Which was the one thing I was worried about. "Poly?" I suggested.

Lane shrugged. "How do you think Olivia would feel if Gabby made a move on Xander?"

"Or Gabby if Olivia tried with Roman." Fuck, but that was going to get ugly. "Ok, so this is something we need to bring up with her, but how? And with her mom in the room?"

"Let Elena take lead," he suggested. "If Gabby looks like she's embarrassed, I'll ask Elena to step away with me. I mean, we all know I'm not an expert on love triangles. Not with this fate thing in my head."

I nodded. "Ok. I also don't want Elena to be upset about us openly talking to her daughter about this stuff. Sex will come up, Lane."

"Elena's a realist about it," he promised. "She also wants Gabby to not treat her sexuality like it's related to her self value. I'll buffer the mom, but I think this is one of those things that has to be done. If she's truly going to do this - "

"She asked about betas," I whispered. "She meant Nik. Lane, she's already got one human, maybe two. If she takes the tiger as well?"

"And possibly a fox," Lane realized. "Ian, she's bridging

the species. She doesn't care what they are. She cares how they work with her, and that girl has a little too much charm for her own good."

"Yeah, she does," I agreed, "but she's going to need it if Wolf's Run becomes a multi-shifter sanctuary. That she's a convert?"

"Means she's not biased to thinking that our way is the only one," he finished, nodding to show he agreed. "Let's make sure we don't screw that up."

"Glad we're on the same page." And I opened the door, gesturing for Lane to go first.

The pair of us made it to the living room just as Seth passed Gabby a very pale coffee. I nodded at him when he lifted his chin at me, silently asking if I was ready for one. Then I claimed one of the chairs. Gabby took the corner of the couch, Elena was in the middle, and Lane moved to the cushion on her other side. Pax took the other chair, leaving Trent and Seth as the delivery boys this time.

"Thank you," I told Trent when he brought my coffee over. "So," I said, looking at Gabby, "you realize this was an important thing, right?"

"Means I'm the dominant alpha of my generation, right?" she asked.

I nodded proudly, glad she'd paid attention to us. "Exactly. Since I also want to claim you as my heir - as I have no intention of having kids of my own - it has even more weight. If Ashley ever has kids, they will most likely inherit the business. That means Wolf's Run as a community. But, I currently am a part owner, and you will inherit that half. That means the houses can never be separated from the pack, but you will always have to work with the other partner. It prevents any one of us from becoming too powerful or money-hungry."

"Kinda smart, actually," she said.

Which was why I liked this kid. She could conceptualize things like that very easily. "But you asked me about betas, and that's not an easy talk. It involves a lot more than just running the pack. Gabby, your betas will be your life partners, just like mine are. These four guys will grow old beside me. If I ever retire, they'll have the option of moving into their own homes and starting their own families the same way Patrick Green did, but it's also not a requirement."

"You mean that you could all live together forever?" she asked.

I nodded. "And our mate with us. There's nothing saying we have to separate when I pass on the pack. And yes, I do plan to retire from this position instead of die. My father's situation was a little different. The betas he grew up with didn't all live to retire. Patrick replaced one. The other followed my mother when my parents divorced."

"Why?" she asked. "I mean, if he was Henry's beta, why did he follow her?"

I glanced at Elena and she nodded, all but giving me permission. "So, you know Ashley's my oldest sister, right?"

"Yeah?"

"We have two more siblings. Twins, born between us. Ethan and Alison. The thing is, while they're my siblings, we're all pretty sure one of Dad's betas is their biological father. Their birth certificates have Dad's name on them, and none of us care, but James didn't move to be closer to my mom. He moved to be closer to his kids."

"Oh." She nodded. "That's actually kinda cool."

"That's how most wolves work," I told her. "You, Gabby, are not most wolves. First, you're a convert, and there has never been a converted pack leader in history. Secondly, you just asked me about adding a tiger to your betas. Now, normally, I'd say that's a very good idea. Here's where the catch comes in - you are not like other alphas. You are supposed to see your betas as siblings or partners, not boyfriends."

"But - " she tried.

I just lifted a hand. "I'm not saying you're wrong. Don't think that I am. I'm saying it's different, and that means there are going to be a few complications. Things we'll have to figure out. For starters, it's pretty common for mixed beta groups to be romantic with each other."

"I used to date Ashley's other beta, back when I was with her," Lane said.

"So," I asked, leaning over my knees, "what happens when Olivia ends up with Roman?"

Gabby paused, her eyes immediately jumping over to her mother. "It's not like that," she said.

Elena just patted her knee. "And now you see how hard it was for me to talk to you about my boyfriends, huh? It's ok, Gabby. We both know that we're wolves now. We know you're going to be an alpha. I also know that this is something you really can talk to us about."

"But Olivia says she doesn't think of Roman like that," Gabby told us.

"She might in ten years," I countered. "What will you do, Gabby? Your place, as the alpha, is to share everything you have with them. Your home, your authority, and your happiness. If you caught Roman and Olivia in bed together, which one are you kicking out?"

"Neither!" she hissed.

Which was the right answer. "Ok, and how would you feel about it?"

She picked at her lower lip, clearly thinking hard. "I like that Roman likes me most. It makes me feel special, I guess? I love him, Ian. I really do. It's just that Olivia is like my sister, you know? And it's kinda weird to think about her like that, but it's not like they'd leave me. I just..." She pulled her knees up under her, proving she was not as comfortable about this as she was trying to pretend. "What if he liked her more?"

"Doesn't have to be a 'more,'" I assured her. "I mean, what if your mom liked Lane more than me? It's just different, and that's ok. We're wolves. That means we're happiest in a pack, not in couples like the rest of the world tells us."

"So it's ok if she dates him and I date him?"

I nodded. "It is if that's how you're running your beta group. This is the kind of thing that all of you are going to need to talk about, be open and honest about, and not try to hide. That's why it works with us. I know when my betas are with my mate. I know when someone wants to make plans..." I looked over at Trent who shook his head, making it clear that he still hadn't asked for that date, so I kept going. "I have no problem talking with them about things that I will not talk to you about."

"You mean sex with my mom," she groaned.

I just winked at her. "You and I don't talk about that. Deal?"

"Deal!"

Seth chuckled from his chair. "I'm gonna make that a universal rule!"

Elena just shoved her face into her hands. "And now I'm the one over here dying."

"It's ok, Mom," Gabby said. "Just means you're a badass, right?"

"So are you," Elena told her. "I was so worried watching you, but you just dodged everything. One day, I want to be as good of a wolf as you are."

The smile that put on Gabby's face was amazing. No matter how much praise I heaped on her, those words from her mother put them all to shame. The girl looked like she grew two inches in that moment.

"But," I said, hating that I was about to ruin the moment, "if you're dating your betas, and you're thinking about adding non-wolves to your group, that means there's something else to consider. You won't be fifteen forever. One day, you might want to have pups, Gabby. The problem is that I have no idea what happens if a tiger and a wolf cross."

"Would Bridget know?" Elena asked.

I could only shrug. "No idea. She's confident that we can't cross contaminate each other, but that's very different from a child. You also have humans in your beta group. They can get infected, and I'm well aware that most kids do not wait until they're eighteen to have sex."

"Ian!" Gabby moaned.

"Bear with me," I begged her. "All I'm saying is that you need to think about this. Roman with Samantha?"

"Pretty sure Sam's asexual," Pax said.

I just waved that off. "Let's use them as an example

anyway. If Sam gets exposed before she's old enough to move out, then what? She'd be separated from the pack. We'd have to explain this to her parents - or hide it from them. It's complicated, and you are the alpha, Gabby. That means you need to think about all of this and make rules for your betas. Condoms do work. Never mind the fact that you can still get pregnant. Now, just to put it out there, we'll all help you if there's ever an accident, but you're fifteen. If you're considering sex with any of those boys, regardless of what they are, you talk to Dr. Bridget. You need to think about exposure and pregnancy, young lady."

"And now you're really acting like my dad," Gabby grumbled. "Mom's already given me the sex talk, and so you know, she didn't do it in a room full of people!"

"But this is your family now," I reminded her. "And this talk? It's about your beta group, not just sex. It's about the fact that you aren't doing things the way they've always been done - and that's a good thing. It just means that this is going to get embarrassing and complicated at times, but all six of us are here to help. Even if your mother is blushing more than you are. Even if Trent's now hiding in the kitchen so you won't see that he isn't any better. Sex happens. It's how we get the next generation. It's not something to be ashamed of. But for us? It's not as easy as it is for humans."

"We have lycanthropy," Seth said. "Gabby, Nikolai is bisexual. He likes girls too. Betas don't go away when you get out of high school. This thing? It makes us loyal in ways most people can't understand. The idea of Ian setting me aside? I don't know what I'd do with myself. It's like losing a parent. I'd say a sibling, but you're an only child. I love that man like a brother, ok? Your betas will feel the same."

"Ian's our whole world," Pax told her. "I can't remember the last time I talked to my parents. I also don't care. I have my family right here. My mate, my brothers, and my alpha. It's a family we chose, but it's still a family, and now you're a part of that too. Ian claiming you as his heir? That kinda makes you like our kid. Not a pup in the pack, but ours, Gabby."

She looked over at her mom. "See, I told you they feel like my dads."

"Don't tell me," she said. "Tell them."

Gabby just turned those big amber eyes on me. "You do, you know. That's why I wanted you to dance with me. But they do too. Pax is like the grumpy dad who makes me do my homework. Trent's like the artistic dad who helps with my acting. Lane's like the dad who threatens my boyfriends." Then she smiled at Seth. "You're like the cool dad who buys the alcohol for the parties."

"Not gonna happen," he told her.

But the look on his face? I couldn't tell if he was trying not to smile or cry. It also matched the feeling in my own chest, because that little girl? She was mine, and in that moment, I swore I would find a way to make that official. I wanted her to call me "Dad" and introduce me that way to others. I wanted her to scream at us that we weren't fair. I just wanted... this.

CHAPTER 28

Somehow, Ian managed to make it through our chat with Gabby. The end result was that he'd stand behind anything she decided so long as she could justify it. If she wanted human betas, he'd support her. A tiger? That was fine too. Six, eight, even ten betas? If she could tell him why, then he'd help her make it happen - but she had to justify her decisions well enough to make him agree.

Right now, Gabby officially had Olivia, Roman, and Samantha with her. She said they'd been testing Theo to see if he'd benefit the pack - which impressed me a little. She'd also realized that betas really did work best in pairs so that they could have each other's backs. That was part of why she wanted Nikolai, yet his new romance with Theo made her want to wait just a bit. To be sure it was more than just lust, she said. Plus, she also thought that one of the foxes might be a real benefit, but she didn't know them well enough to be sure if any of the three would work with her.

Which meant my daughter was actually thinking this through. Gabby had this vision of a place where everyone was accepted for what they were, and not asked to bend themselves to fit into someone else's mold. It had all started with the bears, grown when she met the tigers, and now that she knew about foxes and other creatures, her plans were expanding. Of course, her version sounded a lot like a utopia, but she was a bit more realistic than that. Not much, though. After all, she was still fifteen.

But sometime over the weekend, the foxes finished moving in. That was why, on Monday, the youngest was sitting in the back seat when Roman came to get Gabby for school. Olivia was beside her. Zaria, I thought the girl's name was, but I'd been getting her and Ridley confused for the last couple of days. Sheridan, at least, stood out because I'd actually met her.

She also started her first shift on the gates that night. I'd made it clear that she could wait another week, but Sheridan wanted to prove that she was taking this seriously. When I headed into the office on Tuesday morning, she was just getting off from her first night of training, walking her way back to her home.

"You know you can drive," I told her. "Just park in one of the spaces here. Makes it a lot easier when it rains."

She gave me a tired smile. "Thanks. I actually let Ridley have the car so she can either find a job or get into school. Told her I didn't care which." Then Sheridan waved at her chest and the Wolf's Run shirt she was wearing. "I approve of the green, though. Goes with my hair."

I just laughed. "I think that's proof that you're

exhausted. No one is supposed to like their work uniform. If you want, we've got a coffee pot in the lobby."

"Oh, no." She waved me off. "There's a Keurig in the guard shack. I'm so over-caffeinated, I'm vibrating. But hey..." She took a step closer, closing the distance between us. "Thank you, Alpha. The house is amazing. The job is a dream come true. The community? Lev's bear friends are here, and rumor has it that you might be taking more of us weirdos."

"Not weird," I assured her. "It's just that wolves work in a pack. If all three of you - types, I mean - can help us figure out how to make this work, then doesn't it make sense? The strength of the pack to shelter those shifters who are all too often isolated. The power of bears and tigers to help when we're just not big enough? The intelligence or cunning of you foxes? I mean, those are all generics, but the idea of it? That we could all bring something new and unique to a community like this?"

"It's never been done before," she told me. "Not once. Not even to fail. Wolves are wolves. Foxes are foxes. If we meet in public, we smile, nod, and pretend like it never happened. This? A Sisterhood of women to lean on? A Pack Alpha who doesn't seem to put his kind above ours, but rather makes fair decisions? Yeah. I'm all in. If there's ever anything I can do, just let me know?"

"I will." Then I pointed up the street. "But I think sleep is the first thing on your list. Go. To. Bed. Sheridan."

"Good morning, then, Alpha," she laughed, waving as she started walking again.

I was smiling when I walked into the office, amused at how happy Sheridan always seemed to be. I wasn't sure if it was because she was so young or if maybe it had more to do with being a fox. Either way, I liked her. She was the kind of person that felt like a pleasure to be around.

Unfortunately, the joy of my morning only lasted until I opened my email inbox. Right at the top was a message from Karen, of all people. It was short, sweet, and to the point. Hidden Forest Pack was officially demanding reparations for the loss of two of their wolves. She listed out the reasons why they felt this was valid, and what they expected in response: a million dollars per wolf.

And, she noted, if Wolf's Run was unable to pay, they would claim our pack and its assets instead.

I grabbed my phone, sent a text to Ian that Karen was still being a bitch, and let him know I was forwarding him an email from her. With that handled, I kept going, sipping my coffee while I worked through a dozen of the typical inquiries. One caught my eye. The woman said she'd heard that our community encouraged wildlife, and was wondering how diverse the natural population was. I sent her back the usual response, then added in a paragraph about how it seemed that making a nature preserve inside the community walls had been attracting a few different species, so we were trying to nurture that as much as possible.

It was all vague and subtle enough that if she was some bird watcher, she wouldn't clue in. But, if this was yet another non-wolf shifter, then I wanted her to understand that we were willing to consider her. Just reading that note Scott had made with the request for a single tree made me want to ensure that no one else became that desperate.

It also made me realize just how lucky I was. For once, I wasn't the one getting the bad breaks. I was finally the person who could help others. Not only was this the right thing to do, but something inside of me was demanding it. That maternal thing again, I supposed. I figured this was similar to how Ian's protective instinct worked, except that he wanted to fight to help and I wanted to just offer a cozy blanket and a shoulder to lean on. Flip sides of the same coin, right?

Ashley came in right about the time I finished the first group of emails. She was late. Very late, and there was the subtle scent of sweet grass about her. My lips curled in a smile.

"Long night?" I asked.

"Weekend," she corrected. "I will have you know that when everyone left the trails on Friday night, I was invited to have another beer, so I did."

"With the bears?" I couldn't stop grinning.

"Jax, actually. And I may have had one too many and climbed that beast like a tree." She flicked both brows up, clearly proud of herself. "And the next morning, Vic caught me in the kitchen and made it clear that he has no problem with that. And so I ended up spending the day there. Yeah, and I'm not sure exactly how it happened, but I woke up in Scott's bed this morning, so I kinda had to run home for a shower and office-friendly clothes."

"You don't know how," I said, latching onto that part of her story.

"Well, there was a little Vic, a little Jax, and then Scott joined in, and I may not have slept at all on Saturday, then Sunday we had a repeat, so I kinda passed out early, but I swear it was on the couch."

I just grabbed her coffee cup. "I'm refilling this. You go

sit down because I'm sure you ache too much to be standing. Bears? Really? Are they..."

"Hung?" she asked. "Oh fuck, yeah. Today, I get to be the one sitting so I can recover."

"Deal."

Because I did not want to ruin this for her. The last thing Ashley needed was some reason to cut those men off. Now that I knew how long she'd gone without having any kind of serious relationship, I was determined to make sure that she at least tried with these guys. Didn't matter if they were bears. I didn't give a shit if anyone approved or not. If those men could make her happy - one, all, or some - then I had her back.

The hard part, though, was not quizzing her. I wanted to ask. I longed to know how she felt about them, but I knew better. Instead, we spent most of the day giggling about sexual positions and the problem with being pinned into bed by men so much larger than ourselves. While falling asleep in between them was nice, the next morning? There was nothing quite as awkward as trying to get out of the covers, on top of them, and then crawling to the foot of the bed to go pee!

And the inquiries didn't stop. I couldn't be sure, but it felt like the word had gotten out that Wolf's Run was considering non-wolf shifters. One person said they had an exotic cat, legal, and asked if they'd be allowed to keep it. A mountain lion, evidently. I let him know that there were conditions on such things, and if he'd like to come into the office, we'd be happy to explain it all.

Another was curious about coyotes in the area. I responded that there weren't any, but that this was a wildlife-friendly community, and we did not trap or kill the local animals, but rather tried to make sure they could exist in a way that wouldn't threaten the other residents to preserve the ecology. In truth, I was starting to feel a little proud of my answers. It wasn't like this subtle double speak was easy!

Then, just at the end of the day, my phone rang. "Wolf's Run, this is Elena," I answered.

"Well hello, shoe girl," the man replied.

I didn't even need him to tell me his name. This was Damon. I could feel the hair on the back of my neck rising, but I fought back the urge to growl. "What can I do for you this time, Damon?" I asked.

He chuckled. "You know, Karen says you're a weak and passive little thing. What changed, woman?"

"Mm, that is really none of your business, but if you have to know, it was running that bitch out of here."

"And right into my pack. Thank you for that, by the way. Now, about our request?" he asked.

I knew he meant that email, the one about the reparations. "I'm afraid that's been sent to management. You're going to have to wait your turn like everyone else, but I wouldn't count on a favorable outcome."

"My people died!" he roared, forcing me to lift the phone away from my ear.

"Then be a better leader," I told him. "If you expect Ian to manage your pack, then maybe you should just step down now."

"Oh, that's not how it works, you stupid human," Damon sneered. "Don't think I missed how your mates - and even that Langdon bitch - hovered over you protectively. You see, some of us fight our own battles, and you owe us. I lost two good men. Two! And they were successful wolves. My pack is suffering because yours exists, and I intend to get that back, one way or another."

Then the phone was snatched from my hands. I looked up to find Ashley there, pissed, and leaning over my desk. "Damon, this is Ashley Langdon, Elena's beta. Now, let me make this very clear so you don't misunderstand. You will get *nothing*. I don't care how long you chase after my brother. It doesn't matter if you went to the same school, the same university, or even dated his exes. If you want to get ahead, then lift yourself up and stop looking for handouts."

"Fuck you, Ashley," Damon said, and I could hear him through the handset.

She chuckled. "Yeah, I'm not that desperate. You have no claim on Wolf's Run. We cannot be held responsible for some psycho shooting at our pack. More than that, we can't be held responsible for defending ourselves against it. Those hunters you keep whining about? They were incited by a mentally-disturbed high school boy - not us."

"I've now lost three wolves because of you!" the man roared.

"Thought it was two," Ashley countered.

"And Seth," he said. "Oh, but you see, that one *is* Ian's fault. I turned him. I was responsible for him. He stole him from my pack. Yes, Ashley, I've thought this through. Pay up, or I'm coming for Wolf's Run."

"Try it," she snarled. "Do you honestly think you can best Ian in a fair fight?"

"Fair?" The man scoffed. "Ian is a weak Alpha. He let a teenaged boy disobey his orders and what did he do? Nothing. He allowed his mate's child to be turned, and the punishment for that? Not a thing. His pack members ignore him, knowing full well that he's not a threat. Why do you think I'd be scared of him? My mate nearly killed his, and all Ian could manage to do was kick her out? Yeah, I think I've got this. Wolf's Run will be mine..." He chuckled. "Unless you pay."

"Go play in the street or something," Ashley snapped, and then she slammed the phone back into the cradle. "Dick."

"Ash?" I asked. "What is he talking about?"

"Ian is fair. He's not a tyrant, Elena, but Damon? He is. He's convinced himself that because Ian didn't kill Roman and didn't destroy Karen that he's not strong enough to fight back." She pushed both palms down onto my desk and let out a heavy sigh. "He's wrong, but he's also not going to stop. If you get any more calls like that? Just hang up on him, ok? If that asshole wants to challenge my brother then he needs to come in here and do it."

"What about the reparations, though?" I asked.

She rolled her eyes. "It's his excuse. If he tries to attack us for no reason, other packs will attack him. If he has a reason - even a weak one - it gives him justification for this bullshit. Kinda like the UN or something, I guess. If you're going to declare war, you have to have a reason and follow a few steps. If you don't, you're branded a criminal, and there are enough wolves in this world to make that suck."

I just nodded. "You should probably know that he seems to think I'm still human."

"Good," she said. "I mean, your eyes are dark for a wolf, but a lot lighter than they used to be. Believe it or not, that's a good thing. It will make him less likely to try to claim you as his prize."

The breath rushed from my lungs. "He can do that?"

"He can try," she clarified. "Some wolves think it's sexy. But no, wolf culture isn't rape culture. He's just trying to look impressive, and you are too smart to get wet panties over a man acting like a self-absorbed prick. Besides, what can he really do? This is Wolf's Run. There's a reason we made this place into a fortress."

I just hoped she was right.

CHAPTER 29

When Ian got the email from Karen, he was pissed. After hearing that Damon called Elena, I was too. Not that the idiot could do anything, but if he was pushing this hard, then Damon was clearly up to something, and I would not allow my mate to get hurt in the process. So on Wednesday, we made a check of the community security features. They were all still working.

Then, that evening, I headed over to Ashley's to do a little digging. Damon said he'd lost two pack members to hunters. That meant they'd been wolves, so there wouldn't be much in the news about a few animals being killed. Still, an increase in the local wolf population should be mentioned somewhere. Probably on a rural forum or something, but I'd found nothing.

Ashley, however, was a bit better at this. She ran through Twitter first, got a few leads from hashtags, and then dove in. Eventually, in some tractor owner's forum, she found it. Just northwest of town, ranchers were reporting a surge in wolves being seen during daylight. That was right around where Damon had parked his Hidden Forest pack, and the idiot was letting his members run as wolves in broad daylight?

He was basically asking for it. The only concern was that the numbers didn't match what we knew of his pack. Hidden Forest had always been a small community. They had a trailer park out on land someone was leasing for something. The last we'd heard, he had just about twenty pack members, but this? It sounded like there were easily fifty wolves. A big pack, and they'd been seen taking down one man's cow, if the story was accurate.

"You think they're that dumb?" I asked Ashley.

"In all honesty?" She looked up at me. "Yeah, I do. This is Damon Shaw we're talking about. Lane, he wants wolves to be exposed. He thinks we're the more advanced people. He's not trying to be careful. He's trying to prove he's better than Ian, and he has been since they were kids! The fact that you saved Seth, helped him turn, and made him into a functional wolf?" She shook her head as if that should say enough.

"You know Seth wants revenge, right?" I asked.

Ashley nodded. "Not surprised. Damon and his friends jumped him, Lane. They changed his life. Maybe it was for the better, but who can be sure? Of course he wants revenge. What Damon did to Seth? It may as well have been a form of rape. He took Seth's humanity without consent, and I can't say that I blame the guy for being pissed about it."

"But he's a wolf now," I hissed. "He's stronger, better, and he has us."

She just nodded. "And maybe he didn't think there was a damned thing wrong with himself before." Then she sighed. "Lane, don't get me wrong. I'm glad Seth's in the pack. I like the guy, and he makes Elena happy. He's a wonderful beta for my brother. None of that changes the simple fact that Damon bit him, and the man wanted to kill him. Seth's just proud enough to want to get a piece of his own back."

"I can see that," I admitted, because I probably would feel the same if I was him. "But where did he get the extra wolves?"

"Maybe he's taken over another pack? Could explain his sudden interest in threatening to do the same here." She sighed again and scrubbed at her face. "If he's won one dominance fight, he'll feel like he's top dog. He's also convinced that Ian's weak because he didn't kill Roman or Karen. Damon can't tell the difference between compassion and strength, and Wolf's Run is quite the prize."

"The life Damon's always wanted," I grumbled. "Ian can take him, though."

"Make sure of that," she said. "I want you training with him. Push him, Lane. Make my brother work for it. Two of you, three, or all of you. I don't care, but make sure that if Damon ever does show up here and makes it a challenge that my brother will win easily."

"Promise," I said, aware that her eyes kept jumping to the clock. "Have someplace to be?"

"No, it's just..." She gave up and just laughed. "Dinner date."

"Vic?" I asked.

She bit her lips together and didn't answer for a long

moment. "Scott, actually. Um, I kinda spent the weekend with them."

"And they're cool with that?" I asked.

"They sure didn't complain," she shot back. "Jesus, Lane, don't start giving me shit about this, ok? Yes, I know they're bears. I know nothing can come of it. They're also nice, and - "

I grabbed her arms, making her look at me. "And they make you happy, alpha. They're pack. They're strong - maybe even stronger than you. They're loyal. I know all of that, and if you don't think that I checked to make sure they were good enough, then you don't know me very well. I let those men help me teach Elena to walk as a wolf. I approve of them, but none of that matters. Ashley, the only thing you need to be sure of is if they make you happy."

"For now," she told me.

I just moved a hand to the back of her neck, making her look up at me. "Don't push them away because someone else hurt you. They're bears, Ash. Not wolves. They aren't with you because they have to be. They get no benefits in the pack for it. If anything, they're risking a lot. How would those guys know that Ian just wants his sister to find someone who can keep up with her, or that no wolf stands a chance?"

"He said that?" she asked.

I nodded. "Ash, subtle is not something you're good at. Vic's almost as bad. Jax basically drools when you walk into the room - or area. Scott? He's the quiet one, but his eyes follow you like he's hunting prey. Yeah, we noticed. We also haven't said a thing because Ian's hoping you'll tell him. He doesn't want you to feel like he's pushing you one way or the other."

"Who knows?" she asked.

"We all do. Pax and Trent figured it out when you called them, I guess? Seth said Vic tipped him off. The man was a little too adamant that it was just a drink. No man just has a friendly drink with a woman like you. And Elena said something when I was bringing her home. She didn't mean to, so don't you dare blame her."

"She doesn't understand," Ashley said. "To Elena, they're just men. She has no idea that my family would lose it."

"Yeah, well, I made Ian think about it. Took him all of sixty seconds to figure out that maybe, just maybe, a bear will be enough to keep up. Bridget says they can't make you sick. No one needs you to have kids. So, if this becomes more than a little fun, we're all with you, ok?"

"I'm not ready for anything serious," she said.

I just smoothed back her hair. "I know, alpha. I also know that you won't ever be. Just don't push them away because you think you have to. Toy with them for days, months, or even years. You're the strong one here, and they're lucky to have your attention." Then I let her go and closed her laptop. "Now, should I tell Elena you're going to be late to work tomorrow?"

Ashley just ducked her head and laughed. "Tell her there's a chance." This time, when she sighed, it sounded relieved. "Thanks, Lane. You're too good as a beta to have been wasted with me."

"And yet I'm still as loyal to you as ever," I promised. "Just let me know if those bears need a little talking to. As in a hint." With one last smile, I turned and headed for the door.

"Pretty sure they've figured it out," she called after me. "Night, Lane."

"Night, Ash!"

Closing her door behind me, I started walking the block back home. In front of Elena's house, there was a pair of cars. One was Roman's, but the other? I'd never seen it before, yet the boy standing beside it had black hair, and was tall and muscular enough to stand out. I was pretty sure that was Nikolai. I hadn't even thought about him being old enough to drive, but it made sense.

It also made me feel old to think that Gabby would be driving in a year. Seth had already said he'd be teaching her, but Trent wanted to help as well. I had a feeling they wouldn't be the only ones. Me? I'd stay home with Elena, because I wasn't sure my nerves could take that. Gabby behind the wheel? I'd claw the seats to death or end up going lycan beside her.

I jogged across the street just as Elena peeked her head out the door and yelled Gabby's name. She was holding something up. A phone, it looked like. Gabby groaned, ran back to grab it, then hurried to the car again.

"Hey, Lane!" she said.

"Where are you all off to?" I asked.

She grinned. "Running as a pack. Sam and Theo want to see the trails, and Nik can see at night, so we'll be out a few hours." Then she winked. And no, it wasn't subtle.

"Go play," I laughed before looking up at Elena. "Got a message from Ashley," I called to her.

As the kids drove away, Elena held up a finger and ducked back inside. A second later, she was back, wearing clothes that made it clear she'd planned to have a lazy afternoon at home. For a moment, I felt bad. I hadn't meant to drag her outside.

"What was that?" she asked as she shuffled across the lawn toward my driveway.

"Ashley wanted you to know there's a chance she'll be late to work in the morning. Sounds like she has a dinner date with a bear."

Elena smiled. "Good. I can hold down the fort this time. She's done it often enough for me."

So I tilted my head to my place. "I need a shower, but if you're all alone..."

"The kids will be gone until ten," she said, just a little too casually.

It was just after seven. A few hours alone with her? Well, away from the kids, at any rate. I'd take it. "Can I make dinner for you?"

"No," she said, turning me toward my own house and giving me a push. "You guys can stop with the spoiling already. I can't remember the last time I cleaned my own house, Lane!"

"Yeah, but you have to take care of Gabby," I pointed out. "And there's five of us - "

"With your own place," she broke in.

"And still five. Elena..." I stopped and turned to her. "We do it for each other. It's easy to pick something up and put it away. It's also one less thing to weigh on you, and this is an easy way to show we care. Dishes, laundry, vacuuming. It means Gabby has time to worry about her betas, you have time to worry about your daughter, and we get the joy of worrying about you."

"Yeah?" she asked, lifting her chin to look up at me. "So when do I get to worry about making *you* happy, Lane?"

A smile claimed my lips. "That's not how this works, little bunny."

"No?" So she stepped closer. "What if I want to brush the tangles from your hair, or maybe spoil you a bit? How am I supposed to do that if you're always handling it before I get the chance?"

"Kinda proves my point, doesn't it?" I teased. "If I can do all of that and help you before you even get a chance, maybe it means you have enough on your plate." Then I leaned down to kiss her forehead. "You won't win this one, Elena. You make me plenty happy just doing what you do. I like watching you learn to be a wolf. I love the chance to spend the night with your arms around me. The fact that you let me treat Gabby like she's my own? So far as I'm concerned, you spoil me plenty. Now get inside, because I can see the hair standing up on your arms."

"Doesn't feel fair," she grumbled, but she did go.

"Now, if you want to let me give you a very long, very skin-to-skin massage," I offered just as she opened the door. "You know, to work out those aches."

"Who's getting naked?" Seth asked, proving at least one of my roommates was home.

"Trying to convince Elena that she should," I said.

He sat up, his head peeking over the back of the couch. "Where's Gabby?"

"Trails," Elena admitted.

Seth just caught my eye and smiled. "Well, then I think a naked massage is a great idea. Ian, Trent, and Pax are at Henry's. Something about splitting the business assets so it's not officially held by the Alpha and can't be seen as a pack asset anymore."

I just looked down at Elena. "Tell me you don't ache after your running lesson."

"Without lying?" she asked. "Kinda can't."

Seth just chuckled. "I'll get a blanket and some massage oil. Get comfy, Elena."

She just kicked off her shoes and headed for the living room. "I blame you for this, Lane."

"Uh huh," I agreed.

Because that woman was about to be very naked in the middle of my floor. I couldn't quite find a problem with this idea.

CHAPTER 30

Seth tossed the blanket down on the arm of the couch. Lane worked me out of my clothes, pausing to steal kisses along my arms or back. The only problem was that when I tried to return the favor, he laughed and stepped out of my reach. Seth moved in, almost like it had been scripted.

"We're spoiling you," Lane reminded me.

"Oh, is that what we call this now?" Seth asked. "I was just trying to get my hands on my mate's body."

"She's been using all those new muscles as a wolf," Lane reminded him.

"Same thing," Seth countered as he eased my pants and panties to the floor.

"I am not about to be the only one naked in this room," I told them.

"Yes," Lane said, "you are." And then he sat on the couch, pulling me down in his lap.

Yeah, he was hard, and I could feel it through his jeans,

but he ignored it. Instead, his hands moved to my back, kneading at the muscles on either side of my spine. Seth cleared his throat pointedly, then gestured to a tube of massage oil on the end table. Lane had to lean to reach it, but he still didn't let me up. I could feel his hardness pressing into my rump, though.

Then Seth knelt in front of me and lifted my leg, working at my bare foot. "Believe it or not, Elena, we really do like to spoil you."

I moaned when he found a sore spot. "I'm kinda getting that impression."

The words were barely out of my mouth before Lane's hands were on my back again, but this time, they were slick. He pushed both of his thumbs upward, right along the length of my spine, and I moaned, letting my eyes close to enjoy this. Seth's hands made their way across the bottom of my foot, focusing on any place that earned another sound, but sometimes those were for Lane instead.

The men didn't seem to care. Seth eventually moved to the other foot, then up to my calf. Lane's hands shifted to my shoulders. In truth, I really did ache. Bridget's medicine helped, but the last thing I needed was to become dependent on that, so I only used it when I had to. This? It worked a lot better, in my opinion, and the pair of men were a lot more tempting than swallowing a foul-tasting pill.

But there was something about sitting on Lane's lap, completely naked, in the middle of their living room. As Seth's hands moved higher, I felt the need to squirm a little more. Then Lane's lips found the back of my neck. I relaxed my head back, giving him more room, so he kissed again just as Seth's hands began to work the aches from my inner thigh.

I moaned.

So Seth bent, kissing the spot he'd just rubbed. My legs relaxed a little more, spreading for him, and he murmured against my skin. The next kiss was higher. Lane's hands moved lower, sliding across my ribs. Then back up until he found my arms. There, he kneaded my biceps, guiding my arms tight against my body.

Then Seth flicked the tip of his tongue across the junction of my legs. One of my hands clawed at Lane's leg. The other reached for the back of Seth's head, holding him right there. Lane simply kissed my neck, but I knew he wasn't oblivious to what was happening before him.

"You sure you still want those pants on?" I asked him.

He chuckled softly. "Spoiling, little bunny. And I told you that you were made to be eaten."

Seth flicked his tongue across me again, spreading my folds. My nails scraped across Lane's jeans. "I thought you were supposed to do the eating."

"Not necessarily, no." Lane sounded just a little too amused. "I'm supposed to make sure you're taken care of. Seth? He's been dying for a taste." And then Lane spread his legs, effectively forcing mine wider in the process. "Believe it or not, Ian isn't the only one who likes to watch you."

Then Seth leaned in just a little more and sucked at my clit. With Lane's arms around me, holding me against his chest, there wasn't much I could do but take it - and moan. He had one pinning my right arm to my ribs. His hand on that side was pressed against my belly, keeping my hips from thrusting. The other arm was pressed between my breasts with his hand resting just at the base of my throat, tilting my neck toward his lips.

"What is mine is his," Lane whispered against my skin. "And you, little bunny, are very much mine."

"Yes," I breathed just as Seth's tongue flicked over my clit. "Lane..."

"Sometimes," Lane said, "you don't have to do anything but take." He kissed at the corner of my jaw, but his eyes were on what Seth was doing between my legs. "Does that feel good?"

"Yes," I panted.

He murmured his appreciation and kissed the spot just beneath my ear. "Did you want him to stop?"

"No," I whispered. "I want more."

Seth immediately pushed two fingers into me, but his mouth never stopped. He licked, he sucked, and he pumped his hand into me until I didn't care about anything else. My hips tried to buck, but Lane's hand held me still so Seth could have his way with me. My breasts ached to be touched, the nipples so hard, but neither of them tried. Lane just kissed me again, then again, watching every single thing Seth did, and I could feel him throbbing beneath my ass, proving he very much enjoyed the show.

And there was something about being restrained that made every pass of Seth's mouth and hand feel that much better. I couldn't help. I could only take, and it was so good. I felt the sparks shooting straight through my core, my body so very close, and the most I could do was whimper with desire. My head fell back against Lane's shoulder, my body completely in his control, and then Seth sucked at my clit again.

That was all it took - I lost control, struggling to bite back the cry of passion that tried to break free. My thighs clenched, but Lane's legs were too strong. My back arched, thrusting my breasts forward, and that hand pressing on my belly intensified the pulses of pleasure coursing through me as I came so hard.

"More," Lane said.

Seth leaned back with a chuckle. "Oh, so you go last now, hm? I'm ok with that. Make room."

Lane shifted me forward, sliding my ass toward his knees, but Seth was pulling off his shirt. His pants came next, although he only opened them, pushing his jeans and underwear down to his thighs before leaning back in. One of his knees pressed between mine and Lane's. The other foot landed between my spread legs, and Seth leaned over us both with his dick in his hand.

"Seth?" I gasped.

His mouth brushed mine. "I'm not worried about being close to him, but you can still tell me to stop."

I shook my head. "Kiss me again."

He did, and then I felt Lane's lips on my shoulder. A moment later, Seth pressed into my body. My hot, slick, and very stimulated body. I sucked in a breath as I stretched around him, but I still couldn't do anything with my hands. My left, the most free of the two, could only reach far enough to let my fingertips brush across Seth's denim-covered thigh.

Then he thrust, pushing me back into Lane's chest. The three of us didn't really fit on the couch like this, but the guys didn't seem to care at all. Seth braced one arm against the back. Lane pressed his face into my neck, ignoring the man so very close to him, and Seth began to pump, driving me higher all over again.

Pinned between them, I felt like their toy, and I loved it. Turning my head allowed my mouth to find Lane's, and he kissed back hard. Seth leaned over my other shoulder, panting as he thrust himself into me harder and harder. I gasped against Lane's mouth. Seth's chest slid across my breasts with each thrust. Lane's fingers moved lower, caught between mine and Seth's body as he sought my clit. Then he began to make slow, lazy circles. I tried to clench my jaw. I struggled to breathe, keeping my noises to myself, but it was futile.

I cried out with pleasure, and Seth pumped into me again. "Scream, baby," he begged, sliding into me one more time.

Long, hard, deep strokes that took my breath away. And yet, the only release I had was my voice. I panted, I gasped, I prayed to God and called out both of my lover's names, not caring about any of that. All that mattered was the feeling growing inside me, building like a dam about to burst, and I wanted it so badly.

My hips tried to move. That only made Lane press harder, sending sparks straight up my clit. I could feel Seth's belly sliding against Lane's hand, rocking that touch with each thrust, and I just let it happen. These were my mates - my men - and I'd never imagined anything so sensual in my life. This was all for me. Every touch. Every kiss. Every inch of Seth's dick sliding through my body. It was all mine, and with one more thrust, I stopped trying to hold back.

I came hard, clamping down on the man inside me. My body jerked, shoving my shoulder into Lane's body, but the man simply purred in pleasure. Seth pumped into me only one more time and then he groaned as warmth filled my body. Then he gasped, his lips right beside my ear.

"Move," Lane ordered.

Seth sucked in a breath, and then extracted himself from my body. He staggered back a step, proving he was as spent as I felt, but Lane didn't care. The moment Seth was out of his way, Lane lifted me to my feet, standing only a second later. I felt him pull off his shirt and turned to look, only to see him smile deviously.

"Floor," he said, popping open the button on his jeans.

Seth's hands caught my arm, and he guided me to the carpet. Like me, he was still breathing hard, but while Lane got out of his pants, socks, and shoes, Seth stole a kiss. The first was fast, but the second was a little deeper, easing me onto my back. Then his hand found the side of my face and he turned me toward him.

The moment I was on my side, Lane dropped down behind me. He kissed my arm, completely ignoring Seth. Then my shoulder, making his way to my neck. There, he bit. Just once, before shifting to spoon up against me. I pulled my mouth from Seth's to look back, but Lane was waiting. He took his turn kissing my mouth, his tongue exploring quickly as Seth shifted to lie before me.

"Leg," Seth said, guiding my top knee up.

Lane caught it, pulling my calf across his thigh, spreading me. Then he angled himself into place, pressing against my opening. My ass was pressed against his hips, my back against his chest, and Seth was sliding his hand across my curves, watching me like he was starving. Lane eased himself in.

"Oh, that's nice," Seth breathed, moving his palm from my ribs to my breast.

I felt the rough skin tease across my achingly hard nipple. Seth's cognac eyes were locked on my face, judging my reactions, so he did it again, even as Lane eased partially out of my body.

"Kiss him," Lane told me.

My hands were free, so I caught the side of Seth's face and pulled him toward me. Our mouths met and Lane rocked into me again. Every time he buried himself in my body, it shoved my lips against Seth's mouth, but neither man cared. Tongues tangled. Bodies writhed. Hands teased and taunted. I could barely keep track of which one belonged to who, but I also didn't care.

Someone was holding my hip. Someone toyed with my breasts. Lane's teeth threatened the back of my neck, and his lips kissed it all away. The whole time, he pumped into me from behind, the three of us spread across the floor without shame. It was wild, almost feral, and I couldn't get enough. I rocked back, driving Lane deeper, and gasped against Seth's mouth. He drank it in, kissing me even harder as praise.

"Bite her," Seth hissed. "Stop teasing her."

"No," Lane said, thrusting even faster.

"Please," I begged.

He groaned beside my ear, but still wouldn't bite. Instead, Seth ducked under the other side of my neck and nipped at my pulse. "Mine," he whispered.

As if that was some kind of dare, Lane's teeth finally closed on the back of my neck, pressing hard enough to make me cry out. My core clenched, and Lane growled in the back of his throat, but his teeth didn't let go. Not until his arm reached around my chest to hook on my shoulder. But the moment his teeth released, Lane pulled, driving my body onto his the way I really wanted: hard.

My beast fucked me hard, but this was more than that. These men loved me. This wasn't empty or meaningless sex. It meant everything. It was us, my mates, loving without limits. This was honest, open love. This was what it meant to be a wolf, and pinned between them, I wanted nothing else in the world.

My gasps turned to moans. The moans became cries. Then, that turned into one single scream of passion as my body could take no more and I lost control. Seth kissed my open mouth. Lane let out a long, low grunt and tried to keep going, but it was just too much. He came, clinging to me desperately as it took us both together, and for a moment time seemed to just pause.

Then I remembered to breathe again. Lane sighed against the back of my neck, and Seth pushed damp strands of my hair from my face. Carefully, Lane shifted his hips, withdrawing from my body, and then he twisted. A moment later, that blanket landed across all three of us.

Seth pillowed his head on his bent arm, a soft smile on his lips. Lane hugged himself against my back, his cheek pressed against my shoulder. I loved it all. No, that wasn't it.

"I love both of you," I said softly, reaching back to hold Lane closer, but my eyes were on Seth's. "I love that I can."

"You're just so perfect," Seth whispered. "So very beautiful, and you're ours."

"Mine," Lane mumbled.

Seth chuckled. "Which means ours, in case you for-"

He didn't get to finish the thought because Lane's

phone began to ring. Both men immediately sat up, but even I knew that ringtone. That was Ian.

"Got it," Seth said, flinging off the blankets so he could grab the pants making that sound. He pulled it out by the third ring and swiped immediately. "Yeah?"

Then his head whipped around to look at me. I heard him make agreeing noises, but Lane kept his volume turned down too low for even my new wolf hearing to make out what Ian was saying.

Then, "Be there in five," and Seth hung up. "Both of you, get dressed. The kids were attacked at the trails. They're at Bridget's. Gabby's fine, but Olivia got torn up pretty bad."

CHAPTER 31

The three of us piled into Lane's truck and raced over to Bridget's. When we got there, the street was packed. Cars had been parked anywhere they would fit. The door to the house was open, making it clear an entire crowd was inside, plus more outside in the yard, and yet, when Lane parked and I jumped out, a woman pointed to the side.

"Clinic," she said, meaning the large building set beside the house like a detached garage. "Your pup is there, Alpha."

"Move!" Lane roared, clearing a path by the power of his voice alone.

The last time I'd been to see Bridget as a doctor, she'd treated me in her home. However, it appeared that her clinic was now fully functional, and by the way the pack was gathering, I knew this was going to be bad. When we got closer, I heard a scream. Thankfully, it was short and didn't sound too bad.

A man yanked open the door, holding it so I didn't even have to slow down. Lane and Seth were right behind me, but when I burst into the waiting area, the first thing I saw was Sampson Delaney, and the man was covered in blood. Samantha was blotting at a wound on his head. Strangely enough, the old man was letting her.

And in the corner, Vic stood with Theo and Nik. I didn't see Lev, but couldn't worry about that yet. Roman was sitting in one of the chairs. Xander was beside him with a hand on his shoulder, looking as if the boy was offering his best friend some emotional support. At the back of the room, I saw Jax. Beside him was Scott. A second later, I realized that the men with their backs to us were Trent and Pax.

"Where's Gabby?" I asked, not even caring who answered.

Trent spun to face me and crossed the room while answering. "She's fine, Elena. She's with Olivia. Bridget's stitching up the girl's leg and Gabby's holding her hand. Ian just took Heather in there."

"What happened?" I demanded.

It was Roman who answered. "We were on the trails, Alpha. Nikolai was hanging back with Theo. Gabby, Olivia, and I were running up the creek bed. Samantha got tired, so she went back to start a fire. No big deal, we thought, and then we just..." He lifted both hands to rub at his eyes. "We weren't alone."

"Wolves," Nik said from the other side. "I don't know everyone here yet, but the guy was colored like a husky, but brown, and he came at us growling."

Theo chuckled. "He didn't expect to see you shift, though."

"No," Nik agreed. "I moved between the wolf and Theo, roared, and he took off, but I could see others in the trees. Theo grabbed our stuff and we tried to head back for the cars, but it was dark, and he only had two legs, and so we weren't moving too fast."

"We heard Olivia scream," Theo breathed.

"So did I," Vic told him, picking up the story. "It was the sound of a hurt wolf, and Ashley immediately knew something was wrong. I was expecting to find someone who'd slipped down the bank or something. Ashley and the three of us went to help."

"May have been the only thing that saved me," Theo said. "Because as soon as Olivia yelled, it was like the wolves were everywhere. Nik was trying to keep them off me, but there were at least five around us. I put my back to a tree, knowing what happens if I get bit, but there were too many for Nik, so I yelled for help."

"Which I heard," Vic said. "I went to them. Ashley, Jax and Scott went to Olivia."

"And," Sam said, turning to look at me, "I heard it too, so I was initially trying to get back into the trails when a wolf moved before me. She was growling, her hair up, so I ran for the car - but I was all alone until Sampson showed up."

"Was wanting to have some time to run alone," Sampson grumbled.

"You saved me," Samantha breathed.

Sampson just blew that off. "I just wanted to make it clear to you kids that my teeth still work."

"What happened?" Lane demanded.

Sampson's head snapped up, and the man swallowed at the fury in Lane's tone. "I run at night, beta, so I can have a little quiet. I was walking across the parking lot when I saw the wolf stalking the human beta, and it wasn't one of ours. Never seen that bitch in my life. She made a lunge and the girl ran, but no way she could outrun one of us. I just made sure to put myself in the middle. Figured that would make it clear enough that the beta's allowed here, right? 'Cept that bitch didn't care. She came at me." He paused, looking over at me. "I put her down, Lane."

"Tore her throat out," Samantha breathed. "You saved me, Mr. Delaney."

"Weren't for you," Sampson grumbled. But he reached over to pat her knee, and it may have been the kindest gesture I'd ever seen the grizzled old wolf make.

"How'd Olivia get hurt?" I demanded.

Roman pushed out a breath. "We had like ten on us. I'm pretty sure they were all converts, though, because none moved like they were really used to having four legs. The three of us were caught between them, but holding our own at first. Then, it was like they all rushed in at once. Gabby went after one, I was on another, but Olivia went for someone trying to get Gabby, and another got her. Before we even knew what was going on, there were two on her, and one had her leg." He drew a line from his hip to his knee on the outside of his thigh. "Tore her open bad." Roman lifted his far arm, showing a set of bites running the whole way up. "Then they hit me. Gabby was still fighting, but she was losing. Just outnumbered, you know? And that was when Ashley and the bears arrived."

"Who attacked us?" I demanded.

Trent stepped before me and grabbed my shoulders. "Olivia said she saw Karen."

The Hidden Forest pack. Damon said he was coming

for us, and Karen knew all the ways to get in and out of the community. The only question was what they'd planned to do. Had this been a scouting mission that went wrong because the kids were out so late? Not many people went running after sundown on a random Wednesday night.

Or had they intended to attack the entire community?

I turned, looking at the injuries on everyone in the room. The bears had nicks and scrapes all over them, proving that not even they had made it out of that unscathed. Nikolai looked like he'd been beaten pretty badly. The boy was definitely going to have a black eye. Sampson had clearly been chewed on. The only ones who weren't hurt were the humans - and Xander.

"Where were you?" I asked Roman's best friend.

"Home," Xander said. "I came here when I heard, Alpha."

Which explained why he was fine. That only left one more question. "And the other wolves?"

"Gone," Scott said. "Sampson killed one. We hurt quite a few. Ashley tore the hell out of a few more. Sounds like Nik may have mortally wounded another, but they didn't expect us. Three bears, a tiger, and five wolves? I know there were more of them than us, but not that many more. Fifteen at most? Hard to count with everyone moving in the dark, but about - "

He was cut off by the clinic door being wrenched open too hard. "Nikolai!" Lev bellowed as he rushed in.

"I'm fine, Dad," Nik told him, rushing forward to catch his father. "Olivia got bit pretty bad, but we're all ok. I'm fine."

Lev just wrapped his arms around his son and hugged him so hard. The same way I wanted to hug Gabby, but she was busy. The guys said she was fine, and I believed them. Still, it seemed the panic of a parent was a universal thing, but where were the others?

"Roman, where are your parents?" I asked.

"Bridget's house," he said. "When we got here, Ashley sent Bridget out, but didn't follow. Mom said something about how the Sisterhood will handle the questions because you had more to worry about. Dad's with her too."

"Heather's with Olivia," Theo said. "Ridley and Zaria are serving as Ashley's go-fers if she needs anything. Sheridan and, um, I think his name's Mitch? They locked down the gates."

"I barely got in," Lev said. "Was at work when I got the call. Are all of you ok?" He looked over at Samantha. "Bit?"

"No," she assured him. "Sampson protected me."

So Lev looked at Theo. "And you, boy?"

Theo just looked up at Vic. "I will say that being thrown on the ground under a bear is probably the most terrifying thing that's ever happened to me, but no wolves could get through him and Nik."

"Thank you," Lev told Vic.

Vic nodded. "I tried to keep them off Nik too, but your son? He's as vicious as you are."

"That's my boy," Lev praised, rumpling Nik's hair before hugging him again. "Zaria wasn't with you?"

"No, she was home with Ridley," Nik told him. "Unpacking, she said. If she had been, I would've watched over her, Dad."

"I know." Lev just sighed, slowly looking up at me. "What happened?"

"Another pack," I told him, hearing a door open down the narrow hall.

I wasn't the only one. Everyone turned to look, and Ian walked toward us with his hand on Gabby's shoulder. My daughter looked rough, like she'd been in a brutal fight, but she was all in one piece. The moment her eyes landed on me, she smiled in relief.

"Mom," she breathed, coming toward me with her arms out.

I grabbed her and hugged her close. "Are you ok, *mija*?" I asked. "They said you're not hurt too bad, but I mean *you*, Gabby." And I caught her face between both of my hands, making her look at me. "Are you mentally ok?"

She just nodded. "I was so scared, and I'm still a little freaked out, but I'm fine. Olivia had to get stitches, but Bridget said she'll heal. No school for a couple of days, but nothing too bad."

"Not as bad as it could've been," Ian finished for her. "Hidden Forest came through the culverts and false gates."

"False gates?" I asked.

Trent lifted his hands to demonstrate. "We have 'wildlife' gates back there. Places where the wall overlaps and doesn't line up. Looked at straight on, it's a solid wall, but anything running along the edge would realize there's a gap about the width of a person. Sideways gap, like an S turn, but no actual fence or gate."

"Because wolves don't have thumbs," Lane explained.

"Those'll have to be closed off," Ian decided. "And we need grates over the culverts. I want this place locked down so no human can make it in, and no wolf can make it out."

"We'll help," Vic offered. "Get some rebar and we can close the culverts so the water can still pass through. Will mean cleaning it out more often so the debris doesn't make a dam, but we'll handle that too."

"Get me a welder and I'll make it permanent," Lev offered.

"We've got one," Ian assured him. "I'll get you a key to the shop. You guys are welcome to use anything in there." But he shoved a hand across his mouth. "How do we close the false gates?"

"Metal gates," I said. "Like wrought iron. The type with the sharp points at the top. The slats will be wide enough for small animals to get through, but not a wolf. If you make it eight feet tall or more..."

"I can build those," Lev said. "What I can't do is build them and install everything."

"You build it," Vic told him, "and we'll install it. Muscle's not a problem."

Pax slapped the bear's shoulder. "We'll start installing the mounting brackets for the gates. I'd prefer they can be opened again if necessary, so we'll want them to swing, but we'll also want them secure enough that no one can simply shift and open them."

"Keypad locks," Lane said. "Give the code to the community?"

Ian shook his head. "For now, I want a padlock on those. This place was made to protect us from humans. The banks and terrain outside would make it hard for people on two legs to make it inside, but wolves? No.

Wolf's Run is on lockdown, and if the pack doesn't like it, they can talk to me."

"Why is another pack attacking us, Alpha?" Jax asked Ian.

Ian just sighed. "I don't know. I know who it is, but I have no idea what he thinks he's going to accomplish."

CHAPTER 32

Lane and Theo helped Heather get Olivia home that night. Ian took Lev and the bears to see the warehouse of equipment Wolf's Run had available. I asked Seth if he'd stay and help Bridget with the crowd of people wanting to know what had happened and who had attacked children in our community. Ashley promised that she had it, but I figured the presence of one of Ian's betas sure couldn't hurt.

Just as we were getting everything under control, a girl slipped into the waiting area and made a straight line for Gabby. Her hair was a deep, dark red, the kind that could easily be mistaken for black in the wrong light. Her eyes were a warm, orangey-brown shade with hard dark lines around the outside of the iris. Striking, but they made her stand out among so many wolves.

"We're going to need a story for school," Zaria said. "Olivia's going to miss a few days, and all of you look like you got beat up. I was going to say that you got mugged outside the movie theater, if that's ok?"

"Why?" Roman asked. "I mean, who'd come after a group of teens?"

Zaria huffed at him in frustration. "Maybe someone who thinks the kids from Wolf's Run are rich? Maybe you'd all been too loud, or did something to piss them off, and they caught you on the way back to your car. Olivia tripped, cutting herself on something in the parking lot - which is why there's no police report - and the others ran."

"That works," Gabby said. "Thanks, Zaria. Can you tell the other kids and make sure it's common knowledge?"

"I'll help," Samantha said. "No way I'm getting out of school tomorrow. Told Mom that Roman's car had a flat on the way home, and we're waiting for a ride."

"I'll take you," Nikolai said.

And that was pretty much it. The kids had this. The parents had this. Our pack had this, yet I still felt like I needed to do more. Trent and Pax took Gabby and me home. The guys pampered both of us, but I caught Trent pulling Gabby aside to look at the cuts and scrapes on her. He said something, the look on his face serious, and she nodded. Then the man hugged her, looking like he'd been as worried as I was.

But the Hidden Forest pack was gone. One woman had been killed in wolf form. The bears took her body outside the walls and left it there. The hope was that her family would be able to collect her if they wanted. If not, nature would take its course, and no human would see anything but an animal.

At work, Thursday, I kept waiting for a call from Karen or an email from Damon. Something, most likely a threat, to let us know why they'd gone after the kids. It never came. Ashley was pretty sure the kids had merely been in the wrong place at the wrong time - or right, depending on how we looked at it. Because if they hadn't been there, how far into the community would those wolves have come?

"But what's their big plan?" I asked. "Seriously, Ash. I mean, what good does it do for a pack to kill off our members?"

"Recon," she guessed. "Elena, I have no idea. Damon keeps saying he's going to make us pay, and maybe that's what he's trying to do?"

"Oh, because that's not obvious at all! We're supposed to be hiding from humans, and he keeps blaming us for being noticed, but this? Isn't it going to be even more obvious? Isn't he just asking for us to be exposed?"

"I'm not sure he actually cares," she said as she pulled a chair over to sit beside me. "Look, I know you're doing great as a wolf. The problem is that you can't get centuries of history in only a few months - and it's not all good."

"What do you mean?"

"We're stronger than humans," Ashley said. "We heal better. We're adaptable. The problem is that humans outnumber us in the millions to one. Locally, it's probably more like hundreds to one, but still. No matter how strong we are, we will never win against those odds, so our best bet is to hide, to blend in, and to do everything in our power to prevent revealing what we are."

"Which makes sense," I agreed.

"But," she continued, "not everyone agrees. There are wolves in this world who want to have that fight. They know that the more people we bite, the more will turn. In an all-out war, the tides will eventually turn. The only question is who we're willing to lose in that process. Me? No one. Damon? Everyone. See, there's something you need to know about him."

"He used to be in the pack?" I guessed.

"No," she assured me. "His family was never allowed. His father hated Henry. I don't even know how that started, or why. It wasn't much of a problem, so far as I knew. Just two men who didn't like each other. But Damon's a few years older than Ian. The boys went to the same prep school. In truth, most wolves who could sent their kids there. It was a small, elite place that knew what we were. It was also the idea that started Wolf's Run. A hidden place where wolves could be themselves without fears."

"A wolf prep school?" That was actually impressive.

Ashley nodded. "It closed a few years ago. Someone saw something, rumors were running rampant, and it was eventually exposed. A fire destroyed all the evidence - faulty wiring, the police report said. But, to so many, it was proof that this idea will never work. To Ian, it was a sign that it was possible, but we'd have to be more careful. The walls were his solution. No one can accidentally see anything if they can't get in to see it."

"Makes sense."

"But Damon went there," Ashley continued. "He started out a few years above Ian. My brother didn't care. He had plans, had responsibilities, and he intended to change the world. Kinda like Gabby, in a lot of ways. He kept testing out of courses, doing summer classes to get ahead, and moving up a grade until he was in the same classes as Damon. Naturally, that didn't sit so well with such an arrogant alpha."

My mouth flopped open. "Ian was bullied?"

"Damon tried," she admitted. "The problem was that Ian didn't care. He had his betas, and they were now in his class as well. Ian had the money to get and do whatever he wanted. Damon was there on a scholarship. My brother isn't an ugly guy, so he got the girls, and Damon? He's always been a dick. In his eyes, my little brother was everything he wanted to be, and Ian made it look so easy."

"That doesn't mean it was," I pointed out. "He took extra courses, and clearly had to study!"

"Ah, but my father wasn't a poor man, even back then. My mother's family had connections. Those two things together meant my family began to succeed. We went from upper middle class to more. Dad was thriving as an attorney, he reinvested his money and made more, and he started a few businesses. Ian drove a new car; Damon had a beater like Roman. Ian had nice clothes, but Damon's were from Walmart. My brother didn't care, but Damon always did."

"And all of this is because of what happened when they were kids?" I asked.

"It didn't stop there," she told me. "Ian could've gone to any school he wanted. Trent was in love with drama, so they went to the school that was best for him. That was around the time that I lost my beta and mate, so Lane moved up there to keep an eye on them. And to bond with them, but that was never really spoken out loud. I always knew that Lane needed to be a beta. I was failing him, so Ian said he'd love to have a roommate who could buy the beer. Thing is, Damon went to the same university. It's the closest, so easier for him to afford everything."

"Shit," I breathed.

Ashley nodded. "Damon tried to say Ian was following him. Ian laughed it off, which actually hurt Damon's pride more. Ian lived in an apartment. Damon was in the dorms. They were both business majors, but while my brother was excelling, Damon was struggling. He partied too much, skipped too many classes - according to Ian - and his grades were paying for it. He got put on academic probation, his scholarships, grants, or whatever he was using to pay weren't enough, and then Seth was the last straw."

"Why did Damon attack some random guy in front of Ian's apartment, though?" I asked.

Ashley sighed. "Ian thinks it was a coincidence. I think Damon waited until Seth was close enough that he could point the finger. My guess - and I have nothing at all to base this on except what I know of the guy - is that Damon planned to kill Seth, was going to blame Ian somehow, and force Ian to either go to jail or expose himself as a wolf. Believe it or not, my brother used to be a bit of a hothead. He had a long fuse, but once it burned out, nothing would stop his fury."

"And now, Damon just hates Ian," I realized. "He's done it for so long that he knows nothing else? I mean, why is this such a big deal?"

"Because my brother - hell, my entire family - has

everything Damon wants. Success, money... You name it, and we had it. Damon grew up in a pack with nothing. We had a nice house. He lived in a run-down mobile home and had to move often so they wouldn't get caught. Ian got his degree, Damon ended up dropping out of college. It was as if so much of their lives paralleled, but Damon always got the shitty version."

"So did I," I shot back. "I didn't grow up with a silver spoon, but I worked to make my life more comfortable, and now I'm hoping to make Gabby's even better! It's how it works."

"Unless you think you deserve it. If you blame things like bad luck and good luck, or if you're the kind of person who can't accept that it's ever your fault - and Damon is. He's also strong, Elena. The man is a beast of a wolf and a brute of a man. He's an alpha, and the vicious kind. He's killed his rivals instead of letting them submit. When Ian talks about tyrants, it's Damon he's thinking about."

"Oh." Because what else could I say to that?

"So," she said, "this isn't over. I think Damon has finally convinced himself to challenge my brother. I think that asshole has some trick up his sleeve, and I'm willing to bet that he sent his pack in here to scope out the place, hoping for some advantage."

"And Karen's probably egging him on," I grumbled.

"Or she's the trick he has up his sleeve," Ashley countered. "She's a wolf from some very old bloodlines. She's his mate. To Damon, that's proof that his luck turned, or he deserves this, or some shit." She paused, grunting at the annoyance of it all. "I just don't know, but I have a feeling that we need to have a backup plan. That's why we're separating the finances from the pack. For now, my father is holding Ian's shares of the business. Wolf's Run is a completely independent, but wolf-owned, corporation. The pack is Ian's. The two things are not combined, so if my brother does lose, Damon will still get nothing."

"And Henry could kick the pack off his property?" I asked.

Ashley canted her head. "He could. He also won't. Dad's still an alpha, Elena. He still cares about these people. But he could charge Damon rent. He could restrict his access. We can make it uncomfortable enough that Damon would never succeed as the Alpha. The only problem is going to be convincing my brother that if he loses, he has to run."

"Leave?" I asked.

She nodded. "Which is where you come in. If Damon is going to win, you have to beg Ian to go. Swear you will follow him. If Ian runs, he'll lose a lot of his pride, and that will hurt more than you can imagine, but he'll live. Damon won't kill him. I don't care if my brother is the Pack Alpha or nothing. All I care about is that he is alive."

"I'll make him swear it," I told her. "And I think the guys will be on my side in this."

She caught my hand. "Thank you. Just tell him that you love him. Not his money, not his status, and not even this place. Elena, I know you. You don't need anything fancy, but my brother wants to give it to you. But, if you can convince him that what you need is him and your mates? If Gabby can help? Look, I want my brother to win. I just don't know if he can, because Damon's big - you saw him."

"Almost as big as Lane, yeah," I agreed.

She nodded. "And he doesn't care who he hurts to get what he wants. Ian does. That could get him killed."

"No," I decided. "If he can't win, then he'll run, and we'll all still be together."

"Thank you," she breathed.

CHAPTER 33

Damon didn't call on Thursday, so I called him that night. The conversation was short and directly to the point. I told him where his pack member was, that she'd attacked one of mine, and how she'd refused to submit and had been killed. Damon tried to rant at me, but I merely hung up. There was nothing to discuss about this.

But after seeing the gash down the side of Olivia's leg, I couldn't pretend like this hadn't happened. I stopped in that night to check on Gabby and make sure Elena was still holding up, but I couldn't stay. I left Lane with her instead, and headed home. A hot shower didn't help. Neither did the whiskey. Sometime around two am, I gave in and just let it out.

The roar came first, and then I swiped everything from the closest shelf, sending books and papers crashing down. When that wasn't enough, I slammed my fist into the wall. I had to destroy something. To vent the fury building inside me. My pack had been attacked. My pup! Worst of all, I hadn't been there.

I'd convinced myself that we were safe. Humans had left us alone, my pack was thriving, and we were finally happy, and now this? Of all the things to fear, it was another wolf, and that was more than I could take. I wanted to make something pay - anything - but all I had was the stuff in my room - things - and they didn't feel pain or shame. So I let them all have it.

Then a hand grabbed my arm. I turned with a snarl to see Seth standing there in his pajama bottoms, wearing no shirt, and from the look on his face, the man had just jumped from his own bed. It stopped me cold.

"This is what Damon wants," he said. "Ian, we're fine. The kids are going to be ok. The bears protected them. Nikolai's worth as much as two wolves already. Gabby and her betas weren't stupid, because you trained them to think fast. They're fine."

"Olivia was torn open, Seth!" I growled.

"And you made sure this pack has a doctor who could put her back together. She's fine. Gabby says Olivia's making the most of skipping school, and it sounds like she's talking to Xander again."

"But Damon..." I tried.

He palmed the back of my neck, looking right into my eyes. "He'll only be more pissed if you don't give a shit. Damon hates you because you can't be dragged down, Ian. Don't start now."

"I'm going to chase that asshole from this town," I decided.

"And risk losing Wolf's Run in the process?" he countered. "Hidden Forest is just outside what is considered polite distance. Stop and fucking think about that, Ian. Of all the places he could be, Damon set up here? And before the Langdons owned this land, where was he?"

"Just on the other side of town," I grumbled. "He moved about six months after we did."

"Exactly." Seth shook the back of my neck as if trying to rattle that into my mind. "He's chasing you. He wants to *be* you. The only way that can happen is if he tears you down to his level. You didn't have to save me, but you did. You didn't have to take the bears and tigers, but you did. You are a leader, Ian, not a tyrant. You help your entire pack thrive, not just the most dominant few."

"But he went after Gabby," I breathed.

"I know," Seth said softly. "Next, he'll probably go after Elena, but Ashley knows that too. So does that little Sisterhood those ladies have made. When that fails, he'll try to attack Henry. He's hitting as close to you as he can, and aiming for what he thinks are the weakest links. There's just one problem."

"They're not weak," I realized.

"Exactly," Seth said. "And as much as I want to rip that man's throat out myself, I'm not going to make a stupid mistake that plays into his plans. Neither will you. Now, we can fight this out in the back yard - because this mess is going to be a bitch to clean up in the morning - or we can drink it out."

I clasped his shoulder. "You were meant to be a beta, Seth. And a good one."

"Thanks, Alpha." But he cocked his head back toward the hall. "I'm also awake now, and I promise I don't mind a few grass stains in my fur. Might also help me sleep a bit."

"No growling, snarling, or barking," I told him. "The girls are sleeping next door."

"Elena is still not a girl," Seth teased. "But yeah, I can fight quietly." Then he punched my shoulder lightly. "Just know that if you leave marks on me, both of us will be answering questions."

That made me chuckle, which helped push that fury just far enough away for me to realize Seth was right. I needed to burn this out. Side by side, we headed downstairs and out back. Then, for the next two hours, we sparred as only wolves could do. I had to admit, Seth was a quick fucker, and almost as flexible as Gabby. He wasn't a strong wolf, but he didn't need to be. He also wasn't a weak one. He was the kind of wolf that always managed to survive.

And he made me work for it. Every time I tried to grab him, he was gone. Whenever I lost my temper, he snuck in to get a nip. I was panting before I expected, and exhausted by the time we were done, but it felt better. I finally felt like I could think again. Together, Seth and I shared a dash of whiskey, and then we both found our beds again. Sleep took me quickly.

The next morning, I made sure my beta had the strongest coffee I could brew waiting for him. Next door, Gabby got a ride to school with Roman, and then I saw Lane walking Elena across the street to the office. Trent and Pax staggered in sometime after that, smelling like they'd had quite the night with their mate. Thankfully, the pair headed to the showers to fix that.

But we were all going to head out together. I didn't even need to say it. My betas knew we were being targeted, and that meant no more running around alone.

We'd make it subtle, but someone would keep an eye on Elena and Gabby as well. Then, almost like providence, I saw Sheridan walking up the street after her shift had ended.

I raced to the front door, pulling it open just to yell, "Sheridan?"

She froze, her head slowly turning back. "Alpha?"

"Hey..." I made my way outside and down the drive. Without needing to be asked, she came toward me. "Can you do me a favor?" I begged. "You and your sisters. I need someone to keep an eye on my father."

"Ok?" she asked, sounding a little wary.

"He doesn't have betas like I do. He doesn't have a Sisterhood like Elena. I just..." I groaned, knowing I was making a mess of this. "Sheridan, is there any way that you and your sisters can spend time with him, watch him, or something? If this pack tries to hurt us again, they will come after my betas, my mate, or my family - and everyone else is protected."

She nodded quickly. "Of course! I'll send Ridley over to ask him something today. Anything, Alpha. We're glad to help."

"Thank you," I breathed. "I know you foxes aren't big enough to hold off a wolf, and I would never ask that of you. Just, if anything happens, let me know? Or my mate, betas, even my sister."

"Yeah," she said. "Not a problem. Henry's nice. He kinda reminds me of my grandfather."

"I owe you one," I told her. "And if you give me a second, I can give you a ride home."

"I don't mind walking," she promised.

I just gestured around us. "We had wolves in here the

other night. I'd feel better if you had Mitch drop you off from now on."

"I'll just drive tomorrow," she said. "And if a wolf does come after me, Alpha, I'm small enough and fast enough to get away." She just pointed up the street. "See all the parked cars? Ever heard a fox scream? I'll be fine, Alpha."

"Ian," I told her. "Just be careful?"

"Always." The little vixen wiggled her fingers in a wave and started walking again, but now there was just a bit of a skip in her step.

Damn, but I liked these new shifters. My whole life, I'd been led to believe that our kinds would never work well together, but that was a lie. We did. Beneath the creature we could change into, all of us were just humans with a little something extra. That humanity was our common bond, and kindness brought it to the surface.

Which was what Gabby had been trying to tell me. Diversity would make Wolf's Run better. Not for some vague ethical reason, but because it brought more to the table. Foxes were small and fast. Bears were strong and powerful. Tigers were agile and terrifying. Wolves? We knew how to bring all of that together to work as a whole.

I thought about that throughout the rest of the day, trying to think of ways I could make this place more alluring to shifters besides the ones we already had. We'd figured out how to market to wolves. When I was over at Dad's the other night, we'd made plans to look into buying the land out back to increase the nature trails. Yeah, it would mean building more and moving the back wall - not necessarily in that order - but I had a feeling the pack would love a little more space to run.

And Ashley had mentioned the lot beside us. I had no

idea what kind of price tag we were looking at, or if the company could even afford it, but another twenty houses would mean a lot more space for shifter diversity. If Gabby could hold off the Hidden Forest pack with just three bears, one tiger, two humans, and five wolves? I could only imagine how comfortable we'd be with lions, eagles, and more.

Thankfully, the day passed with nothing untoward happening. My phone stayed silent. Elena sent me a cute meme she'd found. Probably one Gabby had sent her, but I wasn't complaining. Lane claimed her lunch hour, and the whole day, not a single thing broke. I was as tense as could be, second-guessing everything, but the full moon was coming next week. That probably had something to do with it.

But just to be safe, I pulled up at the office just in time to take my mate home. On impulse, I decided that I'd claim her for the night. If Seth wanted to join me, that could be fun. Granted, I also wouldn't complain if Trent and Pax needed another round, but they had been with her last night. And if she just wanted to fall asleep? I could definitely deal with that.

"Hey," she said, climbing into my truck before I could even get out. "Gonna give me a ride?"

I just chuckled, aware I'd been caught. "I was thinking about inviting myself over tonight, if you're ok with that?"

"Always," she promised as I put my truck in reverse and aimed for our homes.

One day, that would be home, singular. I was pretty sure that my current place wouldn't be big enough, not with Gabby still living at home, but we could manage if we had to. Ideally, I'd get a bigger house built. One just for our crazy little family we were building - but I was still waiting on Trent and Pax, and those guys were trying so hard to make sure they got this right.

On impulse, I parked in her drive, deciding that I already had everything I needed at her house. Elena opened her door to get out, then hit me with one of those things that a man never wants to hear.

"Ian? I wanted to talk to you about something."

My balls crawled into my throat and my blood fell to my toes. "Please tell me it's nothing bad?" I asked as I got out.

The problem was that she didn't answer. Elena simply made her way around the truck and over to me. Evidently, we were going to do this here and now. Gabby was home, and this was bad enough that she didn't want her daughter to hear. My heart began to beat a little faster.

"Damon," she finally said, looking up to meet my eyes. "Ian, Ashley told me all about him. Your history with him, Seth's, hers, and more. She said he wants to challenge you."

"Yeah," I breathed.

"What if you don't win?" she asked.

I just pressed my palm against her cheek. "I'll win. I've been sparring with the guys, making sure I'm in shape for it. I will win this, Elena."

"But what if you don't?" she asked, leaning into my hand. "Ian, I love you. More than that, Gabby loves you. You're like the father she always wanted, and you come with the guys. We aren't with you because you are the Pack Alpha. I didn't even know about wolves when we met."

"I know," I assured her. "I never thought you were with me because of rank."

"No," she groaned, stepping back. "Ian, listen to me. Damon sent his pack here for something. One of them died because she was going to kill Samantha, and Sampson killed her first. Died, Ian. Ashley said that Damon's the kind of wolf who won't accept your submission. What I want to know is what you plan to do in the unlikely event that you don't win?"

"I have to," I said.

Her eyes darted away and she pulled in a slow, measured breath. "I want you to promise me you'll run, ok? If you're losing, if you know you can't win, I want you to run before you submit."

"We'll lose our homes," I hissed.

"I don't care about our homes!" she shot back. "I care about *you*, Ian. And if you go, then your betas will follow, and we'll be right there with you. Gabby and I don't love you because you're the Alpha, or because you have money, or even because we live here! We love you because you're a good man, and you can't fight back if you're dead." She paused to swallow, then her eyes found me again. "Please? I know it's a lot to ask from you, but please, Ian? Promise me that if Damon does challenge you, and by some chance you can't defeat him, that you will run - so I can follow."

I stared at the beautiful tawny color of her eyes, watching the moisture well up in them, and I did the only thing a man could do in my position. I nodded.

"I swear, Elena. I would rather be a poor, broke wolf and have you than leave you at his mercy. I'll run, but only if I can't win, and I need you to trust me on that."

"I do," she promised, just as a car came speeding down the road, going much faster than the posted limit.

Without thinking, I moved to stand before her, turning to see what was going on - and then breathed a sigh of relief. I knew that car. I also knew the punk teenager behind the wheel.

"Roman," I bellowed as he pulled up in front of the curb. "What if a pup had been in the road? Drive slower!"

He ignored me, rushing out of the car to walk straight up to me. The boy's eyes were on the ground, refusing to look any higher than my feet. Even worse, he didn't even try to glance at Elena.

"Alphas," he breathed, "I think we have a problem." He paused to lick his lips. "Theo has a headache. A bad one, and he can't shake it. Says he has a cold."

"Does he?" Elena asked.

Roman just pushed his hand across his mouth and shifted his feet like he wanted nothing more than to run. "Um, when Hidden Forest attacked? Uh..." His eyes jumped up, seeking her instead of me. "He and Nik were alone. We knew they were alone. They went off specifically to *be alone*. The problem is that Theo said something about trying to pull on his pants with wolves charging him, and now he has a headache."

"Fuck!" I snarled.

CHAPTER 34

"What did they do?" I demanded, stepping around Ian to see the boy. "You all know better than to expose a human."

"We never talked about it with him," Roman said. "Nikolai, I mean. He's a natural-born. We thought he knew, but now I'm not so sure. And, um..." His face was turning very red, very quickly. "I mean, I know that's why we have to use condoms, but maybe it broke? Look, I didn't ask what they were doing. I didn't even think about the pants comment until Theo started saying he's got a headache. Olivia said I can't tell her mom, so..." His eyes finally moved to Ian. "I came to you, Alpha."

"That's the right thing," Ian assured him. "I need you to talk to Nik, ok?"

"Ian," Roman said. "Sir, I can't... I mean, what do I ask?"

"Wait," I begged. "If Theo's just sick, that's one thing. It's basically spring, Ian. He could actually have allergies."

Then I looked at Roman. "Go get Gabby and call her out here."

He nodded and then took off for the house. I turned to Ian. "It never slows down, does it?"

"Not really," he admitted. "Is it bad if I say I'm glad you're helping now?"

I huffed out a laugh. "It's kinda sweet, actually. Like an inadvertent compliment."

So he caught my hand. "No, it was a very blatant one. You are the perfect Alpha Female for this pack. You and your Sisterhood keep this place running in ways I would never think of." His fingers squeezed mine. "How are we handling this?"

"Step by step," I told him. "Lev doesn't know his son is into boys. We don't want to make that into a mess if we don't have to. Nikolai deserves to choose when he tells people. There's just - " I paused as my front door closed too hard and my daughter jogged toward me.

"Mom?" she asked.

"What does Theo know about exposure?" I asked. "Have you talked to him about condoms?"

"Yeah," she said. "No sex with a wolf without one..." Her eyes went wide. "Oh crap."

"What?" I asked.

She looked back at Roman. "Blow jobs."

"Shit," he breathed.

"What?" I asked.

Gabby just flailed her arms as if she was thinking and trying to make me stop all at the same time. "We told him that it's bloodborne, and that he has to be careful. We told him - and Samantha - about accidents, Xander getting shot and why we had to clean it up, that it can pass through mucus membranes during sex which is why condoms have to be used. I don't think any of us told Theo about, you know, in the mouth."

"I'm dying," Roman mumbled, sounding like he was talking to himself.

"You're not alone," Ian assured him. "But, you two need to find out what exactly happened. Someone needs to talk to Lev. Someone needs to talk to Theo. Was he even exposed, or is this just a seasonal allergy problem? The flu? Humans get sick easier than we do, and we should rule that out before worrying."

"They didn't mean to," Roman insisted. "I know that much. Theo has been talking about whether he'd want to wait to turn until after high school or college. He kept saying that he didn't want to go off to school and be alone, so it might make more sense to just wait until he had his degree. He didn't intend to turn now, Alpha. This *wasn't* intentional."

"Kinda got that impression," Ian reassured him. "Look, I know I told you kids that would get you kicked out, but I meant another trick like you two pulled. Accidents happen. We just have to make sure..." He paused, pulling out his phone. "Wednesday, 3:19 pm"

"Moonrise," I realized.

He nodded. "Lane bit you right around thirty, maybe thirty-two hours before. It takes the virus twenty-four hours to activate, so a bite too late wouldn't trigger on that moon, but rather the next."

"Roman bit me the week before," Gabby pointed out. "I felt sick all week until about two days before. That's when the fever hit."

"It's Friday. If Theo is going to turn, then he'll do it in

five days. So, you two find out exactly *what* they did. Get into their personal lives, Gabby. Make one of them tell you. Semen, blood, anything. I need to know. Even if there was exposure, we can't rule out something normal. Elena, have Ashley run to the store for every allergy drug she can find. Make sure she doesn't go alone? Take Vic, just in case Damon's out there." He blew out a breath. "And cold meds. I'll talk to Heather."

"No," I said. "You talk to the betas, because if this boy is exposed, he's not going to run like a wolf."

"Fuck," Roman groaned. "And I'm not sure Nik's ever seen a tiger turn. If we ask Lev..."

"If it comes to that," I decided, "then I'll talk to Lev. Just..." I pointed at his car. "Go see what's going on. If Theo won't give you all the details, then make sure Nik does."

"Yes, Alpha," Gabby said, grabbing Roman's arm to drag him towards the car.

The kids headed one way, so Ian and I headed toward the house. "Can you tell if this is lycanthropy - or whatever version - by looking?" I asked him.

"No," he admitted. "Not at this stage, I mean. When the fever hits, sure."

We made it inside and I immediately turned. "Ian, be honest with me? What are the chances that this boy has a headache that no medicine can touch and it's just allergies?"

"Slim," he admitted. "Elena, you've seen him and Nik. Those boys? They're what, sixteen, seventeen?"

"Sixteen."

He nodded. "Believe it or not, I remember being that age. You know what I thought about the most? Putting my dick into things. For me, it was girls. For them, it's each other. The problem is that boys can't get each other pregnant. They don't have the rest of the world telling them to wait, to be sure, and all of that. They're either hiding it from everyone or open and have no reason to care."

"Ok?" Because I couldn't say that he was wrong.

"And look at how long and hard you thought about the problems with condoms? They break. They could come off. And blow jobs really aren't that great with one on. At least, not for me. If Gabby stressed mucus membranes and sex with a woman, what are the chances that those boys are going to think anal isn't ok? Or Gabby could be right, and maybe it was a blow job. Maybe Nik thought pulling out would be enough? I don't *know,* but if I can come up with all of those things this fast, what do you think is going to happen?"

"Theo's about to become a tiger," I breathed.

He just stepped closer, lowering his voice. "And what do tigers do? They climb, they jump, and most importantly, they fight. It's easy for us to get wolves through the conversion here because we can keep them in. Lev? He could leap those walls without trying. He could scale the trees - " But Ian paused. "So can bears. Shit. This might work." Then he rubbed my arms. "Go talk to Heather. She needs to know what's going on either way. I'm going to drop in on Vic and hope like hell that my sister is either not there or wearing clothes."

"Knock," I told him as I shifted out of his way. "And text the guys?"

"On it," he promised.

For a moment I just stood there with my eyes closed

and breathing slowly. Around me, the house creaked and settled, almost like it was complaining about being empty. In my head, a million thoughts spun. All of them came back to the very same place: Theo. That poor boy. All he'd wanted was to find someone who could care about him, and now this?

But he'd known what Nik was before anything happened. I'd watched him pet that tiger's head. Maybe this wouldn't be the end of their relationship, but rather the beginning? Although, it meant that Lev would find out about his son. And if he decided to toss the boy out?

I glanced up the stairs, thinking about that spare bedroom I had. We'd find a way to make this work. Hopefully, it wouldn't tear apart the happy pack we'd just made. But if Lev had a problem with his son being gay, then what other option did I have? Nikolai was only sixteen years old. He needed to have a safe home and a parent he could rely on. Hopefully his father, but I would be better than nothing. And if the boy did have to tell his dad, then I would offer to stand with him, because there was nothing more important than a little moral support.

Decided, I pulled out my phone and sent a text to Ashley. First, I warned her that her brother was on the way to the bears' house. Then I asked if she could clear out the closest store of all allergy and cold meds for a kid with a headache that wouldn't go away. Almost immediately, I got a text back.

Ashley: Not with the guys. What kid?

> **Elena:** Theo. Two days ago was the night they were attacked.

Ashley: Crap. I'm on it.

Elena: Do not go alone! Damon could be in town. I don't care who you take, but Ian suggested Vic.

For a moment, my phone was eerily silent. I dimmed the screen and woke it back up, but Ashley wasn't answering right away like she always did. Had she already left? I was just turning to the window when it vibrated again.

Ashley: He's actually ok with that?

Elena: He likes the guys, so yeah. But he's headed up there, so meet him there. My quiet weekend just became hell, and I'm going to need your help.

Ashley: Always. What first?

Elena: Bears, then the store. I'm going to talk to Heather about the boy in her house.

Ashley: Good Luck. I'll stop there when done.

Dropping my phone back into my purse, I headed to my bedroom. If this was going to be a long few days, I didn't want to be wearing my work clothes and heels, so I changed. Then, on impulse, I grabbed another t-shirt and carried that back to shove into my purse. I remembered how frantic I'd been when Gabby was sick, and I couldn't imagine Heather would be any better. Theo might not be her son, but she'd taken him in, and Heather seemed like the kind of woman who'd care just a little too much - even if she didn't always show it.

Only then did I grab my keys and head out for my car. If this was really happening, we'd have a lot of trips to make and things to consider. As I backed out of the driveway and headed up the street, I just hoped that Damon would be too busy with his own pack to pick on mine now. And yes, this was *my* pack. Maybe Ian was the Alpha, but I was his mate, and this? It fell under my domain, right?

I was still giving myself the mental pep talk when I arrived to find Gabby and Olivia standing in the front yard. The moment I stepped out, both girls turned to me, looking as worried as I felt.

"What?" I asked.

"I think I screwed up, Mom," Gabby said. "Roman's upstairs talking to Theo, but when we asked if he and Nik may have fooled around, he kinda, um, smiled?"

"He had that 'yes I did' look," Olivia said.

"And the risk of exposure through sex is low," I reminded them both. "Maybe he's just coming down with something."

"Like what, Covid?" Olivia asked. "What are we going to do?"

"First," I told them, steering both back toward the house, "we're going to talk to Heather. Then, we're going to see what Theo tells Roman. Depending on that, we'll do whatever we have to so we can take care of him, right?"

Olivia stalled out. "I kinda didn't want to tell my mom," she admitted.

"Why not?" I asked.

Desperately, she looked to Gabby, hoping for a little

help. "Just tell her," Gabby said. "Mom's cool. She's not going to screw you over unless she has no other choice, ok?"

"What?" I asked again, hoping to convince Olivia to just tell me.

The girl closed her eyes, scrunched up her face and just said, "Sometimes Xander and I would say we were going running at the trails, but we were really, you know, doing something else."

"Sex, Mom," Gabby clarified.

"And you think that's what Nik and Theo were doing?" I asked.

Olivia nodded. "I know we'd said something in front of Nik. And those two wanted to be alone. They were all over each other, like holding hands and kissing and stuff. And Nik said he knew a nice quiet spot where Theo wouldn't even have to climb down the creek."

"And he didn't have a shirt on when Vic was standing over him. He put it on when we were going to Bridget's," Gabby added. "I mean, Nik was naked, but he was shifted, so I didn't really - " She stopped. "Oh, crap. When they were talking about the wolf coming at them? Like, that first one? Nik didn't say anything about tearing off his clothes, getting stuck in them, trying to strip, or any of that. And you know he would've. Or they would've come at him if he started getting undressed, because, that's like..."

"Shifting in our clothes can be done," Olivia said, "but it's like tying ourselves up. Pants are easier to get out of than shirts. Most of us know that the time to lunge is when the other person starts taking off their clothes, and those wolves weren't here to make friends - but Nik never said he stripped."

"Because he already had." I nodded. "Sounds like we might need to start making plans. Come on, girls. Let's go talk to Heather, because it sounds like this is going to happen."

CHAPTER 35

The girls led me inside, and then I told them to go check on Roman and Theo. Immediately, they escaped, not needing to be told twice. Across the room, Heather's brow furrowed in confusion, but I just waved her at a chair. Letting out a heavy sigh, I took another for myself.

"This looks serious," Heather said. "Am I talking to the Alpha Female or Elena right now?"

"Both," I said. "Heather, Theo may have been exposed."

The air rushed from her lungs. "When they were attacked? I didn't think he'd helped Olivia. He and Nik were on the other side..." She just let her sentence trail off. "Shit."

"Yeah," I agreed. "We're not sure yet, and Roman's trying to ask, but they're teenagers."

"And boys," she groaned. "No, I'm with you. Same reason I put Olivia on birth control last summer. I swear I was so much older than that when I was their age, you know? It's like being sixteen feels so grown up, but it sure doesn't look like it on the outside."

"I know," I groaned. "The problem is that Lev doesn't know about Nik."

"They told me," Heather admitted. "Nik's terrified that his dad will react like Theo's did. I mean, I can't even imagine kicking a kid out because of something like that. What difference does it make, you know?"

"Trust me, I know," I told her.

"But what if Lev does?" Heather went on, waving her hand upstairs. "I can't just let them share a room!"

"I'll take one," I told her, "and you can worry about the other. I was going to say I'd take the tiger since I live beside Ian and the betas, but..."

She just laughed. It was the dry and tired kind. "Shit. Kids! Well, Kim's offered to help too. Bridget and Ashley made it clear that they're willing to take the kids if we ever need a break, but we both know that Ashley's not exactly a good influence and Bridget's too busy."

"Yeah," I agreed. "But we can make this work. Henry will help too. He loves kids, and that man has a four-bedroom house. Worst case, there's that."

"He was a good father to the pack," Heather told me. "Cheryl didn't make the cookies and lemonade. Henry did. Granted, Kim's husband reminds me of him. The trick is going to be keeping these kids from living with the one they're trying to sleep with, and that's not going to be so easy."

"We'll worry about that when we get to it," I promised. "But, if this boy is - "

Gabby came thundering down the stairs, moving at

her top speed. "Going to get Nik," she called as she made a rush for the door.

"Take someone!" I barked at her.

She stalled out just as her hand grabbed the doorknob. "Front yard, Mom. I texted him to get over here now." Then she rolled her eyes and kept going.

"I have no clue how you do it," Heather laughed. "She really is a true alpha. I thought Xander was bad, and since I'm not an alpha myself, he keeps pushing."

"But you're a mother," I countered. "I think that trumps all else."

"I'll make damned sure it does," Heather laughed. "I'm also about to put all of these kids to work, because if that boy is going to turn, my house is about to be packed full of people."

"Start making a list of what you'll need," I told her.

"Broth," she said without thinking. "That was my soup you drank when you were fevered. My mother's recipe. I think her grandmother's, but not sure. Mom taught it to me, at any rate, and we Stuarts have been making it for the converts for as long as I can remember. I made sure Bridget had the recipe, just in case, but it seems to be the only thing most of us will eat when we're that bad off."

"What's in it?" I asked.

She smiled. "Um, lots of salt and protein. Egg noodles. There's a cup of brown sugar, just for a little extra energy to fight off the change. The goal is to keep someone hydrated and nourished until they can finally shift, and everyone seems to drink it."

"I have a feeling we'll need a batch. Plus stuff for the crowd. Toilet paper? Paper plates?" I was trying to remember what I'd used most when Gabby had turned.

"We'll send Ashley," she said. "And once these kids stop long enough to talk, I'm calling Bridget."

"Call her anyway," I decided. "It sure won't hurt."

Heather pulled out her phone and dialed. A moment later, Gabby came back inside, dragging Nik with her. From the ashen color of the boy's face, I already knew the answer. Yes, Theo had been exposed, and no, Nik hadn't meant to.

"Talk to me," I ordered.

But it was Gabby who came over. "Mom, I'm sorry. I think I screwed up bad."

"Just talk to me, *mija*," I begged.

She nodded. "So, we told Theo about sex and condoms. And about blood. We also said that kissing was safe. I mean, I clearly remember the whole talk about how saliva breaks down the virus so kissing wasn't a problem, and um, I was thinking, you know, normal. But..." She shifted back and forth nervously. "I didn't think about the blow job thing. I mean, that's just blatant, right? But, um..."

"It's not sex," Nik blurted out.

"It's called oral sex for a reason," I told him. "Now, blush as much as you want, and stammer as bad as you need, but tell me exactly what happened."

"He, um, kinda..." Nik glanced at Gabby, but she just waved for him to go on. "He sucked my dick but he didn't swallow." It all came out in a rush, the words tumbling over each other.

"But you came in his mouth?" I asked. "So, he spit?"

"Mom!" Gabby groaned.

"Go upstairs if you can't take it," I told her, "but this is important. I'm not asking to be nosey. I'm asking so we can take care of Nik's boyfriend."

"Yeah," Nik finally said. "We, um, were fooling around, and he kinda did that, and I said he had to be careful, but the mouth's fine, I thought."

"Saliva is fine," I told him. "Just like with HIV. But if he has a cut in his mouth? Bit his tongue? There's still a risk. A small one, but a risk. The problem is that seminal fluid doesn't have the same digestive enzymes to break down the virus. Yes, I asked Dr. Bridget all about this. So, you basically gave him a mouthful of infection, Nik, and there's a very good chance he caught it."

"No," Nik breathed. "But he wanted to wait. He wanted to be a wolf!" Then the boy's head snapped up. "Dad."

"We're going to figure this out," I promised.

"You don't understand," Nik snarled. "My father will kill me. How exactly would Theo, of all people, end up a tiger and not a wolf, huh?" And he slapped his chest. "Because of me, and that means he's going to... Fuck."

"Hey, hey, hey," I said, pushing to my feet to wrap the boy in my arms. "It's ok, Nik. We'll figure this out together. Your pack is here. We're going to make sure this works out."

And slowly, the kid's arms closed around my back. His face pressed against my shoulder. For a long moment, that was all, but then he gasped, proving he was fighting so hard not to cry.

"It's ok," I soothed. "Your dad seems to be a good man, and maybe he'll be shocked, but we're not abandoning you. I promise, Nikolai. You're a part of this pack now, and I will take care of you."

"How do I tell my dad that I like guys?" he whimpered.

"One word at a time," I told him.

He pulled back to look at me. "Can you do it? I mean,

just tell him it was an accident, and, um, if he hates me, then I don't have to see it?"

The boy's hands were shaking, but he was trying so hard to look tough. His chin was up, his face was as close to stoic as he could get, but his eyes were a bit too wide and his skin much too pale.

"Nik, this is something you should probably do. That way you can answer questions and - "

"No," he whimpered. "He'll hate me, Elena. You don't understand. Dad grew up in Russia, and that's not ok there. Men are men, and when they like other men, they were beaten to death!"

"And he doesn't live in Russia now," I countered. "Nikolai, your father seems like a fair man."

"So long as I'm manly enough," he breathed. "Please, Elena? He's going to know. If Theo turns, Dad will find out, and..." He paused to swallow. "Just... Please?"

"Ok," Heather said, moving closer to turn Gabby for the stairs. "You kids go make sure Theo's ok. Find out if there's anything he needs. Elena and I have to talk to Lev anyway, because we've never seen a tiger turn. So, there's no reason we can't tell him for you while we're there, Nik. Right, Elena?"

"Right," I agreed, watching as Nikolai visibly relaxed. "Ian and the betas may be over while we're gone. Just tell Gabby to deal with it." I grabbed for my keys. "Is your dad even home, Nik?"

"Just got home," Nik told us. "Gabby sent a text saying she had to borrow me, so I barely had time to say hi before I was leaving to come here."

I nodded, then pointed at the stairs. "Go take care of your boyfriend. He's probably feeling pretty miserable. If you need anything, Heather and I will both have our phones."

"Thank you," he breathed.

Then Heather turned me toward the door and started walking both of us that way. As soon as we were in the front yard, she paused, letting out a heavy sigh. "Did you see him? He was terrified."

"Yeah," I agreed. "Do you think Lev would really kick out his son? Especially after what I heard happened to his wife?"

"But Nik has a point," Heather reminded me. "Some men - like Theo's father - judge their sons on these stupid ideas. Times like this? It's exactly what our Sisterhood is for. If Nik can't tell his dad himself, then I dare that man to try to come through us. Tiger or not, he's never seen what it's like to threaten a she-wolf."

I had to laugh at her vehemence. "Right. Well, having seen Nik in his cat-form, I have a feeling we'll probably be running as fast as our wolfy legs will carry us. But, on the upside, at least you'll have a little more of a chance, right? Since, you know, next week are my running and jumping lessons."

Heather laughed at that. "I think we'll be fine," she promised. "It's also why I'm coming with you. So, drive on, Alpha."

We headed to my car. Heather took the passenger seat, but Lev's place was just right up the street, about two blocks away. It was close enough that we could've walked if we wanted, but this wasn't the kind of night for a lazy stroll. No, things were falling apart, and I had the worst feeling in the pit of my stomach.

Because if that man rejected his son because of who he

loved? God help me, but I might tear apart a tiger with my bare hands. I'd actually liked Lev. I'd respected him. He'd been a single father for a long time now, and I knew just how hard that really was. He always seemed so proud of his boy, and he'd taken in those fox girls as if they were truly his family. For him to be so paternal and yet Nik so terrified of telling him?

I was braced for the worst when the pair of us made it to the front door and knocked. From the back of the house, I heard the man yell "Just a second!"

So we waited. Then we waited a little longer. I could hear him moving around inside thanks to my super-special wolf ears, but I couldn't make out what he was doing. Just as I turned to ask Heather if she could tell, the steps came closer. The deadbolt clicked as it released. Then, Nikolai's father pulled open the door.

The man was standing there in nothing but a pair of jeans. Jeans that were zipped up but not yet buttoned. His hair was wet and I could see the droplets on his chest. The scent of some masculine soap wafted in the air.

"Alpha?" he asked. "Heather? Is Nik ok?"

"Can we come in?" I asked.

Beside me, Heather just nodded. When Lev pulled the door open wider in a clear invitation, I elbowed her, aware that her eyes were still hanging on his almost-open jeans. Granted, who knew that tigers had abs like that? Sure, the hair on his chest might be a little salt-and-pepper-colored, but it was over some rock-hard muscles.

"What's going on?" Lev asked. "Did the kids get jumped again? I told them to stay off the trails until we had all the gates and grates put up."

"No," I said. "Actually, this seems to be a little leftover

from the last time they were out. Lev, what did you teach Nikolai about not exposing others?"

"The usual," he said. "Never donate blood, if he goes to a hospital without me, then he should say there's a chance he's been exposed to HIV so they'll be careful, and that he can't have sex with a human girl."

Heather groaned. "And when his teenaged hormones went stupid? Did you tell him about condoms?"

"Uh..." Lev was looking from one of us to the other. "I told him that when he was ready, he had to use protection. He didn't want to get a girl pregnant or have her turn. Why? He said he wasn't interested in Samantha. She's just Gabby's friend and doesn't like him that way." Then he stopped. "Did he infect a wolf? I thought the doctor said - "

"No," I broke in. "No, Lev, it seems there's a chance he infected Theo."

"What?" Lev asked, looking from me to Heather and back. "In the fight? The boys were pretty beat up, but - "

"Before the fight," Heather said. "Evidently, some of our kids are making out on those trails while the others are running around as animals."

I clasped his arm. "Lev, Theo has a headache that no medication is easing. Two days ago, he and your son were intimate, and yes, it was consensual."

"My son's gay?" he asked. "But... he's always had girlfriends."

"Bisexual, it seems," I told him. "He didn't realize that oral sex counts as exposure. The boys thought spitting it out would be safe enough, and now Theo's got symptoms of whatever your version of this is called."

"Nikolai asked us to be the ones to break it to you," Heather added.

"Fuck," Lev breathed, turning away just to grab his keys and wallet from a side table. He turned back to the door but stopped again. "Shirt. Shoes." And then the man rushed towards the back of his house.

I just looked at Heather. "Is he pissed?"

"He seems worried," she said.

And then Lev was back, rushing for the door the pair of us stood before. "Wait," I told him.

"I'm not fucking waiting," the man roared. "There's a boy who's about to have the worst few days of his life, and my son doesn't know how to handle this on his own. Get out of my way, Alpha, or I'll make you."

"If you hurt him," I warned.

Lev just turned to me, his eyes so close I could clearly see how they were green in the center, fading to yellow at the edges. "I'm his father. I'm supposed to protect him, and I'm not doing a very good job, so I'm about to fix that."

Then he just shouldered me aside and kept going, leaving the door standing open behind him. Heather was gaping at me. My heart was pounding. As quickly as I could, I grabbed my phone and started walking to my car. "Close the door, Heather."

But in my hands I was typing out a notice to Gabby that Lev was on his way and might beat us back, but I was only seconds behind. The problem was that I still didn't know what that man intended. He was pissed, but I wasn't sure whether that was directed at himself or his son.

CHAPTER 36

I pulled up in front of Heather's house just as Lev strode through the door without seeming to knock. The pair of us piled out of my car and ran to catch up. I hit the stairs to the second floor just as the man reached the top, storming down the hall as he followed the kids' voices. I felt like I was chasing him, but Lev barely even noticed I was there.

Then he turned into the last room on the right and the kids all fell silent. "Nik?" Lev asked.

"Dad," Nik breathed just as I reached the room.

For a moment the pair looked at each other, then Lev shoved a hand over his hair. "Is your, uh, friend ok?"

"Boyfriend, Dad," Nik corrected.

"I didn't want to presume." Lev looked like all of his determination had just evaporated. "Is he ok?"

"He's probably exposed to this because I was too fucking scared to ask you about it!" Nik shot back. "So, no.

Theo's not ok, but I'm going to make sure he will be, and my alpha's going to help."

Lev rushed forward just to wrap his son in his arms. "Don't you ever think I'll stop loving you, boy. Not ever. You are my son. Gay, straight, or bisexual. All I've ever wanted for you was for you to be happy, and I'm so sorry I let you down."

And Nikolai relaxed, finally hugging back as he melted into the man. "Really?"

"Really," Lev promised. "And we're going to get your boyfriend through this, ok? I never even thought to tell you. Shit, I was embarrassed to tell you about this stuff, and I'm sorry. I just..." He ran his hand over his son's dark hair. "I saw you with the girls, and I just assumed that was it. Nik..." He turned, looking across the room until he saw Theo. "Either of you. The only thing I hate is that people might make this hard on you two, but I'm not gonna be one of them. All I want is someone who treats my son the way he deserves. That's it, Theo, and if that's you, then I don't have a damned problem with it, ok?"

"Really?" Theo asked.

Lev nodded. "That's the truth of it. I remember what it was like growing up in Russia where some things just weren't done. I didn't like it then, and I want no part of it now." He tousled the back of Nik's hair, then moved over to squat before the bed Theo sat on. "Head killing ya?"

"Yeah," Theo admitted. "I tried turning down the lights, but it didn't help."

"Not gonna," Lev told him. "Now, I don't know how it is for wolves, but you're going to feel like this for a couple more days. Dry eyes, the worst migraine you can imagine, and every muscle and joint in your body will ache. Take long, hot baths while you still can, because when the fever hits, it'll only get worse, but we'll take good care of you."

Theo nodded. "Gabby says that sometimes wolves have trouble turning back, but the alpha can help them. But tigers don't have alphas, so what happens then?"

"You'll turn back," Lev promised. "If you want your boyfriend to kiss and hold you again? Yeah, that means you gotta turn back." He dropped his hand on Theo's knee. "All you have to remember is to keep your claws to yourself, ok?" Then he pushed himself up. "I need to talk to the Alpha. Nik, let me know if he needs anything, ok?"

"Thanks, Dad," Nik said, still looking completely wonderstruck.

When Lev turned to find me still standing in the doorway, he tipped his head down the hall, silently encouraging me to walk with him. Then he closed the door behind him, giving the kids a little extra privacy that we didn't normally allow. Heather leaned on the wall across the hall, but she didn't say anything, just gestured for us to go first.

When we made it downstairs, she finally said, "I just want you to know that if you'd torn into that kid..."

Lev huffed out a laugh. "You honestly think I'd break my son's heart because of who he loves?"

"Theo?" I countered. "He's here because his father did."

"Good point," Lev admitted. "But no." He pointed at a chair and glanced at Heather, seeking permission to sit. "Mind?"

"Make yourself comfortable," she said. "When this happens in the pack, we all converge on the house to offer help, so I'm pretty much bracing for a very long weekend, and I'm about to call work and tell them I'm going to need a few days off. Beer?"

"Would love one," he told her, but his eyes dropped a bit when she turned for the kitchen.

I just crossed my arms, pulling his attention back to me. "Vic said that bears don't run. They hunt the moon their own way. What do tigers do?"

"Oh, we hunt it. That's the thing, though." He gestured for me to sit. "I promise I'm not going anywhere, and I'm certainly not picking a fight in a wolf's den. Sit down, Elena, because Heather's right. This is going to be a very long weekend, but it also means we have time to talk about this."

"Where's Ian?" Heather asked as she returned carrying a bottle for Lev and two glasses of wine for us.

I took the smaller. "Last I heard, he was talking to Vic. Ashley's supposed to take one of the bears with her when she goes to get some medication. Hopefully, we'll find something that will work."

"Yeah, and Bridget said she was going to talk to Ashley," Heather countered. "I think that was right about when Nik showed up, though. So, yeah, little redirect there."

"It's fine," I promised. "I'm not Ian, ranked high enough to get my panties in a wad because someone had a better idea. I just..." I paused for a drink. "This place was built for wolves, guys."

"It's not too bad for us either," Lev countered. "The problem is going to be keeping that boy out of the trees. I'm pretty sure that Nik and I can keep pace with him. If you wolves can keep him off the walls, then even better. The one thing you must know, though, is that he's going to have some very big teeth and very sharp claws, and he may not realize that you wolves are his friends."

"We'll make it work," Heather told him.

"You, uh..." Lev tipped his head at the couch. "Mind if I crash for a few days? I figure Nik's going to be feeling really guilty about this, and I don't want those kids thinking they have to do this on their own."

"I'd honestly love the help," Heather told him.

From there, we started making plans. From food to space, ideas were thrown around and discarded. At some point, Trent and Pax showed up, saying they'd finished putting up the last grates in the culverts. One less thing to worry about while we all focused on Theo, they insisted. Ian and Lane came later, weighed down with a few dozen plastic grocery bags.

"Dad's contribution," Ian said as he headed to the kitchen.

I hopped up to help. "Where's Ashley?"

"She and Bridget are researching," he said. "Bridget said no to our idea about allergy medicine, but she has a theory about easing the headaches. She just wants to make sure that therianthropy reacts the same across species."

I just nodded at him because half of that went over my head. "Doctor's on it, then," I said. "That's all I need to know."

"Yeah. Let me go get the rest of this."

He left, and Lane took his place, dropping at least six overly-full bags onto the counter. "Are you holding up?" he asked.

"Well, my idea of a lazy Friday night just went out the window. But yeah. Lev's been telling Heather about how tigers react on their first shift. I have a feeling that the rest of the pack will converge on us shortly, right?"

"Just waiting to hear if we're locking the gates," he admitted. "So, are we, Alpha?"

Which meant that I could make that call. For some reason, it felt like a big thing, but I knew it wasn't quite that complicated. Locking the gates just meant that no humans would be allowed in for the next few days, people had to be extra careful when driving - just in case Theo became delirious with his fever - and that the risk of someone seeing the wrong thing had gone up.

The pack members could still leave and come back if they had to. There was a way to get in and out, but the community would be on high alert. If they didn't need to go out, they wouldn't. Instead, they would all try to find some way to make Heather's life a little easier so she could focus on the boy she was now raising.

And now Lane was saying that I could basically alter everyone's plans for the next few weekends. All it took was one order, and the whole pack would listen to me. I didn't need to check with Ian, and in the last hour or so, it had become pretty clear that this really was Theo turning.

"Yeah," I decided. "Lock the gates, Lane."

He grabbed his phone and dialed. Then, "Sheridan? Lane, beta. I need you to lock the gates. We have a convert. Mitch will tell you what to do, but it's Elena's orders. The community is pack only to prevent any exposure until the moon sets."

Then he ended the call, put his phone back in his pocket, and opened the first bag. It seemed he was going to help me put all of this away. Sadly, I wasn't quite sure where most of it went.

"We're winging this," I told him.

"You put things in the fridge," he said. "I know where the rest goes. I've probably spent more time in this house than yours."

I glanced back at him quickly. "Really?"

Lane caught the look on my face and laughed. "Not like that, little bunny. Heather's been with the pack longer than I have. I helped her move in - along with the other guys. You're cute when you're jealous, though."

"More shocked," I corrected. "I was trying to figure out why no one had mentioned anything between you two before."

"Didn't exactly date," Lane reminded me. "Flings weren't something encouraged in the pack, and after Karen, you know why."

"Good point." I found a bag of mostly refrigerated things, grabbed it, and started putting it all away. "Lane? How are we going to keep a tiger from getting on the roads?"

But from the other room, Lev heard. "You're going to have the pack run the walls," he said. "If there's a whole group of monsters between him and that direction, he'll turn away. I'd suggest splitting into groups so you're not always trying to flank him."

"How big will this tiger be?" Lane asked him.

Lev chuckled. "Not quite as big as a black bear, how's that? Theo? He should be a bit smaller than Nikolai. Doesn't mean he'll stay that way."

"All that matters is now," Lane assured him. "Ian and I can handle a cat the size of Nikolai. The five of us could probably deal with you. Add in the bears?"

And Lev smiled. "They won't be scared of his claws, either."

"We can do this," Lane said, almost like he was finally accepting it himself. "With all of us together, we can make sure he pulls through this."

"Yeah..." Lev moved into the kitchen and took one of the bags, but he didn't start emptying it immediately. "There's just that one catch, and Theo's already figured it out. We don't have alphas."

"How do you make your kids shift?" Lane asked.

"It's just something parents do. Stops working right around the time they can do it themselves. It's kinda how we know it's coming."

"Shit," Lane breathed. "So how do we help him shift back?"

"You helped me," I said. "Not because you're an alpha, Lane, but because your voice cut through everything else. You told me how, and I could try that. I wanted to, because I wanted to be human again. I had things I wanted, and that made me listen to your directions and actually try."

"So what does Theo want?" Lane asked.

Lev just chuckled. "Sounds like Nik. And I don't know if that thing between them is serious, fleeting, love, lust, or whatever. Also doesn't matter. Those kids? They're his friends. His family abandoned him, but this pack took him in with open arms, and those kids have been his shield." He paused to look at both of us. "Don't you remember being that age? How strong those friendships were and how intense everything felt? We'll use that."

"Because Theo didn't have a lot of friends before that video," I realized. "And what do we all want most in this world? Someone to love us. Someone we can count on. Someone who actually cares, and who will stand beside us." I was nodding. "So, we make sure that Theo knows that if he wants to keep that, he has to turn back, and we'll make sure he has everything he needs so that can happen."

CHAPTER 37

The weekend became a blur of people coming and going from Heather's house. Somehow, Elena managed to keep track of it all. My mate was amazing, and the more I got to see her in action, the more impressed I was. At home, she was such a sweet and sensual woman, but like this? She had the same charisma as Ian, knowing just what to say to make people feel valued. There was just one problem: she didn't know when to quit.

The first night, I convinced her to curl up with me on the couch for just a moment. Running my fingers through her hair relaxed her just enough for sleep to take hold. Ian and Seth took over, while Trent and Pax headed out to check on our houses and the others who couldn't be here. Sadly, problems didn't stop just because one boy was going to turn this month.

But she woke up before the sun even rose. All day Saturday, she made trips upstairs to check on the kids, alternated with Heather to get them to sleep, and spent time talking to Theo. Kim and David showed up, sending Heather back to bed, but Elena wouldn't stop. They'd done it for her, she said. Twice. And while she was right, I hated that she was running herself to the bone for this.

I finally convinced her to come home with me for a few hours. Ashley and Kim said they'd call if there were any problems. Gabby needed a ride back for new clothes and a shower anyway. So, deciding that I wasn't above playing dirty, I asked Gabby to help me get Elena to sleep, and it worked better than I imagined, because Gabby ended up napping as well.

Four hours. That was all she allowed herself before my mate was up and running again. The woman was wearing me out, but when Seth said he'd take care of her while I got some rest, I about bit his head off. The guy just smirked, making it clear I'd basically proven his point. So I gave in. Ian and I headed home, trusting the other betas to call us if there was a problem.

There wasn't. Theo's symptoms were right on track with what we had as wolves. His headache got worse, his body ached more, and then on Sunday, he was well and truly sick. The boy began to vomit, and none of the teens knew what to do, but Nik still wouldn't leave his side. The mothers of our pack didn't seem to care, though.

Elena, Kim, and Heather were the worst. Bridget checked in as often as she could, and often stayed all night just in case. Ashley tried, but she didn't have that same maternal instinct as the others. Instead, she took care of them.

The neighbors brought meals. Jesse, one of our quieter pack members, organized a group to check the trails, making sure the Hidden Forest pack hadn't come back. The bears made plans for Theo to "hunt," as they called it. Together, those three moved anything from the walls that the boy might use as a way to get over. Slowly but surely a plan was being formed.

It was early on Tuesday morning when the fever hit. Elena was stretched out on the couch, fast asleep. Ashley was sprawled in a chair with her legs thrown over. Bridget was on the floor, using a decorative pillow for her head and a throw blanket over her legs. Gabby came down the stairs at her usual pace - which was loud - and not a single woman stirred.

"Shh," I said.

"Lane," she hissed. "He's burning up and mumbling."

"Send Samantha home," I told her. "She can't help anymore."

"She won't leave," Gabby hissed.

So I pushed myself from the chair and moved to Ashley. "Hey," I whispered. "Wake up, Ash. I need a driver."

"Mm?" She pried open her eyes.

"Theo's running a fever now. Samantha can't stay. I'll get her out of the room, but you'll need to take her home."

She groaned. "You're awake. You drive."

I just glared. "I am not leaving my mate. Get your ass up, because you're doing this, alpha."

The growl in my tone made her suck in a breath, and Ashley sat up, pushing away the last fog of sleep. "Yeah. Ok."

Then I gestured for Gabby to go first. Together, we made our way upstairs, and she pointed at the last room. Not Olivia's, but Theo's. Evidently, her little group of betas hadn't been willing to go very far either. Quietly, she opened the door, and I followed her in.

Not surprisingly, Nik was on the bed, curled up against Theo. Roman sat on the floor beside them, a bucket within his reach. Xander was sleeping in the corner, his head resting on a pile of clothes. Olivia and Samantha, however, were sharing a blanket and pillow in the way that only teenage girls could manage.

"Sam," Gabby breathed.

But it was Theo who heard her. "Can't see it," he mumbled. "So dark."

"Shh," Nik whispered to him. "It's supposed to be dark. Just close your eyes, babe."

"Water," I told him, keeping my voice as quiet as I could. "He'll be thirsty, and if you can get him to take broth, let him have as much as he wants. He'll be up in spurts from now until the moon rises."

"Who wants to get broth?" Nik asked.

"On it," Xander muttered, proving he was now awake.

But looking around the room showed me a few too many sets of eyes, and they were all watching me. I turned to the girl I wanted. "Sam, it's time for you to go."

"No," she hissed, sitting up. "Lane, I'm here to help."

"And in a couple of hours, that boy is going to stop thinking and start reacting. He will be convinced that everyone in this room are monsters. He will bite, Samantha, and you are still very human."

"But, can't I..."

"No," I said. "I'm sorry, but he's not going to be a puppy. He's going to turn into a tiger that is big enough to think you're his next meal. And when they turn, they don't understand. The fever burns so hot, the senses are so distorted, that everything you think of as normal is confusing and terrifying. Wolves run, Samantha. Tigers? They hunt, and you are his prey. I need you to go home."

"I can stay downstairs and help Bridget," she said. "Something, Lane. I can't just go home, not with him like this!"

"The whole pack is helping," I told her. "I know you want to, but right now, the rest of us need to take care of you too."

"Mom will make me go to school," she finally said. "I mean, she thinks that's where I was yesterday, and..."

"Go to my house," Gabby decided. "I know you've barely slept, so do that today."

I had a better idea. "I'll have Ashley take you to Henry's. You can keep him updated, but there's a catch to this."

"Anything," she promised.

"You make sure he doesn't try to run with us. When the moon hits, you keep him there, because he's lame. He couldn't get away from Theo. And if that happened..."

She nodded. "I can do that. And I'll get texts about how he's doing and I can tell Henry. It's just... I don't want to be sitting in class wondering if he's ok. Olivia and I kinda made up a thing that said the group of us were going to be out for a Langdon sponsored holiday, you see." She scrunched up her face. "We didn't ask, but it kinda sounded like the sort of thing someone would pull their kids from school for. Um, and we kinda forged it."

"It's fine," I told her. "But it's time to go, Samantha. He's only going to get more violent, and I don't want you getting hurt."

"What about Olivia?" she asked.

I turned back just in time to see the girl in question throw off her blanket. She was wearing shorts to sleep in, and down the length of her leg was an impressive bandage. That was from the fight on the trails, and she was going to be just as lame as Henry.

"You too," I decided. "Both of you, off to Henry's."

"I can't get bit," Olivia said.

"And you can't run," I countered. "Olivia, you will go with Samantha. If I have to carry you down the stairs, I will."

"Maybe just help me up?" she asked, thrusting out a hand.

I did better, reaching down to grab her by her waist and lifting her to her feet. She giggled, but that made Theo moan. Nikolai just smoothed back his hair, crooning softly to reassure him. It actually seemed to help.

"Nik, when he turns, you stay right with him," I told the boy. "No matter what. And if you have to throw him down to keep him from leaving the community, you do that. He will bite you. He will claw you. It doesn't matter, because you will heal. If you care about that guy at all, you will take it, do you understand me?"

He nodded. "I do. I'm trying. I didn't mean to do this to him, and now I have to make sure he's going to be ok."

"And we'll help, but tigers are bigger and stronger than wolves. We're going to need your help."

"Dad too," he told me. "He swore he was ok with this."

I glanced back to make sure the girls were actually leaving, then turned back to Nik. "How's Theo taking this? Is he ok with what's going to happen?"

Nik licked his lips. "He was a little bummed that he

wouldn't get the pack thing the wolves have, but..." Nik paused as Xander walked back in.

"Got broth," Xander said, holding up a thermos. "Plus water and a cup." Those were in his other hand.

"I can do this," Roman told him. "You deserve a break too, Nik. Go ask Lane your questions."

Nik just leaned in to kiss the side of Theo's face, then worked his way off the bed. Like the other boys, he was still wearing his jeans, but Nik had lost his shirt somewhere. He also didn't seem to care. In truth, the kid looked completely exhausted, but I knew that feeling.

"Come downstairs and eat something," I told him. "When you're done, send the next. Start taking shifts, and make sure all of you get some sleep, ok?" And I turned him for the door.

He shuffled, but the boy went. By the time the pair of us made it downstairs, Ashley had the girls and was headed for the door. She smiled at me but didn't stop. Samantha lifted her hand in a wave to Nikolai, but Olivia gave her a friendly nudge. The rest of the women were still out cold, so the pair of us stepped around Bridget and didn't stop until we were in the kitchen.

"Coffee?" I asked him.

"Nah," Nik said. "If Roman can get him to eat, I think I'll do like you said and sleep." But he did open the fridge. "So, what's it like to be a beta?"

That was not the question I'd expected. "It's like having a very close group of brothers."

"Don't have one," he said, leaning back with a leg of fried chicken in his hand. "Lane, what I really want to know is how this works. My friends keep talking about these things, like instincts and feelings. I don't have them, but I feel like I have something else."

"What else?" I asked, immediately thinking about my bond to Elena.

"Um, Gabby," he said. "The first time I met her, it was like she was my best friend in the world. Roman and I get along great. I mean, we give each other shit, you know? But it's..." He paused to take a bite, thinking. "Have you ever had a friend crush? Like, you just met a person and you immediately knew that you could hang with them?"

"Yeah, with the guys," I told him.

"No," he said. "I'm not a wolf, Lane. I don't submit."

"You do," I countered. "I've seen you do it to your father. You say, 'yes, sir,' and don't puff up to him."

"He'd smack the attitude out of me," Nik countered.

"But that's submission," I told him. "It's nothing more than respecting someone else's authority. The same way you don't cuss in front of Elena."

He chuckled. "Dad told me that we don't talk like that in front of ladies. She's a lady. Kim and Ashley too."

"Not Heather?" I asked.

"Or Gabby, Sam, or Olivia. They all cuss as much as me. I don't mean that like being a lady is bad or anything. It's just that I know they won't be offended."

"Elena won't either," I assured him. "Trust me, Seth can make most people blush when he's on a roll. All I'm saying is that all those signs of respect? That's what makes a pack work. The tie you feel to help those around you? That's the pack bond. It's stopping for long enough to care. I don't think it's some strange ability that wolves have and no one else gets. Even tigers have families, Nik. You understand the feeling; you just think you shouldn't be allowed to have it."

"But I kinda do," he said. "I feel like a bouncer for Gabby. She's the brains of this operation. Roman, Xander, Olivia, and I are the muscle. Samantha is the organization, and Theo? He's like the heart. He's the one who points out when something crosses a line or could help."

As the boy talked, I counted them, and that made six betas for Gabby. Six. Oh, maybe they weren't all her official betas yet, but I had a feeling it was going to happen. Just seeing those kids camped out upstairs to take care of Theo proved it. He was one of their own. They would bend and break rules to put him first - and had.

"You want to know what it's like to be a beta?" I said, bringing us back to his question. "Well, I've had two alphas. First was Ashley. I still feel that tie to her, though. I probably always will, but Ian doesn't mind. Those two are my family. Henry all but raised me. They may not be the family I was born to, but they're the family I got to pick. That's the tie. When you can disagree so much that you'll throw punches because of it, get back up, and go have a beer? That's the bond, Nik. That's what it's like."

"Because family is forever, right?" he asked.

I nodded. "Real family is. Doesn't mean we always get it right the first try, though."

"Why'd you leave Ashley?" he asked.

"She left me," I corrected. "See, I failed her as a beta. I let her get hurt so bad that she couldn't recover. I kept thinking of physical problems. I forgot that sometimes the worst wounds are to the heart and mind. Betrayal can destroy a person, and she doesn't want to be an alpha. She might be the strongest one I've ever seen - "

"Stronger than Ian?" he asked.

"Oh yeah." I huffed at that. "Ian knows it, too. The only wolf I've ever seen who might be stronger?" I leaned toward him and lowered my voice. "Gabby, and she's just a kid."

He sucked in a breath. "Really?"

"Strong enough to make a tiger ask if he's feeling the pull of a beta? Yeah, I kinda think so. Nik, what you kids are doing? It's impossible, so keep doing it. When someone tells you that you can't, don't listen. If you can, then do. I mean, just look at this. You have a wolf pack turned out to ease a tiger's first shift. Sometimes impossible is just another word for 'never been done before.'"

"Then can you help me with Theo?" He bit his lips together. "They said that you talked Elena into shifting back when the alphas couldn't make her. Tigers don't get alphas, so maybe that will work?"

"She listened because she loves me," I told him.

He nodded. "I haven't known Theo that long, but I really like him, Lane. I also don't want him to die because I didn't say no."

"Then beg," I said. "If he can't do it on his own, beg. Ask Gabby what it felt like. Try to describe what you do to change bodies. Get the words right so you can explain it to him, and then beg him to just listen and try one more time. If we have to, we'll run that boy until he can't even swipe at us, and that's when it will be your turn."

"Thank you," he breathed.

"Now finish that, have some more, and then sleep, Nik. Your boyfriend is going to need you at full strength, and none of us wolves will be able to keep up."

CHAPTER 38

Sometime Wednesday morning, I fell asleep on Pax's lap. I woke up to the sound of Heather's bedroom door opening, but when I opened my eyes, it wasn't her walking out. It was Lev. At first, I thought nothing of it. Not until Heather stepped out a moment later. Even more interesting, they both had wet hair, as if they'd timed their showers a little too well. Almost simultaneously, or something.

It made me chuckle, which woke Pax. He sucked in a breath, shifted to get a little more comfortable - and then sat straight up.

"It's 2:30," he said, nudging me. "Moonrise is at 3:19. Who's with Theo and the kids?"

Lev heard him. "Ian's up there right now. We need to make sure all the kids are up."

"And get Theo outside at least ten minutes before," Lane said. "Seemed to help Elena."

"Carry him to the trails, maybe?" Lev asked.

Lane shook his head. "He'll fight us if we try to hold him for too long. They always do, and I don't want to be holding a terrified tiger."

I just reached for my phone, whipping out a text to the group I'd made. It was short, simple, and to the point, notifying them that we had half an hour to be ready. Moonrise was coming, and this was going to be an all hands on deck scenario. Right after I used the bathroom, washed my face, and got a little coffee in me.

The next half hour was nothing but chaos as all of us tried to squeeze past each other, get the last minute things done, and forget nothing. People were messaging that they'd head this way. Someone mentioned that we should block the road so Theo had to head to the trails. Others agreed, so the pack started moving. Then the yelling started from upstairs.

"Cut it off if you have to!" Ian said, his voice carrying too easily in the house.

Lev immediately surged for the stairs, climbing them two at a time. "What?" he asked.

"We need him out of his clothes," Ian said.

"Nik, pull his pants. Ian, hold him. Someone get me some fucking scissors," Lev demanded.

That meant we were close. I wanted to grab my shoes, pull my hair back, or something, but that would be pointless. "Guys?" I asked. "Make sure the kids stay out of the way. I'm going to deal with the mob we're forming."

"I'm with her," Lane said, trailing after me.

The pair of us walked outside to find a surprisingly large group of people clustered together. At least thirty of them, although that was a very wild guess. In the center was a man I only vaguely knew. He'd moved here long before I had, but he'd been pointed out to me for one specific reason: he wasn't a wolf. Jesse, it seemed, was an African Wild Dog, turned when he was in Africa for a business trip, although he lived in America - and the man was giving directions.

"The trick with large cats," he said, "is to keep moving. If one targets you, turn back. He'll be confused by the next wolf coming at him. We're faster over distance than a tiger," he told everyone. "They pounce, though, so work as groups. Three of us will be enough to make him run the other way, especially today." Then someone pointed, letting him know I was standing a few yards behind him. "Alpha," he said in greeting.

"Jesse," I replied. "Have you been around tigers who are turning?"

"Nope," he said. "The pack that helped me through my conversion hunted lions. Well, it's more true to say they chased them off. It was pretty much the only education I got on how to use my body. If I didn't get eaten, I was deemed good enough to live."

"I think I like our way better," I said.

He flashed me a smile. "So do I." Then he pointed at the people. "I've split us into five groups. One for each side of the trails, based in the corners, and another to float, helping where it's needed. Then there's you and your mates." He canted his head. "And your daughter with her betas. I'm assuming you'll all be running together."

"And us." That was Vic as he walked up the street. "Elena, think you wolves can steer him into the trails?"

"We'll make sure of it," I said.

Lane dropped his hand on my shoulder, moving closer to my side. "Yes, Vic. I think we can."

"Yeah, well, I can't make that run and keep up. The three of us are going to be just inside the trees. If he goes up a tree, can someone do that sharp bark thing you have?"

"It means now," Lane told him. "But yeah, we'll sound off for you. He's going to move fast, though."

"Trust me," Vic said, "I've run with Lev. Jax, Scott, and I will be spread through the area. If he attacks anyone, we'll come get him off. I promise that your yelps of pain hit our ears hard."

"Thank you," Lane told him.

I just pointed back up the street. "Go, Vic. They're about to bring him out, and he'll turn as soon as he feels the moon."

"Then let's get ready," Jesse called to the others. "I'd rather we were wolves before he turns instead of after. A few seconds could let him get away from us."

I leaned closer to Lane. "Make sure Ian knows about this, would you? I mean that he's helping out?"

"Jesse always helps," Lane told me. "He will also never ask for credit. Says he's just happy to have a pack. Now strip, woman, because he's right."

There was a definite feeling of anxiety in the air. I was pretty sure it was the voices. Everyone was just a little too quiet and talking just a bit too fast. Lane followed me over to my car where I pulled off my clothes, tossed them inside, and then shifted to a wolf as quickly as I could. He smiled down at me, stripped, but wasn't quite as ready to change forms.

"I want to make sure they have the hands if they need them," he said just as the kids began to make their way out.

Up and down the street was nothing but wolves. So many wolves, and we came in all colors, shapes, and sizes, yet every head was turned toward the front of Heather's house. Gabby and her betas quickly shifted to match us. A moment later, Trent, Pax, and Seth joined them. Heather took a little longer. Then, finally, Ian and Lev carried Theo out between them with Nik following to work the door.

"Nik," Lev said. "I want you shifted. The Alpha and I will as soon as he's moving."

But Ian still pulled off his shirt and kicked off his shoes, not caring where they landed. Lev canted his head and made a face like that wasn't a bad idea, then did the same as soon as Ian was back to support Theo. When Nik changed into a tiger, the crowd of wolves moved, each one trying to get a look. Nik made a soft sound that I could only describe as a tiger's laugh.

Then it happened. The sun was still in the sky, but the moon didn't care about that. Still, I felt it the moment the moon came above the horizon - and so did Theo. The boy screamed, his body twisting in the most unnatural way, and then it began to dissolve like smoke. The substance twisted, almost like it was fighting itself, yet there was nothing else for the men to hold.

Lev shoved off his pants and changed, and Ian was only a split second behind him, yet my eyes hung on the cats. Where Nik was orange and striped the way I'd expect, Lev was paler, almost golden. His stripes weren't as thick, and some had interesting splits, where Nik's were dense and closely packed. On the upside, that meant it would be easy to tell the pair apart.

Then Theo found his form. His back was a slightly

darker orange than Lev's, but not as much as Nik's. The difference was his stripes. They weren't black! Instead, they were a darker shade of his coat, clearly visible, but more red than anything else. The cat's belly was pale, possibly white, but I didn't get the chance to be sure before he was moving - and fast.

The wolves along the street all began growling and barking, making themselves as obvious as possible. In the delirium that came with the first shift, Theo didn't know what they were, but he knew enough to avoid them. That sent him up the street the way we wanted. When he hit the intersection, the wolves headed to block him off. Again, they made a lot of noise, but this time I added my voice with them, and Lane was right there with me.

Theo just turned away. Nik was on his tail, keeping the pace and all but driving him forward. Ian fell back, but Lev rushed ahead, flanking Theo's other side to keep him going straight forward. There were only a couple of blocks between Heather's street and the parking area for the trails, and I was pretty sure there had to be at least fifty wolves around him, herding this boy whether he liked it or not.

It didn't take long before I was losing ground, the rest of the pack getting away from me. I'd only been a wolf for a month, and while I could do many things, running flat out wasn't one of them. I simply didn't have those muscles built up yet. Still, I moved as fast as I could, glad that my legs were working the way I wanted, and Lane loped at my side. Evidently, he'd meant it when he'd said he was with me.

Up ahead, Theo hit the trails, immediately grabbing at a tree. Even from halfway down the street, I heard the roar of a bear and saw the cat jump away, vanishing into the forest. That was the moment the pack began to split. Four different groups broke off, making straight lines for their assigned positions. Each group was a slightly different size, but they moved together, proving this had been coordinated.

By the time I reached the entrance to the trails, everyone was gone, but I could hear the wild crashing of the animals all around me. I paused, trying to get my bearings, and my eyes jumped to the horizon. For me, catching the moon had been so important. Some kind of mental pull that had taken over my thoughts completely. Bridget said it was tied to the tidal force of this virus, so Theo would feel the same thing, right?

On impulse, I moved east. That was the direction of the moon, so the way he'd be inclined to go. Lane rubbed his head against my hip, making it clear he was still there, and we chased the sounds of so many large animals moving at once.

Then a rush of barks caught my attention. A moment later there was another roar, but this one did not come from a bear. Then I saw Theo again. The problem was that the boy also saw me. He turned, those green and yellow eyes locking on my small wolfish body, and then he came toward us. Lane shoved before me without hesitation, and his form began to blur.

My mate grew, stretching up toward his human form, but not completely. He also appeared to get bigger! Theo skidded to a halt, his attack thwarted, and the massive cat hissed just as Lane solidified into his lycan form. The monster chuckled, leaned forward, and then growled louder than I'd ever heard a wolf do before.

Behind him, I was frozen, staring at the red color of his back, the tail coming from his bare ass, and the blend of human and canine features. He was beautiful like this, but also terrifying, and I wanted to make sure that he stayed right between me and the cat that would gladly kill me right now, but it was a standoff. Theo hissed again. Lane took a single step forward.

That was all it took to break the cat from his fear-induced standoff. Theo spun and bolted, heading east again, but the moment of pause had been enough for Lev and Nik to catch back up. Lane didn't seem to care. He just turned to me and squatted down.

"Ah oo ood?" he asked from that strange mouth.

It took me a moment to realize that meant, "Are you good?" but then I nodded to show I was. They could talk? We could communicate in that shape? No wonder so many people had called werewolves things from nightmares. In any other situation, hearing something that looked like him talk like that? I would've been screaming.

But it was Lane, which made it kinda funny. While he shifted back to a wolf, I chittered in amusement, and then we started moving again. Sadly, this time Lane edged me back toward the parking area. Clearly, my awkwardness meant that I'd just been sidelined. I didn't try to fight it, but I still wanted to watch. I wanted to help in some way, but Lane was probably right.

Trying to keep up with a tiger was stupid. If I got in the way, someone could get killed, and so far, it looked like they had this. Deciding to make one last stand, I moved between the trees, finding a space away from the obvious trails, out of everyone's way, but still just deep enough into the woods that I had a chance to see my daughter and mates pass by.

Lane huffed out a heavy sigh, circled around me, and then laid down on the dirt. When I kept standing, he whined softly, then did his best to jerk his head, summoning me closer. Making a wild guess about what he meant, I moved to curl up against him, and he immediately threw a leg over my shoulder and started licking at the back of my head.

But that felt really good. I leaned back, making it even easier, so he shuffled around. While Theo continued his mad dash through the woods, our pack called out his location as best they could, and the tigers did everything in their power to contain the new shifter, Lane and I just listened. I knew I was safe here with him. I knew I couldn't really help. I also didn't want to leave.

Slowly, the shadows began to shift under the trees, growing longer. Still we waited. The sun drifted across the sky. I waited a little more. At one point, I saw Gabby and her pack running flat out, their bellies near the ground, and then they turned. All of them were focused in the same direction, which meant they were herding Theo.

And still it went on. Time felt like it passed so much faster when I was in the middle of this, but Lane was right. I wasn't that good of a wolf yet. I was just happy he hadn't sent me to Henry's like they had the girls. I wanted to be here. I needed to help somehow, even if that was just checking on my pack when this was all over.

At some point, the feeling began to change. No longer was the crashing and roaring frantic. It became teasing, then playful. Eventually, wolves started heading for the seating area. Tongues were hanging low, but we still got wags from tails as they passed. Then I finally saw him again. Theo seemed to be thinking, and the boy looked like he might even be enjoying himself. Just across the creek, I watched him leap up to hug a tree and then mock-bite at it. Nik pounced at Theo's tail, looking just like an oversized house cat, and then Jax grabbed Nik in a hug and fell over, pretending to wrestle.

Gabby and her betas rushed in to bounce between them, and Theo tried to bat at one. The paw caught, but there were no claws, and Xander was pushed into the dirt. Theo immediately jumped back, but Xander just hopped up again. The two boys looked at each other for a moment before Xander rubbed his face against the tiger's to nibble at his neck.

Friends. I didn't even need to know them to realize that was what it all meant. The cats, the bears - and then I saw the triplet of foxes mingling with the other wolves. All of us were here, and we were all just fine. We were friends. No, this was pack, and it was actually working. This was all going to be just fine. One way or another, Wolf's Run would find a way to make it work.

CHAPTER 39

I t had taken a while to get Theo turned back to human, but when the boy was so tired he could barely move, Nik had shifted to talk him through it. When that hadn't been easy, Elena had come over to help, making it clear that he wasn't expected to get it right on the first try. She hadn't either. It didn't matter how long it took, she was going to stay right there with him, and they would help him.

Thankfully, Lane had done like I asked and kept her safe. While she focused on the boy, I pulled him over to the side, hoping none of them were paying enough attention to listen in.

"Is she mad at you?" I asked, keeping my voice down.

He chuckled at me. "No. She couldn't keep up with the pack on the street before Theo hit the trails. As soon as we got in here, she tried to follow the sounds, but she wasn't rushing. When Theo came at her and I had to scare him off - "

"What?" I hissed.

"I went lycan. Bigger, hairier monster. He hissed. I growled. He left."

"And if he'd attacked?" I asked.

Lane just shrugged. "Old wolf, young tiger? I think I could take him. I also would never let him touch her. Kinda why you asked me and not Seth."

"Yeah," I admitted. "I also needed Seth, because not many of us can keep up with a cat." I gave both arms a swing, feeling the burn of overly-used muscles. "I'm going to hurt tomorrow."

"Well, I got her to cuddle with me as a wolf, so I'm ok with this," Lane promised.

But something was happening. Elena had moved to hold Theo's head in her lap, and she was calmly stroking the tiger's fur. The boy's eyes closed and all the tension faded from his body. Nikolai moved to sit beside him, leaning in to press his head against Theo's shoulder. For a moment I thought they were about to take a nap. The whole group looked just a little too comfortable. Then the tiger lifted a paw to pull Nik closer.

"You need hands for that," Elena told him. "Don't push. Don't try to be a human, Theo. Reach for what you want. Feel the cells of your body moving to get there. Pushing will shove it all away. You want to reach for it, like if Nik's hand was just an inch too far away. Reach, make yourself go there, and then you can hold him again the way you want."

Something began to happen. The tiger's form blurred. His arms stretched and his legs changed their angle. It wasn't happening fast, but it was definitely happening, and the whole time, Elena kept stroking the boy's head. Her eyes weren't closed, though.

"She can watch now?" I asked.

Lane nodded. "I think so. Since she shifted, she sometimes forgets to look away. Besides, her kids need her, and I think that trumps everything else for that woman."

"God, I love her," I breathed. "She's so amazing."

Lane just slapped my back. "Yeah. We found a good one."

"You did," I reminded him. "Lane, I'm so glad you were fated for her. She's everything we've ever needed."

"This mean you're not going to care when I call her mine?"

"Not at all," I assured him, "because I keep doing the same thing. Pretty sure the others do too. You know Seth's got it bad, right?"

"Mhm. You know Trent's idea for a date keeps getting thwarted. We need to make sure that can happen, Ian. I'm pretty sure Pax is in love. Trent? He needs this. He has to prove to himself that he's not with her because we are, just so he can be sure his feelings are really his. Not yours, not Pax's, but his."

I looked over at Lane. "Little over two weeks until Gabby's big play. Let's make a date out of that, and then those two can take her out on Saturday. And if something comes up? We don't tell them."

"Deal," he agreed. "And then?"

Ian smiled. "Then we all need to have a very serious talk with Gabby about our intentions."

He nodded, but across from us, Theo was almost there.

The boy was more blur than form now, and starting to resettle into his human shape. Elena just kept talking, telling him that was it, not to stop, and that he had this. Then, almost like elastic breaking, his form snapped into place and Theo gasped, sucking air through his very human mouth.

"Someone pick him up. There should be a car out there to take him home. Let's get Theo into a bed where he can recover and sleep this off." And I looked at Nik. "If you can't lift him, we'll help."

"I can," Nik promised, scooping Theo into his arms.

"I have the car," a woman called, waving for him to follow before she shifted into a wolf again.

Elena just waited for Nik to get Theo, then for others to pass her by, and then she stood. I watched as she dusted herself off, glanced around to check for her mates and daughter. Finding everyone milling in the group around her, she made a straight line for me.

"Ian," she said when she was close enough. "You and the betas need to go home and sleep."

"And you," I countered.

"And Gabby," she added. "Theo's fine, but the rest of us are running on fumes."

"My place?" I offered.

Evidently, I said that just a little too loud, because Pax made his way over. "Trent can crash with me. That will give Gabby his bed. Elena has her pick."

"You good with that?" I asked Trent.

He just shrugged. "Sure. I also know that all the adult materials are in his room, which means mine's teen safe. I'm guessing Lane's going to make room for Elena with him?"

"I am," he said.

Trent nodded, but the sly twist to his lips made it clear he'd also heard that slightly possessive tone. "Right. Elena, take them home. I'll get Gabby and drop off the rest."

Somehow, we managed to make it all happen. I was honestly exhausted, but Theo had made it through just fine. So far, we had quite the track record of successful - and injury-free - conversions. Not too shabby. But Gabby had to make sure that Olivia and Samantha knew Theo was ok. That meant a trip back to Heather's to get her clothes and phone, plus ordering the other kids to go home and let the boys sleep.

Finally, I found my bed and fell into it alone. It was earlier than I usually went to sleep, but so far as I cared, it was still night, so good enough. The moment my eyes closed, I was asleep.

When they opened, the first thing I noticed was that it was still dark. The second was the woman pressed against my side, still breathing softly. I turned to find Elena sprawled on top the covers, almost like she'd come to ask me something and hadn't quite made it that far. I eased the covers out from under her, got her properly into bed, then curled up around her and was back asleep.

When I woke again, she was gone. Downstairs, I heard the sounds of dishes and pans. My stomach growled, letting me know it wanted in on that, but I had to do something first. Staggering from my bed, I barely remembered to pull on pants before crossing the hall to claim the shower. That helped, but I could still feel the exhaustion of the last few days making me slow.

But when I made my way downstairs, it wasn't Elena in the kitchen. It was Gabby and Seth. The pair of them were working on something that definitely smelled like breakfast. Gabby saw me first, flashing a smile as she turned to reach for a cup.

"Coffee, Ian?"

"Please," I mumbled, moving to claim a stool at our bar. "What are you doing?"

"When was the last time we all ate?" Seth asked. "I figured I'd make food, wake everyone, and if they go back to sleep, then that's what they do."

"Where's Elena?"

Gabby giggled. "I think she's with Trent and Pax. Heard them talking outside my room. Kinda sounded like she'd been in bed with you, went to the bathroom, and bumped into Pax. So, yeah, she's asleep somewhere."

"She was in my room last night," Seth said.

"Mine too," I admitted.

Seth nodded. "Checking on us, I think. Her alpha instincts are going pretty strong after that run."

Gabby came over to set the cup of coffee before me. "Is that a good thing?" she asked. "I mean, if my mom's an alpha, is that a problem for you?"

"No," I promised. "It's actually great, Gabby. And so you know, she's an amazing Alpha Female. I know you've never seen one before, though. See, we pick our mates because we love them. Sadly, love isn't always a good qualification for helping others, though, and that's what the Alpha Mate is supposed to do. Their duty to the pack is to be a buffer between me and their complaints."

"Like, an ambassador or something?" she asked. "You know, that whole thing where you can tell someone who'll tell someone?"

I nodded, not quite understanding how she got

ambassador from that description, but her idea sounded pretty close. "Yeah. Plus, her little Sisterhood?"

"Ashley says she's Mom's beta," Gabby told me.

Even Seth stopped moving at that news. "What?" I asked.

Gabby nodded. "I heard her do it. I just didn't think that the Alpha Mate got betas. Then again, what happens if one alpha mates another? Do the betas kinda merge?"

"No," I said. "Usually, the Pack Alpha's betas stay 'on the job' and the others eventually fade back to their own lives. Kinda like how Dad's betas have moved on now that he's not leading."

"That would suck," Gabby grumbled.

But I was still stuck on what she said. Grabbing my cup, I made some excuse about needing to check something, and headed for the den. There, I grabbed the land line and dialed Ashley's cell. It took all of four rings before she answered.

"What's wrong?" she answered.

"Nothing," I said. "At least I hope not."

She sighed in relief. "Why are you calling me from the house and not your own phone?"

"Because I'm still wearing pajamas and don't want to walk upstairs. Ash, what's this about you being Elena's beta?"

She groaned, but there was something about it that sounded amused as well as annoyed. "Who told you that?"

"Gabby, actually. So what's going on? You know Alpha Mates don't get betas."

She scoffed. "Fuck the rules, Ian. Fuck traditions. You know what that shit has gotten us? My mate ran off with my beta. Your mate's daughter should be taught that she's

379

not good enough to be your heir, and our father should be dead because one of us had to kill him. Every time we say screw it and just follow our guts, things work better. So, that's what I'm doing."

"And what does your gut say?" I asked, making it clear I expected her to answer.

It took just a little too long for her to answer. In the background, I heard her moving, sounding like she was getting comfortable in a chair. Next, there was a sip - probably coffee - and then a sigh.

"My gut says that Gabby's going to be the Pack Alpha that we need. It says that there's something about both her and Elena that we've never seen before. Nothing too big, mind you. I mean, they aren't going to start throwing magic or sucking blood. It's just..." She murmured, clearly searching for words.

"You don't have to be official," I told her. "I just want to know where your mind is, Ash."

"Ok, look." She pulled in a breath. "If the pack is like a family, you're in the position of being the father. You're the one who sets the rules and protects us from everything outside and each other, right?"

"Right."

"But Elena? She's the mother. She nurtures us. She makes us feel just a little special, guides us to be better, and feels like a safe place where we know we'll be taken care of. It's not just me, either. Those foxes? They adore her. The Sisterhood? We're basically her backup. If she needs an extra set of hands, she calls us. That's like her betas, right? And we have bears, and tigers, and will probably get more. We both know it. Never mind the size of this pack. Ian, you can't run this on your own. Not even with your betas. You're going to need a hell of a lot more than just the five of you to deal with all these people. And yes, I said people, because we're not just wolves anymore."

"But we're still a pack," I reminded her.

"Exactly," she said. "We're a pack because Elena found some common ground and Gabby's reinforcing it. Those two? They transcend the lines we've always known. Now, I can't tell you if it's because they're converts, but I don't think so. Seth's a convert. David's a convert. So what is it about them that makes them feel so damned safe and easy?"

I had to pause to think about that, because I knew what she meant. I wouldn't have picked those words myself, because Gabby wasn't safe. She was a little hellion, and more than willing to pick a fight, it seemed. She led the way my father had shown me: by example. She was also willing to put her foot down and set boundaries, but they were always fair ones.

What was different about them? I agreed that there was something, but I couldn't quite put it into words.

"Is it just because she's nice?" I asked.

"No," Ashley said. "I promise that nice doesn't make me want to follow anyone else's orders. And Ian? I follow Elena's. I don't even think about it. It's not a conscious decision. I simply work as an extension of her the same way Trent and Pax do with you. So, if that doesn't make me her beta, then what the fuck do you call it?"

"You think she's an alpha?" I asked.

She just chuckled. "I think she's the damned den mother, Ian. And so you know, I think Roman's becoming the same thing. The more time he spends with Gabby, the more he works to build the bonds with the people around her. He's the social butterfly, the one who makes sure that Gabby has a place to lean that's strong enough to hold her up, and an understanding ear for those who've been on the wrong side of that girl's attitude."

"But what do you even call that?" I asked.

"I have no idea," she told me. "It's new, Ian. I think Roman's learning from them because he wants so hard to make up for his mistakes. I think Elena is flying blind, so what we see is what we get. Most of all, I think that we don't have a tradition or wolf law to describe this, so fuck it. Let's make up our own. It's not as if we're a normal pack, right?"

"But Elena isn't my beta," I pointed out. "That means they aren't the same."

"Isn't she?" Ashley countered. "Isn't her word the same as your law? Who closed the gates for Theo's conversion, Ian? Who do you go to when you need something handled gently? Who have you begun to rely on to help with the softer aspects of leading your pack? Elena? Why, because she's a woman?"

"Of course not!" I snapped. "She's just better at that than..." Fuck. The words were halfway out of my mouth before I realized what she was saying. "Oh."

"Exactly," she said. "You use her as an extension of yourself. Like a beta. You also like to get her naked and do kinky things to her body. Like a mate. Turn that down to teenage mentality, and you have Gabby and Roman. So, what the fuck are we calling this new thing?"

"A miracle," I decided. "Ash, I don't have a good word, and I don't even care. I just need to figure out how to manage my mate having her own betas."

"Her Sisterhood," she corrected. "Or Brotherhood,

when Roman does it. Either way, they're going to be the den guardians."

I just chuckled. "And there we have it. Den Mother. Den Father. The Alpha Mate doesn't have betas. They have guardians."

"Nah," she teased, "We're still the Sisterhood of Being Too Old for That Shit. But sure, guardians sounds pretty impressive too. Have you also noticed that we're all alphas or very strong beta types? Me, Kim, Heather, and Bridget. Those last two should've bonded with an alpha, but never got a chance. They're both also damned close to that line between strong-willed and leader types."

"Shit," I breathed, realizing she was right.

"Look," she said, "don't overthink it. Those kids don't need any more pressure on them, and whatever Elena is doing is working. Sometimes, little brother, it's ok to just let nature take its course. For now, just rest, recover, and don't forget that Gabby's play is coming up."

I groaned. "I know. Trent and Pax want a date night with Elena. I might ask for a little help so that can happen."

"Sure," she agreed without hesitation. "But why do I think this is something of a big deal?"

"Trent wants to be sure before he says a triplet of words. I need them on board."

"For?" she asked.

I leaned back in my chair and smiled. "I'm not letting the perfect woman get away from me, Ash. I'm also not going to tell you because I know you can't keep a secret from your alpha."

"Size seven and a quarter," she told me. "And just remember how long I knew her without telling her I was a wolf. I can keep a secret. It's Lane you need to worry about."

"He's already on board," I promised. "Seth too. Just waiting for the twins."

"Then we'll make sure that entire weekend is perfect," Ashley promised.

CHAPTER 40

Theo was back to school by Monday. The boy was slow and still aching, but he said he was fine. The week after, Gabby started the final dress rehearsals for her play. Trent jumped right in, helping with the final touches on her costume. The funny thing was that Nik also helped, giving her tips on the stripes for her Cheshire Cat and asking pointed questions about why she was portraying her character that way.

And every evening, we all crowded into Ian's place. Between myself and the guys, plus Gabby and her newly-forming group of betas, mine simply wasn't big enough. Trent moved some of his clothes into Pax's room, and the pair cleaned up Trent's so that Gabby could use it any time she needed. I couldn't say we were moving in, but the fact that I bought my daughter a toothbrush for their place said a lot.

When I stayed over, I slept in Lane's room. First, because it wasn't on the same floor as my daughter.

Second, because it had an attached bath and a bed big enough for a little extra company. Somewhere in the last month, I'd gotten over being embarrassed about Gabby knowing what was going on. Plus, from the looks the boys she hung out with were giving her when she wasn't paying attention, my little girl was going to end up building her own harem.

Theo was the one who surprised me the most. Not that he gawked at my daughter, but he didn't seem to mind when Nik did. Plus, he and Roman were getting to be pretty close friends. The boy seemed to be adapting well to his transformation, but unlike Nik, Theo still had that need to be with his pack. Ian made quite a few comments about it.

Although, with Gabby's play coming up so fast, my own wolf lessons got put on hold. Heather and Lev worked together with Gabby and her betas to make sure that Theo could at least shift with control and walk as a tiger. Those few hours every day were also the only time it felt like I got to actually relax. My mates would make dinner, I'd sneak in a hot bath in Lane's tub, and for just a little bit, everything else got put on hold.

Until the day finally came. Yes, it was a high school play, but for Gabby, this was a Big Deal, capital letters and all. That Friday, Roman brought her straight home after school. I was still at the office, but they stopped for a minute to say she was headed back. As soon as I got off work, I hurried home to change. I picked a nice dress and heels, and had just pulled them on when Ashley walked into my house, yelling to let me know she was there.

"What?" I asked, peeking my head out of my bedroom. "I didn't know you were going to the play!"

She just rolled her eyes. "Gabby's been talking about this since she got here, Elena. After Gerardo, the pack wants to make sure that she has one hell of a cheering section. Her betas are all going. Your Sisterhood. Ian and his betas. Then there's Dad. I talked the guys out of suits, but Roman's insisting on ties so she knows we take this seriously. Lev had to find something that would fit Theo, but they're at Heather's making this work."

"Speaking of Lev and Heather," I said.

Ashley just grinned. "Do not mention it. Do not breathe a word of it. Nothing is happening, she swears."

I nodded to show I understood. "Gotcha. Well, make sure she knows that I have enough space for the kids to spend the night with Gabby when she needs a little excuse."

"Will do. Now, can I borrow your curling iron? We're on a schedule, woman."

The pair of us got down to work. Ashley used my bathroom sink to fix her hair and touch up her makeup. I sat down before my vanity in the bedroom and did the same. The pair of us were just finishing when my doorbell rang. No one used my doorbell!

"I think that's for me," Ashley said, hurrying out of the room.

I slipped on my heels and followed in time to see her laughing and opening the door as wide as it would go. On the other side was Vic, Jax, and Scott, but behind them my mates were struggling not to laugh.

"So, I see this is going to be an event," Ian teased.

"Ashley just said she needed an arm to hang off of," Vic assured him. "And, well, we have room for one more in the truck."

"Oh." Ian nodded as if accepting that, but the corner of his lip was curled a little too high. "Because, when my sister dresses like that, it means you should definitely take her out to dinner afterwards. I mean, whichever one of you is brave enough to ask her, that is. Or all. Might be safer if you deal with her as a group."

Scott ducked his head. "I thought the big brother was supposed to give the subtle threats, Alpha."

"Nah," Ian said. "She's the oldest of our bunch, so I had to learn how to keep up. Trust me, I'm not worried about Ashley taking care of herself, so no threats. You piss her off and you get to deal with her."

"Cute," Ashley said, but while she tried to sound offended, she was failing. Badly.

Then Lane cleared his throat. "We have someplace to be, ladies. Which one of you is running late?"

"Not me," I assured him as I grabbed my purse. Then I squeezed Ashley's arm so I could slip past. "Meet you there?"

"And everyone else," she reminded me. "Henry's bringing Bridget, just so we're not all cramped, so save room for them?"

"Can do," I promised.

On the way there, we talked about the girls, because Samantha had the leading role of Alice in this play. Gabby was the Cheshire Cat, who was probably the second most important character. All of us wondered who'd taken on the Jabberwocky. Mason had been cast to play it, but that boy was now in jail, awaiting his trial. Granted, it looked like his attorney was going to use an insanity defense.

We arrived to find the school entirely lit up and parents all making their way into the main doors. Some were dressed up like us. Others looked like they'd just gotten off work. Then there were the other kids. Gabby clearly wasn't the only one who had invited the people she knew to come watch.

We were almost at the doors when someone called my name. I turned to find Bridget hanging on Henry's arm and waving, but the commotion made someone on the other side notice us. That was David. He and Kim had their daughter, Julia, with them.

Inside the doors, Roman and Gabby's betas were all clustered at the side, looking at a poster. I tried to see, but couldn't quite make it out. There was a picture of a football player on it, and he was wearing the school colors.

"Who's that?" I asked when Roman moved to join us.

"Hm?" He sounded confused.

"The poster you're looking at," I explained. "Friend of yours?"

"No. He's one of the jocks. Ran away a few days ago. The school has those up all over trying to get his friends to rat him out. Evidently, we're not the only ones who can keep secrets. I mean, you haven't managed to see Gabby's costume yet." And he grinned.

I just rolled my eyes and reached out for Ian's arm. Together, we led our pack into the auditorium. The place was huge, but this was also a very well-funded school. The group of us headed down to the middle of the center section, and then carved out a healthy chunk of unclaimed seats. Ian and I went in the middle. Lane was on my other side, with Seth beside him. Trent and Pax flanked Ian.

Behind us was Henry and Bridget. Kim and her family

sat to Bridget's right, saving four seats on Henry's left, most likely for Ashley. Then Heather and Lev arrived. A moment later, it was Jesse and another single man from the pack. Ashley got there soon enough, but I couldn't believe how many of us there were. Roman had moved the betas to a row just behind Henry, and it felt like the entire center block of seats was nothing but people from Wolf's Run.

"So," Henry asked, leaning forward toward me, "is this the big culmination?"

"Actually, no," Trent said, answering for me. "This is their first live performance. After this, they start doing school competitions. If they're scored well enough, then they'll advance. I can't remember what order it goes in, but there's a competition for district, regional, and state."

"Then I'm glad we paid for good props and costumes," Henry said. "I told that Mr. Bell to let me know if they needed any more funding, because my granddaughter deserved only the best."

"You aren't buying her way into next year's play, are you?" Bridget teased.

Henry just smiled. "Oh, no. I made sure he knows Samantha's one of my projects too. I bought both of them starring roles for as long as they want them."

"Henry..." Trent groaned.

Ian's dad waved him down. "Relax. I know better than that. I told him that we had some kids from the neighborhood in school here, and I felt that drama was a good influence for them, so wanted to make sure the arts had as much of a chance as the sports. I didn't name names, Trent." Henry's smile turned fond. "I know how much acting meant to you when you were that age. Believe it or not, I listened."

Then the lights began to dim. They didn't immediately go out, but those who were still standing and talking moved for their seats and the noise of the audience dimmed to a buzz. Then, a man in a suit - Mr. Bell - walked onto the stage holding a microphone.

"Good evening," he said to the audience. "Tonight is the first official performance of this year's long play. These students have been learning their lines and improving their acting for months now. To show appreciation, we ask that the crowd remain quiet during the scenes. Calls of encouragement to one student could distract another, ruining their night. Applause is acceptable at the breaks." He paused and stepped back, gesturing to the curtain. "And now, I present to you, *Alice in Wonderland!*"

Naturally, we all clapped even as the lights dimmed the rest of the way. The curtains began to pull back, the spotlights turned on, and the breath fell from my lungs. The stage was magical. Yes, it was all hand-painted plywood and tricks of lighting, but it was so much better than Gabby's last school. Then Samantha walked onto the stage and I forgot to think of anything else.

The girl was Black with natural hair that fell behind her in tight ringlets. She didn't look like the typical Alice, but Samantha also didn't try. She wore a dress, but it wasn't the pastel blue with a white apron we'd all learned from the Disney movie. Hers was pink and yellow and fell to the middle of her calves, more appropriate for the time period this was supposed to be set in.

And Samantha could act. A smile broke out on my face.

A moment later, Ian's hand slipped into mine. Lane moved his to my knee, and I didn't think anything of it. I no longer had anything to be ashamed of this was us, watching our pups have their big day, and it felt right to do it together.

When Gabby finally came onto the stage, she looked like a psychedelic tiger. Her dark hair had been streaked with colors. Her face was painted orange and white, but her stripes? They were in all the shades of the rainbow. She wore nothing but a spandex bodysuit - painted to give her stripes - with mittens shaped like paws and slippers that matched.

"Wait for it," Nik said behind us.

Because when Gabby acted, she was a cat. Ok, a tiger, but still. Her arrogance was real. Her pride was almost palpable, yet she was friendly, curious, and somehow a little mysterious. Then came the best part: the moment she disappeared.

The spotlight on her changed color, and all of those stripes seemed to glow. The orange of her skin turned black. One more change of the light, and my daughter became nothing more than a shadow made of UV reactive stripes. As the spotlight dimmed, so did her glow, until she slipped behind a prop and was simply, completely, and totally gone from sight.

In the balcony, someone clapped at the effect before being hushed, but the play continued. It was good. They were good! When the final act was done and the curtains closed, I wasn't the only one jumping to my feet to give the kids a standing ovation. A glance down my row of seats showed Trent beaming proudly.

The kids came out for one last row of bows, but the lights were growing brighter, letting them see just how full this auditorium was. Gabby and Sam were in the middle. The girls clasped hands with each other and the actors on the other side, and then the whole line of them bowed.

"That's my girls!" Roman bellowed from behind us.

"Best Alice ever!" Olivia screamed.

"Best cat!" Nik added, making Gabby look up with a grin, proving she'd heard it.

Then it was over except for the shuffling out. I turned to Ian, about to ask him if he'd mind me sneaking around back. Instead, I caught Jax reaching over for Ashley's hand.

"So, about that date?" he asked. "Maybe the group of us could buy you dinner?"

"Of course," Ashley said. "We just have to make it out of here."

Then Trent reached around Ian. "Hey, I think we can sneak around the side to see Gabby," he said, pointing at a door.

"Coming with," Pax said. "The rest of you going to wait here or shuffle back to the cars?"

"Here's good," Ian told him. "We don't want to make too much of a fuss, right?"

I did a little dance to make my way around Ian, then Trent found my hand. He led me toward the aisle, but Pax fell in behind me, clasping my shoulders so I wouldn't get lost in the chaos. Together, we all made it down to the front where it was open, then aimed for a door at the side. Passing through that put us in one of the random halls of the school.

Lockers lined the walls. Doors down the way were all wood with long, narrow windows set off center. It even smelled like a school, if stronger because of my new wolf-improved senses. Yet the guys both paused and turned to me instead of continuing on.

"What are you doing tomorrow night?" Trent asked.

"Uh..." I wracked my brain. "Nothing. Why?"

"A date," he told me. "The two of us have been trying to ask you out on an official date for far too long. Something always went wrong, so we decided not to say anything until Gabby's play was over. You know, so we didn't jinx it."

"Drama students," Pax groaned playfully. "But we're serious, Elena. The three of us, together. A nice dinner, maybe an event?"

"Not a movie," I told them. "I'm far too old for that."

Trent scoffed. "You're not, but I was thinking more about something where we could actually spend time talking."

"Star watching in the park?" Pax offered.

"It sounds perfect," I told them. "Just one question. What am I supposed to wear? Casual? Fancy?"

"Sexy," Trent told me. "Attire should match tonight's event, and our goal is to make sure that tomorrow is even better."

"Time?" I looked between the two of them.

"Eight," Pax decided. "Ian already said he'd keep an eye on Gabby."

I couldn't have stopped the smile if I'd tried. "Oh, he did, did he?"

Trent ducked his head. "Busted. No, it was to remove one more hiccup, because I've been waiting to take you out like you deserve since before you were a wolf. That night in the hot tub when you said you wouldn't be ashamed to be with us both?"

I reached over and caught each of their hands. "Guys, I can't imagine a single reason to be ashamed. I'm the woman with the hot men, right? Trust me, it's not a problem at all to show you off to the whole world."

CHAPTER 41

Pax and I had a plan. We'd spent all night working on it, so I sincerely hoped that this wouldn't fall through. As I trimmed up my beard and styled my hair, I realized my hands were trembling just a bit. Yes, I was nervous. I had good reason to be, because I wanted to be sure that this thing with Elena wasn't just a fluke.

I liked that woman too much. I adored her daughter. Being with them made me feel as if I belonged there, and the way Gabby treated me? I could finally understand Henry's obsession with being a father. Evidently, it was a whole lot like being someone's hero. The fact that Elena seemed to approve of how I acted with her kid?

This really had to work.

I was just finishing when Pax stepped into the bathroom beside me to focus on his own hair. The two of us were dressed to complement, and a sneaky little text to Gabby had helped us out with the right colors. I knew it was stupid, but it seemed like the perfect little detail to prove just how invested Pax and I were in making this work.

Gabby had said Elena's dress was burgundy, and she'd even sneaked in a picture. Sadly, the dress was still in the closet, not on our mate, but it helped. Now, Pax was wearing a shirt that was pretty close to the same color with a black tie. I had on a black shirt, but my tie matched Pax's shirt. We were going for full suits tonight, but mostly because one of us would have the chance to loan Elena our coat. Maybe both, since her legs might get cold too.

Then I grabbed the Bluetooth speaker, Pax went to the kitchen to get our big surprise, and the pair of us headed to my truck. Our stuff went in the back, along with a bottle of chilled wine. Once that was all secure and out of sight, we headed to Elena's house. When we reached the door, I looked over, so Pax knocked. The man looked as anxious as I felt.

Of course, it was Gabby who opened the door. "Mom!" she yelled. "Your mates are here."

"Be good," Elena told her. "If the boys - any or all of them - are coming over, tell Ian, ok?"

Gabby made an X over her heart. "Promise. Any idea what time you're coming back?"

"Late," I answered for her. "Eleven, maybe midnight."

She just grinned. "Have fun, you three. Call if you get arrested."

Elena groaned, shaking her head at her daughter's bad joke. I simply offered my arm. "You look stunning, Elena."

Because she did. The dress was tight across her body, showing just enough cleavage to make my eyes keep dropping, but it was loose across her legs - and short. The hem hit the middle of her thighs, making her legs look even longer. Something about her had changed since she'd turned, but I still hadn't figured out what. The only real difference I could name was how her smile seemed just a little easier. And those wine-red lips? I really wanted to kiss them.

"So, do I get to know what's in store for me tonight?" she asked, looking over at Pax.

He just gestured to the sky before pausing to open the passenger door for her. "It's nice out tonight, the sky's as clear as can be, and we promised you stars."

She laughed as she climbed into the passenger seat. I took the driver's, since it was my truck, and Pax ended up in the back with our dinner. When Elena turned to say something to him, she noticed the blanket, but I was pretty sure she had no idea what we were truly doing. Pax's answer had been just vague enough to keep a little of the surprise for later. I just hoped she liked it.

Thankfully, the drive was short. While Wolf's Run was being built, we'd all been wolves living in the city. Ian had taken an apartment to be close to the construction, which meant that we'd had nowhere to go on the full moons. Someone - and I couldn't remember who - had found this quiet park. There was a baseball diamond, a playground, and beyond that was a large, open field for flying kites. Beside that was a nice-sized pond that spilled out of a miniature forest.

That was our destination. It was quiet, it wasn't exactly popular, and it would have a perfect view of the sky. We'd be just far enough away from anyone else that we wouldn't need to watch our words, and yet anyone could see her with us. This counted as public. It was also away from the rest of the pack, which meant that for once, we wouldn't have to share her attention with anyone else. And, if this went like I hoped, I had something very important to say to her.

The conversation on the way over was easy. We kept it to simple things, mostly what Gabby had said about her play and how excited she'd been. The girl was basically on top of the world, and from the sounds of it, this was the first play she'd ever done where no one tried to make her feel bad about it. Instead, we'd all come, and Elena said that had meant the world to Gabby.

Yet the moment I pulled into the park's parking lot, Elena fell silent. She looked out the window, and a little crease formed in her brow. "I might be a bit overdressed for this," she teased.

I simply gestured to my suit. "I don't think so. Pax? Can you grab our dinner?"

And that was when she figured it out. "An evening picnic?"

"We have food, wine, and even dessert," I said, grabbing the blanket and speaker from the back seat. "Pax cooked, and I selected the music. There might even be dancing. What there won't be is any reason to worry about saying the wrong thing."

"Ok," Pax said, tilting his head. "This way. Our destination is a little open area beside that pond. If your shoes won't make it, then Trent is going to carry you."

"I think my shoes will be fine," she assured us. "Don't want to wear you out too early."

Under the light of the waning moon, we hiked across the grass. In the middle of that field, we found a soft spot.

Elena squeaked adorably when her heel sank further than she expected, so I swept her into my arms and kept walking, refusing to let Pax leave us behind. He chuckled, but Elena wrapped her arms around my neck and leaned in.

"You smell good," she said.

"Oh, I will not stop you from getting closer for a better smell."

So she did. I could feel her breath on the shell of my ear and her fingers pressing against the back of my neck. At that moment, I knew it was going to be a very long dinner, yet I still wanted it. I wanted to do more than throw her in a bed sometimes. I wanted this, her complete attention on only us.

When we reached the little grassy area, I set her down and spread out the blanket. Pax put the cooler in one corner, then helped Elena down. She'd taken a spot in the middle, which was perfect. While Pax started looking for our food, I went for the wine.

"Our glasses," I said as I began to work the corkscrew into the top, "are very fancy plastic. Our wine, however, is your favorite white."

"I completely packed this backwards," Pax groaned, pulling out a tray I recognized. "So, Elena, hold this for - "

Just as he leaned toward her, the cork came free with a loud pop. The problem was that the angle was aimed right at him. He ducked. The tray of cupcakes tipped. Elena yelped as the food tumbled toward her and wine began to well from the end of the bottle. And of course, the cupcakes landed right on her, icing side down.

One hit her calf. The other her thigh, just above her knee. The last smushed into her dress and slowly slid down the side. Wine gushed over my hand before I was smart enough to lift the bottle again, and the whole thing was ruined. All this work, all of our careful planning. Everything had just fallen apart in the first five minutes we were alone.

Then Elena began to giggle. "Dessert first?" she asked, swiping at the icing on her dress.

Pax's eyes dropped to her leg. "Oh, you have no idea how tempting that offer is." With a laugh, he dropped to his hands and knees to lick at her knee.

But that only made Elena laugh more. She tilted her head back and didn't try to stop it. I could see the tears welling up in her eyes, and my lips curled in response. This wasn't funny, but something about her was just so infectious. Then she grabbed the cupcake from her lap and pushed it at Pax, smearing his nose with what remained of the icing.

"And Trent's covered in wine," Pax chuckled. "Yep, we officially suck at dating."

"But it's my favorite white," she giggled, leaning far over to grab my hand.

That, she pulled to her lips, sucking at my sticky finger. She had to pause to laugh again, but she looked happier than I'd ever seen her before. I'd been so focused on being perfect for her that it seemed I'd overlooked the most important thing. Elena never asked us for perfect. She tackled insanity on a daily basis and made it look elegant. This woman asked for almost nothing in return, yet I'd been shooting for the moon just so I could keep up.

The sound of her childish laughter was the most beautiful thing I'd ever heard. The sight of Pax licking at her knee was so very fitting. The simple fact that our date was now a complete disaster and possibly the best night of my life? I didn't think. I didn't give myself time to change my mind. I simply opened my mouth and the words fell right out.

"I love you, Elena."

If anything, her smile grew a little more. "Yeah?" she asked. "I just made a mess of our date!" And she started giggling again.

"A tasty one," Pax said as he shifted to sit beside her. "And I love you too. That's why we wanted a moment alone, so we could finally tell you that."

"Both of you?" she asked, looking from me to him. "And you waited to tell me together?"

Her smile faltered, but the look that replaced it wasn't her being upset. It was the look a woman had when she was overwhelmed with happiness. Then Elena reached up for me, all but calling me to her, and I obeyed. Dropping to my knees beside her, I leaned in to caress the back of her head.

"There are some things we've always done together," I admitted. "So, Pax was waiting on me."

"And you're sure?" she asked. Her eyes searched mine for a moment before she turned to Pax. "Because I don't want you to feel like you have to say this just because everyone else has."

"Honey, hearing you say that to Ian that night? I've never been so jealous in my life. I want it too. I want you. As a friend, lover, mate, and so much more. I want to lick icing from your knee and ruin our big plans together. Yes, I'm sure that I love you."

Then she turned to me and my guts clenched. "I didn't prepare a speech," I mumbled. "But yes, I'm sure. I just want to know that this? It's not because we're simply comfortable, or because you feel like you have to be with us. When you're around, my worst days become my best. I can't stop thinking about you, Elena. If this isn't love, then I have no idea what else to call it."

She bit her lip and nodded. "I was waiting for you to say it first. I..." She glanced over at Pax. "I love you both. All five of you, if I'm honest. And I know that's not fair, but this feels so right to me, and I can't say that I have a favorite or a best. All I can say is that I don't want any of this to change. I love you, Pax." Then her eyes returned to meet mine. "And I love you, Trent. I knew I would from the moment you jumped right in to help Gabby with her play. Maybe I just have a weakness for men who are good with kids, or... I dunno. But if this isn't real, you both are going to break my heart."

"Not going to happen," Pax said as he leaned in to kiss the side of her neck. "Not without breaking ours too."

"Fuck dinner," I decided, and pushed forward to claim her mouth.

Elena met me halfway, yet when her hand clasped my neck, I was pretty sure she left a little icing behind. Oddly, I couldn't think of anything more perfect.

<u>CHAPTER 42</u>

My mouth found Trent's, my hand reached back for Pax, but my mind was stuck on one thing. They loved me. Both of these men had done all of this just to have the chance to say it. I didn't even care about the cupcakes or wine. Dinner suddenly seemed very unimportant. I just wanted to wrap my arms around both of them, kiss my men, and be right here, right now.

Trent's tongue explored my mouth and he crawled just a little closer, pushing me back into Pax. I felt a hand move around my waist - Pax's - then up, pausing just beneath my breast. The sound of our lips, the rustling of our clothes, and the new leaves blowing in the gentle breeze were the only sounds close by. This little area was like an oasis from the world, sheltering us from sight without trapping us away.

So I grabbed Trent's hand again, lifting it even as I broke our kiss. The moment my mouth was free, I sucked at his middle finger, but my eyes held his. Behind me, Pax groaned his approval.

"If you keep that up, this will go from a date to an exhibition," he warned.

So I released Trent's hand and turned to face Pax. "There's no one out here."

He just trailed his hand up the side of my neck until he cupped my jaw. "There could be. Elena, we wanted to impress you. To show you that we're worth the trouble."

"But that's the thing you don't seem to understand," I told him. "Neither of you are trouble. You're always worth it. Pax, so far as I care, nothing's changed. I still want to hear about your adventures with the latest contractor or Trent having to crawl into a drainage culvert. I like having the chance to notice that you've all but moved in together because Gabby and I spend too much time at your place." Then I looked back at Trent. "I want to be surprised that you stopped at the office again to give me a ride home, or went out of your way to give me a ride that half-block to work because it's raining. But I also want the rest of this."

"Which 'rest'?" Pax asked.

My eyes held Trent's. "Thinking of you both naked, wrapped around me, and showing me that I'm worth desiring. The way you two work seamlessly together, and never make me worry about if you're too close, touching each other, or things like that. When I'm with you - dressed or naked - I always feel completely comfortable, even when I'm so far out of my depth."

Trent's eyes made a trail down my body. "So the fact that I keep thinking about taking you out of that dress, out here where we could get caught, isn't necessarily a bad thing?"

My nipples were so hard I could feel them grind against my bra with each breath. "Yeah, that's not bad at all."

Pax murmured his approval beside my ear, and then I felt his hand move to my back. Trent caught my face, keeping me from turning. Pax's mouth teased the skin just beneath my ear. Then he found the top of my zipper, and slowly - too slowly - eased it down.

"I want you looking at me," Pax whispered. "Kick off those shoes, slip out of this dress, but this time, it's just us."

And Trent smiled. "*Then* I'll have my turn."

He only let go of me so I could shift to my knees and pull my dress off. My shoes stayed halfway across the blanket. Then, while they both watched, I reached back for my bra. The clasp released, but Pax was shrugging off his suit coat. While I worked my panties down my legs, he slipped his tie free. Then he passed it over to Trent and reached for me.

"That's the most beautiful thing I've seen," he breathed, turning me to face him. "My mate, bare under the stars? This is perfect."

"Close," I told him as I reached for his pants.

Pax just rolled onto his knees to match me, then fumbled at his belt. After that, he made quick work of opening his pants, but he only pushed them so far down. Enough to bare himself, allowing his hard dick to spring free. My eyes dropped to it, but Pax wrapped one arm around my back and pulled me right onto his lap.

Then Trent grabbed my arms. A loop slipped around my left wrist, yet when Trent pulled it behind me, I made no move to resist. That was why Pax had handed over his tie, and I wasn't opposed to a little bondage in the woods with my mates. The moment I moved my other arm back to make it easier, a devious smile curled Pax's lips higher.

The tie was barely secure before Trent leaned in, holding me in place. That was all it took for Pax to reach down and angle himself, dragging the head of his dick across me. I sucked in a breath when he pressed against my clit, so he did it again, then again, his eyes watching my chest as my breathing came a little harder.

"Cold?" he asked.

"No," I promised, because my nipples were so damned hard, and I just wanted him to touch them.

Instead, it was Trent. Clearly, their idea of alone was a lot different than mine. I also didn't care. Trent's hands cupped the weight, his fingers pinching those hardened nubs between them before sliding across the tips. I gasped, feeling the sparks make my core throb for its own attention. Pax just dragged himself across me again.

"Oh, now you're ready," he purred. And then he found my entrance and pulled me down onto him.

I wanted to grab at him, to hold myself in place and lift myself back up. I couldn't, not with my wrists bound behind my back. I couldn't cling to his body or reach back for Trent. All I could do was feel my body stretch around my man, loving just how good he felt. My thighs gripped his, Pax's hands found my waist, and the man eased me up just enough so he could pull me back down. Slowly, taking his time about filling me again, he taught me his version of making love.

Because that was what this was. This was Pax giving me everything he had, and I could feel it. Just us. Only our bodies were connected, but Trent was still here, still a part of this, and it was somehow perfect. I let my head fall back, knowing there was a strong shoulder there to support it. While Trent toyed with my breasts and kissed the line of my shoulder, Pax pumped into me, using both his legs and arms to bring us together.

The first moan slipped out, sounding so loud in the still night air around us. As if that was more than he could take, Pax pressed his mouth against mine, kissing me like he couldn't stop himself - and I matched him. Our tongues dueled, our bodies collided, and I took it all. The feeling of being so exposed only made every touch that much sweeter - and I loved it.

This was his way of showing how badly he needed me. He wanted to look at my body, lose himself around me, and he didn't care about anything else. Not his clothes, his partner, or who might see, and neither did I. I'd made this man lose control. I'd seduced him by just being myself, and it made me feel so beautiful, and there was a power in this feeling that I'd almost forgotten.

Then he pulled his mouth away just far enough to whisper, "I really do love you. So much, Elena, that I can't think of anything else. I love you."

Then he thrust a little deeper. My back arched so I could take him, and another moan escaped. I could hear a car in the distance, but it was far away, so I didn't care. Another thrust made my legs clench. The cool breeze on my skin was like a lover's kiss, touching me everywhere and making Pax's hands feel even hotter. The next time he pulled me onto him, I felt my core tense, warning me I was close.

"Please," I whimpered. "So close."

As if that was an order, he doubled his efforts, moving faster, driving deeper. Trent's hands began to flick my nipples, and my skin slid against both of their shirts. They were both so close, so focused on me, but when I turned my hand to cup Trent, he angled his hips away from my reach. This was for me. It was their form of giving me everything, but I wasn't sure I could take any more.

My legs began to tremble. My pussy clenched, gripping Pax each time he slid into my body. I was panting around my moans of passion, and I'd stopped caring about it. I just wanted one more thrust, another little bit of friction to send me over the edge. Pax gave it, and my climax hit hard. I gasped, tensed, and shuddered around him, feeling my mate pump into me again as he lost his own control.

A groan slipped from his lips, and Trent immediately began releasing the bonds around my wrists. The moment I was free, I caught Pax's face on both sides and leaned in to kiss him the way I'd wanted. Drowning myself in him as the last grip of my orgasm let me go.

"I love you," I breathed against his lips.

"Good," Pax said, and then he pushed me back.

Trent was right there, catching my shoulders to guide me down onto the blanket. As soon as I was lying safely, he yanked open his pants, shoved them beneath his ass, and shifted between my legs. As he slid into my body, he reached for my mouth, merging us completely.

"Mine," he whispered against my lips and then he began to rock.

This time, I could hold him. My arms wrapped around his back, my legs around his ass, and we writhed together. Every time he thrust, I pressed myself just a little deeper, taking a bit more. His tongue swirled around mine. His hand turned to trail across the line of my face, but he just kept going.

My body was still sensitive, still humming from what Pax had done to me. I'd barely begun to come down from my last climax before Trent was driving me higher. Every time he rolled his hips into my body, I sucked a breath against his mouth. Each moan I let out, he swallowed. My hand found the back of his head, tangling in his hair, but that only made him work my body harder - and I loved it.

I loved them. The man buried inside me and the one putting himself back into his pants beside us. I loved that Trent lost himself in my body completely and that Pax watched us without shame. I loved the feel of their strong arms holding me against them. I loved that being near them was always filled with some kind of passion, even if it masqueraded as control. I just loved these men.

Most of all, I loved that I didn't need to be ashamed of it.

There was nothing wrong with having five mates. There was no shame for loving them all. Instead, this had become my strength. These guys reminded me that I was more than my age, more than simply a mother, and so much more than someone to do the tasks they didn't want. With them, I was a partner, someone to be respected, and the most beautiful woman in the world. The more I tried to give, the more they gave back, and it was the fantasy I'd never quite been able to put into words.

But when Trent pulled his lips from mine to gasp for breath, still working me so hard, my eyes flicked open. I felt every muscle in his body moving. I heard the soft moans of Pax's appreciation. I could taste my lover's kisses on my tongue, but my eyes saw only stars. So many pinpricks of light shining above, and it was the last thing I needed.

I turned Trent's face toward me, our eyes meeting in the darkness, and I breathed, "Mine."

His breath caught, his hips thrust into me hard, and together, we both went over the edge. My back arched as the pleasure took over, but he was right there to hold me, pressing his face against the side of my neck as he rode me through it, driving me just a little higher, and then finally groaning as he could take no more.

As the breath rushed out of his lungs, Trent whispered, "I love you too, Elena. Only you."

<u>CHAPTER 43</u>

Late Saturday night, I got a short text from Pax that simply said, "Done." He didn't need to explain. I knew exactly what he meant. It seemed my betas had managed to declare their love to our mate, and Elena returned it. I tossed my phone away with a relieved sigh and finally managed to find sleep.

The next morning, however, I started making plans. I'd never hidden my end goals from the guys, but I still checked to make sure they hadn't changed their minds. When Trent and Pax finally made it home around noon, we all got to hear about their catastrophic attempt at a date, but they both agreed that, if anything, it simply convinced them even more.

So, this was a go. Lane, of course, was thrilled with the idea. So much so that he was the one who asked Gabby to find a subtle reason to sneak over to our house. The little brat replied that it would be easy, since her mom had just laid down for a nap. He still made her promise to leave a note on the fridge in case she woke up. Not a text, though. We didn't need to risk waking her.

Less than ten minutes later, Gabby was tapping at the front door. Seth hurried to let her in. The rest of us moved into place, leaving the main chair in the living room open for her. When Seth led Gabby back, the girl eyed us with well-warranted suspicion.

"What's going on?" she asked. "This all feels very 'Mission Impossible.'"

"Sit," I told her, gesturing to the chair I usually used.

She did, and Seth moved to the floor in front of the TV. Her eyes jumped to him, aware that she'd just been given pride of place. It seemed that my little protégé had some very good instincts when it came to understanding wolf dynamics. Then again, it was part of what made her such a good alpha. She didn't just understand our ways, but also the other shifters.

"Am I in trouble?" she asked. "Ian, I promise I haven't done anything. I mean, I had no clue that Theo and Nik were, you know..."

"This is not about that," I assured her. "But, Gabby? We do have a little problem, and it's something we need your help with."

"Ok?"

I glanced back at the guys, and they all nodded, giving me the go ahead. Yet when I turned back to Gabby, my insides twisted and my fingers tingled. Nerves, I knew, but it wasn't a feeling I was used to. Still, this could be the most important moment of my life.

So I blew out a breath and just said, "We need to know how you feel about your mother getting married again."

Her eyes narrowed. "I dunno, Ian... Kinda depends on

who she'd be marrying." And her lips tensed as she fought a smile.

"Us," I admitted. "Gabby, we want your permission to ask Elena to marry us."

And the girl's face went slack. "Mine? Why?"

"Because marrying her means becoming a family with you. Because your opinion matters to her more than anything else. This relationship we have isn't just between the six of us, but you too. If we marry her, you'd have to move again, because we're honestly tired of living apart. I know it's not far from my house to yours, but when the two of you aren't here, we miss you both."

"It also means we'd legally be your stepfathers," Lane added.

"And you all want to marry her?" Gabby wagged a finger at the group of us. "Guys, I don't think it works that way."

"Legally, no," I admitted. "As the Alpha, I'd be her husband on paper. But we're wolves, so we've made our own traditions. While the government might not recognize my betas as her husbands, the pack would."

"What about *mis abuelos*?" she asked. "They'd want to come to her wedding, and that would be hard to explain!"

"Two weddings," Seth said. "The real one here, for us. Then we'd have a formal one for her family where we're just the best men. It's not actually uncommon for wolves, I've been told."

Gabby's lips finally curled again. "So, like, does that mean I'd get to call all of you my dad?"

"Hence the second part of this question," I told her. "If you're ok with us proposing to your mom, and if she says yes, then Henry says he could file paperwork for me to legally adopt you. I'm not sure if that's what you want, though, because it would mean changing your name."

"To what?" she asked.

Pax chuckled. "Gabriella Sofia Langdon. The heir to the Langdon empire. Ian's legal daughter, and the next Alpha of Wolf's Run."

The girl pressed her hand to her mouth and her eyes jumped back to me. "Really? You want me to be your daughter?"

"I do," I admitted. "And Ashley your aunt, and my dad would be your Grandfather - not *abuelo*. Not convinced he could actually say that."

"Grampa," Gabby decided. "That would fit him better."

"So?" I asked. "Does that mean we get to have permission?"

And the little heathen grinned, shifting in her chair to face me as she crossed her arms. "I dunno, we might have to come to terms. Where will we move to?"

"I was thinking here," I admitted. "Then, in about three years, you and your betas could move into the little house next door."

She slowly nodded. "Rooms?"

"You can have mine," Trent told her. "Right beside the bathroom upstairs."

"And Mom's?"

Lane chuckled. "I was thinking about having her share mine."

Gabby made a face. "Guys, this is going to be weird, isn't it? I mean, you could just give me the downstairs room, and then all of you'd have the second floor."

"Not happening," Trent laughed. "You've already

proven that you like to take little trips outside at night. So, no."

She just sighed. "Well, it was worth a try." But the smile still hadn't left her face. "And yes, you can all ask my mom to marry you, but I'm not going to be the flower girl. Just don't even think it."

"Ring bearer?" Seth suggested.

She scrunched up her face and shook her head. "Nope."

"Well, what do you want?" Pax asked.

"I think we should let Mom pick, but I'm definitely the daughter of the bride. And you guys know she'll say yes, right?" Gabby stabbed a finger at Trent. "I heard you three giggling when you came in last night. My mom doesn't giggle, guys. She never did before she met all of you, and now she's so happy that she has to say yes, but you can't divorce her. You can't ignore her like my dad used to. If you're going to be a part of my family, then you *all* have to love her. Like, really love her, ok? Because Mom is the best person in the whole world, and I know you need her as much as we need you."

"I promise, Gabby," Lane said. "I need her too, and I need these guys, so it all works out."

"And no kids!"

Seth lost it, turning his head away even as he failed to smother his laughter. "How about one?"

"No!" she insisted. "I'm fifteen. I don't need to wake up to a baby in the house, and that's just gross, ok? No kids, guys."

"I was thinking you," Seth admitted. "Just you, Gabby."

She tilted her head a bit as she realized what he meant. "Yeah?"

He nodded. "Never wanted kids," he admitted. "Not

really a fan of babies. You, though? I can hang with you. I mean, I could probably even get used to getting called Dad or something, but I'll probably get all embarrassed."

"I want something cooler," Pax decided. "I dunno, like Big Daddy."

"Gross," Gabby told him. "Not happening."

He just laughed, making it clear he hadn't been serious. "Gabby, so far as I care, you can call all of us your uncles. Would probably make it easier at school."

"No," Lane said. "I don't want to be an uncle."

"She'll figure it out on her own," I told him. "It's not like there's a switch that flips, and all of you still call Dad Henry. So maybe she doesn't give you personal names. Do you honestly care?"

Lane just sighed, clearly wanting to say yes but knowing better. "She's my pup too, Ian."

"I know, Lane, but she has a few opinions of her own. Elena hasn't even said yes." I turned back to Gabby. "Are you willing to help when it's time? We might need a little interference to make sure she doesn't run off just when we have our big plan ready."

She nodded. "I'm in. Also, Mom says diamonds are boring. She never really liked her last wedding ring, either. It was too big and always got caught in her hair. She didn't complain, but sometimes she'd just huff, you know? And I can't count how many times she'd pick a hair from it, but Gerardo wanted to make sure she had this big rock that he could show off. It was like she was his little trophy, you know? And I was supposed to be the little doll, but it didn't work."

I just sighed. "Gabby, I'm sorry, but I hate that man a little. I know he's your father, but - "

"He's not," she told me. "Remember, he signed the papers."

"I meant biologically," I explained. "But as far as I'm concerned, the only good thing he's ever done?" And I pointed at her. "So, any advice for what kind of ring we should look for?"

She immediately pulled out her phone, crossed her legs under her, and began to search. "Yeah, we've talked about it. I mean, in general type of talk, not like, about you guys or anything. How are you going to ask her?"

"No idea," Trent grumbled. "We kinda thought we'd get a ring first, then go from there."

"Well, she'll want something to remember, but nothing too fancy. Don't corner her in public, because she told me that sucks. Everyone's looking at you, and then you feel like you have to say yes, and you always wonder what you would've done if you'd been alone."

"Because that's what Gerardo did," I realized.

She nodded. "Big family dinner, and he popped the question at the table. Oh, and it was *his* family. The same ones who have now forgotten that I ever existed. I mean, except my cousin, but you know how it goes." Then she paused. "I have a question."

"Ok?" I asked, bracing for the worst.

"Well, we can't wear rings when we shift, and I haven't seen a lot of men in the pack wearing them. David, but he only started shifting when Mom did. So... How does that work?"

"She can wear the ring or not," I explained. "Ideally, she can wear it at work, so any of our new applicants know she's off limits."

"But you won't wear a ring?" she asked.

I just ducked my head. "First, I would never expect her to buy five different wedding rings, so it's more of a practicality. Second, I would if she asked. See, Gabby, that's the thing. I would do pretty much anything if she asked. We all feel the same way."

"But if you don't get a ring," she pressed, "then how do the women who come in know you're all taken?"

"You have an idea," Pax realized.

Gabby grinned. "Have you seen the silicone ones? They're safe to work in, and they stretch, so they'd work if you shifted, right? Lev said that's what he and Nik's mom had. Wasn't comfortable as a tiger, but if they forgot, they didn't lose a finger."

"You think I need to get your mom a cheap, stretchy ring?" I asked.

She rolled her eyes. "No. Mom needs a nice one. She's human enough to want it. I'm saying that she should get all of you one. Would that work? And then you would be visibly married when some lady moves in next door and checks you out in the garage."

"What?" Seth asked, leaning forward. "Oh, I didn't know about this."

"I mean..." Her words turned to a mumble. "I may have said something first, and Mom tried to make me be polite, but she was looking too."

"Please don't ever check me out again," Seth teased. "We can pretend like that never happened, right?"

"I was just looking at your tattoo," she insisted. "I mean, because I was a stupid human back then. That's my excuse, and you can use it."

"Deal," he said.

Then Gabby held up her phone. "And this is the kind

of thing she likes. Personally, I think you should get a yellow stone. You know, like our eyes. Plus, she has skinny fingers, so nothing too big. And if you need help, I've totally got your backs."

I eyed the picture she was holding up and just nodded. "Pretty sure we can make that happen. Thanks, Gabby."

"No problem, Dad."

My heart stalled out first, but immediately swelled, and I looked up to see if she was joking. She wasn't. My pup had just called me Dad, and I was pretty sure it was the best feeling ever.

CHAPTER 44

Monday, Ashley helped us out. She told Elena that she needed some womanly advice and headed home with her. Elena texted me to say she'd take care of her own dinner tonight due to some best friend time. Gabby was heading to Olivia's to help her still-healing beta and check on Theo. In other words, the five of us had a few hours to sneak out and not even be noticed.

I texted Ian. He let the rest of the betas know. Then, as soon as the coast was clear, we piled into Ian's SUV and headed into town. Everyone had some idea about the rings we should get, but they'd forgotten the most important thing.

"The jewelers are humans," I reminded them. "They think marriage is a one man, one woman type of thing."

"It's not that bad," Seth insisted. "Men marry each other now, and women, and poly is a thing. I'm pretty sure the sales clerks at some jewelry store have pretty much seen it all."

"They also won't be upset if they get a commission," Trent pointed out.

"Not hiding this," Pax said. "The fact that we have to be just the roommates or friends for the rest of our lives is bad enough."

Ian was noticeably silent, so I turned my attention to him. "Thoughts?"

"Not really," Ian said. "I'm the one who gets to claim her when the rest of you can't, so I think this is one time that I don't exactly get a say. I also happen to know that Elena was only worried about what Gabby would think and making things hard on her daughter at school or such. So, if we call her our wife, I'm just fine with that."

I felt a smile slowly growing on my face. "Not yours, huh?"

"Lane, she was yours first. We all know that." He glanced over and then back to the road. "You're the one fated to be with her. If you wanted to be the legal husband, I could actually go with that. I'd hate it, and I'd be as jealous as Trent, Pax, and Seth are, but I also know that my love for her will never trump your need."

"Nah," I decided. "It's easier if she marries you, but thanks for saying it."

Because he didn't have to. Ian was the Pack Alpha. By our rules, she was his mate, not mine. I just got the side benefits. The simple fact that he openly called her ours was pushing the boundaries of a traditional mating more than any of us wanted to admit, but the pack accepted it. Granted, they could also see that she was all of ours. This wasn't a case of scratching an itch when the Alpha was away. This thing we all had was real.

It was more than friends, more than Ian simply making sure his betas were taken care of - or his mate. This relationship we had was the epitome of why we all worked so well together. When Ian said that what was his was ours, he meant it. Not to show us up or remind us of his dominance. He truly believed that he owed us that much, and we felt the same way right back.

Then Seth had to ruin the little glow I had going on. "So, are we going to be like, co-husbands or something?"

"No," Trent said before anyone else could react. "I'm not your husband, man."

"Oh, but you'd be Pax's?" Seth leaned over to slap his arm. "I see how it is. You love me less."

"Guys," Ian begged.

But they didn't care. "Co-mates is just as bad," Pax said. "And no, I'm not mating you or Trent, Seth."

"Partners sounds like we're gay," I pointed out. "Before you say it, I'm not gay."

"Guys," Ian said again. "We're all her mates. She's our mate. You're my betas. I'm your alpha. That's it. You don't need some title for this."

"What if we want one?" Trent asked. "You know, because introducing Lane as my mate's mate is going to be a mouthful."

"Another beta?" Ian suggested. "How do you usually introduce him?"

"Uh, as Lane," Trent admitted.

"There you go." He slowed the truck and turned into a shopping center. "Now, try not to embarrass me today? I already have one kid."

"Asshole," I grumbled.

Although the truth was that I was happy for him. Gabby calling him "Dad" had been something he'd needed. I wanted her to feel the same way about me, but he had a point. I still called Henry by his name. I'd never wanted to replace my own parents, so while I felt like Henry had been a father to me for most of my life, he was still Henry.

It wasn't the word that mattered to me so much as having Gabby feel like I was someone she could run to when she needed help. Any kind of help. To pick a shirt for a date, make a boy leave her alone, or if someone tried to attack her. I was going to be the man who made her feel safe, and if I did it good enough, then one day, she'd start to say my name in a little different tone, and that would honestly be enough.

But first, we had to get Elena to agree to marry us. Granted, when the five of us walked into the quiet little jewelry store, three different salespeople looked up. A girl to the right was faster than the others, though.

"Can I help you, gentlemen?" she asked.

"We're looking for a wedding ring," Ian said.

She smiled. "We have a selection of women's rings over here, and beside them are the men's." And she moved to the area she'd just indicated until the glass case was before her. "So, who's the lucky man?"

"We all are," Pax told her.

"So, you're having a group ceremony?"

"One wife," I said. "Five husbands."

"Poly thing," Seth added.

The poor girl's cheeks were getting a little brighter, but she nodded. "Lucky her. So, did you have something in mind that you were looking for?"

Just like that, the biggest hurdle was handled. Oh, I knew Pax had pushed the issue just so he wouldn't get left out, but I actually agreed with him on this. I didn't want to remember buying Elena's ring as a moment when we'd all been forced to keep our mouths shut, and I also didn't care what this girl thought about me.

"You have any yellow stones?" I asked. "Topaz, diamonds, don't care. She likes yellow, though."

"Amber," Trent corrected.

"We have a collection of yellow diamonds, since colored gems are so popular right now." And she pulled out a tray with fake, velvet fingers on it. That she set on the glass before us.

"She doesn't like diamonds," Seth reminded us.

"Needs something to remind her of us," Ian said. "I like that color." He pointed to another ring in the case.

"That's a blue topaz," the girl told him. "So you know, our jeweler can replace the stones with something else. There's a fee for that, but often the cost of the stones traded out makes up for it. Do you know her size?"

"Seven and a quarter," Ian said.

"How?" I asked. "When did you figure that out?"

"Ashley asked for us. I have no idea how, and it sounds like she did it a while ago."

"Another partner?" the girl asked.

"My sister," Ian corrected. "Her best friend. She says she wants Elena to be her legal sister, so she's been helping."

"Oh, so a surprise proposal?" the girl asked.

I listened to the guys explain to her about how they had her daughter's approval, and that while yes, this was a surprise proposal, it wouldn't be too big of a shock. The salesgirl was smiling at the story as if daydreaming, but my eyes were scanning the available rings. I wanted this to be perfect. I liked the colors Ian had picked, but not the setting. That one had a really sharp stone that was set very high.

Gabby had mentioned Elena hating getting the previous one caught in her hair, so she would need a lower setting. Then it sounded like my mate would never take her ring off if she could help it. She'd wear it in the shower, on her days off, and even in bed - with us. I wanted it to be so comfortable that she didn't have to think about it. That she could simply accept this the same way she'd accepted all of us.

Then Seth knelt down beside me. "What about that one?" he asked.

"No, that one," I said, crouching beside him. "A yellow stone in the middle of the engagement ring, and the conforming band can have a single diamond for Ian and four of those blue topazes for us."

"Alternating," Ian countered. "Topaz, diamond, topaz, and so on. There are five of the little diamonds in it now, right?"

"Yeah," I told him. "And it's not too much - the band looks delicate enough for her hands, but thick enough that she wouldn't snag it."

The other guys moved to look, all of us crowding over each other, and the salesgirl lifted it out. "You guys are cute, you know that? I should warn you, though. This is one of our more expensive options..."

"Don't care," Ian said.

So she placed it on the glass between us. "It's a

beautiful ring, but be aware that it will take a week to ten days to reset the stones with the colors you want."

"That's fine," Ian promised, lifting it up. "Pax? Can I borrow your hand?"

"Not marrying you," Pax joked, but he offered his hand.

Ian just pushed the ring onto the first knuckle of Pax's index finger. "Your skin tone's the closest to hers. What do you guys think?" And he looked right at me.

"We need one of the diamonds that's actually yellow. Not the faded, but the bright color."

Ian nodded. "Like her amber eyes."

"This color for the blue ones," Trent said, pointing at another ring. "More turquoise than blue. It would look better with her skin, right?"

Pax just looked over at the girl. "Can we engrave the inside?"

She nodded. "Yep. That's common with our wedding bands. With that ring, there's not a lot of room, though. It would need to be a short phrase."

"Just want two alpha symbols and four beta. The alphas in the center."

"Nice," Trent said.

The poor salesgirl was looking between us as if lost. "Personal meaning, right?

"It is," I assured her, then turned to the guys. "What do you think? Is this the one?"

The problem was that they all just looked back at me. "I like it," Ian said.

"My taste sucks," Seth pointed out.

Trent and Pax were both nodding. "If you're happy with it, Lane, then we are. Is this the one she needs?"

I looked at the ring still on Pax's finger. It felt right to me. I could almost envision it on her hand. With the colored stones, it would be just enough to draw the eye - not too much, though - and it had meaning. Those five little diamonds were what had caught my attention. Five of us. The stone in the middle was one of her, elegant, perfect, and beautiful.

"I think that's it," I finally said. "Guess we didn't need all day to make this happen, huh?"

"When it's right, it's right," Ian said as he turned to the salesgirl. "Now, what do we need to do to make all those changes? And I want the yellow diamond in the middle to be just the right color."

"We have a chart for that," she assured him, holding out her hand for the ring. "Now, if the group of you will head down here with me, we can customize this to be everything your fiancé needs. If you'd like, I can get you the forms to fill out for financing while we're at it."

"No, we're good," Ian promised. "This is the only wedding ring we're ever going to buy, so we got this."

"Lucky lady," the girl joked.

But all I could think was that we were the ones who were lucky. Now, we just had to convince her to say yes. She loved us, and we all loved her. Somehow, we had to make it clear that for us, that meant forever, and this was going to be the perfect ring to do so.

<u>CHAPTER 45</u>

The guys surprised me on Tuesday with lunch. Not just one or two of them like usual. This time, it was the entire group. Ian ordered pizza, and we all took over the breakroom. When Ashley saw, she looked a little disappointed, and I had a funny feeling why.

"Lunch date?" I teased when she immediately turned to leave.

Ashley paused and stepped back. "Not anymore."

"Go," I said. "Or tell them to come here. Either way. I'll listen for the door."

She just sighed, letting her head drop. "Elena, your boyfriends are a little intimidating."

"To yours?" Ian teased.

Ashley just thrust an arm out at him. "See?"

I waved Ian to silence. "That's not intimidating, Ash. That's him being an annoying little brother. Tell whichever guy or guys this is to bring you lunch. I promise that I'll keep my mates in line. Because..." And I looked at the guys. "If they aren't nice to my best friend's crush, I would be heartbroken - and then Lane would have to kill you."

Lane just chuckled. "I would, too."

"Fine!" Ian said. "Tell the bear of the day that I'll be nice." But he couldn't help himself. He turned to his sister with a smile. "So, Goldilocks? One is too big, one is too small, so which one is just right?"

She lifted her middle finger. "Bears are hung better than wolves. Be nice or I'll tell Elena exactly why we don't screw in our other bodies." And she shifted her hand so her thumb and index finger were only two inches apart. "Dog dicks."

"So, if they get all flustered, do they hump the air too?" I asked.

"Bye, Ashley," Pax said, leaning back to shut the door.

"Do you?" I asked.

Seth tittered. Immediately, the group all looked at him. "What?" he asked. "I didn't say anything."

"We don't talk about this," Lane told him.

And now I was very curious. "Which part?" I asked. "And which one of you did it?"

"Wasn't me," Seth promised.

"Don't blame us," Trent said.

Ian just took a very large bite of pizza, but not a single one of them would look at Lane, so I did. He ducked his head, but I just waited. Then his cheeks began to get red. At the other end of the table, Pax stood.

"Drink?" he offered, clearly trying to change the subject.

"But I almost had him!" I groaned.

"Trust me, you didn't," Ian promised. "Besides, what happened as kids, stays as kids, right, Lane?"

"We will never speak of this again," he grumbled.

At this point, I didn't even care what he'd done. Watching the five of them cover for him so smoothly? It was actually sort of adorable. It also proved that they all knew - including Seth, who hadn't even been there. Oddly, that made it even cuter somehow. When people said that boys would be boys, this was what they should be talking about.

But of course, the lobby door had to choose that moment to chime. With a sigh, I pushed back my food and stood.

"It's probably just Ashley's date," Lane said.

"I promised to check," I reminded him as I headed for the door.

When I peeked out, I saw a woman hugging her arms to her chest. Unlike most of our clients, she wore raggedy jeans and a very tired jacket over an oversized tee. I paused, lifted a finger to the guys, and then headed up the hall to greet her.

"Hi," I said politely. "Welcome to Wolf's Run. Can I help you?"

Her head snapped up and she looked at me with honey-colored eyes. "Are you her?"

"Which her?" I countered. "I'm Elena."

"The Alpha bitch," she said, huddled into herself like she was terrified. "She's the one I'm supposed to talk to, so get her."

"I'm her," I promised. "The Pack Alpha mate. Are you ok? Come, sit down."

She just shook her head. "I can't. I'm supposed to deliver a message."

"From who?" Ian asked as he moved behind me. "And so you know, I'm her mate."

The girl swallowed. "Damon says he's still waiting. He demands his reparations or he's taking your pack. Pay up or suffer the consequences."

A grumble proved that we weren't alone. Glancing back, I saw Lane in the hall, looking like he was ready to rip this poor girl apart. I just gestured for him to stay and moved closer.

"I get the impression you don't want to be here," I told her. "It's ok. We don't hurt the messenger. C'mon, just sit down, and I'm sure we can find a way to help."

Her eyes jumped to Ian, then behind me. "Your pack killed Charlotte! Tore her throat out and tossed her into the woods!"

"The woman who tried to attack Samantha," Ian realized. "And the man who did that didn't want to. He gave her every chance to run, but she wouldn't."

"We can't!" the girl snapped.

"Ok," I said, soothing her as much as I could. "I get that. We're also not going to hurt you. What's your name, anyway?"

"Evelyn," she mumbled.

And the girl couldn't have been more than twenty-three. She looked younger than Sheridan, in my opinion, but I was just guessing at that. Her hair was just a little dirty, her clothes looked ready to fall apart at the seams, and she trembled. No matter who had sent her, this young lady needed help, and I was going to give it.

"Sit down, Evelyn," I said as I caught her shoulders.

She flinched, huddling into herself even more, if that was possible. "Damon said you'd kill anyone who stepped foot into this territory. He said that's why we need an army."

"And you're safe now," I promised, guiding her into the closest chair.

"Elena..." Ian warned.

I just looked back at him. "This girl is scared. She's not much older than some of our pups, so don't you 'Elena' me. Whatever she has to say can wait until she knows we're not going to hurt her."

"And when she tries to attack you?" he asked.

"Then I'll get out of Lane's way," I promised. "Back off, Ian. If you want to help, brew her one of those cups of hot chocolate."

"Yes, Alpha," he said, moving to do just that.

Evelyn's eyes went wide. "I thought he was the pack leader?"

"He is, but a smart man knows when his mate has been pushed too far." I took the chair beside her and leaned closer to gently rub her shoulder. "Why did Damon make you come here if he said we'd hurt you?"

She moved her hands to her lap and clasped one over the other. "I'm his least favorite mate. He said I could be replaced."

"And you still came?" I asked.

She nodded. "He has my baby. Our baby. Said that if I don't come back, he'll give him to Karen."

Pax just growled, turning away to slap his palm against the wall. "Pax!" I snapped when the girl flinched.

"Sorry," he told me. "I just hate that bitch."

"But she's from the old families," Evelyn reminded him. "We have to respect that."

He tapped his own chest. "Romero." Then he pointed at Lane. "Blackwood." Trent was next. "Powell." And finally to Ian. "Langdon. Honey, old lines are running around this place and baring our throats to Castillos."

And then the door chimed again. Ashley stepped in with Scott right behind her, but they both paused at the sight of us. The girl whimpered, making both look at her.

"Shit," Ashley breathed. "Where are you from?"

"Hidden Forest," I answered for her. "One of Damon's mates, sent to give us a message."

"Here," Ian said, passing the little paper cup to Scott. "Maybe you'll be less terrifying to her than I am."

Scott took it, but only moved close enough to hand it to Ashley. Immediately, the girl began pushing back, trying to get away from him. "Bear?" she asked.

"A little bear," he promised. "Sweetheart, there are enough wolves in this room to make me run if I tried anything wrong. Not gonna hurt you. I'm actually kinda fond of wolves."

"Uh..." Trent just flicked a finger at her. "She's with the pack that jumped the kids the other night."

"Yeah, that kinda changes things," Scott admitted. "Why did you people go after our pups anyway?"

"We didn't!" she said. "Damon sent us to leave a message. Thanks to all of you, our pack is suffering. Our members are being hunted by humans. People are suddenly very interested in wolves now - because of your children! Damon says we have to stop you before our kids are the ones paying for it. He knows where they go to school now, thanks to that little stunt." She finally opened her hand. "And we can fight fire with fire."

On her palm lay a class ring. A boy's. I held out my hand, silently asking if she'd let me see it, and she passed it over. A quick look proved that it belonged to Gabby's high school. The graduation date on it was for this year. The symbols on the side were the school mascot and a football player.

"Whose is this?" I asked.

"The more of us who die, the more of us we have to make," she said, pausing to sip her cocoa. "Damon said that if we want to stop living like animals, then we have to take what we deserve."

"You know he's lying, right?" I asked. "Evelyn, if you want to do better, all you have to do is leave your pack and come here."

"Oh, and you'd give some nobody like me a home?"

"They gave one to me," Scott pointed out. "I'm not even a wolf."

"Damon knows you have bears. He said he knows how to kill them, too." She licked her lips. "And lions."

"Tigers, actually," I corrected. "I don't know what Damon's told you, but this place? We're making it safe for our kind. A home, Evelyn, but also a fortress. So when you talk to Damon, you let him know that we're not worried. We're also not going to let him threaten us. But..." I caught her hand. "If he tries to hurt you or your baby, you run here. When they ask at the gate, you tell them to call me. Me, not anyone else, and I don't care what time it is. If you ever want out, I will help you, but I can't do it *for* you. See, that's what Damon wants. He thinks he can bully and abuse his way to success instead of actually working for it. We can't help him. Even if we paid the money he's asking, you wouldn't see a dime of it. He'd either take it and run, or he'd spend it all on himself and then try to threaten us again."

"But what are we supposed to do?" she asked. "He's taking mates instead of betas. He's named Karen as his second in command. She's the Alpha Female, and I don't even know what that makes us."

"So leave him," I said, braced for her to make the same rebuttal as most women in her situation - that she loved him, or how he was the father of her child.

Instead, she lifted her chin. "I can't. We weren't asked our opinion. Damon claims every female over eighteen first, and discards the ones he doesn't like. Those are given to the best fighters. Being Damon's mate is safer, and it's not like we have anywhere else to go. Our families think we're dead. That's why Charlotte fought, don't you see? She had to, because if she came home wounded, he would've given her to the other converts to work out their new instincts."

"Shit," Ashley breathed. "Oh, girl... You can't go back there."

"He has her kid," I told her. "She has to. He sent her here to deliver his message but made sure she would have a reason to return." Then I looked at her. "So you give him a message from me. Let him know that if he touches my pups or any member of my pack, it will be the last thing he does. He already ran from my shoe. I promise that my teeth are much worse."

"You were supposed to be human," she told me.

I smiled. "Well, I'm not. A lot has changed since Karen

436

was here, and she didn't exactly have the inside scoop even then."

"But you won't be able to stop us," she said. "Elena, you seem really nice, but you don't know what you're doing. Just pay the money, ok? He wants to see Wolf's Run burn. He hopes that we'll get exposed in the process and that humans will come after you next. He wants to make the Langdons pay for what they've done to him, and he's not going to stop until it happens."

"And we aren't going to just roll over, because he'll only come at us again," I reminded her. "His threats won't work because he's already proven what kind of man he is. If we want to take care of our pack, we have to tell him no."

"There are more of us than you," she breathed.

"Can't be," Ian said. "His pack was no more than twenty people."

"Not anymore." She sucked back the last of her cocoa and offered me the empty cup. "I have to go back, but were you serious? I mean, about coming here?"

I nodded. "I am. No mother should ever have to choose between protecting her child and herself. That's the whole reason to have a pack, right? If yours isn't doing that, then it sounds like the wrong pack."

She pressed her hand over my arm. "Thank you. You're the nicest Alpha I've ever met. Damon says that means weak, but I think he's wrong."

"He is," Ian told her. "Good luck, Evelyn."

"Thanks. I think I'm going to need it."

She was barely through the door before I let out a rush of breath and just shook my head. "What the fuck?"

"You told her too much," Seth said gently, moving to sit beside me. "Elena, you don't have to share everything."

"I only told her we don't have lions, we have tigers," I countered. "Not how many. Not that they were all we have. I convinced her that we're not the bad guys, but we are the strong ones. If you don't think she's going to tell her friends about this?"

"She's got a point," Ashley admitted. "And if Karen didn't know about the other shifters or that Elena's a wolf, then he'll doubt the rest of her knowledge."

Lane just leaned his shoulder against the wall and smiled at me. "See. Told you you're strong. I think that today you just made an enemy into a friend. Nice job, Alpha."

"Yeah, but I'm more worried about something else she said. He knows where our pups go to school, Lane." And I held up the ring. "This came from someone, and it had better not be one of ours. I need to call Gabby."

CHAPTER 46

I got ahold of Gabby between classes. She promised that everyone from Wolf's Run was at school. No one was missing, and she'd seen all of them recently, but she promised to text just to be sure. When she asked why, I told her that Damon had made a threat and I just wanted them all to be very careful. In response, Gabby assured me that they'd put the buddy system back into effect.

So who did the ring belong to? I spent the rest of the day trying to figure it out. Sadly, Evelyn's visit ruined my lunch date with my mates - and Ashley's - but I was starting to get used to that. The guys headed out to double-check the community perimeter. Scott promised that he'd have the other bears grab a few things from their job just in case we needed to do any repairs. Just to be safe, I also called Bridget and gave her a head's up. She immediately put in an order for more first aid medication and supplies.

In her office, Ashley was doing her own last-minute checks. She called her father to double-check on the status of the company. She also ordered emergency supplies, including a fire extinguisher for both the office and the guard shack for the front gates. I managed to talk her out of buying the guards a bulletproof vest, though, since teeth were more likely to be an issue.

The problem was that we really had no idea what to do, so we were completely winging it. It didn't take a genius to figure out that Damon would try to ambush us somehow. After all, he'd already done it once. But when that didn't work, what would come next? In my head, I had visions of some medieval siege with his pack parked outside the walls trying to smoke us out. I knew it wouldn't work that way, but that was sure what this felt like.

So, when we got off work, I decided it was time for a pack council meeting. First, I sent a text to Ian, but the idea of a council baffled him. He was the Alpha. This was supposed to be his responsibility. I countered with the simple fact that a few more minds never hurt, and he agreed. Then I invited everyone else who'd been helping so far - including Gabby and her betas.

So, an hour after I got off work, we headed next door. The street was already lined with cars, and quite a few of them were parked in front of my place. When we walked in, Ian's house was a lot more full than I'd expected. I saw Roman and Kim around the corner. Lane and Seth were in the living room talking to Henry and Vic. Jax and Lev were in the kitchen helping Trent with something. Bridget, Scott, and Ashley were out back with someone else, and it took a moment to recognize Jesse. Then there were the kids.

Teenagers were everywhere, but Gabby quickly rounded them up and sent her betas to the den. I even saw Samantha in the group, which meant this was truly an all hands on deck situation. I paused for just a moment to be a little proud of myself, but was startled out of it by a pair of arms wrapping around my waist.

"The council was a good idea," Ian said beside my ear. "It also means I'm going to need a bigger table, so we're eating outside tonight."

I turned in his arms to face him. "You cooked for this herd again?"

"Providing for my pack," he teased, reaching up to tap my nose. "So, I filled everyone in on what happened except Gabby. I'm assuming you told her?"

"I did," I assured him. "I'm just not convinced I should drag her into this. Ian, she's only fifteen!"

"And my heir," he reminded me. "Elena, we both know that she's not going to hide safely at home if anything happens to her pack. She might say she will, but she'll just slip out the back and keep trying to save the world. At her age, she thinks she's invincible. So, how about we put her in charge of something that will keep her out of the way?"

"Like what?" I asked.

"I don't know yet, but something she'll find important that's a lot less dangerous," he said. "I mean, did you know that Theo wants to be a doctor? Maybe we can make them stock medication or something? First aid?"

"Wait, Theo wants to be a doctor?" I hadn't heard that.

Ian nodded. "He's always planned to do neurosurgery, he said, but he's starting to think that maybe general practice is a better idea after seeing what Bridget does for us. She's even offered to give him a letter of recommendation." He smiled. "And, since he's a tiger, he won't have pack withdrawal while he's in school."

"And Nik?" I asked.

Ian leaned a little closer. "Caught him watching Roman earlier. Funny thing, so did Roman. I think Gabby's got quite the little mess on her hands, and the truth is that I have no idea how to make that easier. But Sam? She's going to college too, and she's close friends with Theo."

"Do you think they'll last through the separation?" I asked. "Most kids grow apart."

"Most kids aren't like us," he countered. "See, I realized something. This pack? It doesn't work because we're wolves. It works because we're humans - at least a bit. It works because we all want a community, and regardless of what kind of beast we become, that human desire to have a safety net is still there. So, let's make Wolf's Run that place. A sanctuary for girls like Evelyn, bears with no trees, and tigers trying to raise foxes. Who knows, maybe we can add in some lions to our tigers and bears, right?"

I laughed at the *Wizard of Oz* reference. "I think that's a great idea, Ian, but first, we have to find a way to make Damon leave us alone."

"Yeah, and you're not going to like my idea."

"Remember what you promised me?" I asked.

He nodded. "I do. If I'm going to lose, I will run first, and trust Lane to get you and the rest out. But, if I challenge him for *his* pack and lose, I don't forfeit *my* pack, I simply don't win his. If I do win, he's gone and no longer a problem."

My heart paused. "You can't do that."

"I can," he countered. "I'm not saying I will. I'm simply saying that it needs to be on the table. Our agreement still holds, though. If I lose, I run. My pride will heal. The only downside is that it means he'll come right for us."

I just tipped my head to the side. "What about Ashley?"

"Huh?" He clearly wasn't following.

"You always say she's the strongest wolf you've ever seen, right? Everyone talks about her like she's unstoppable. Could she beat Damon? If you lost, could she challenge him and then win? Would she be allowed to give the pack back to you?"

He huffed out a laugh. "Yeah, actually. That just might work."

Then a sharp whistle pierced the air. "Food's done!" Pax bellowed. "Table's outside, pick a chair. No rank, no worries. Just sit down beside who you want, because we're going to be at this a while." Then he tilted his head and looked into the den. "Hey, pup? There's a blue cooler by the fridge for the under twenty-one crowd."

Gabby groaned as she tromped out of the den and into sight. "Practicing the dad jokes?"

"Hey, I gotta start somewhere," Pax joked.

I couldn't get the smile off my face, so Ian turned me to the backdoor and guided me forward. "You know," he said, "she called me Dad the other day. I'm not sure if she was joking or not, but I kinda like it. You ok with that?"

"I am," I promised. "I also told her that it was between her and the five of you. So, congratulations, I suppose? You have a bouncing teenaged girl."

He laughed, leading me to a chair in the middle of the table, on the same side as the hot tub. Lane took the chair on my other side. Like always, Seth sat beside him, then Trent and Pax took the chairs beside Ian. Henry took the spot at the head of the table. Ashley claimed the foot with Scott and Jax on her right, then Vic and Lev on her left. Bridget was down by Henry, but the kids were spread in the middle across from me. Gabby had taken the chair that faced Ian, actually.

"I'd like to call this meeting to order," Seth said as he gestured to the dishes before us. "Food is free for the taking. There's a red cooler over there with alcohol, and a blue one with soda and bottled drinks. Now, we eat while we plot."

"Where's the ring?" Ashley asked as she leaned over to fill her plate.

Ian took mine and did the same. "You have it, Elena?"

So I pulled the thing from my pocket and placed it on the table. "I do."

But Gabby's face looked confused. "What ring, Mom?"

"The girl who showed up had a class ring from your school," I said. "We were afraid it may have been one of our kids."

She just thrust her hand across the table. "Can I see?"

So I let her. She looked at it the same way I had, then offered it to Roman. His brow furrowed, and he turned it to look inside, then passed it down to Samantha. She just shook her head before showing Olivia. When they were done, the kids passed it the other way. But when it reached Theo, I knew he recognized it.

"That's Jonah Sims," he said. "The number on the inside? It's the one on his jersey."

"The guy that's missing?" Olivia asked.

Theo nodded. "I think so."

"What guy that's missing?" I asked.

"The one who supposedly ran away," Roman told me. "You asked me about it at Gabby's play."

Crap, I remembered that. "Ok, so why did Damon's mate have it?"

"What if Mason wasn't the only one who believes in werewolves?" Samantha asked. "Maybe my video didn't convince everyone?"

"No," Xander assured her. "Sam, no one believes we're real. It's how we get away with this."

"Wait," Gabby said. "Damon had this. The boy's missing. What if the Hidden Forest pack killed him? Was Jonah a hunter?" She looked at Theo.

"I don't know," he said. "I looked at his ass while he was working out. You've reached the extent of my knowledge."

"Have a thing for checking out strange guys' asses?" Nik teased.

"Not at the table," Lev said before Theo could even reply. "Manners, boys."

But the pair shared a grin. Unfortunately, their cuteness did nothing to help solve the problem. We now had a class ring that had belonged to a human who was probably dead by now. Besides the implications that would cause with the police, it still didn't explain why Damon was using this as some kind of a threat for us. Unless...

"Did he hang out with any of the wolves?" I asked. "Maybe date one of the girls?"

They all shared a look. "Don't think so," Gabby said. "We mostly stick together. I mean, I kinda knew Sam before I was a wolf, and Theo was an accident. The rest of the time, it's really just us."

There went that idea. "So what's he planning?" I asked.

"She kept talking about an army," Ashley said. "Sounds like Damon took over some other pack, increasing the size of his."

"Where?" Gabby asked. "I mean, Wolf's Run has the community. Wouldn't a big pack be noticed in a normal neighborhood?"

"It's a mobile home park," Ian told her. "Paradise View, or something equally as bland. The landlord doesn't care so long as the rent gets paid, and the more wolves who move in, the louder it gets, and the more likely everyone else is to move out. Packs traditionally pick places that are more transient. Not the kind where people own their homes and rent the lots, but where the whole thing is just one low-cost rental that no one cares about."

"Like some kind of meth lab sorta place?" Sam asked.

He nodded. "Cops raid looking for drugs, find nothing, and think we're just a bunch of redneck freaks."

"But..." She gestured to Ian. "You're not really very redneck."

"The more generations a family has," Henry told her, "the more we know what to prepare for. Converts have it the hardest. Often, they lose their career, their social groups, and even their families. Then, they start all over from the bottom, but the government doesn't know anything has changed. So you're still buried under student loans but unable to work in an office because the fluorescent lights whine and you can't stand it - as an example."

"But your family's been wolves for a long time, so you're a little more settled?" she asked.

Henry nodded. "Exactly. And then we encourage our

kids into careers that benefit the whole, and that compounds for the next generation and the one after that. Wolf's Run has been a pack since the eighteen hundreds, Samantha. We Langdons were wolves even before that, but our pack had a different name. Youngest child, and all that."

"Wow," she breathed. "So, Damon's a convert?"

"First generation wolf," he corrected. "But a wolf in the wrong pack won't settle. Can't have a life if you're always moving to avoid being caught. Hard to get a job if you're never in the same place for more than a year. At least, not a good-paying one."

"There has to be a better way," she said.

Henry just spread his arms. "Welcome to Wolf's Run. A chance for even the converts to be stable and have a secure future. That was my dream. Ian took it a step further and wanted to prepare for humans learning we exist. And now there's you, Gabby, and you're pushing to include other shifters. I can't say I'm opposed."

"That actually makes a lot more sense," Gabby said. "Like Black people having no generational wealth because of things like what happened in Tulsa. We minorities can't catch up, and that makes us angry. Damon's just doing the same thing, right?"

"Right," Seth said. "The problem is that he doesn't want help. He wants to show the world he's better. That man is looking for a way to expose wolves to humans but come out without endangering himself."

"Us," Gabby realized. "Damon wants to see Wolf's Run destroyed. But why?"

"Because if humans accept us, then his problems are solved," Vic told her. "But if humans react like they always have, then we'll be the ones beaten, chased out, and scorned. We'll be the ones losing our homes, our investments, and everything else - and that man will no longer be in second place. He'll be ahead for once, because someone else pulled this pack down to nothing."

"Not my pack," Gabby said, looking over to Ian.

"Not my pack," I agreed, doing the same.

He just dipped his head in acknowledgement. "And not my pack either. So, let's see what options we have to protect ourselves, because the only one I've come up with is very, very bad."

CHAPTER 47

O ver the next few days, things settled down into something like a routine. I went to work, worried about my daughter at school, and got a text every day from her at lunch saying she was ok. Then, at night, I relaxed with my mates while talking about how to make Damon leave us alone. The problem was that Evelyn had said they had more people than us - but how? If Ian did go into their territory to challenge the man, would he even make it out alive with that many people around?

Pax and Trent had called a few relatives to see if they knew anything about this guy. The response always came back to him being a radical, one of those people who thought that a war with humans would result in wolves being recognized as some kind of master race. In other words, like a racist, but far worse. And from the sounds of it, Karen was using her name and lineage to push the man's buttons.

I knew how easy it was for me to convince my own mates to change their mind. Asking nicely, feeling strongly about something, or even putting my foot down had the same effect with Ian as it did anyone else who cared about my opinion. He listened. Often, he wanted to make me happy, so he would change what he'd planned to do. I did the same for him. It was a pretty normal thing, I thought.

Karen, on the other hand, was using that same reaction to make this unhinged man into some kind of weapon for her revenge. I was sure of it. Sadly, there was no way to prove it. But when I took that into consideration, the idea of Ian challenging Damon became even less likely to work out for us. Karen wanted my mate, not her own. She wanted the prestige of Ian's last name, but she didn't care about things like his feelings. That fucking bitch would destroy everything else if it meant she could finally achieve some stupid status that actually meant nothing.

And among all of that, I was still sneaking in a few wolf lessons. I'd learned how to run now, so I could actually keep up with Bridget. Seth, however, left me in the dust - but I'd get there. My problem wasn't going fast. It was doing that while trying to avoid the branches, holes, and other hazards on the ground. I could also jump, and my daughter had taught me how to chase my tail as practice on turning and bending. Needless to say, I'd never again laugh at a dog for doing it.

Theo was doing even better. When the kids got home from school, they went straight to the trails. Often, one of the bears was home, so whoever it was made a point of keeping an ear out for any problems on the trails.

Thankfully, we had none. On Thursday afternoon, the kids came piling into my house laughing about something, and come to find out, Theo had climbed his first tree as a tiger. He'd also required Jax's help to get down, and Nikolai thought it was the funniest thing ever.

But on Friday, the kids were noticeably absent. Gabby was home - upstairs on her computer - but the regular insanity of having a teenaged alpha wolf as my daughter was simply missing. They didn't come over before dinner. They didn't drop by to steal some food, and when it got dark, there'd still been no word from any of them. I'd been a mom long enough to know that when the kids were too quiet, it meant they were up to no good, so I headed upstairs.

"Gabby?" I asked, tapping at her door.

"Yeah, Mom?"

I opened it to see her texting furiously on her phone. "What are you doing and where are your friends?"

"Oh, they're hanging out tonight," she told me as she dimmed her phone and tried to casually set it aside. "Why?"

"Are you doing something stupid?" I asked.

She just sighed. "No. I would like you to know that I am not. Roman is home too. We had no idea, but Samantha got it in her head, and Nikolai said he knew where, and they could all fit in Theo's car, so Olivia decided it would be fun." She scrunched up her face. "They went to see the Hidden Forest pack, Mom."

"What?!"

I turned, immediately heading downstairs because I needed my phone, calling back, "What were you thinking, Gabby?"

"I told them not to, Mom. I didn't even know about it until they started texting me!"

"And you should have come right to me!" I snapped just as I reached my purse.

My phone was still on the top because I hadn't put it on the charger yet. Grabbing it, I woke up the screen and started tapping out a message to Ian, letting him know that the kids were making a mess of things again. I hit send, and he replied a second later.

Ian: we're coming over.

That was it, but it was enough. "Gabby!" I roared up the stairs. "Get your ass down here. Your Alpha's on his way, and you'd better have a damned good excuse!"

She was halfway down the stairs when my mates piled through the front door. "What's going on?" Ian asked.

"I didn't know until a few minutes ago," Gabby said.

"No?" I asked. "So why are you home alone, and Roman's at his house? Why are you making sure that you're exactly where you're supposed to be, Gabby? Do you think we're stupid?"

"Roman's grounded for getting detention at school!" she told me. "No going out this weekend. I asked Olivia what she was doing, and she said hanging with Xander. Nikolai and Theo were being cute all day, and I didn't want to be in the middle of that. Sam just said she couldn't hang out tonight. I did *not* know, Mom."

Ian's head whipped around to her. "What didn't you know?" he demanded.

"You were all talking about the Hidden Forest pack, and you basically told Sam where it was. She used Google

Maps to see it, but those images are outdated, you know? And all of you were talking about an army, and how the pack used to be small, but that woman said it isn't anymore. Sam said we need a head count, because you can't plan a defense if you don't know what you're up against. And Nikolai said that if they got the intel, then it would prove we're doing our job as your backup." She licked her lips and lifted her chin, proving she wasn't scared at all. "I told them to come back. That's what I was doing when Mom came upstairs. I was hoping to call them off before they got there, but..." And she lifted her phone to show a picture.

Pax snatched it from her hands. "That's Hidden Forest all right." Then he enlarged it, moved it around, and passed it to Lane who was beside him. "If Damon finds out that our pups are in his territory, do you know what he'll do, Gabby?"

"If he's feeling nice, he'll capture them, hold them for ransom because he wants that money, and force Ian to submit to him. If he's not, he'll kill them. I know, Pax. That's why I want to scream at them too."

"You need to be harder on your betas," Lane told her as he passed the phone to Trent. "They do this because you run your group like a democracy. It's not. You, Gabby, are the alpha, and if they won't obey, they can get rolled or get replaced. Pick one."

"Maybe for you," she shot back. "I want to have betas who'll tell me when I'm wrong, who'll have better ideas, and who'll take risks without fear of punishment from me. We're all supposed to be on the same side, ok? And that means they'll screw up sometimes. More when they're trying to impress someone - like all of you!"

"Don't put this on us," Seth told her. "Ian makes it very clear that he's proud of you kids. I'd like to think the rest of us do too, so don't you try to make this our fault."

"No..." Gabby groaned. "I don't mean like that. I mean that you're always doing things for us, so we want to help. We don't want to be the burden, you know? Nikolai wants his dad to see that being a wolf's beta can work. Theo wants to pay the pack back for giving him a home. Samantha wants to make sure she's a part of this. Olivia? Ok, she just likes the thrill of it, but Xander's been trying everything to apologize for challenging me. Even submitting!"

"He wants to be your beta," Trent told her.

"But he's an alpha," she countered.

Pax shrugged. "So am I. I would've been a weak alpha, and while I can lead, I'm not very good at it."

"And you were never given the chance to lead," Ian told him.

"Happier as your beta," Pax promised. "I have a feeling Lane would've matured into an alpha too, if he hadn't lost so many years as a wolf."

"Guys!" I groaned, cutting them off. "Can we please figure out what we're going to do about the kids?"

Ian just pointed at Gabby's phone. "Tell them to get their asses back here - now - or they'll all be looking for a new pack," he ordered.

But just as Gabby's phone was once again in her hands, it vibrated. The girl let out a relieved sigh. "They're already coming. Sam says they have something we need to see." Then she started typing. "I'm telling them to come here, leaving off the fact that you're pissed, but making it clear you're with Mom."

"I'm not pissed," Ian told her.

"I am," Lane said. "How dare they risk themselves like this?"

"But that picture?" Pax asked. "Ian, have Gabby show you. It's Damon's trailer, and there are at least a dozen wolves hanging out, and more in their canine form. It means that girl was right. His pack has grown, and how many trailers is the pack renting?"

"And that should've been done by Jesse," Ian countered. "He just smells like a dog, and that's easy enough to explain away. Damon wouldn't suspect him as anything but a normal human." He flailed a hand toward Gabby. "Those kids? If they get caught? Damon would kill them - and I don't want to be the one telling Heather or Kim that their kids aren't coming home."

"Or any of them," Seth added. "I'd rather go blind into a fight on their turf than risk our pups! I haven't worked this hard to learn how to be both a strong man and a strong wolf just to lose it all because a group of children can't wait for us to do things safely!"

"I didn't know!" Gabby insisted.

Seth just turned to her. "Then get order in your pack, girl, because right now you don't have any. Your betas aren't working for you, they're working with you, and a pack needs a leader. Otherwise, it's just chaos."

She pulled in a breath and lifted her chin in defiance, "Maybe that's - "

"Stop!" Seth snapped, cutting her off. "Don't you dare try to say it's how I was raised. There always has to be someone to take responsibility. One point where things always come back to, and that means the final say. It's you, Gabby. For us, it's Ian. If someone dies, it will be his fault.

Ours too, but his for not sending us out sooner. His for not seeing the signs. His for not being strong enough of an Alpha to stop it." And he lifted a brow. "Or you can just keep saying you didn't know, it's not your fault, and trying to push away that responsibility, but it doesn't make for a very good leader."

She nodded. "Ok. Should I call Roman over too?" Then she looked at Ian. "Maybe you can? I mean, since he's grounded? Because Sam's message sounds like she got something big, but I'm not asking because they're supposed to be on their way back, and I don't want to do anything to convince them to change their minds."

Ian just nodded. "I'll call Kim."

"No," I told him. "I will." Then I looked at Gabby. "And if you think this is over, just know that you're wrong. You are fifteen years old. I have no idea what you kids think you're going to do, but saving the pack? Not. It."

"More like the world," Gabby admitted. "Because if Damon wants to let humans know that we exist? That's not going to end well, Mom. We're trying to make sure that doesn't happen."

"That's our job," I told her. "Not you, a girl who can't even drive yet."

Gabby just dropped her head. "I was just trying to help."

"No," Lane told her. "You, Gabby, were trying to be the hero, and you didn't stop to think about who is running around behind you constantly picking up the messes you make." And he pointed right at me. "So, until you can remember that we're all on the same side, you go sit and think about this." And he pointed at the couch, making it clear exactly where Gabby was supposed to sit.

My daughter obeyed, surprisingly enough. I just dialed Kim and waited for her to pick up, trying to figure out how the hell I was going to explain this. I decided to just keep it simple.

"Kim?" I asked as soon as she answered. "For once, it's not your son making a mess of things. It's my daughter. Her betas are up to something, so Ian and I need all of them. Can you send Roman over to my house?"

"Yeah, sure," she said. "Is it bad?"

"I don't know yet," I admitted. "I'll send Roman back when we're done and have him fill you in, ok?"

"Good luck, Alpha," Kim said, sounding as exhausted as I felt. "Kids, right?"

"Exactly."

CHAPTER 48

R oman arrived a few minutes before Theo pulled in. As soon as I heard that car, I opened the front door and stood there, making it very clear they were busted. Samantha, Xander, Nikolai, Theo, and Olivia all got out, but when they saw me, they moved a little slower. Clearly, my "mom-stare" still worked.

"Inside," I snapped. "Now!"

"Elena," Olivia tried, "we need to tell Ian about what we - "

I pointed to the living room. "He's already here."

I swore all five of them ducked their heads and dropped their shoulders at that. They also walked a little faster, though, so I considered it a win. Once they were inside, I closed the door, but Ian just pointed them to the couch. He and his betas were still standing - glaring - just in front of them.

"What," Ian finally demanded when they were sitting,

"were all of you thinking? Do you know what Damon would do to you for trespassing onto his territory?"

"Yeah, but - " Xander tried.

"He would kill you," Ian went on. "You first, Xander. The moment you tried to mouth off, he'd cut your throat if you're lucky. If you weren't, he'd throw you to his betas and have them tear you apart. And do you honestly expect me to believe that you could fight off five, six... ten adult wolves at the same time?"

"We weren't that dumb," Nikolai snapped. "Have a little faith. Jesus."

Ian's head just turned to Gabby. "And you're going to allow your beta to talk to me that way?"

"Ian..." Gabby said.

"They answer to you, Gabby. That means this? All of this? It's your fault. You are the alpha here, aren't you? And you didn't even know where your betas were? How are you going to explain it to their parents when they don't come back? Because that's on you. How will you make Kim stop crying? How will you explain to Heather that not only her daughter, but her foster son are just gone? And Lev? Nikolai's all he has left of his family, but you were willing to throw that away without even talking to the rest of your pack."

"That's not how it was," Xander snapped.

Ian's head just turned to him. "No? Why, because you were the alpha in charge of this? Are you taking her betas?"

"It's not like that!" Gabby said. "I should've asked why they were all busy, Ian, and I'm sorry."

"You'd better be," he told her. "Because if they made one mistake tonight. If Damon saw them and decides to

459

take it out on us? Then that's on you. Every person who is hurt will be your fault. Do you see how this thing works yet? Being the heir to the pack isn't always fun and games. It's also not some movie where a little editing will make it work out. This is real life, Gabby!"

"I'm sorry, Alpha," she said. "I should've done better."

"Which is why you're grounded," he said. "I may not be able to keep you home, since that's your mother's domain, but I can keep you from being a wolf. One week, all human. Let's see if you remember how nice it is to have a safe and protected community where you don't have to hide what you are. See if you think it's worth risking that for a few bragging rights."

She nodded. "No shifting," she agreed.

But Nik couldn't take it. The boy shoved to his feet. "We're the ones who fucked this up, and you're only punishing her? What kind of bullshit is that?"

"That," Ian snapped, "is how it works. All of you are supposed to be extensions of her. That means she's the one who will always pay when you screw it up. Just like she is now." Then he lifted a brow. "Still fun, Nikolai?"

"No, if you're pissed, you take it out on me," Nik said, shoving forward.

Both of his hands hit Ian's shoulders, shoving the Alpha back a step. I gasped, jumping out of the way. Lane immediately moved before me, but Seth was also in motion. He grabbed Nik's arm, shoved the boy's shoulder away, and stepped forward with Nik's arm now pinned behind his back. Two steps took the kid toward a chair. Then, Seth shoved his own knee into the back of Nik's, forcing the boy down until his face was flat on the cushion.

"An alpha is never alone," Seth warned him. "You attack him and you attack all of us. Know your place, kid."

The sound Nik made was rage, but I could only describe it as a hiss. An almost cat-like one. Then his form began to blur. Immediately, Gabby shoved to her feet.

"Don't do it!" she ordered. "Nik, you screwed up, so deal with it. If you want to be one of my betas, then you will realize that Ian's not just the wolf I listen to, but he's also one of my dads. That means you crossed a line."

Nik snarled under his breath. "This isn't fair, Gabby."

"This is a pack, Nik. All for one, right? Sometimes it sucks. Most times it's good, but if you shift, we're done."

The boy just sighed, relaxing in Seth's hold, and then nodded to show he was good. Slowly, Seth released his grip. When Nik still didn't struggle, Ian's beta stepped back, but the others were all tense and watching. This was the first time I'd ever seen that side of them. No, I hadn't missed Lane moving to guard me either.

They worked like a team in a way I hadn't expected. From where I was standing, it felt like Ian had sent the most gentle of his betas to deal with this, almost like judging the weapon against the threat. And from the look in his eyes, I was pretty sure that having Ian fight was kinda like pressing the button to release the nukes.

Then Sam propped up her tablet and turned it to face us. Lifting a brow, she pressed play. "Ground us if you want, but I think this is kinda important," she said.

At first, I couldn't make out what was on the video. There was a lot of darkness and a bright spot in the middle. I wasn't the only one who moved closer to get a better look. It seemed the bright spot was a fire burning in a metal barrel. In the darkness were two different mobile homes - one on each side. This had to be the yard space between them. And there, sitting in a lawn chair, was Damon, shirtless.

Then two men dragged a third up before him. The men said something but their voices were too low to make out. Just random mumbles coming from the cheap tablet speakers. The man being held tried to struggle, doing his best to get free or fight back, but the others were simply too strong.

And then Damon shoved off his pants and shifted. The wolf was brown and white, but not in the typical pattern. More like Bridget, yet not as striking. Without warning, it simply lunged forward, sinking its teeth into the struggling man's leg. There was one thrash, and then the wolf released and backed up, shifted into Damon again, and began to pull his pants back on.

He flicked a finger and the pair of men took their captive toward the mobile home on the right side. As they got closer, a curtain opened, someone's head appeared, and then a light came on over the door. I watched as they dragged the now-injured man inside, clearly against his will, and the video ended.

"They're making converts," Olivia said. "I know you can't hear it on the tape, but Damon told the guy that this would either be the best day or the worst day of his life. Welcome to the new army."

"Shit," Seth breathed.

"Yeah, that's not the worst part," Samantha said, tabbing back through the time stream of the video. When she got where she wanted, she dragged at the screen, enlarging a corner. "That window in the mobile? I didn't notice this until I was just trimming it down to show you." And she tapped to play again.

There, at the back of the room, visible through that window, was a man. A young one. It looked like he had a chain around his arm, and he was pulling at it. Then, all of a sudden, he stopped and looked at the window. Sam paused the video again.

"That," she said, "is Jonah Sims. The missing football player who supposedly ran away. The boy whose ring Damon's girlfriend gave you."

"He's chained up in there," Olivia said. "Damon's making converts, guys. That's how he got so many wolves."

"How many?" Trent asked.

"A lot," Olivia told him. "The whole trailer park is filled with people who have amber eyes. There are wolves lying in yards and running across the street. I saw a symbol for the Dry Creek pack on a car, so maybe they merged?"

"Where's that pack?" Gabby asked.

Ian scrubbed at his mouth. "Next county over. I'm honestly more worried about the bite."

"Full moon's coming next Friday, Ian," Nik pointed out. "He's got at least two waiting to turn. How many more has he shifted? And those wolves that attacked us on the trails?"

"Damon was there," Gabby said. "I saw that same wolf, I just didn't know it was him."

"Fuck," Ian hissed, glancing over to me. "If he has that many new wolves?"

"Younger men, too," Pax pointed out. "Looks like eighteen and maybe mid-twenties."

"Think he's scouting?" Trent asked.

I was so lost. "Scouting?"

Trent huffed like he wasn't sure how to reply. "Um, sometimes packs need new blood. It's not unheard of to go looking for able-bodied men and women, tell them what we are - slowly and over time, mind you - and offer to make them wolves. Some call us insane. Others think it's amazing and want to be converted."

"Keeps our lines from getting a little close," Pax admitted. "It's also not a very common practice. Kinda like marrying girls the day they turn eighteen. It's legal, technically, but kinda gross at the same time."

Ok, I could see that. "Normally, you just, what? Wait to see if you get caught? Or..."

"Lovers," Ian admitted. "Boyfriends, girlfriends. We meet humans, we become close, and we offer to bring them into our society first. Kinda like moving in together. Sometimes it's an 'accident,' like with Theo."

"Not many who are attacked live through it," Seth admitted. "Most wolves are very careful to finish the fights they pick with humans. Animal attacks, you know."

"And now Damon is scouting humans?" I asked, trying to put all the pieces together. "Is this because of what Mason was ranting about?"

"Makes sense," Nik said. "The idea of werewolves was put in people's heads for just a moment, then disproven. But in those few days, some thought it would be the coolest thing ever. Damon clearly knows about that, since he's been holding it over Ian's head. Maybe he heard a few people talking? Or figured out some way to talk guys into it?"

I was just nodding slowly, letting all of that sink in. "And a lot of them," I breathed. "Anyone know how many accidents there've been on the roads in that area where someone hit a wolf?"

Samantha grabbed her tablet and began typing. The rest of us just waited while her brow furrowed, her mouth fell open. Then she gasped. "Oh, that's not good," she breathed.

"What?" I demanded.

"Damon was saying there've been hunters shooting at his pack, right? That's why he says he deserves reparations?" And she turned her tablet toward us. "The red dots are wolf sightings. The orange ones are livestock killed by them. The black ones are the ones hit on the road." Then she dropped her tablet back on her lap. "Guys, those farmers, or ranchers, or whatever they are, outside of town? Yeah, they're not shooting wolves because we were on the news. They're shooting them because there's been an explosion of them."

"You sure?" Ian asked.

"Listen to this," she said, and started reading. "*Last year we had a rabbit problem. This year, it's wolves. Are any of you really shocked at how many adults are out there? I lost a calf to a pack. Now, I'm shooting any of them I see. Got motion lights and my gun by the back door. Endangered, my ass.*" She looked up. "It's on a Facebook group for the area."

"That means he's turning them and keeping the ones who make it," Seth breathed.

"How many black dots?" I asked. "Sam? How many people have they killed because Damon wants his army?"

"One hundred and thirty-seven," she breathed. "Those are just the ones that this group knows about. How many wolves got hit and the car didn't stop? How many ran away only to die later?"

"And if even half survived," Ian realized, "that's a lot of new wolves with no idea what's going on. Some of those guys are going to be pumped up on their new strength and senses..."

"And they won't know not to be seen as lycans," Lane added. "He wants to expose us."

"He wants to see us take the fall," Gabby corrected. "The finger was pointed at us once. If werewolves are seen here again, and caught on tape by someone who isn't tied to our pack? Then what? Sam can't do that again! It won't work twice!"

"And we need to get those boys," I decided.

"We can't," Ian said.

I just turned to face him. "That boy is still in high school, Ian. The other one? He's probably Sheridan's age, at best. They're barely more than kids, and they're going to die if we don't help them. You made sure I knew all about the risks of turning outside the walls. I got horror stories about people being hit by cars. Even Bridget said it! So we need to figure out how the fuck we're getting those kids out. They didn't ask for this, and I will not just stand here and pretend like I didn't see that."

He leaned in. "I can't go onto Damon's territory, Elena. If I do, I'd better challenge him. If his pack is made of converts? What are the chances that they're going to join in? Or stop me if I run? They don't know how this works!"

I licked my lips. "What about me?"

"No." That was from Lane.

I just lifted my hand, begging him to wait. "What about me, Ian. If I went there, what would Damon do? Say, I tell him I'm there to deliver a message?"

Ian just caught my chin. "No." He sounded just like Lane.

"What would he say?" I demanded.

It was Seth who answered. "He'd hear you out, probably give you a time limit so he could laugh as you ran, and then he'd chase."

Nik just leaned back and crossed his arms. "I can get in. Theo too. Sam's human, so if she parks and looks at a map, she could probably get away with it. Just leave the phone on like she's asking a friend for help because she's lost."

"No," I told him. "This is not the kind of thing that teenagers should be handling. I agree that those kids need help, but there's a reason all of you have parents."

"Then what about the bears?" Gabby asked. "They won't smell like wolves. We know where Jonah's being kept. We can show them how to get in, get out, and bail before the pack knows what happened."

"And I'm guessing all of you forgot about the chains?" Ian demanded.

Xander shrugged. "Bolt cutters. Pax has a pair. Wasn't that thick of chain. More for holding a dog and less for logging."

Ian's jaw clenched. "I don't like it."

"And you still know it has to happen," I said, reaching up for his hand. "Can you really live with the idea of those kids being killed because Damon wants to get even with us? We have to help them."

"He wants to get even with me," Ian countered. "Not you, not even this pack. He hates *me*, and he's turning people to get his revenge? No, I'm not ok with it, but I hate the idea of risking the members of my own pack even more, Elena. This is a stupid idea."

"So help me plan it better." I crossed my arms and lifted a brow.

He just closed his eyes, sighed, but then my Alpha nodded. "Fine, but you're the one driving the car, and you can't do it alone."

"No, I think this is something for my Sisterhood," I decided.

CHAPTER 49

"No," I said again, making Elena glare at me in frustration.

This debate had been going on and off since the kids had come back last night. I loved this woman more than I could put into words, but she simply refused to listen to reason. Her heart was in the right place, but the problem was that my mate had no clue how to fight. She shouldn't need to! She had us.

Still, she'd played through almost every possible scenario for how to get that high school boy out of Damon's trailer and into Wolf's Run. She kept talking about how frantic his mother must be, and I got it. I could actually understand her concern, because I felt it too. The difference was that I knew that her life was worth a hell of a lot more than his - at least to me.

So, we'd discussed it last night until our voices were closer to yelling than talking. That was when Lane had snarled at me that we needed a break. I'd been sent home by my betas. Lane and Seth had spent the night. Trent, Pax, and I, however, had kept talking about it, because we really couldn't go into Damon's territory. If we could, this would've been a lot easier.

So, this morning I'd come over and made breakfast as a peace offering. She'd accepted it, and then immediately went right back to trying to save those people. I loved her dedication. I adored her stubbornness. I was, truthfully, in awe of her bravery. Sadly, there was just no good solution for what was going on over in the Hidden Forest pack.

"Ok," she breathed, sitting down at the table across from me. "So, how would you do this, Ian?"

It was the closest she'd come to giving in. "You won't like it," I warned her.

"Tell me anyway," she mumbled, reaching up to rub at her forehead.

"So, you'd need to buy a case of beer and put both Gabby and Olivia in the cutest grungy clothes they have -"

"What?!" she roared, shoving back to her feet in an instant. "Are you fucking insane?"

I heard the thudding of Lane's feet a split second before he burst into the room, but I ignored it. "You asked. I'm simply answering your question, and I did warn you that you wouldn't like it." I tipped my head at her chair. "Please, Elena? I'm hoping that if I lay this out, you can think of a way to do it even better."

"Bunny?" Lane asked.

"I'm fine," she promised, dropping back into her chair. "I'm also trying to decide if it's too early to start drinking whiskey."

Lane just moved behind her to rub her shoulders

lovingly. "You know I'm going, right, Ian?" he asked.

I nodded. "I assumed you would. I just really need you to not be seen. If Damon thinks the leadership is behind this?"

"Think he'd recognize Red?" he asked.

"Probably not," I admitted. "It was night when you tore into him, and fast."

Elena reached for her coffee. "Ok. What's the rest of this plan, Ian?"

"You're not going to like it," I said again.

"And I'm holding coffee, so I won't lose my mind this time," she promised.

Oh, she was killing me. The worst part was that I actually thought this idea had a chance of working. Not a great chance, but a decent enough one that I was willing to listen to her scream at me. Having grown up as wolves, and from well-respected families, Pax, Trent, and I had pulled quite a few stupid stunts as kids. Not all of them were just for fun. Some I never wanted my father to know about, but a little privilege and a lot of teenage hormones had fueled us back then.

"So," I tried again, "beer. Gabby and Olivia need to be as sexy as possible - "

"Ashley and I can do that," she countered.

I just lifted a brow. "Baby, while I may love a real woman, most of those guys in the Hidden Forest pack are closer to Roman's age than mine. They're looking for girls who are right around eighteen, and I know Olivia can do a few miracles with makeup. Pushup bras, show a little skin, and men that age forget to think. That is what you need, and I'm sorry, but you are not the slutty type. Gabby could play it up."

"Yeah," she admitted. "She could."

"Then," I said before she could say this was a bad idea, "you'll send the girls to the back of the trailer." I paused. "First, scout with the tigers. Those guys can see in the dark, you know. When they give the all-clear, then you send in the girls. The wolves - Kim, Ashley, Roman, and Xander - sneak as close as they can to cover the retreat."

"The girls can't carry out the converts," Lane pointed out. "They're going to be sick, Ian. Migraines and just starting the delirium."

"Which is why she needs to take our bears." I glanced up at him and Lane nodded.

"Pax's plan?" he asked.

"The three of us worked out as much as we could," I explained. "Pax said to use the other shifters. I wanted to use the foxes for the scouts, but at night, tigers can pull double duty."

"Makes sense," Lane said. "So, then what?"

I looked back to Elena. "When the girls go inside, the bears push closer. All they'll have to do is get the two boys out. Bears will rush in and carry them back. Our wolves will slow down any pursuit, and since the men in that video were all dressed, the time it takes for them to strip is going to work in our favor."

"Where am I?" Elena asked.

"Driving the first SUV," I told her. "Heather will follow you, and she'll be using Dad's SUV. That will give you enough room. Now, we'll need someone with medical experience. I don't care if that's first aid - Lev might know some - or Bridget. I'd really prefer not to send our doctor out, because if anything goes bad, I'd prefer she's prepping for surgery."

"I can agree to that," Elena said. "I know some first aid."

"You're going to be driving," I told her again. "See, you'll need to keep the trucks running, because when this happens, it needs to happen fast. We'll have Sheridan at the gate. Samantha will be here working as a runner. I want to keep Theo, too, because the boy doesn't know his body yet. You'll just need a reason to convince him."

"Telling him no should work," she decided. "But I know what you mean."

"Now," I said, continuing, "the girls get the converts out. Our wolves let them get to the bears. The bears carry the boys to the SUV. I'd love it if Gabby and Olivia can shift and bolt, but it might be easier to just run. That depends on how far they are from your trucks. See, you don't want to be too close or Damon will notice vehicles just hanging around."

"And if the entire pack comes at us?" she asked.

"Tigers," I told her. "Elena, that's going to stop a lot in its tracks. Plus, you have an extra bear. You remember how you reacted the first time you met those guys? I promise Damon's pack will be the same. They will stop. They will be confused. There aren't a lot of other shifters. Wolves have been successful, but the rest? They're rarely seen. I mean, most of us can list one or two in our lifetimes, and we're wolves."

"And then we just run for it?" she asked.

I nodded. "You'll need to have everyone look out for two partners. So, Gabby watches Roman and Olivia, as an example. Roman watches Gabby and Nik. That way, before you take off, you'll have someone screaming to wait if someone got left behind. Set up a rally point.

Someplace that if you pull away, they keep running and you'll get there to pick them up."

"Basic hit and run stuff," Lane assured her.

She looked up at him, then down to me. "You've done things like this before?"

All I could do was sigh, but Lane didn't have that problem. "Yeah. Between school rivalries gone wrong and packs sneaking in for control of safe land, it happens enough that we all learn to fight. Not just because it's some ancient traditional holdover. We settle our disputes with teeth and claws. Diplomacy only goes so far, and sometimes, it makes a much bigger impression to hit a pack in their beds and remind them that we are the stronger wolves."

She just nodded. "Not anymore, ok?"

"That's why we built Wolf's Run," I told her. "As a boy, I thought it was just what everyone did. When I got older, I realized that humans are so much more civilized, and I wanted that. I learned how to hold my temper. I made myself. Not because I don't have one, but because I'm not barbaric, and wolves aren't beasts."

"No," she agreed, "we're not. So, how do we do this without the kids?"

And we were right back to her problem. She wanted to snap her fingers and fix this, or call someone to do the dirty work for her. She just didn't understand that men like Damon weren't going to cooperate with the police. They'd rather kill them, and the cops wouldn't see the wolves coming.

With Karen pushing him, he'd probably do a lot worse. Never mind that the woman was our biggest problem. I still didn't know what to do if she spotted the girls, because she would recognize them. If that happened, the only chance would be if they ran, and I wasn't convinced that either one would do it.

"Elena, you can take Sheridan and Ridley and leave the teens at home, but is that really any better? We've taught Gabby how to fight. Olivia's been learning since she was a toddler. They can hold their own, and are you sure the vixens can say the same?"

"No," she muttered. "I just hate the idea of using more kids for this."

"But Damon's picking them young," I countered. "You need the kids because they're the ones who won't stand out. You need the boys because they will not let anything happen to the girls. Gabby's group is tight. Her betas are impressive, even if I keep pushing them for more. Xander's a hot-headed little shit, but Olivia directs him well."

"And you're taking their moms," Lane pointed out. "I mean, not Xander's, because his parents tend to always be at work, but Kim will watch out for him. Besides, do you honestly think that a pack of she-wolves protecting their pups is something Damon really wants to mess with?"

"We shouldn't have to do this," she said. "This whole thing is just wrong!"

I nodded in agreement, but what could I say to that? Try to tell her that there were bad people in the world and that being a wolf didn't always make it better? Sadly, that helped no one. So I decided to try a different route.

"Elena, in all my life as a wolf, I've never seen an alpha like you. And yes, I'm convinced that you're an alpha, because I feel the strength in your eyes when you stare at me. I see it when you push yourself just a little harder. But where most alphas tell others what to do, you spend your time trying to fix it. You turn that strength and pride into love and nurturing. You are the den mother. You make people feel safe the moment they lay eyes on you - and what's this? It's a situation where they need a safe place to run."

"But I don't do anything," she insisted.

I just canted my head and shrugged. "I think you do a lot. I think that wherever you lead, we all want to follow. I think that your quiet strength is what drew me, Lane, Trent, Pax, and Seth to you, all in our own ways. I think it's why Vic and Lev and Sheridan all found it so easy to fit in here. I think that you have this ability to make anywhere you are feel like home. I also think that Gabby has it too."

"What is 'it'?" she asked.

"No idea," I admitted. "But it's a power that we've all noticed. Sampson Delaney likes you. He doesn't like anyone!" I chuckled. "I have a funny feeling this power is called humanity, but I'm not sure it's because you were human."

"Selflessness," Lane said. "You gave the bears more than three trees. You treated the tigers like nothing more than a normal family. You gave the foxes a chance to do it on their own. Over and over, you're racking up these little debts and you have no intention of ever collecting them, and we can feel it. How do you think this boy is going to react when you get him out of there, help him shift, and stand with him as we explain it to his family?"

I answered before she could try to push that off. "He's going to feel like he owes you his life. And you? All you'll think is that it was a shame he was in that situation in the first place. You'll never think of yourself as the hero. Not when you're bending over backwards to take care of Gabby on your own or planning to invade another pack's territory. You just do what has to be done, but we still notice."

Lane bent and kissed her head. "People follow where you lead, little bunny. If you're going to do this, though, you're going to have to lead."

She just nodded. "I will. But, if I pull this off, maybe I get a nickname that sounds a little tougher than 'bunny'?"

"No," I said before Lane could. "Sorry. That one's going to stay. You are soft, adorable, and..." I stopped myself before I got into trouble.

"Good to eat," Lane added, mimicking my thoughts. "Told you, little bunny, and it seems Ian agrees."

"Very tasty," I assured her. "I'm more than willing to give a demonstration. I'll call in a few friends if it means you'll give up this plan to save some guy you've never met before."

"Not happening." She sounded almost apologetic. "Ian, someone has to do this, and since no one else is, that means it's falling on me."

I just dipped my head in acknowledgement. I didn't quite agree, but I could see that she had to, and I wasn't dumb enough to tell her no again. Even my sweet, kind, and gentle mate had a limit, and I was pretty sure this was where she'd drawn her line in the sand.

"Then I will keep the pack safe until you're back, Alpha. Just..." My eyes jumped up to Lane. "Make sure you all come back, ok?"

"She'll make it home fine," he swore. "I'll make sure of it."

CHAPTER 50

I spent the rest of the day making plans, getting supplies, and calling everyone whose help I needed. Samantha and Theo were livid to be cut out. Thankfully, Lev jumped in to side with me, telling Theo that he wasn't ready yet, and Nik needed to have his full concentration on this. Heather told the boy to watch over Sam while we were out, and that seemed to help a bit.

But the bears were all in. A little more than I expected. Scott's knowledge from previously serving as a Marine would be helpful. He not only had the first aid experience we needed, but the man showed up to Ian's place with three guns. One for me, one for Heather, and a military-style assault rifle for himself. Just in case, he said. Then we went over the plan. When that was done, Sam pulled up Google Maps, and we picked out our route, and then we went over the plan again with more details.

At midnight, Henry arrived with his SUV, pulling it up next to the curb. When he walked into the house, he tossed Heather the keys and headed over to the table where Samantha still had the map pulled up. His eyes scanned it, then he turned back to me.

"Elena, these boys are going to be confused and probably scared. If they need to be tied up to get them here, then do that. I'm going to wait with Bridget. Sheridan's on the gate tonight. If there's anything else you need, Alpha, your pack will be ready and waiting."

"I'm still not used to that," I told him.

He just smiled. "You've more than earned it, and you haven't even been a wolf a year yet. Take care of our kids, ok?"

Ian just caught my hand. "I want you to call me when you're on your way back so we can get you in without stopping. Samantha and Theo both have Sheridan's number too. If you have any problems, she'll have the gate open. You're going to head straight to Bridget, because the clinic is the only place we have to ease them through this right now."

"When's the moon?" I asked.

"Friday, just after one in the afternoon. It'll be a day run."

I nodded. "Then let's make sure they're alive to make it."

I tried to turn away, but he caught my hand, pulling me back. Then his lips found mine. There was something frantic about this kiss, and I knew that was his own worry, but mine matched. So I pressed into him, not caring about the kids in the room. All too soon, he pulled away.

"Be careful," he breathed.

Then Seth moved beside me, reaching up to turn my

face toward him. Trent's lips found my neck, and Pax kissed my shoulder on the other side, then the three of them hugged me so hard.

"We love you," Seth whispered. "So you'd better come back, because I don't want to do the whole dating thing again, ok?"

"Promise," I said, glancing back at Trent and Pax to make sure they knew they were included in that. "Take care of Ian, guys?"

"Take care of Lane," Pax told me.

Trent met my eyes. "I'm proud of you. Terrified, but proud."

Then it was time. I turned for the truck, shooing the herd out before me. We had this balanced out pretty well. There were fourteen of us in total. Gabby and Roman were with me, along with Lane. Xander and Olivia were with Heather. I got Ashley, but Heather got Kim. Lev told Nik to ride with us so each truck had a tiger as well. Then Scott climbed into the back with his gun, leaving Jax and Vic to ride with Heather.

As we pulled out, I looked over at Lane. "Guess you count as a bear, huh?" I teased.

"Shit," Scott laughed from the back. "I saw him in his mid-form. What do you people call it?"

"Lycan," Ashley told him.

"Yeah, that," Scott agreed. "Well, he's about as big as me as a bear. I think he counts."

Then Ashley leaned forward, between the seats, and snagged my phone. I gave her a confused look in the rearview mirror, because I was currently leading this caravan, and I kinda needed that for directions. Then, she did her leaning trick again and passed Lane my phone while handing me a Bluetooth earpiece.

"Heather has her headset on," she said. "So you get to use mine. I just paired it. Lane? Can you clip that phone holder to the air vents? Angle it so Elena can see where she's going. Then call Heather?"

"Can do," Lane assured her, making his words into truth.

A ringing started in my earpiece. "Yeah?" Heather answered.

"Evidently, we're supposed to be connected," I told her.

She just laughed, but there was something nervous about it. "Well, I'm trying to convince myself that this is just like chaperoning for a school trip. Not that I've ever done that before, but it feels a little less insane."

"Tell me about it," I mumbled.

But I couldn't stop thinking about that boy. It was Saturday night. In six days, he'd turn into a wolf. Somewhere out there, his mother was probably crying herself to sleep - if she slept at all. I knew our plan was good, and since Damon's pack didn't have any walls or protection around it, we could do this. We wouldn't even drive into the trailer park. Samantha had actually found some quiet dirt road with only a pasture between us and the trailer we wanted.

That didn't mean the drive was quick. It was twenty minutes from Wolf's Run to Hidden Forest. In the back seat, the kids were talking about their own parts to play. I heard Roman swear that he wouldn't rush in unless she called his name. Not yelled for some reason, but called his actual name. But the moment we left the city limits and started seeing nothing but country around us, I realized I'd forgotten one thing.

"Gabby?" I asked.

"Yeah, Mom?"

"As soon as you're out of this truck, you are the Alpha. That means aborting this is your call, you understand? These people are our pack, and while we want to save those guys, it's not worth losing one of ours to do it, ok?"

"Yeah," she agreed. "I actually know that, Mom. I promise that if it's too risky, we'll abort."

Then I made the final turn. Warning Heather first, I shut off the lights and drove slowly down the dusty gravel road. We didn't want to go fast because our brake lights would still illuminate the plume of dust, so I just let the truck coast, searching for any signs in the distance of the place we wanted.

"You have reached your destination," the GPS said in my ear just as I saw the pair of trailers.

Oh, they weren't the only ones. I also knew this was exactly where Samantha had been when she took her video, because the angle was the same. So I coasted forward just a bit more - enough to see the back side of the trailer I wanted, and then parked. I had no idea why they had set the mobile homes on the lots sideways, but right about now, that was a good thing.

"Heather?" I asked. "Can you see the fronts of those mobiles from where you are?"

"I can," she promised. "Can you see the back?"

"Yep. We ready?"

"Everyone's getting naked here," she told me.

It wasn't much better in my truck. The only one not taking off her clothes was Gabby, and that was because she had a specific part to play. Then it was time. Ashley warned us to turn off the overhead lights first, and everyone piled out. Immediately, they began changing. Three bears, two tigers, and so many wolves. The only one who didn't go was Lane, yet he was sitting in the passenger seat beside me naked.

"Coming?" Ashley asked him.

"I guard her," he said, gesturing to me.

She nodded and then found her wolf, heading for the ditch on the far side of this street. The bears, however, moved behind the trucks. It was the tigers who went first. Lev was on the right, Nik on the left, and the pair slipped into the grass a little too easily. I watched the barbed wire fence shift when they slipped between the strands, and then they were gone.

"That's a little impressive," Heather said. "I know they're in that field somewhere, but damned if I can see where."

"No kidding," I agreed.

But the trick was going to be getting the girls through that. It looked like some kind of pasture, but I didn't see any livestock in it. The problem was that there was a lot more open grass than trees. The moon wasn't full, but it was well over half, and that meant we could all see easily - even Damon and his pack.

It felt like it took forever. The cats were just gone. I could see forms moving between us and the fire barrel, but no one seemed panicked. And while it was hard to count, I was pretty sure there were only three or four people outside. Then, before I was really ready, Nik was back. He made a chuffing noise at Olivia. That was the sign, and the entire pack began to move.

The wolves followed the same path the tigers had. The girls had to duck and weave through the fence, but once they were on the other side, they crouched, taking their time about getting there. Beside me, Lane's hand gripped the door a little too hard, hanging halfway out of the open window.

"So," I said, talking to Heather, "you want to tell me what's going on with Lev while we wait?"

"He's just helping me raise a teenaged tiger," she replied.

"Uh huh." I swallowed when my voice climbed, betraying my nerves. "So, those shared showers are some kind of cultural thing?"

"You've seen his abs," she hissed. "Yes, I slept with him. Bridget says it's fine and not a problem, so there's no reason not to. Just a couple of adults. There's nothing to it."

"So why are you denying it so hard?" I teased.

She almost laughed, but the sound was more breath. "I don't want to jinx it," she admitted. "He's a shifter, Elena. He gets me, he doesn't mind the kids, and my shower drain is no longer acting funny. I mean, he helps out, you know? It's not just the sex. It's..." She paused. "Nice," she decided.

"Does she know Ashley is with the bears?" Lane asked, proving he could hear her on the other end.

Heather huffed out another laugh. "Yeah, I do. She said her brother's ok with it. That means this isn't going to be a problem, right?"

"I don't see why it would be," I told her. "I know wolves traditionally didn't date other shifters, but we didn't live with them either. I think it's time to do something..." I stopped, my eyes watching the fence on the far side. "The girls are across the pasture."

"I see that," Heather agreed.

Then Lane sat up. "That - "

Gabby and Olivia were still trying to slip through the strands of barbed wire when someone walked away from the fire. The girls had nowhere to go, and no way to explain what they were doing. My heart froze as I waited, but the silhouette just kept moving to the back of the trailer. That was when the bears decided to move into position.

They made no effort to go over, under, or through the fence the way everyone else had. Instead, Vic walked right up to a section and simply pushed it down. The strands of wire gave way. The metal posts were pulled out of alignment, leaning precariously just before the wire snapped, and then the path was clear. Scott and Jax pawed at the strands, scraping them out of the way, and the three bears trundled their way forward.

I had no clue how they'd pull that off on the other side without getting caught. That was too close to the wolves, wasn't it? But it didn't matter because the wolf who'd moved away from the fire was now visible against the narrow side of the mobile home. Clearly, it was a woman, and she was carrying something. Our entire group had paused, but the woman simply headed for the back door and walked in like she belonged there.

That was when Gabby and Olivia hurried forward, keeping to the shadows. I was actually a little impressed with them. The six pack of beer they'd been "sent to deliver" was tucked under Olivia's arm like a football, but

I kept wondering if the bottles were clanking or if something else would give them away.

All too soon, the girls reached the back door, and just like the woman before, they walked in as if they belonged there. The big plan was that a pair of cute girls showing up with beer might be enough to distract the men. If they could, they were going to try to get the guys out without hurting anyone. If they couldn't, the plan was to knock the captors unconscious - with a bottle of beer if nothing else.

But nothing. I could hear Heather breathing through my earpiece. Lane's hand hadn't moved from the top of the door to the handle. His entire body was tense and ready to run, and mine wasn't much better. I could almost feel the pistol tucked between my seat and the console, demanding that I grab it and go protect my daughter, and my heart was pounding so hard I could hear the blood rushing through my ears.

And then the back door opened again. First, a guy staggered out. Behind him came a woman. It was too far away for me to be positive, but I was *pretty* sure that wasn't one of *our* girls. This one seemed to have something in her arms. Then, just behind her, came another guy. Lane released the door latch but didn't quite push it open, and my mind was screaming to know what was going on.

Then Gabby and Olivia came out carrying another girl between them.

"Shit," Lane breathed, jumping out.

But he didn't shift, and he didn't leave. Instead, he hurried to the back, leaning through the open window to grab Scott's gun. With that in his hand, wearing absolutely nothing, Lane raced for the gap the bears had left in the fence. I just strained my eyes to see a little more, trying desperately to figure out what was going on. Our wolves were moving into place. The tigers had to be up there somewhere. The bears were in place to cover the retreat.

And that was when everything went wrong.

CHAPTER 51

"Evelyn!" a man yelled from the fire. It sounded like Damon.

Jax reared up to shove his full weight on the fence.

One of the people with Gabby tripped, staggered, and slammed his hand against the side of the mobile.

And the whole time, Lane was running toward them just as fast as he could go, but the thump on the house had been heard. The men around the fire were all starting to move, trying to figure out what was going on. Gabby and Olivia began to walk a little faster. The girl held between them stumbled, clearly in worse shape than the guys. The other woman - hopefully Damon's mate Evelyn - shoved one of the guys forward.

All of it came to a head just at the back corner of that mobile home. One of Damon's men came around the side, saw the group - and froze. Ashley surged forward, shoving between them with her teeth bared. Roman

488

shifted to human, grabbed the closest guy, and hauled him back toward the fence. For just a moment, I thought we were going to get away with this.

And then Damon came to see what the hell was going on. "They're stealing our converts!" he yelled - and then shifted.

But the man didn't have the chance to do anything else before the tigers were rushing forward. Lev roared. Nik just swiped, knocking Damon's legs out from under him. Vic and Jax got the fence down just as Lane reached them. My mate dropped the rifle beside the smallest bear and then shifted to his wolf. Vic and Jax followed, but Scott held his ground, standing on his hind feet to roar loudly.

The three big men reached Gabby's side and changed back to humans. Jax picked up one of the guys. Vic got the other. Lane grabbed the girl from between Gabby and Olivia, freeing the teens to rush back toward us. The two girls were still dressed, so they couldn't easily shift, but the pack was moving in to protect them. Then Gabby snagged Evelyn's free arm, pulling her along with them.

Wolves were rushing in from all sides, but we'd picked the one direction they didn't expect. Once Gabby, Olivia, and Evelyn were through the gap in the fence, the bears and Lane followed. Scott dropped back to all four feet, shifted into a man while crouching, his hands on the ground, and then straightened up to brace the gun against his shoulder.

"Move!" he bellowed.

That was all it took. Roman and Xander turned to follow their pack. Ashley paused for just a moment, but Kim barked as she passed, convincing Ashley to follow. Lev and Nik, however, were taking their time about it.

The pair backed toward the fence, hissing and swiping at anything that got too close. It was enough to let the rest run halfway across the field before Damon's pack even figured out what was going on.

Then four wolves rushed in, right at Lev. Sadly, they'd picked the wrong tiger. Lev clawed the first, sank his teeth into the second, jumped the third, and swiped at the last. In that moment, I knew why he'd wanted his son with him. One tiger was terrifying, but two? The sight of them covering for each other made the rest of the wolves hang back, too scared to attack.

Somewhere in all the commotion Damon shifted, and he wasn't willing to quit. Snarling, he made a dash at Nik. A sharp crack rang out, the dirt puffed up between the two, and Damon just jumped back. That had been a gun. Scott's gun, I realized.

"Come on, come on, come on," Heather called.

"When you're full, go," I told her. "Get the converts out of here. I think that's Damon's mate, and if it is, she has a baby."

"Fine, but I'm stopping at the highway," Heather told me.

"I'll be right behind you," I promised, watching as Lane and the bears jump-ran through the long grass with the converts in their arms.

Then Scott said, "Time to go, kitties!"

Both tigers spun, retreating to the fence line. There, they turned back around as if they'd done this a few times. Then Scott turned and ran, making it about fifty feet before he stopped and called out, "Go!"

The tigers and human-bear alternated like that, covering each other as the wolves tried to recover. The problem was that more of the wolves were flanking, slipping through the fence, into the pasture, and racing for the side. They wanted to cut us off, and I wasn't sure our group could stop them.

Then the gun went off again and something yelped. "I *will* shoot you," Scott bellowed. "Back the fuck off and let us go. If you come at us, you will not like what happens!"

The wolves paused, milled and looked confused. Damon barked something, but I hadn't learned very many of those yet. The tigers, however, raced back to Scott's side, each one pressing against him, and Scott began to walk backwards. It was almost as if the cats were guiding him. Step by step, the three of them held off Damon's entire pack, and I could hear a wolf growling from here.

Lane, Vic, and Jax finally crossed over the last section of fence. "Put them with Heather," I told him. "Fill her up first and she'll go."

Gabby and Olivia were right behind them, and now I was *sure* the woman with them was Damon's mate. The same woman who'd come to my office. The one who'd wanted out. The girls helped her into Heather's truck as well, and then they split. Olivia climbed in. Jax and Vic helped their converts into the back seat, but Lane went for the trunk. Olivia leaned over the back seat to help as he laid the girl down in the open space, closed the door at the back, and then Lane headed for me.

Then Gabby began giving orders. "Xander, Kim, Jax, with Heather. Everyone else with Mom. Let's move!"

Wolves began jumping into trucks. The bears closed doors. Jax took the front seat beside Heather, and she pulled out, heading up the road without waiting. In my truck, the kids all moved to the back seat. Lane claimed the passenger seat beside me. Scott and the tigers were still making their way backwards, almost to the fence, and the wolves were all getting closer.

"Let's go!" Lane yelled. "Everyone's in."

Scott just turned and ran, heading for the back. He managed to open the hatch just as Lev and Nik jumped through the back door and both men began to shift, but the wolves thought this was their chance. A round of shots burst forth, much louder this close, and someone yipped in pain. In the rearview mirror, I watched as Scott crawled halfway into the back, still hanging out the door with the rifle on his shoulder like some military hero, and then Nik closed the door beside him.

"Go," Scott told me. "Drive fast, Elena, because there's more coming."

A lot more. I eased the truck into motion, terrified I'd drop Scott out the back, but he was good. Just as I hit twenty miles an hour, he leaned out, caught the open door, and pulled it closed, securing himself into the trunk.

"Do we have everyone?" I asked. "Heather? Guys? Is anyone missing?"

There was a long moment while I listened to Heather asking her passengers the same thing. Then, "No, we're good," she said. "Tigers and Scott are the only ones unaccounted for."

"I got them," I promised. "Let's just get home."

Sadly, it couldn't be that easy. "Faster, Elena!" Scott called. "We've got wolves bearing down on us." Then, "Shit, how fast can you fuckers run?"

"About forty miles an hour," Lane said.

"Forty?" I asked, glancing at the speedometer. "I can't do that on a gravel road!"

"Yes," Lane said, "today, you can do a lot more than that."

I turned on my headlights, clenched my hands on the wheel, and tried my best. I didn't bother to look at how fast I was going. I just did what I could to keep this SUV on the road and heading the direction I wanted it. Beneath the wheels, the gravel slipped, making it feel like I was driving on ice, but we'd just stolen four people from Damon's pack.

I knew that wolf was going to be pissed.

Up ahead, I could see the tail lights of Heather's truck barreling down the road the same way I was. In my ear, I could hear her talking to the people in her truck. Then a baby began to cry. That made it five people we'd stolen, and one was Damon's child.

"Shit," Nik breathed. "They're pacing us."

He was looking toward the passenger side of the SUV, but I couldn't turn my head to see. Even that quick glance in the rearview mirror felt like a big risk when going this fast on this bad of a road. Instead, everyone else looked, including Lane.

"Someone check a map," he demanded. "I want to know where they come out, and we need to avoid that."

Which meant they were on the road parallel to us. The one that ran through the trailer park. From what little I could remember, that curved back around while ours went straight to the highway. We'd have at least a little lead, but I had a funny feeling they knew exactly where we were going.

"Heather, we have wolves in cars, and they're going to meet us somewhere before we get home I bet."

"Shit," she laughed. "Driving fast is one thing I can do,

plus I've got three sick people in the car with me. If the cops stop us, well, the wolves won't mess with us. Just make sure everyone has on clothes."

"Get dressed!" I demanded.

"Kinda don't have my clothes," Vic said.

"Me either," Scott pointed out. "And this cute little pair of jeans?"

"Those are mine," Roman said, snatching them from his hands.

"Highway," Heather said, and then I saw her truck slow down.

It didn't stop, though. Instead, she turned left and took off at top speed. When I got closer, I realized why. The end of this road had a clear view of the highway, and there wasn't another car in sight. So, naturally, I did the same. The moment the tires were on asphalt, I felt a lot better about the pace we were going.

"So," I said, "we have a bit of a clothing problem in my truck."

"I told the ones in mine to put on what they could find," Heather said. "I think Scott's gun is going to be a much bigger problem. Just... don't get arrested." And then she began to pull away, clearly putting on the speed.

My friends were all crazy, I decided. The worst part of this was that it had been my idea, but we'd done it. Somehow, we'd just stolen these kids right out from under Damon's nose. Now, if he wanted reparations, at least he'd have something worth asking for.

But we weren't done yet. "Someone call Ian," I said. "Gabby?"

"On it," she promised, wiggling around in the back seat to get to her phone. Then, a light flared in my mirror.

"Hey," she said, sounding like he'd answered. "We're headed back, got four. Three converts who will shift, and a woman with her baby. I guess that means it's five, huh?" There was a pause. "Hell, I don't know," Gabby said. "I do know that they were chasing us in cars, and I'm pretty sure they know that we're the ones with tigers and bears. So yeah, I figure they can't be too far behind us. No, I don't know how fast they're going. Ian! The bears are naked."

"And Scott has a gun that we can't explain," I told her.

"Yeah," Gabby said. "Scott brought the firepower. I mean, the guy's a total badass, but we don't want to get pulled over." She paused. "Oh. Well, ok. Yep. I'll tell her, and I'll call you back when we're close." Then she hung up.

"Tell her what?" Nik asked.

"Ian said drive fast, you've got a good attorney, and that there's some crazy guy chasing you, Mom," Gabby said.

I just hoped he knew what he was doing, but I pushed the pedal a little harder. This was so far out of my comfort zone, but I was making it work. I was also panicking a little inside. It seemed that I really wasn't cut out for being the hero type.

CHAPTER 52

It was 2:14 am when we pulled onto the street that would get us back to Wolf's Run. So far, we hadn't seen anyone chasing us, but there had been a few close calls with too many headlights behind us. Heather and I had split up, using city blocks to get lost in before getting back on the main road. It seemed it had helped.

"Someone call Sheridan, or Ian, or... I don't even care," I ordered.

"On it," Gabby said.

I heard her talking, and it sounded like that was to Ian. Our pair of SUVs were moving just a little too fast for this road, all but begging a cop to notice, but the grand entrance to the community appeared before us. The highly-manicured flowerbeds set off the metal letters against the brick wall proclaiming the community name, and it looked like salvation right about now.

"Gates are open," Gabby called out.

"Hear that?" I asked Heather.

"Oh, I *see* that," she promised as she turned into the drive. "I'm going right to Bridget's!'

I was no more than five car lengths behind her, but when I slowed to make the turn, I saw something behind me. A lot of somethings. It was the middle of the night, so there shouldn't be that much traffic on the road. I could easily count five cars, and I had a feeling that was just the first wave. As Heather sped around the first turn, I lowered my window, then slowed down as I got to the guard shack.

"I think we have some behind us," I warned Sheridan. "I don't want you outside the gates."

"I'm ok with that," she promised, waving me in.

I kept going, aiming for the office parking lot, but what I saw behind me made me even more impressed by my community. Sheridan did something. I didn't even know what. A line of metal pillars, each one as big around as Gabby's waist, began to rise from the ground right in front of the gate. Behind that, the metal strip I'd always assumed was a weight plate turned, revealing sharp metal points. A tire strip, of sorts. The lights in the guard shack turned off, and then the little vixen hopped out and ran between the closing gate.

With only a foot left before the community was completely secure, the first car pulled up. We were piling out of the truck, so the driver decided to do the same. It wasn't anyone I knew, but he looked pissed, and his partially-renovated muscle car was still running.

"Give us back our packmates!" he demanded, yelling at the top of his lungs.

Sheridan answered him the way I wanted to. The girl

lifted her middle finger and grinned. "Ours now, big boy. First rule of wolves: the bigger bitch always wins."

Gabby giggled. Ashley murmured her approval. Vic just cleared his throat. "I'm, uh, borrowing the truck because I still need some pants."

"Same," Lev said from the back seat.

Which was when I saw Ian jogging across the street toward me. "Elena, take the pups to the clinic." The rest of his betas were heading for the doors to the office.

"What's going on?" I asked just as he reached me.

Ian caught both sides of my face. "I'm so glad to see you, but you didn't think this would end here, did you? We're sending out a pack-wide alert. First, that you're back. Second, that Hidden Forest is coming for a challenge."

"No," I breathed, realizing what he was saying. "You fucking knew he'd do this?"

Ian just turned me back toward the SUV. "He has to, just like you had to do this. Get the Sisterhood set up there as a second line of defense, because that's where they'll go next. Damon's going to want his converts back - and his child."

In that moment, I realized why he'd wanted to leave it alone, but he'd let me run with this. This man had allowed his entire pack to be risked because I'd wanted to help these kids. Now, how many more had I just put in danger?

"Ian..." I tried, pausing to turn back.

He just pressed a kiss against my lips. "I'll run if I have to, Elena. If Damon wins, there's nothing saying Ashley can't challenge him. Any pack member, actually. We have options."

But Vic heard. "Any of us, Alpha?" he asked Ian, leaning out the window to be heard.

And Ian began to grin. "Technically, yeah," he said.

Vic chuckled. "I could handle being called the Pack Alpha. I'm also easily bought out. Don't act like a stupid dog, ok?"

"Watch my girls," Ian told him. "That includes my sister."

The men shared a look. Something had just been settled, but it wasn't Ian whose opinion had changed. No, Vic was the one who'd just found comfort with their agreement - but the guy at the gate was still ranting at Sheridan. The fox was still taunting him, but now there were three cars instead of just one. From the traffic on the street behind him, I was starting to wonder if the entire Hidden Forest pack had followed us.

And my guts clenched. "An army," I breathed.

"But we're a pack," Ian said. "Go. Protect the weak ones, Elena. This is *your* fucking den. These are your pups. Every last one. The pack will listen to you as much as they do me, so get ready for this to get ugly. And if it doesn't? Then we lose nothing. I'd rather be safe than sorry."

I climbed back into the truck, along with everyone else - and then Lane whistled. "Sheridan!"

The girl spun, raced across the street, and climbed into the back just as I started the truck again. There wasn't really enough room, so she claimed a spot on Vic's hip, sitting awkwardly because the guy still wasn't wearing pants.

"I need to stop by my place," she said.

"And mine," Lev added. "Heather should be at the clinic with our clothes from earlier."

"We need to hit the trails," Scott said. "Jesse's been grouping the pack into defensive chunks - teams, of a sort."

"But aren't we safe?" I asked as I drove. "The walls, the grates. They can't get in, can they?"

Lane reached over and caught my hand. "They can. One way or another, they will. If we don't give back their converts, they'll use that as an excuse to come and take them."

"Why didn't anyone fucking tell me this!" I screamed, needing to just get it out.

Lane's thumb swept gently across my hand. "Because you're hard to deny. Because you were right."

"Because," Lev said, leaning forward, "if it wasn't this, then it would've been something else, and at least five lives are worth fighting over."

That made me feel a little better, but not much. When Ian had said going into Damon's territory would mean he wasn't risking Wolf's Run, I'd assumed that meant Damon would just lick his wounds and find another way to complain. I'd never imagined a man driving his entire pack across town to assault an upper-middle-class housing community!

There were supposed to be cops to prevent things like this. Then again, if no one called them, they wouldn't come, and none of us wanted humans to see what these men really were. Sampson had already killed a woman, but there had been no legal repercussions because she'd just been a wolf. It also hadn't seemed real. I'd been told, but I hadn't seen the dead animal. That had made it a little too easy to push from my mind.

When I pulled up in front of Bridget's house, everyone piled out. The naked men went straight for the SUV parked in the drive. The kids headed for the clinic with Gabby leading the way. I turned off the truck, thought about it for a split second, and then rolled down the windows and left the keys in the ignition. If anyone needed to get something or pick up someone, we wouldn't have to double back to find keys. Then I followed my daughter.

Inside, the clinic was a quieter version of chaos. People were sorting out their clothes. Ashley and Kim were helping Bridget get the sick boys into rooms where they could lie down. I didn't see the other girl, but Evelyn was soothing her baby, who was still making unhappy noises.

"Alpha!" she gasped when she saw me. "If Damon asks, you can send us back. That should appease him."

"No," Kim yelled back at us.

I just held out my arms. "Can I see the little one?"

"Derek," she told me as she offered her baby. "I named him after the wolf on that show."

Under the blankets, the little boy was adorable. He couldn't have been more than four or five months old, and the boy was wonderfully fat. But the moment his childish eyes landed on me, his face lit up in a smile and all of his fussing stopped.

"Hey, you," I whispered, setting him on my hip. "Aren't you a cutie?" Then I looked at Evelyn. "Why'd you come if you just want to go back?"

"I don't want to go back," she insisted. "I also know that Mia had no idea smiling at a guy in a bar would earn her this. And he's going to make her his mate, just like he did me."

"Are you a convert?" I asked.

She nodded. "Most of us are. Damon picked me up when I was just out of high school. He bit me, he turned me, and then he claimed me. For a bit, I thought it was so romantic, until he took the next girl. Alpha's prerogative, he said."

"Shit," Xander groaned. "I joked about that stuff, but that's just sick."

"Now you see why it's not funny," Olivia told him.

Xander nodded, then simply turned to Gabby. "Alpha?" he asked. "Make sure I never become like that?"

"Then be my beta," Gabby said. "Did you know Pax is an alpha? Ian's betas are all strong. They all work to make him even stronger, and they don't just do what he says. They push him, Xander. I'm not losing Olivia, but I'll gladly take you."

He paused for a moment, looking at his friends. "All of us?"

"Six," Gabby told him. "Two tigers, a human, and my three best wolves. I don't know how else to balance us than to have more than just wolves, and that means a bigger group."

"But I can stay with Olivia?" he asked.

She nodded. "Fuck those outdated traditions. Wolf's Run isn't like any other pack, right? So that means we can't be like any other leadership group. I'm the alpha of our group, and I will take the responsibility, but I need the strongest betas I can find, and I need to know that you aren't just going to tell me what I want to hear."

"Then yes," he told her. "I'll roll over for you later, but

count me in." And he caught her hand. "You're a better wolf than I'll ever be. Now let's protect our pack."

"Whoa!" I snapped. "Where do you kids think you're going?"

Gabby just turned to smile at me deviously. "We didn't steal a few people just to throw them to the wolves, right? Ian sent us to guard the medics. First, that means we need to get some backup. We're going outside, Mom."

I didn't try to stop her. That didn't mean I didn't worry, but if Gabby was going to stay back here, buried in the center of this community, it was better than her trying to stand by Ian's side. I was the one who'd brought all of this on us, and yet I couldn't make myself regret it. I simply hated Damon a little more for being unreasonable.

"You," I told Evelyn, "are not a possession to be passed around because some man decides it. Derek here? He needs to grow up and learn that some of the strongest wolves are women. And this place? It's a sanctuary. We're not using you as bait or leverage. If you want to stay, then stay, and we will fight for your right to make that decision."

A slow clap proved that my little speech had been heard. "There she is," Ashley said. "That's the Alpha Female of Wolf's Run."

I just handed Evelyn's baby back, clasped the woman's shoulder, and turned to my best friend. "I learned from the best, right?"

"No, Elena." Ashley turned me to the rooms at the back. "You changed the rules. For as long as I can remember, the Alpha Mate was a position for social functions. You? You made being the second in command into a powerhouse. That's why Karen hates you. Ian listens to you. Hell, half the time he rolls over for you. And this?" She pushed open the first door.

A small bed was placed against the wall. A cheap white blanket covered the girl in it. Sweat stood out in drops on her skin, and she looked pallid and uncomfortable, but her eyes still turned to the sound. They were wide with fear.

"Twenty years old," Ashley told me. "Waitress at a local bar. She did the same thing so many of us have and smiled a little nicer to get a better tip. This is how Damon paid her back."

"I didn't even like the guy," the girl, who must be Mia, said. "I was just working! But when I went to my car, he and two others jumped me in the parking lot. The man changed into a wolf and bit me! And he says I'm going to become a monster."

"A werewolf," I told her. "Just like me, just like half those people who saved you tonight - including the two girls - and just like your doctor."

"She's..." The girl shut her mouth hard.

"A wolf," Ashley said. "The good kind. The man who kidnapped you? He's not. None of us want to hurt you, but you're going to keep getting sick until Friday. That's when you'll turn. We will help you through it, make sure you're safe and protected, and then you can decide where you want to go from there."

"Where am I?" she asked.

"It's a medical clinic," I explained. "There are two guys in the rooms next to you."

"Jonah?" she asked. "Damon hated him. He said the punk talked back, and he'd pay for it one way or another."

I nodded. "Him and the other guy. The one who just got bit."

"Christian," she said. "They chained us up together."

"And we're going to get you three through this together," I promised. "I know it seems terrifying, and I know you think this has to be a bad joke, but it's not."

"I saw them," she broke in. "The werewolves. I know it's real because I saw them change!"

"Soon, you'll be able to do that too," I assured her. "And when that happens, you'll become just as strong as they are. No more assholes grabbing you without your permission, because you'll be able to make them pay for it."

And the girl smiled weakly. "Yeah, that does sound like an upside. I just wish my headache would go away. I'm so tired, and I ache all over."

"So get some rest," I told her as I pulled Ashley back out of the room. But in the hall I turned to my best friend. "He kidnapped her?"

"And was planning on raping her until she gets Stockholm syndrome and gives in," Ashley added. "Elena, Evelyn was telling them all about it on the way back. From what I know so far, it sounds like Damon had a pretty good little system. He turned anyone he wanted to. The women he made his fuck toys, until they either got strong enough to fight back or bored him. The men? Those he used as his thugs. He didn't care if they got killed in the process, because he could always make more. And when Karen showed up?" She waved her arm indicating everything around us. "She convinced him to build the biggest army of converts he could. Evelyn said they'd have fifty converts shift each moon."

"So there's more?" I asked.

Ashley just shook her head. "They were planning to attack before next weekend. They said they were ready, so they didn't need to turn anymore. These? Jonah screwed up Damon's order at McDonalds. The boy wasn't upset enough about it, Damon said, so he turned him, saying he hoped the boy learned his lesson. The girl was a spontaneous thing because she made his dick hard. The other guy? He got in Damon's face at a bar or club. I'm not sure, but this is his punishment."

"Asshole," I breathed.

Ashley just nodded. "Karen finally found her perfect mate. Someone with a title, who loves her last name, and who's just as fucked up as she is. Together? They're dangerous, Elena."

"And they're currently coming to pick a fight with us," I pointed out. "They're not going to stop, are they?"

"Not unless someone makes them stop," Ashley said.

I just looked over at her. "You know I'm too old for this shit, right?"

"You and me both, sister," she agreed. "How about we kill a bitch tonight, hm?"

"And wine tomorrow," I decided, not even feeling guilty at the idea. Evidently I was more of a wolf than I'd realized.

CHAPTER 53

E lena left, but more cars and trucks kept arriving. Many drove past. I could hear them slow and turn, most likely into one of the properties around us. Then a newer pickup turned into the outbound lane for the community, effectively blocking any of us from leaving. The door opened, and Damon stepped out. From the passenger side, Karen did the same.

Behind me, I heard the office door open and steps moving closer. That was probably my betas, but I wouldn't turn to check. I stood on the median just inside the property, maybe ten feet behind the secured gates. Too far for one of them to reach through and grab me. Close enough to make it clear I wasn't backing down.

One by one, my betas fell in at my sides. Seth to my right, Trent and Pax on my left. I missed Lane's presence, but I felt better knowing he was with Elena. None of us said a thing, watching as Damon adjusted the tail of his shirt, closed the door of his truck and headed around the front to offer Karen his arm like she was some elegant lady.

"Well, well," Damon almost purred. "So you do exist, Ian."

"And you're still taking my castoffs," I taunted. "What do you want, Damon? This isn't your territory."

"Gonna piss on it?" he teased.

I just smiled. "Already did. You know, when I roam around in here freely as a wolf. Take a deep breath. That smell? It's called success."

Damon huffed, trying to laugh like he was amused, yet I knew that had hit a little too close to home. Beside him, Karen glared. Her eyes jumped over to Trent and Pax, then she looked to Seth. Not a single one of my betas moved. They just looked back as if they didn't care at all. In truth, I had a feeling they honestly didn't.

"You took something of mine," Damon finally said. "I want it back."

"Can you describe it?" I asked.

"My mate!" he snarled.

I just pointed at Karen. "Who's that?"

"She's my first mate. You have my third - and my son."

Well, that explained things a little more. Too bad for him, I agreed with Elena on this. "Mm, I don't think I do. No one here is being held against their will, and if your mate left you, then clearly she's no longer your mate. Most of us call that getting dumped."

"She doesn't get that choice," Damon snapped. "I made her, and I'm not done with her."

So I looked over at Karen. "Is he done with you, then?"

"Please," she grumbled. "If he wants to rut on a few

girls, then that's his privilege as the Pack Alpha. Oh, you didn't know that I'm not the jealous type? Thought you would've figured that out already, Ian. I mean, I've been banging your betas since they could get their dicks hard."

"Does Damon know I fucked you too?" I asked. "Or did you leave that little part off? He can't even get a natural-born wolf that hasn't been mine first."

"I wasn't yours!" she yelled.

Bingo. From the way Damon looked at her, I knew I'd just hit a sore spot. Either she'd never told him she'd fucked me, or he hated being reminded of it. Either way, the more pissed off he was, the less he'd be thinking when he actually fought me. We all knew that was where this was going, but I wanted to have the deck stacked in my favor before I opened that gate to let him in.

"Oh, Karen, you begged for me," I reminded her. "You tried to chase off my mate so you could have me. Damon was your backup plan, and I'm willing to bet you're the one who convinced him to look at Wolf's Run. Does he know what you think of the trash who live in mobile homes? How does it feel to fit into that category yourself now? Without your daddy's money - or mine - life's a whole lot harder, isn't it?"

"This should've been my pack," she growled.

"I challenge you!" Damon suddenly yelled. "We all know you're a weak alpha. Your mate does what she wants. Your betas claim her as their own! You allow teenagers to invade other packs, go against your rules, and more. You are a weak leader, Ian, and not fit to run this pack."

"Yeah, yeah," I said, flicking a finger toward the brick column between the inbound and outbound gates. "Not the best challenge speech I've ever heard, but I get the point. But here's the thing. You lose? I take any members of your pack that I want. Karen is not on that list."

"You want my converts?" he all but sneered. "Oh, that's almost funny. One of the oldest lines of wolves is begging for a little new blood. Have you all finally interbred too much?"

"Nah." I just tilted my head at Seth. "You make strong wolves. Could've been the thing that set you apart, but you're too stupid to use it."

"Alpha?" Pax asked.

"Open it just enough to let him in," I said. "This is still my territory until he wins. Your pack is still not welcome, and only a fool would declare war on us."

"With your lame father, ditzy sister, and human mate?" Damon asked. "Please, Ian. Oh, and I know about your shifter pets. Bears and tigers, huh? Do they do tricks too?"

"They do," I assured him. "Ever seen a bear's mid-form? I don't even know what they call it, but it's impressive. The tigers? They could be right beside you and you'd never have a clue."

The fact that he glanced over to the bushes was all the gratification I needed. Clearly, Damon had gotten a pretty close view of "my" tigers. But Pax turned the key, and the outbound gate began to slide open. When it was a man's width from the pillar, Pax stopped it. I knew the rest would find a way in if they wanted it, but we didn't need to make it easy.

Damon pushed through the gap. Karen followed behind him. The rest of Damon's pack moved closer to the gate, but weren't dumb enough to follow with us standing guard. Pax closed the gates again, waiting until they were completely secure, then pulled out the key and casually dropped it into his pocket.

A few of Damon's wolves grabbed the metal bars, setting up to watch the show. Some wandered to the sides, which made my guts clench. I didn't trust this man. I didn't trust his pack. Knowing we'd need at least a little room, I began to back up, aiming for the office parking lot.

"So?" Karen asked, sarcasm dripping from her voice. "How soft have you gotten eating nothing but Mexican food while doing nothing to burn it off?" Then she leaned closer to Damon. "Baby, he's a little sexually frustrated. His mate's scared of catching what he's got."

I just pulled off my shirt and tossed it aside carelessly. "Think so?"

I knew I was in good shape. I'd spent the last few weeks working with the bears, tigers, and my betas to prepare for this. The moment Karen had called Elena, I'd known something would happen. No, I hadn't expected *this*, but while Elena learned to walk, run, and jump, I'd been training myself. I was ready. I knew I was, just like I knew that if Damon was truly stronger than me that I'd run.

I'd sworn it to the woman I loved, and I would not go back on that.

"Guys?" I looked over at Seth. "If this goes bad, tell Lane she's his."

Seth nodded. "Understood, Alpha."

Then Damon pulled off his own shirt. Of course the man was built. Where I was fit, he was as broad as Lane and covered in tattoos like Seth. Granted, Damon's were a little more haphazard, looking like they'd been done almost randomly. When I reached the parking lot, I kicked off my shoes. At the same time, my hands were opening my jeans. Damon matched me, refusing to look away.

I wasn't sure what kind of trick he was expecting, though. I could shift, I could run, or I could fight. In order to do a few of those, I'd either need more clothes - like my shoes - or less. Then I heard it. From the back side of the property, a wolf called out, and it wasn't one of mine. Another answered from the side, then the other side of the community. I was pretty sure they were still outside the walls, but we were definitely surrounded.

"You're not getting out of this," Damon told me. "I'm taking Wolf's Run, and I will kill anyone that stands against me."

"And I'm going to make that human bitch pay," Karen added. "Let's see how she likes turning outside of these walls."

Then a howl sounded in the middle of the community, and this voice I'd know anywhere. That was Gabby, and she was calling the entire pack to the hunt. Slowly, I began to smile.

"That's my daughter, Karen, and she's twice the wolf you'll ever be. Her mother?" I pushed my pants to the ground instead of finishing that.

Damon lunged, shifting as he came at me. I managed to jump back, leaving my pants and one sock where I'd been. The other still hung on my ankle, but Damon was tangled in his pants. That meant I had the chance to finish stripping. I wrenched the sock off my foot and threw it with the rest just as Damon rolled from the last of his clothes.

"Idiot," I breathed.

Which made him lunge again, but I was ready. By the time he reached where I'd been, I was a lot shorter and hairier. He hit the ground hard, and I was on him. My teeth sank deep into his flank. Damon snarled and spun, trying to get ahold of me, but I was already moving. My teeth caught his snout and I tasted blood, but his caught my shoulder. Pain flared as my skin tore, but I couldn't stop.

The pair of us wove and dodged around each other. Teeth clacked loudly, but it wasn't enough to drown out the sound of more howls in the distance. I wasn't sure which direction I was facing anymore, but that was too close. Wolf's Run was being invaded, and there was not a damned thing I could do until I finished this man.

Then someone else snarled. I caught movement from the edge of my eye. Damon jumped back, but that was Karen rushing at Pax. Seth was stripping as fast as he could. Trent didn't bother. When Karen moved past, he grabbed a handful of her scruff in one hand, her tail in the other and slung her away. In those few seconds, Pax managed to get both his shirt and shoes off, but Seth was already a wolf.

My beta snarled as he moved between her and his packmates. They had this, but the distraction had allowed Damon and myself to separate. The man rushed me again, so I decided to use Trent's trick. A thought pushed me back onto two legs. As the brown and white wolf snapped, I buried my fingers in his hair, using his own momentum to help swing him up, around, and then down onto the concrete - hard.

The breath was forced from his wolf form in a rush,

but I still kicked, right on his useless, scrawny little canine dick. Yet before he could even yelp, I shifted again and came at him hard. My teeth found the side of his neck. I felt the skin pop as they pierced it, and then I shook, trying to cause as much damage as possible. If I broke his fucking neck, it wouldn't bother me at all.

Damon cried out, his yelp of pain carrying on the night air. Unfortunately, not all the snarls were coming from us. Lifting my eyes let me see Trent and Pax holding Karen back. A glance in the other direction showed some of Damon's pack climbing their way over the gate to get inside. I had a feeling there were more doing the same at other points around the walls. I had to end this. I needed to defend my pack!

But Damon got his feet around, using them to push off my body. I didn't let go, but his skin tore, allowing him to slip free. I jumped right back on him, but the man was ready for that. His mouth found the back of my neck, right above my shoulders. I shifted again, letting him slip through my form just to change into a man and grab his back legs. He bent, sinking his teeth deep into my arm, but I didn't care. I slung that wolf like a cheap sack of grain, slamming him back down onto the hard parking lot.

"We," I yelled before doing it again, "are not," and then again, "beasts!"

The last impact dazed him enough to make him let go, but I was hurting. When I found my wolf again, that leg was lame, refusing to hold my weight, but I didn't have time for this shit. The man would never stop until he was dead. His pack was attacking mine. I needed him out of the way so I could deal with that and protect my mate and pup.

We slammed into each other again, but the wounds were adding up. His bites were weak, but I couldn't dodge fast enough to get away from all of them. That meant I had to deal with his head and everything that came with it. The next time he shoved in to bite me, I grabbed the only thing I could catch: his ear.

Then I pulled.

Damon fell over, squealed, and tried to get away. I thrashed, shaking him as hard as I could. My breath was coming so fast, and I still felt like I couldn't breathe, but I didn't care. I had time for that later. Right now, I was winning. I'd told Elena I'd run, but only if I couldn't beat this man, and I knew very well that I had him.

He realized it at the same time and became frantic. His snarls turned to whimpers. His attacks became desperate attempts to get free. Then he just yanked. Blood filled my mouth, my grip lessened, but my teeth still held him. The man screamed as only an injured wolf could, and then did it again. Something broke, the release of tension made me stumble back, left with nothing but part of his ear in my teeth, and Damon scrambled away. He didn't even need to admit his defeat. Running was the same thing.

I tried to follow but that leg gave out, sprawling me onto the ground, so I shifted back to a man. "Seth!" I yelled. "He's running. He's defeated. Get that bastard off my territory!"

The words weren't even out of my mouth before my beta took off, little more than a streak of blonde and grey chasing the man who'd once thought he could make me submit.

CHAPTER 54

The moment that Damon bolted, Karen tried to follow. Trent grabbed her hind leg and I shifted, wrapping my hand around her tail. Then Karen tried the same trick, but she formed swinging. Her fist caught me right in the mouth, knocking me onto my naked ass. Trent just moved around her, his lips curled in a warning snarl, but I couldn't stop the laugh.

"Your big plan is failing," I managed to get out.

"Fuck you, Pax."

"Did that," I chuckled. "Oh, you have become so pathetic! You know, I actually used to like you, back when we were teenagers. I thought you were the most amazing girl I'd ever seen." I laughed again at the stupidity of it. "But that wasn't enough. We weren't enough. Nah, you wanted Ian. Not once did you stop to think that if we'd fallen in love with you, he would've made it happen, just like he did for Lane."

"I deserved this pack," she hissed.

Trent just growled, making it clear what he thought of that.

"And you!" she yelled, knowing she was pinned between us. "Do you honestly think that human bitch is going to want the two of you? She'll clutch at her damned pearls and run screaming when she realizes what gets you off."

"Not even close," I promised, reaching up to wipe the blood from my mouth, but still laughing. "Go ahead, Karen. Chase your newest lover. Go after mine if you must, but you should know that a lot has changed since you left. Elena has betas. She also has Lane, and he won't give a shit who tried to hurt his mate. He'll kill you."

Trent barked, the sound a sharp correction.

So I decided to translate that for her. "Or, like my best friend says, Elena will."

Karen turned, glared at Trent, and then just shifted, bolting between the pair of us. Trent appeared to consider chasing after her, but Ian was lying on the asphalt a few feet away, and he looked like he'd just had his ass handed to him. Huffing in frustration, Trent shifted into a man, offered me a hand up, and then the pair of us went to our Alpha.

"You hurt bad?" I asked.

"Fucking arm," Ian said. "I'm lame as a wolf. Might be broken." He lifted it to show what he meant.

Trent just pointed back at the barred gates. "Yeah, well they're all inside now. Sorry, but we couldn't stop them."

"You're fine," Ian promised, but the man sounded like he was in some serious pain. "We knew we couldn't. The trick is going to be turning them back. Who's watching the community center?"

"Henry," Trent said. "Samantha and Theo are with him. We ordered all non-combatants and children there. Heather and Kim said they'd guard the outside, which means there will be a few more to help them, I'm sure."

"Lev," I chuckled.

Ian looked over with confusion on his face. "He's into her?"

"Sounds like he's fucking her," I corrected. "Now, let's go find Damon before Seth does."

"Elena," Ian countered.

"Damon," Trent told him. "Elena's fine. She's got Lane, Bridget, and god only knows who else. The only way anyone's getting to Elena is if Elena goes after them first. Damon's the problem, and so long as he's running around, those converts aren't going to know to stop."

"You sure Karen hasn't finally made it to being an alpha?" I asked, the question for either of them. "Because I'm not convinced who they're following, Damon or her."

"Then we'll kill them both," Ian decided. "One way or another, Hidden Forest is done. But guys? I can't fight. Not as a wolf, and I'm one-armed as a man."

"We can," I reminded him. "Ian, this is why you have betas. Let us help, ok?"

Ian looked down at his arm, the opposite hand clasped over the wound. It was clear he didn't like it. "I can't let Hidden Forest take my pack."

"And you are not alone in this. Let's get you looked at," Trent told him. "If it's not broken, then we can get you back into this. If it is? Then you're still the leader, and we are your other arms."

Then he shifted, and I followed suit, but Ian couldn't. His arm was mangled and bloody, ripped to shreds. His body was bitten and battered. He limped beside us slowly, proving he was in pain. The man had clearly gotten the shit beat out of him, and in all honesty, I had no idea how he was still conscious, let alone walking. There was blood in his hair, open wounds on his thigh and back. I couldn't even count them all.

But Ian wasn't the kind of man who'd stop because something hurt a *little*. That was why he'd never been challenged. Too many of us had seen him push far past what anyone else could. Didn't matter if that was something as seemingly insignificant as holding his temper at bay or making something work - like Wolf's Run. He always found a way to make things work. So if Ian was saying he couldn't fight, that meant he was hurt bad.

So tonight, we would fight for him.

Because we would not lose all of this. I honestly believed in not just my Alpha, but everything this pack had become. Once, we'd been nothing but a group of wolves trying to go unnoticed. Then Elena had moved in. Now this place was so much more. The idea of a sanctuary had grown into something bigger. A true safe place for those who needed it. The craziest part was that it made me feel a little bit like some kind of knight. My armor was a bit fuzzy, though.

It felt like it took forever to get to the community center on foot. Mostly because I didn't know what was going on with the rest of the pack. The front of the grassy area was almost empty. The sounds of fighting came from further back, and we followed them, heading right for the building in the very middle. The moment it came into view, I knew we'd just found the real conflict.

So many wolves were scattered around the grassy yard. I knew all of ours, but too many were coats I didn't recognize. A bitch yelped at the side, and another of ours rushed to help her. Seeing one of ours on the ground being ravaged by one of Damon's, I pushed Ian toward the doors.

"Go," I told him. "Get that checked out, get fixed, and see if you can get back into this."

For a moment, Ian looked like he was going to ignore me. His eyes scanned the pack, jumping from scuffle to wounded wolf, and then back to me. But just before he could open his mouth, Trent spoke up.

"Elena's orders, Ian, and you know it. She's as much my Alpha as you are. Go!"

"Tear them apart," Ian snarled - and then he hurried for the doors.

Immediately, I rushed in to help our own. Trent was right beside me. I knew Ian hated this. In truth, I did too, but we were a pack. Our power came from trusting each other to pick up the slack when one of us couldn't. Right now, Ian was the one who needed help, and I was more than willing to rip out a few throats in his name.

These people wanted to take the community center. I'd be damned if that happened. Inside there were all of our most vulnerable packmates, and right now, Ian was one of them. He'd power through his injuries if he had to - possibly dying because of them - but he'd picked his betas to make sure that wasn't necessary. Trent and I shared a look, both of us impressed that we didn't have to wrestle our Alpha to make him get treated. There was no doubt in my mind that if this wasn't quashed soon, we were going to need his strength again. Then another of our wolves cried out in pain.

I slammed into the wolf on our packmate, Trent sank his teeth into the male's neck, and we got him off. The injured wolf rushed for safety, leaving this bastard to us. Too bad for him, he didn't quite move like he knew his body yet - but we did. I lunged. When the guy dodged, Trent was right there to make him pay for it. Teeth snapped. Fur stuck to my tongue, but I was looking for something else. I wanted blood.

The moment I pierced his skin, the wolf yelped and struggled to get free. Trent jumped on him as well. We both kept going, tearing into him savagely until the male could no longer fight back. Only then did we leave him, moving to the next. A glance at the community center showed the lights were on inside. That would make this place a target, but it looked like we were defending it well enough, and none of us wanted the kids inside to be afraid. We just wanted Damon's pack to leave us alone.

But too many were hurt. Everywhere I looked, wolves were injured. Some were bad, others no worse than me. I was just starting to worry when I heard the roar of something that made my hair rise. Something my instincts knew was bad. And then a pale orange and white tiger came around the edge of the building. The black wolf beside him was paired with two greys of different patterns. Behind them came Bridget in her human form, burdened with two messenger bags slung across her body.

That meant Gabby and her betas were working as the guards. I barked at Trent and we hurried to follow, only to see Jesse bringing up the rear. The man was small, about the size of a border collie, and while he was technically a dog, that was where the similarities ended. His coat was brown with black and white patches. His ears were large, swiveling constantly, and I knew for a fact that the little fucker could fight. He was like a cross between a fox and a lion when pushed.

And then everyone around me began to move. Without thinking, I looked to see what they were moving away from and saw a whole line of Damon's wolves. I turned, growled, and braced up. Trent fell in at my side, and for a moment, I was sure the two of us were about to take this on our own. But then our women arrived.

Heather rushed them from the front, snapping at one just to dart away. That made Damon's largest wolves all turn to look - and it was their biggest mistake. Ashley hit one from behind. Kim took the next only a second later. The snarls were vicious, and those women were determined to kill the men they were latched onto. Then Heather rushed past me and slid to a stop, turning back with her tongue hanging from her face. Our eyes met, she nodded, and then a human voice rang out.

"Guard the center!" Gabby screamed from the doors. "Wolf's Run, pull back. The cavalry has arrived!"

Heather huffed as if this had been planned. I turned back to the oncoming wolves just in time for true horror to descend. I had no idea where they'd come from, but Nikolai hit first with Lev right behind him. The first wolf died instantly. The second was clawed so bad I knew he wouldn't live long. Trent barked in excitement, and the three of us charged in to help.

I knew I was a badass. I'd thrown around enough men and wolves to have proved it, yet I'd never fought beside a tiger before. Nikolai sprang into the air, twisted his body, and came down on the same wolf I was thrashing. I felt the moment the tiger's jaws broke the man's spine as the reverberations traveled through his body. The wolf went limp and I moved on.

But someone turned on Heather. I tried to help, but a bitch shoved in front of me, her teeth clacking together only inches from my nose. Heather yelped, but I couldn't help. Then Trent was down, ravaged by two others. I fought desperately, unable to turn back for my best friend or rush forward for my packmate.

Then the bitch coming at me was just gone. A blur of pale orange and black stripes flashed before my eyes, but Lev didn't stop until he got to Heather. Gold drew my attention the other way as I turned to help Trent. I took one of the wolves on him, but Ashley hit the other. The moment Trent was free, he joined in, grabbing the haunches of the wolf I was fighting. Like a toy, the two of us began to pull, ignoring the fool's screams until they finally stopped.

Carnage. The whole thing was complete carnage, but I had no idea where Ian had gone or what had happened to Seth. Lane was with Elena, and she'd be with the teens we'd saved. But where were the bears? How many more wolves were out there? What had happened to Damon?

Slowly but surely, we fought back, breaking the line and leaving dead and wounded behind us. The stench of blood was thick in the air. The fight felt like it was never-ending, but to my left I saw Lev reach over to lick the side of Heather's head. She leaned into it, but there was something so protective about the way the big cat stood over her.

To my left, Nikolai was with Gabby and Roman, the pair of boys clearly guarding their alpha, but Gabby was sticking close to the building. Theo was braced before the doors with Olivia at his side and... Was that Xander? Clearly, they'd just become the sentinels. Behind me, Bridget scurried among the wounded, and Jesse kept pace. Another wolf had joined them, the man's coat just a bit too red to be compared to a coyote.

Which meant we were winning. Slowly but surely, we were pushing Damon's pack out! I couldn't stop to think about the injuries, or if any of ours had been killed, but I couldn't see faces I knew among the dead. Just strangers. Boys who'd been sent here to die. Nothing about this felt good. It felt like a betrayal of everything we were - but pack came first.

Pack always came first. It had to.

CHAPTER 55

Ridley had burst into the clinic panting that the community center needed a doctor. Too many wolves were hurt, and more were going down. I promised I'd send her, and the girl shifted again, turning into a nearly black fox and rushing off to the trails. Within seconds, even the white tip of her tail was almost impossible to see in the darkness.

So I'd sent Bridget to save our pack. Gabby had immediately stepped up. While Elena was still in the room with that high school boy, I gave my pup the rules. She was to guard Bridget, not get in the middle of the fighting, and hold back. The last thing we needed was our doctor getting pulled away because her own guards were doing too much. Let the plan work like it had been designed.

Gabby swore she'd be good, and then they were off. Now, I had to explain to my mate that I'd just allowed her daughter - and a whole group of teenagers - to wade into the mess outside. Just to be safe, I locked the deadbolt on the doors and headed back. Evelyn and her son were talking to Mia. Surprisingly, Sampson had shown up to help. Elena had asked him to talk to the other boy, the older one, and Sampson had agreed.

But my mate was talking to the kid who went to school with her own daughter. When I reached that room, I tapped lightly and then walked in. Both heads turned to see who'd entered, and then Elena smiled. Gently, she rubbed the kid's arm.

"Jonah, this is Lane, one of the leaders of our pack. He's called a beta."

"The guys who chained us up were called betas," he said.

"Betas are the ones who serve as an extension of the leader's power," she told him. "Good leader means good betas. Bad leaders mean bad betas. Lane's a pretty good guy."

The boy huffed out a weak laugh. "Pretty big, too."

"Yeah, um, I was kinda raised by wolves," I explained. "Real ones, I mean. Being in the wrong form for so long kinda, uh... They think it had a few side effects. Like my eyes."

"They're cool," Jonah said. "Are mine going to be like that?"

"More amber," I told him. "Probably about the same as Gabby's."

He smiled. "Yeah, she's cool. Doesn't talk to anyone but the other rich kids, but she's cool."

Elena chuckled at that. "Her pack, Jonah. She's the heir to this pack's leader. Those 'rich kids' aren't all rich. They're just all wolves, like you're going to be."

He nodded. "Ok. And there's no way to stop this?"

"No," she said. "I'm sorry. Once you're infected, you get this disease, but I promise it's not a bad one to have."

"I just want to go home," the kid breathed. "My mom has to be freaking out, and she needs my help. I don't even know how long I was chained up in there. I lost count somewhere, but Mom can't afford all the bills on her own. She - "

"Shh," Elena breathed. "It's ok. For tonight, we're going to make sure you're ok. Tomorrow, we'll get in touch with your mother, ok? For now, just try to close your eyes and rest a bit. I'm sure your head is killing you."

"Thanks, Elena," he said as she stood.

I just opened the door wider, allowing her to slip past me and into the hall. The moment I closed the door, she turned, lifting her chin to look at me. "What?" she asked, knowing that I'd walked in there for some reason.

"Gabby's helping get Bridget to the wounded," I told her. "I made it clear that she's not to fight unless she can't help it. She's got all of her betas except Nikolai, and he's with his dad."

"Ian?" she asked.

Yeah, that was the problem. "No word yet, but the pack's still fighting." I cupped the side of her face. "He's a strong wolf, bunny. Stronger than he's ever let you see. Stronger than me, that's why he's the Pack Alpha and I'm not."

"But Damon's insane," she whined.

I nodded. "I know. I also know that sooner or later someone was going to try this. Wolf's Run is too obvious, and too sweet of a prize. Eventually some crazy Alpha would get desperate enough to try to take it."

"Is this always going to happen?" she asked.

"No," I promised, sliding my thumb along the side of her face. "Once we push this back, the others will be scared to try again. We'll have earned our reputation, have been tried and tested. Elena, we just have to make it through tonight."

"You should be out there," she decided.

"I should be with you," I countered. "Ian has three other betas. Three good ones. If I'm with you, that means he doesn't have to put an entire pack of men protecting the thing he treasures most. Just me."

"Yeah, but - "

The sound of the clinic door shattering cut her off. She turned, but I was already pushing before her, heading that way. As we passed the last door in the hall, it opened and Evelyn stuck her head out. Elena just guided the woman back in, holding a finger to her lips.

"Stay with Mia," Elena ordered.

And Elena stayed with me. The flat of her hand rested on my spine as I moved forward. For a moment, there was nothing, and then I heard a little more of the glass being broken off, almost like someone was trying to clear it out of their way. When I reached the end of the hall, I realized that was exactly what it was, but this wasn't the face I expected to see.

"Karen," I snarled.

Behind me, another door opened. Before me, the woman's head snapped up. "Lane. And here I was hoping you were dead. Where's the baby?"

"What do you want with the baby?" Elena asked, trying to push around me.

I shoved my hand out, holding her back. Then

Sampson spoke up, proving that had been him coming out of the room a second ago. "Alpha, let him do this."

Elena stepped back. I turned my head just enough to see that crotchety old man move to shield her, then my eyes were back on Karen. "Well?" I asked. "Why are you so interested in someone else's child, Karen?"

"That's Damon's brat," she said. "Damon, the man who said he was so strong, but ran as soon as Ian bit him. He lost, Lane, and that means Hidden Forest is mine now. I'm just here to make sure there's no one else who can try to take it from me."

"Get the fuck out of here," I warned, taking a step closer.

"I challenge your Alpha Female!" Karen barked, halting me in my tracks. "Because as the Alpha of Hidden Forest, I can do that. And if I win, my pack joins with yours, we all get to move right back in here, and I'm the second in charge. Might be the long way about it, but I can handle that."

"No," I told her.

"Elena has to," Sampson said.

But Karen looked just a bit too smug - the insane type. "And I'm going to bite your little toy, Lane. I'm going to make you watch as she turns, but she sure won't have these walls to keep her safe, or her little boyfriends to explain what happens next."

"You bitch!" I growled.

"When that's done, I'm going to take that baby, and I'll outrank both you and that relic of a man that Henry let into the pack. That means you will have to stand there and watch while I bash its fucking head in."

Behind me, Elena was almost growling. I half expected

her to shove past me, but she didn't know the rules to our wolf games. "Fine," I said. "This happens outside - not on the broken glass. You both get to strip first, so there's no advantage. Sampson and I will bear witness, and if she runs? I will pull you off."

"If you can stop me before she's dead," Karen taunted.

"And I get to explain the rules to her." I pointed at the door. "Might as well get ready, because it's not like we can keep you out."

She snorted in amusement, but turned back the way she'd come. "Five minutes, Lane, then I'll kill the bitch right here."

"Is there something in the water over there?" Elena asked.

I just ignored that, spinning to grab her shoulders. "Listen to me. She doesn't know you're a wolf. That's going to give you the jump on her. She will bite you, probably a lot. Ignore it. That feeling burning in the back of your mind right now? The one that's making you growl when you think about protecting that baby? Hold it, Elena. Use it. Don't think about what comes next. Don't try to do this the right way. You are a fucking wolf, and your instincts know what to do."

"Lane, I've never - "

"I know," I broke in. "Doesn't matter. You ran hard as a wolf. You jumped. You played. You climbed up trails and down them. That is the wolf you need to be, so don't think about it. Just like when you change forms, little bunny. Reach for what you need, don't push it away. Let the rage, the anger, and even the fear run through you. Bite hard. Hit harder." Then I gestured to my throat. "If you can lock your teeth under here, around her windpipe, she'll submit. If you can grab and tear, she'll bleed out. Bite hard, bite deep, and don't stop biting until you can't take anymore - because when you run, that woman is going to come in here, kill that little baby boy, cut the boys' throats, and tear out both of the girls'. Five lives. That's what you're fighting for. Those five kids that are depending on their Alpha Female to protect their fucking den!"

"Now let's go," Sampson said. "Once you're outside, take everything off. I'll hold it."

"He also won't look," I promised. "Believe it or not, we aren't going to judge you for being naked."

And I led my mate forward, twisting the deadbolt to unlock it. Then I pushed open the broken door and let her step out first. Sampson followed. The old man was being calm and quiet - which wasn't like him. But when I moved to his side, he caught my eye. His were filled with nothing but rage. This little act? It was all for Elena, to keep her calm before her challenge.

But inside, I was seething. That fucking bitch had found the one way to keep me from going after her. If Damon was still the pack leader, we could ignore her. If I knew Ian had claimed the pack, I could ignore her. The problem was that I couldn't prove it either way, which meant Karen got the right to call a challenge, and Elena had to answer it or forfeit everything - including her claim on me.

Piece by piece, Elena took off her clothes, letting them drop to the ground. Across Bridget's lawn, Karen stood there in her full glory, watching as if judging my mate. The problem was that Elena was the more beautiful of the pair. Her hips flared in the exact way I liked. Her stomach was soft, like a place I wanted to lay my head. Elena's skin was warm and inviting. Karen just looked like any other naked woman, and I'd seen plenty in my life.

The moment Elena was bare, Karen took a step forward. "I'm going to kill you, Elena. You ruined my entire life, and I finally have a way to make you pay for that."

"I'm not going to let you touch that baby," Elena told her. "I already held you off with a stick. I think this time will be even easier. I'm not the same terrified woman I was this winter."

Karen smiled. "Good, that'll make this even more fun." Then she lunged, her form shifting as she pushed toward Elena.

I stepped forward, unable to help myself, but Sampson grabbed my arm to hold me back. "Respect your mate," he whispered. "That's a real woman you got there, Lane. Trust her."

Elena had jumped out of the way, but she was still human. Before her was the taupe and white form of Karen as a wolf, but my mate was still on two legs. In my chest, my heart was pounding, because that meant she'd frozen. She couldn't remember how to find her wolf again, and Karen was stalking her.

"Please, little bunny," I breathed.

And then Elena figured it out. Screaming in rage, she reached down, and her form blurred, shifting faster than I'd ever seen it before. That in itself was enough to make Karen stop. She hadn't realized that Elena had turned yet. All the signs had been there, but they were subtle due to Elena's late transition, and my mate took full advantage of it.

The shadow of her wolf body surged in without a growl or any sign of warning. Elena didn't want the show. She had no need to proclaim her power. All she wanted was to protect her den. That had always been her strongest ability, and now I was counting on it to get her through this. My mate's teeth caught nothing but fur the first time, which woke Karen from her stupor. The bitch jumped back, but Elena wasn't scared to get right in there.

And she was moving. Those tawny eyes were locked on Karen's, and Elena's sleek, sinuous body struck over and over, more like a snake than a wolf. Her legs moved. Her teeth snapped. Her ears were pinned back and her tail was held just low enough to be out of Karen's reach. I always heard people talk about mama bears protecting their young, but this? It was my she-wolf, and she had just become a monster.

Karen couldn't even attack. All she could do was back up because Elena didn't give her the chance for anything else. I could hear Karen growling, but Elena? The only sound she made was when her teeth snapped back together. And then she finally connected. Elena's mouth closed on the side of Karen's neck, and my mate thrashed, slinging the paler female off her feet.

Karen cried out, but it didn't stop Elena. She simply pushed Karen into the ground, using it as a chance to get a better bite, and kept going. That was when Elena finally began to growl. Karen struggled to bite back. Bending, she caught Elena's shoulder, twisting let her get the side of Elena's face, but none of those snaps did more than pinch.

That was when Karen began to panic. Twisting, screaming, and flailing her legs for all she was worth, the bitch managed to get just enough leverage to latch onto the side of Elena's cheek, but my mate didn't care at all. The pain only made her jaws clench, tightening around Karen's throat, and this was over.

Karen let go, falling limp in Elena's jaws, submitting completely. "That's it, Alpha," Sampson said. "She's submitted."

Elena paused, her eyes jumping over to me, so I nodded. "Yeah, bunny, you won. The baby's safe."

A sigh came out first, and then Elena carefully released her jaws. Stepping back, she watched Karen for a second, but the defeated woman just lay there, knowing her failure had been witnessed and she couldn't deny it. Then Elena shifted back to human and staggered toward me, proving she had nothing left.

I opened my arms to catch her just as Karen rolled to her feet and jumped, aiming for Elena's back. Time slowed. My hands caught my mate, pushing her at Sampson, and I felt my rage rush to the surface as I watched Karen's body change, growing to her lycan form with her eyes locked on the one thing I couldn't live without.

My heart stopped, my anger grew, and my body changed to match. I could feel the fabric of my shirt straining. My jaw lengthened. My hands turned to claws. This was my woman! Mine, and no one else touched her unless I allowed it. Not my Alpha, not my fellow betas, and certainly not this pathetic and defeated bitch!

Just as Karen's hands closed on Elena's arm, I grabbed the creature she'd become, spinning her around to face the beast I was proud to be, and I slung her to the ground, following her down. The woman's body slammed into the dirt. I crashed into her, but my head was already moving.

No second chances. That was my bunny. My sweet, gentle thing. My treasure to keep very safe, and as my lycan jaws closed on her throat, I decided that I would kill to make that possible.

I felt her strange skin part beneath the power of my jaws, but I didn't stop. My hands held her down, but the rest of my body pulled, and I felt that woman's throat tear. Spitting out the hunk of flesh, I turned back to her, forced myself to become a man again, and leaned closer even as her life poured from the wound.

"Mine," I said. "That woman is my fate, so this is now yours. Just because I play nice, doesn't mean I am."

"Lane?" Elena asked.

"He's fine," Sampson promised, hugging her against his chest. "Don't look, Elena. Just give him a second, and this will all be over." Then he tipped his head at me. "Bunnies, Lane. Be gentle with them."

"Take her inside," I begged, reaching down to grab the hem of my stretched-out shirt so I could wipe at my face.

Then I looked back at Karen's body, the life already gone. "Fucking cunt," I snarled before grabbing her leg to drag her out of sight. "Couldn't even have died as a wolf. Not even as a woman. Gonna have to burn you now."

And then, only when there was nothing left to scare my little bunny, would I go back, because now I knew she was safe.

CHAPTER 56

Damon bolted, and my eyes jumped to my Alpha. The permission was barely out of Ian's mouth before I was going. Unfortunately, those few seconds was more of a lead than I wanted to admit. Even worse, Damon chose the best side of the community, running up the street that led straight to the trail area.

I caught him before the first cross street. My teeth closed on the hair across his lower back. He tried to jerk away, but all he accomplished was sending the both of us tumbling across the street. I went with it, knocked a few paces away, but that made it easier to get back up without Damon's mass slamming into me.

But he just ran again, barking out for help. And he kept barking, wasting his breath - or so I thought until a trio of wolves rushed me from the side. Converts, all of them, and untrained ones at that. The last one tripped on his own paws trying to make the transition from the curb to the street. The first two, however, were a little more of a threat.

I grabbed one and slung him away. Surprisingly, the wolf didn't know how to stop me. The other grabbed my hip, but from the side, so his teeth didn't sink in. I skittered away, then came back hard. A bite to his muzzle, a yank to his ear, then a puncture to his upper leg was enough to make him back the fuck off.

I turned to the one still on the ground but he - no, she - submitted. Damn, but I still felt bad about hitting women, so I left them both, taking off to catch up with Damon again. Thankfully, they didn't follow.

That was the downside of not being natural-born. If we converts tried hard enough, we could learn how to do most things, but there was a very big line between nature and nurture. I'd been raised not to use my strength against women. These ladies, however, were just as strong as the men, sometimes moreso. Ashley was just one example. Kim was another. Then there was Gabby, and while she was a convert, I was going with the theory that being a kid when she turned made it easier.

But right now, that was the least of my problems. Damon knew where our trails were, and he was rushing there fast. His barks had been heard - clearly his voice was recognized by his own pack - and about a block ahead of me, he was starting to pick up a few stragglers. Damon was running hard, and while I was still gaining on him, he was going to make it into the trees before me.

After that, finding the asshole would be a lot harder, so I stretched. I didn't care about the burning in my lungs or the blur of the world around me. I wanted that man. I owed him for what he'd done to me. Yes, I loved being a wolf, but I hadn't been the idiot who'd needed the lesson about consent! He'd taken my human life from me without permission, and I intended to get my pound of flesh back in return. For the scar on my leg, if nothing else.

Because I wouldn't trade all the shit I went through if it meant I had to give up Elena. I loved my mate with a passion I'd never expected. Ian and the guys had become more of a family than my own had ever been. Henry, his family, and the entire pack were like a dream come true to me - but that hadn't been what Damon intended. He'd wanted to take my life, and I'd made myself strong enough to show him what a big mistake that had been.

To my right, I could hear barking, howling, and the yelps of injured wolves. A roar made it clear our tigers were over there somewhere too, and probably the cause of the yelps. Elena should be safe at the clinic. The bears? Hopefully they were with her. That meant I was about to do one hell of a dumbfuck move. I was going to follow Damon and a group of his wolves into what was basically an ambush.

Yet the moment they reached the open area before the nature trails, something small and dark rushed in from the side. A wolf yipped in surprise and jumped to get away from it. Next was a red and black streak. Then a coppery-colored one. It took me a moment to figure out my backup, and then I caught a flash of white.

Foxes!

Those were the girls. I didn't even know who was who, but I knew that a wolf could crush one with a single bite - and those were my packmates! Snarling, I crashed into the closest wolf, sending him tumbling beneath me. A jump got me out of the way but put me in the path of another. The four wolves - three plus Damon - turned to me with their lips raised, and I matched them. Two against one I could do. Three against one was possible, since one of these guys was a convert. But when that one I'd barreled into staggered back to his feet, I knew this was going to be bad.

But I wasn't alone. The sound that came from beside me made us all flinch. It sounded like a cross between some wild monkey and a woman screaming. My head turned that way to see all three vixens standing side by side. The melanistic one with the black and red fur had her lips curled in a foxy snarl. That had to be Zaria. Beside her, the black one was definitely Ridley. That meant the traditionally orange one had to be Sheridan, and her little tail was wagging behind her like a taunt.

Damon turned, letting out a peal of barks to scare them off, but he didn't know these girls at all. Immediately, they rushed in, so I joined them. Sheridan bit at a wolf's belly, never stopping to give him the chance to catch her. Ridley grabbed a tail and yanked as hard as her little body would allow, distracting another. Zaria went for the face of a third, screaming in the way that only foxes could.

I charged right at Damon, but he was ready for me. The guy was quite a bit bigger than me, so when my shoulder slammed into his, I was the one staggering. And then his teeth were snapping at my neck. I felt the burn of the first bite, jumping around to get my own teeth into him. I caught his ribs, felt the skin tear, but then he had my back - and then something roared.

The trees shook. The ground thundered. Damon and I

separated just enough to look back, and six more wolves rushed at us, but they didn't stop - because the things chasing them were even worse. Shadows. The scent of sweet grass and fresh air. Then there were the snuffling grunts that I was starting to get very, very fond of.

I turned back to Damon just as Vic, Jax, and Scott all burst from the trees to stop beside me. Jax and Vic reared up on their hind legs and roared, but Scott was simply picking out his own target, that black head of his swiveling across the line of wolves before us. Damon's pack knew that running wouldn't do them any good. There were at least ten of them, but I figured the odds were in my favor. Three bears, three foxes, and me?

That bastard was going to regret the day he'd targeted our pack.

Scott charged first, rushing the line of wolves. Vic and Jax joined him. The vixens hit from the side. I just waited for them to pass then darted across the back of the line to the one man I wanted most: Damon. He braced, but I no longer had to worry about getting attacked from behind. Right here, right now, this was my chance to get revenge for all of it.

I went for his neck, he leaned, pivoting around me, but I'd expected that. The man was bigger, stronger, but much slower than me, yet the sound of his teeth clacking beside my ear still made me flinch. He noticed and rushed in again, but my teeth were sharp. I caught his lip in them and pulled, swinging my hips around for a better angle. The metallic taste of blood filled my mouth, but I tried to ignore it. It wasn't his face I wanted to bite, it was his throat.

The moment he tried to turn toward me, I released

him and doubled back. Damon whipped his head around the other way, but it was too late. I jumped onto his back, biting at his spine as hard as I could. He went for my hind legs, but I could jump. Without letting go of his body, I threw myself across him, pulling us both to the ground, yet I was facing the way I wanted.

He huffed as he hit, that moment of distraction all I needed. One last push, and my jaws closed on his throat. Using every inch of force I had, I bit hard, feeling something crunch in my mouth. Nope, I did not want to think about that, but I'd be damned if I'd let go. Ian thrashed. Lane thrashed. I was pretty sure even Pax and Trent would, but I was just a little too human for that trick.

I just leaned in, using the power of my teeth, the angle of my body, and the pressure of my jaws to hold his head against the ground. Like he had with Ian, Damon tried to use his legs for leverage. I had to dance around them, making sure he couldn't get any purchase, but I would not let him go. I was pretty sure that my life depended on just hanging on.

And then I heard a woman scream! My eyes flicked over, but there wasn't one here. That had to be a convert. It was the only thing I could think of, yet the roar of a bear proved it wasn't. I tried to count foxes, but that moment of distraction was all it took for Damon to get the upper hand.

The man lunged. His teeth sank into the side of my throat, and he pulled. I felt the burn, then the cold ice of true pain, and I knew this was bad. I also didn't fucking care. Let him kill me. Let him try to tear me apart, but he'd never again do to anyone else what he'd done to me.

The rage of that night so long ago, the fear, and all of the adrenaline coursing through my body built up, and nothing else mattered.

I growled, I snarled, I snapped. He tried to dislodge my teeth. He desperately fought back, but I was done. I was so far beyond done that he couldn't understand. I was the fucking beta of this pack. I'd claimed the Alpha Female myself. I was the man who was supposed to keep them all safe, and nothing was going to stop me.

I darted in for another bite just as Damon turned the wrong way, and it was almost like his throat shoved itself into my mouth. I bit, feeling the skin tear. And then, for the first time in my life, I heaved my shoulders to the side, whipping my head to add more force, and I thrashed as hard as I could. Damon cried out in both pain and surprise, but the sound failed quickly as something inside him broke.

Warmth filled my mouth tasting of copper. Fur wedged between my teeth. My hold slipped as the skin loosened, and the wolf beneath me made a noise I'd never heard before. It was almost a gurgle, but mixed with a gasp, and it was enough to make me back off and look at what I'd done.

Damon's mouth hung open. His entire body heaved as he tried to pull in a breath, but it didn't seem to be working. His tongue lay sprawled on the ground, his eyes were wide and focused on nothing. That was when it hit me: the man was dying. I'd just killed him.

I'd defeated the Alpha of the Hidden Forest pack - and my friends were still fighting.

I forced my body back to its human form and then

yelled, "Enough! Damon is dead. I claim leadership of Hidden Forest and you will all back down now!"

The craziest thing was that it worked. Damon's fight with Ian had been about keeping or losing Wolf's Run. This one was different.

Most of these new converts probably hadn't learned all of our traditions and laws - but they saw *this*. At my feet, their pack leader was dying, and I was the one who'd dealt the final blow. That made me Damon's replacement, and there was no way to dispute it.

The wolves backed off. Their heads turned to see the dead animal at my feet, but that didn't mean they liked it. A few broke off, running back toward the center of the community. Others went the other way, clearly looking to get the hell out of here. But thankfully, not a single one stuck around to avenge their fallen leader. They just ran.

But I turned to see Sheridan in her human form, bent over the red and black body of her sister. "Zaria?" I asked.

When the tip of that crazy-colored tail wagged, I almost cried out in relief. Instead, I rushed over to help. "What happened?"

The girl's leg was bent at an angle it shouldn't be, clearly broken. Sheridan just stroked her sister's side and looked up with tears in her eyes. "One of them caught her."

"Then let's get her to the doctor," I said, ignoring my own pain as I moved around to squat behind her. "I'm sorry, Zaria, but this might hurt. If you need to bite, I promise I won't care." Then I scooped her into my arms.

Someone had to take care of her, and right now, Sheridan and I were the only ones in human form. The

543

vixen screamed again, the sound too human for comfort, but I managed to get her cradled against my chest. Her left front leg just dangled awkwardly, so Sheridan eased her paw up to rest against my arm, preventing it from flopping when we walked. Zaria didn't whimper again, though.

Then Vic shifted to a man. "My house. My truck's there, and we can get her to Bridget's faster."

"Not with the wolves all over," I told him. "Some of them are ours, and we don't want to hit anyone."

"Shit," Vic breathed. "Ok. Elena and Bridget are at the clinic, but..." And he tilted his head. "They're still fighting, and that sounds like the community center. You take her to get fixed - since you're pretty fucked up yourself - and I'll go put a few paws into dogs."

"No," I decided. "You take her to Bridget, because I can stop this."

"Seth, you're done," Scott said.

"How?" Jax simultaneously demanded from behind me.

But I was already easing Zaria into Vic's arms. "I'm now the Alpha of the Hidden Forest pack. I killed their leader, so - "

"And you've got the blood on your face to prove it," Scott pointed out.

"Don't wipe it off," Ridley said as she also shifted to human. "Let them see it, Seth. Zaria will be fine - right, Zar?"

The vixen now in Vic's arms jiggled her nose. The poor thing wouldn't want to shift forms until that was set, because it was an excruciating sensation, but since she was lighter to carry this way, it worked out. Well, besides the weirdness of having a sixteen year old girl being carried by a naked man old enough to be her father.

"Just, take her to the clinic," I told Vic. "Scott? Can I borrow you at least?"

"Sure," he said.

"I'll go too," Jax offered. "That way, if they turn on you, then you've got at least a little muscle."

"Then let's do this," I told them as I reached for my wolf body again.

CHAPTER 57

Sampson had me sitting in one of the waiting chairs, clutching a paper cup filled with water. I'd seen what Lane had done, but I was pretty sure my mate didn't realize that - not with the way he'd reacted. I'd also never seen a murdered body before. The problem was that I hadn't yet decided what I felt about that.

Karen had intended to kill me, so Lane had killed her. That part, I was fine with. The ease with which he'd done it, and the intensity of the man as he'd watched her die was shocking, but it didn't make me love him less. More, possibly. My problem was that he'd vanished right afterwards, and now I was almost sick with worry, but Sampson assured me that he was just getting Karen's partially-shifted corpse out of sight. It would be hard to explain, otherwise.

The kids were fine, though. Evelyn had heard everything from Mia's room, and now she was checking on the others. Things were going to be ok now. We had this, but where the fuck was Lane? I was just about to demand that Sampson go find him when the clinic door swung open. The sound of crunching glass made me flinch, but the sight of Vic - naked and rather impressive - carrying a motley-colored fox in his arms had me jumping to my feet.

"What happened?" I asked.

Lane followed the group in. "Bridget's not here, guys. She went to the community center."

"Shit," Vic snarled. "So did Seth. Damon's dead."

"Karen's dead too," I told him.

Lane's eyes jumped over to me. "You ok, bunny?"

That was the wrong thing to say. All this stress. All of the anxiety, insanity, and fear poured out of my mouth in a single, overly-harsh sentence. "Don't you ever fucking leave me alone like that again, Lane! You hear me?"

And he smiled. "I was just around the corner cleaning up," he promised as he pushed between the crowd to wrap his arms around me. "I'm fine, Elena. You're fine. One of our foxes is hurt, though."

"Right." So I pointed at the door. "Across the street, there's a walkway between those two houses, and the community center is on the other side." I paused to glance back, not surprised at all to see Evelyn standing in the hallway, listening. "Can you hold down the clinic for a few minutes?"

"Damon's dead?" she asked.

Vic nodded. "I saw it with my own eyes. I'm sorry."

The girl sighed, her entire body relaxing. "No, that's a good thing. Go. I'll keep an eye on the converts. Just..." She lifted her hand, paused, then let it fall. "Derek needs formula, and I didn't bring any."

"We'll get you some," I assured her. "Diapers too, I'm assuming?"

She nodded. "I didn't bring anything. I just had him, and you all were there, and I knew this was our chance, so we ran."

"We'll take care of you," I promised, "but right now, we need to get this girl to the doctor and make sure the rest of the pack is all in one piece. Just a bit longer."

"I'm fine, Alpha," Evelyn promised. "Go. I can guard the five of us."

So I waved Vic, the foxes, and Lane back the way they'd come. Sampson, however, didn't follow. "I'll keep an eye on the kids, and clear away the glass," he promised.

Thankfully, it wasn't far. Unfortunately, the sounds of fighting were still loud enough to prove that while the fight had died down, it wasn't yet over. Lane shifted. Sheridan and Ridley shifted. I was once again dressed and not looking to strip, so I walked with Vic, making sure they all knew where we were going.

Ok, Lane could've shown them, but if both Damon and Karen were dead, letting everyone know would end this, right? I wasn't sure how, or what I was supposed to do, but since I was the only Alpha here, I had a feeling I needed to be there. The group of us came out at the side of the large community center, right beside those same doors Gabby had used as her entrance for her *quinceañera*. We hurried, trying to avoid being seen by the groups still scuffling around the front, when a voice called out.

"Hidden Forest!" That was Seth.

My feet froze and my head turned to the sound. Lane shifted, waved Vic and the girls inside, then caught my arm, tugging me toward where my other mate's voice had come from. We hurried, jogging up the length of the building just in time to see Seth, Jax, and Scott walk into the grassy area around the community center. The area was filled with bodies of wolves - both alive and dead - that no longer looked like the beautiful retreat it had been designed to be.

Then Seth yelled again. "Hidden Forest pack! Wolf's Run! Cease fighting! Damon is dead, and I have claimed the position of Pack Alpha. I order you all to stand down."

Growls faded. The snarling stopped. My eyes jumped across the lawn to see that groups were all separating to turn and see what was going on. Seth just kept walking closer.

The man was covered in blood and clearly injured. I pressed a hand to my lips to keep from making a sound, but I wanted to run to him. I knew I couldn't, yet the urge was still there. I could see the gash across the side of his neck and shoulder. It still bled. Across his mouth, chin, and trickling down his chest was more, but that didn't seem to be his. Bites covered his body, dark marks that would become bruises stood out on his skin, and blood had dried in places, making it clear that not all of his injuries were fresh.

Yet my mate walked proudly, completely exposed, straight into the center of that. The pair of bears paced him like bodyguards. That, more than anything else, kept me from panicking, because Seth was not supposed to be the Alpha of another pack. He was Ian's beta. He was my packmate. We could not be separated, yet he'd clearly won the fight - and the spoils that went with it.

Then Ian walked out of the community center. His arm was bandaged and splinted, but like Seth, he was completely naked. "So you claim Hidden Forest as yours?" he asked.

One by one, heads turned to see what was going on. The door to the community center opened again, and Henry stepped out, pausing on the stoop. In the crowd, I saw other faces I recognized, including Ashley. All of them were bloody and disheveled - yet everyone looked, because this was not supposed to be how this ended.

"I do," Seth said. "I have bested Hidden Forest's Pack Alpha, which makes me the top wolf."

"And you're on my territory," Ian pointed out.

Seth just smiled and kept walking. "I am," he said when he was standing right before him. "So I come to make reparations."

And then he just knelt, lifting his chin and tilting his head enough to bare his throat. The men were no more than a foot apart. They both had clearly fought hard, and had the marks to prove it. Ian was tensed, ready to do what was necessary, but Seth just looked up at him, the corner of his lip curled slightly upward. And for a moment, everything else stopped.

They were beautiful like that. The muscles of their bodies on display for everyone to see both of their strength and power. Neither acknowledged the wounds, acting as if they were above that. Even the fact that neither was aroused at all somehow lent an air of authority to the scene playing out before me. It looked like some image from Mount Olympus: the god and the demigod finally coming to terms.

"What do you offer, Alpha?" Ian asked.

"My life," Seth told him. "My servitude. My pack. I

submit to you, Ian Langdon, and give all control of Hidden Forest to Wolf's Run."

"A pack of converts?" Ian asked. "Your life was already mine. Your servitude as well. Why would I want your pack?"

A smile flickered over Seth's lips. "A pack of converts led by a convert strong enough to defeat a natural-born. Why wouldn't you want them? Take those who suit. Release the rest. The decision is yours, Alpha, because we are the ones at fault."

Ian just reached out and palmed the back of Seth's head, still standing over him proudly. "I'll take your pack." Then he raised his voice a little more. "Those who want to stay, may. They will have to find their own reparations with those they've hurt tonight. Those who wish to leave can do so without repercussions, and that will be their payment for the damage, wounds, and deaths tonight. But you have one hour to make this decision, and then my temper will no longer be held in check."

"Hidden Forest will comply," Seth assured him.

Then Ian leaned a little closer. "And you? You stole my kill, Seth." There was a growl in his voice now. "You abandoned your duties to take on another pack. You already swore to serve me, but to make amends for this? You will serve me for the rest of your life. Hidden Forest is dead. There is only Wolf's Run, and you will serve out your days as my beta. Can you agree to this?"

"I can, Alpha," Seth swore.

"Good answer, beta," Ian told him.

Only then did the leader of Wolf's Run let anything but control show on his face. It was brief, but a hint of tenderness filled his eyes before he pressed his head to

Seth's. Still on his knees, Seth reached up to press his hand over Ian's, and the pair mumbled something else between them, too soft to hear.

But I caught one last thing. "Never letting you go now. Might as well just start calling you one of my brothers."

"Not gonna complain," Seth assured him. "Just tell me this is over and Elena's ok?"

"She's ok," Lane called out, making them both look to where we were standing.

"Oh, thank god," Ian breathed as he turned, releasing Seth, and limped toward me.

Seth took longer, but Trent and Pax rushed up from where they'd stopped fighting to help him up. Together, those three headed toward us as well, not caring at all about the people leaving the area, the ones dropping down to sit on the grass to catch their breath, or anything else going on around us. They all just wanted me, and the four of them reached me only seconds apart, each one wrapping his arms around the rest to hold me tightly in the middle.

"You're all hurt," I realized. "Seth, you need to see the doctor."

"It looks worse than it is," he promised. "Half the blood isn't mine."

"Bridget's almost kept up," Ian assured me. "Gabby and the kids - "

"Gabby?" I asked, sucking in a breath as the worry slammed into me.

" - have been helping her with first aid," Ian finished. "The kids are wrapping wounds, putting on bandages, and carrying people when they can't walk themselves. Well, the boys are carrying. Samantha is helping to keep the children calm inside. So far, none of ours have died. The injuries are painful, but all will heal. The only thing we have to worry about now is Karen."

"She's dead," Lane told them, making the guys finally step back so they could see him.

"What?" Pax asked.

Lane nodded. "She challenged Elena. Elena won, but then Karen lunged, shifting into a lycan. Sampson was there, so I shoved Elena at him." But he left off the rest.

"Fucking stupid woman!" Pax groaned. "Why didn't she just stay down?"

"Because she had nothing left," Trent told him. "Two packs in a year? No one else would take her, Pax, and she would never survive on her own. She also knew that Lane is fated and he'd have no other choice."

"I'm sorry," Lane told them.

Pax waved that away. "I'm more upset about the life she threw away than her death," he promised. "You know, she was a happy kid, back before we were all old enough to know we should have real worries. Once, she was actually a pretty nice girl, and I can't figure out what went wrong."

"She got greedy, but didn't want to do the work," Ian told him. "She thought the rest of us should all do it for her, and the more it happened, the more it solidified that belief. This was a long time coming, Pax."

"Yeah, it was," he agreed, looking over at me. "I also knew you'd win. Karen never had the strength you do, Elena. She didn't stand a chance. I'm only sorry you had to go through that."

Lane just murmured, then said, "We'll need to burn her body."

"Probably a few other wolves as well," Ian decided. "I don't know how else to get rid of this much carnage."

Seth chuckled. "Think Jesse can organize that?"

"Jesse!" Trent yelled, turning back to the chaos winding down behind him. "Hey! Jesse!"

"Yeah?" the man called back as soon as he'd shifted to human. "Whatcha need, beta?"

Trent waved him over. "Look, we have a lycan body we have to lose." Then he tipped his head to the mess around the community center. "And this. You willing to get a crew together and do something with it?"

Jesse shoved a hand over his lips. "Can I use the backhoe?"

"Why?" Ian asked. "We have to burn the lycan, at least."

"Yes," Jesse said, "but I can dig a pit, we can dump them all in, add some wood, let it burn down to nothing, then fill it in. Since we have a few pad sites in progress, would be easy to do it there. Once the foundation is over it, no one will even think about it. And before that's done, the disturbed ground won't seem out of place. It's also far enough away that we won't be smelling it all night."

Pax just chuckled. "Yeah, so my keys are up in my jeans, which are in the parking lot of the office."

"Mine too," Ian admitted. "Sadly, this can't wait for morning." He just nodded. "Lane, take Elena home. My home."

"No," Seth said. "Let her check on the kids first, and then take her home."

Ian just caught the man's eye. "Five minutes as a Pack Alpha, and now you're getting uppity, huh? But no, he's right. And the rest of you go with him. I'll get Jesse the keys, make sure Bridget has help, and - "

"Mom!" Gabby screamed as she raced around the corner to throw herself against my chest. "Are you ok?"

"I'm fine, *mija*. You?"

She nodded. "We stayed close, just like I promised, and the only one really fighting was Nik, but he's a badass. No, we're all good. I mean, a couple of minor bites and scratches, but that's it." She looked at the guys, then back to me. "Hey, um, I know you're going to be all worried and everything, but my betas and I kinda wanted to keep helping Bridget until everyone's taken care of."

I nodded. "Ok. I think you've proven tonight that you deserve it. Just..." I looked at Ian. "I'm staying at their place. You can invite your friends to the house, but there's one condition, ok?"

"Mom!" she whined. "I know about the condoms! Please don't do this to me."

I had to fight not to smile. "Make sure everyone's parents know they're ok first. Even Xander's. I know they aren't as active in his life, but go see them. Let them see their child is fine. And then, I don't care what you do, but if you're going to do *that*, then..." I lost control and the grin broke free. "Condoms."

"Not doing that," she said. "I'm fifteen, Mom. I kinda wanna drive first. But I'll send them out to check in, and yeah, we'd kinda like to wind down together." Then she hugged me. "Thanks for being the best Alpha-Mom ever." But when she pulled back, she looked at the guys. "All of you take good care of her, ok?"

"Promise," Lane said.

But Gabby paused, her body shifting like she'd had a thought. "Thanks, Dad." Then she threw herself against him.

Lane paused for a moment before he even remembered to wrap his arms around her. "Yeah?" he finally asked, his voice just a little tighter than normal.

"I have four Dads and a Papa," she mumbled against his chest. "I mean, Pax is a dad too, but a Latino one. So, yeah." Then she looked up into his face. "That's ok, right?"

"It's perfect, little wolf," he promised. "Now go be an alpha before you make me cry."

She stepped back, smiling a little too big at the guys. "I gotta do my thing, right? I think you all should do yours. And since I don't have to listen to it..."

"Gabriella!" I snapped. "Go get in trouble somewhere else."

She left, her giggles proving that she was a little too proud of herself, but Ian glanced over at Seth. He nodded, then the pair of them looked at Trent and Pax. They both shrugged. Lane was last. With a smile, he simply gestured in the direction of our homes.

"Looks like we're walking. I don't even remember where I left my clothes, and right now, I'm honestly too tired and filthy to care. Shall we, little bunny?"

I grabbed his arm on one side, caught Trent's hand on the other, and nodded. The best part was that none of them felt good enough to walk fast, so I didn't have to ask, because my body? Yep, I was definitely too old for this shit, but that didn't really fit with the feeling inside my chest. The one I could only describe as pride.

Elena

CHAPTER 58

We eventually made it back to their place. The aches were starting to set in. Seth's bleeding had stopped, but Trent and Pax both had a few of their own injuries. All minor, thankfully. Still, the first thing I did when I got inside was head straight to Lane's room and turn on the shower. I could feel the crap in my hair, the dirt on my skin from where it had been caught in my fur, and the guys were worse.

Lane guided Seth in just as I got my clothes off. "Elena, make sure all his wounds are clean?" he asked. Seth just tossed up his hands, but Lane headed for the cabinet to pull out more towels. "I promise she's a lot nicer to look at," Lane told him. "Or I can doctor you."

"I'm getting in here with Elena," Seth promised.

He hissed at the temperature of the water, but when I followed, he stepped back and let the shower head spray down on him. There was a lot of blood, and it tinted the runoff by our feet. Reaching over to the side, I got a washcloth and the soap, then began cleaning everything.

We didn't need to talk. He hurt. I was exhausted, but there was something so easy about this. When I got his chin and chest good enough, Seth turned so I could do his back. Then, saving it for last, I worked at the gash along his neck. Thankfully, it wasn't as bad as I'd feared.

When that was done, he returned the favor. The nips and bruises on my body were nothing compared to his. I'd only faced off against Karen, and she'd gone down a lot faster than I'd expected. Granted, she'd been waiting for me to turn my back, so maybe she'd faked the submission? Not that it mattered. I still knew I'd won. It may have taken longer if she'd kept fighting, but I would've still won.

Once we were both clean, Seth guided me to Lane's bed. I fell into it still wrapped in a towel. Seth lay naked beside me, and then Lane took his turn. While he was still in the shower, Trent came to join us. Pax arrived just as Lane turned off the water. When Lane walked out of the bedroom, he paused at the sight of all of us lying naked in his bed - and then the front door opened.

"In here!" Lane called out.

Ian made his way in with wet hair of his own. "Hey, I stopped by your place to get..." He chuckled when he rounded the corner and saw us. "Seems we all had the same idea." Then he flicked a finger at Lane. "Your bed. Might as well carve out your spot. I'll be right back."

"Where are you - " I tried to ask.

But Lane wedged himself in beside me. "Know what I think?" he asked. "My room is big enough for one of those super-sized king beds. If we moved things around, it could become yours. A nice place where you could have as many or as few of us here as you wanted. Sometimes to sleep, others to, well..." He chuckled. "Do other things."

"Move Gabby into mine," Trent said. "It's right by the bathroom upstairs, and it's pretty private for the hall. Also harder to sneak in Roman if he has to walk through all of us."

"I could make the den into another room," Lane pointed out. "Would just need to fix up some walls." He paused as Ian returned, then kept going. "It's not like we really use that space, right? It's empty unless we have company."

"Guys?" I asked. "Are you trying to say something? I mean, I live next door."

"We have more room," Seth pointed out. "And I like you always being with us."

"I miss you when you're not," Pax added.

Ian just moved to the foot of the bed. "It makes sense, doesn't it? I know next door doesn't seem that far, but sometimes it feels like miles. I love seeing you half asleep in the morning - even if you didn't spend the night with me. I want this thing between us to be a little more permanent, Elena. We all do."

I heard him. I really did, I just wasn't quite sure where he was going with this. "Are you asking us to move in?"

"No," he breathed, casting his eyes across the rest before crawling up to sit beside my legs. Then he turned his hand to reveal a small white box. Slowly, he opened the hinged top. "Elena, I'm asking you if you'll marry us."

"All of us," Lane added. "Legally him, but to the pack, it would be all."

"I know it's kinda soon after your divorce," Seth added, "but we're all sure."

"And if this house isn't big enough," Pax told me, "we can build one just for us. Even when Ian retires, we still want us to be together."

"But if we stay here," Trent pointed out, "then when Gabby's old enough to move, she can have your place. Right next door, so we'll always be there to help but not prevent her from growing up."

I had to scoot back and sit up so I could see them all. The whole time, my eyes hung on the pair of rings in the box. A perfect princess-cut stone was the most obvious. It was yellow, but in a shade that almost perfectly matched Lane's eyes. It was the color of a wolf, I realized. Then there was the band that went with it. Five stones, made obvious by the alternating aqua color and clear diamonds, curved around it. The set was amazing, small enough to be tasteful, large enough to be impossible to miss, and designed in a way that fixed everything that had ever bothered me about my first one.

"You want to marry me?" I asked, knowing I sounded like a parrot. "What about Gabby? I need to talk to her first."

"We asked," Ian assured me. "Before we bought the ring, we asked her permission. Elena, I also asked if she'd consider allowing us to adopt her if you said yes. She agreed. Dad can handle all of the legal paperwork, and Gabby will officially become a Langdon, but only if you want this. I'm not pressuring you, and if you're not ready, we'll back off. It's just that..."

"We love you," Pax said. "I know Trent and I took a while to figure it out, but that was just to be sure. Elena, you are so perfect for us, and we kept waiting for that thing that would drive us crazy. The problem, I suppose? Or to realize that we were just, well, distracted by your sexy body and the things you do to us in bed."

I actually chuckled at that. "And you're all sure?" I asked, looking at each of them. "I'm not trying to drag this out, and I'm sure you're all nervous, but each of you is honestly on board with this idea? Not pressured into it by Lane or Ian?"

"Or *me*?" Ian asked, sounding amused.

"You're the Alpha," I reminded him.

He dipped his head in acknowledgement. "Fair."

"No," Lane promised. "This was a group decision."

The other three nodded to make it clear they felt the same way. Hell, they'd asked Gabby's permission! Not my father's, but my daughter's, and now she was calling them all Dad, even if it was still a bit awkward and a little too intentional. That meant it would get there. We would get there, and tonight made it clear that not even the worst thing imaginable could tear us apart.

So I had my answer. "Yes," I breathed. "I'll marry all of you. I don't know how that works, but we'll do it."

"Two weddings," Lane told me. "One for us, here with the pack. That one comes first. Then, when you're ready, we'll plan one for your family and our human friends. That will be the legal one, and if we do them a year apart, you only have to remember one day."

"I like that," I breathed, rolling into him to steal a kiss.

Ian just chuckled and caught my hand, sliding the ring onto my finger while Lane savored my lips. I didn't stop. I didn't look away, because this was my new normal. These were all my mates, and not a single one of them cared what I did with the others. But when Ian released my hand, I had to look.

"It's perfect," I told him, even though I was only wearing the engagement stone. The yellow one.

"The rest comes when you promise to stand at my side and treat my betas fairly," he said. "My equal, Elena, and I think you've more than proven it."

"I like the treating us betas fairly part." Lane caught my hips and pulled me onto him, not caring that Seth had to shift out of the way.

But it wasn't Ian who tugged my towel away. That was Pax. "I am not too sore to do very bad things to you," he warned, catching Seth's eye to point at the side table. "The question is if you are."

Lane was quickly getting hard beneath me, and without the towel, the chill air and bed full of naked men was making my nipples harden. "Never too tired, sore, or dumb enough to say no to that kind of an offer," I assured them.

Seth groaned. "Oh, someone has to have her for me. I'm only good for lying here." Then he passed a bottle of lube to Pax.

"Elena, lift up," Pax said as he moved in behind me.

I did, and then Lane sucked in a breath. "Cold," he hissed.

Then Pax guided me down onto a very hard, very slick part of Lane that I liked so much. My body stretched around him and Trent sat up to find my lips, kissing me softly. I felt the bed shift as the rest moved so they could see, get out of the way, or anything else, but I didn't care. Damn, this man felt good inside me. Trent kissed me slowly, keeping me from looking, and then a hand moved in from the other side, sliding up my thigh, across my hip, and teasing the skin across my belly.

I looked over to see that it was Ian, now beside Lane. Trent had claimed the other side. Then lips found the spot between my shoulders, and I knew that was Pax. Seth just reached down to grab himself, meeting my eyes when I looked over. Then he stroked once. The sight of his hand sliding down his own dick was all the foreplay I needed - or so I thought.

Ian leaned in to flick his tongue across my breast. Lane's legs moved beneath me, driving himself deeper into my body as he adjusted his position. Then Pax's hand found my hip. I felt his dick slide down my ass to press at the pucker, but he paused to kiss the back of my neck.

"Say it's ok," he whispered. "Or tell me if you've had too much tonight."

I just looked back. "I need you too, Pax."

Trent groaned, palmed my cheek, and turned my face back to his just so he could kiss me again. I gasped when Pax eased himself inside my body, but Trent breathed the sound in, smothering it even as Lane's hands moved to grip my thighs. Ian's tongue flicked again, his hand cradling my breast, and I couldn't stay still any longer.

My body demanded that I move, so I did. Lifting up, I could feel both Lane and Pax retreat from my body, and then I simply pressed back down. Lane groaned, fighting against the sensation. Pax slipped his arm around my side, finding my other breast as he pushed closer. They were all so close. Even Seth, angled so his head was next to Lane.

I reached out to catch his hand while his other stroked himself. Our fingers twined together, tying us in this moment. It was the only thing I could keep track of. I could barely kiss Trent back as I moved, sliding my mates through my body. Then Lane's hands found my hips, pausing me halfway down and holding me there. He pushed his hips up, taking over.

Behind me, Pax gasped at the sensation of Lane stretching me and sliding against him. "Fuck, that's good," he gasped.

Lane handled the thrusting, and Pax worked my ass. The feeling of both of them moving inside me was so erotic. Unlike Trent, Lane didn't know Pax's next move, and that was a whole different kind of sexy. Then I felt Ian shift, reaching down to stroke himself while still teasing my breast. Trent let out a sigh against my mouth, evidently aware of what his partners were doing. Then he too grabbed his own dick.

And we all moved. Bodies pressed against each other. My tongue tangled with Trent's. Ian's attentions drove me higher, the sparks of pleasure adding to what Pax and Lane were doing. The whole time, Seth's hand held mine, growing slowly tighter as I lost control, but I wasn't sure if I was squeezing or if that was him. I also didn't care.

Then Ian's other hand moved down to tease my clit. Not a single spot on my body was ignored. I couldn't think of a touch or caress I wanted that I wasn't getting. Pax's mouth sucking at the side of my neck. Lane's abs rippling as he pushed his hips upwards, pumping into me slowly, but not gently. The feel of Pax's body rocking against my back.

We were all too tired, too injured, and too abused to make this frantic. Instead, it was perfect. This was all for me, and it was the hottest thing I'd ever imagined. They didn't care if they touched. None of them felt reluctant or nervous. This was us, and to me it felt like love. Not fucking. Not just to get off, but as if we were proving something.

They loved me.

That was why it all felt so good. These men loved me in a way I'd never imagined before. Not because of what they could get or because of the passion. They loved me. My mind, my body - my flaws and perfections. In their arms, I found everything I'd ever wanted in my life. All those foolish dreams I'd been chasing were now a reality. Growing old sounded like a promise instead of a curse. Forever had once again become a good word, and I'd managed to become so much more than a mother and a maid.

Because most of all, I found myself.

Lane thrust into me again, then again, and I caught at Ian's shoulders for support. That allowed me to feel his arm moving faster, pleasing himself as he sucked and toyed with my nipple. I tilted my head back to gasp, so Trent just kissed the side of my neck gently. On the other side, Pax nipped, his teeth teasing that spot I loved the most. The whole time, he pumped into my ass, a little deeper and harder with each stroke.

The first groan slipped out, so Ian began making circles on my clit. It all felt so good, and only Seth's hand kept me balanced. I stretched, I clenched. I whimpered with the pleasure, but I didn't have to be quiet. I wanted just a bit more, because I could feel my climax building yet still too far away.

Then Lane growled, "Mine," and began to work me harder.

Pax sucked in a breath, pulling his mouth from my

neck to whisper in my ear, "Mine," even as his hand flicked across my other nipple.

My core was clenching. Every inch of my skin tingled with the flood of sensation, and I just took it. All of it. My legs tensed against Lane's hips, desperately trying to enjoy all of this before it was over.

Then Trent's teeth teased the lobe of my ear. "Mine," he breathed before sucking at the soft spot just beneath.

"And mine too," Ian said as his hand pressed my clit a little harder.

Lane only managed one more thrust before I lost control, my orgasm hitting me harder than I could've imagined. My body tensed, my back arched, and I cried out with passion even as both Lane and Pax kept going, kept pleasing, kept loving me the way only these five men could. Then Pax shoved his face against the back of my shoulder and groaned. A split second later, Lane gasped, but he managed to pump into me one more time before simply heaving upwards, pulling my hips down, and sheathing himself to the balls in my body.

Trent's breath caught. Ian groaned. Then Seth's fingers slipped on mine and his jaw clenched as he also lost control. I saw it all. I knew it, but it took me a moment to catch my breath - yet all I could think was that this, right here, was absolutely perfect.

Then Lane began to laugh. "Someone grab that towel?" he begged. "I didn't plan on getting both of your cum on me!"

Pax managed to extract himself from my body just before he snorted out a laugh. "Seriously?"

"Oops?" Trent said.

"Yeah, I'm gonna need that too," Seth pointed out.

Ian just tossed the towel onto Lane. "Let her up, and you can move, Trent."

There was another moment of shuffling, but as I lifted myself off of Lane, it was Seth who guided me down to the bed, right against his tattooed shoulder. The good one that allowed him to wrap his arm around my back.

"Mine too," he whispered before kissing my brow. Then his hand found mine, toying with the new ring on my finger. "Because I'm claiming you forever as my Alpha Mate."

CHAPTER 59

The next day, we were still cleaning up the mess from the assault by Hidden Forest. My Sisterhood had organized groups to gather all the clothes strewn around. Cars were returned to their owners. Keys were found where they'd been tossed. The damage was assessed, but one thing was very good news: not a single one of ours had been killed.

Thankfully, most of the wolves from Hidden Forest had only been maimed as well. Bridget patched up as many as she could. Gabby and the kids had been out until well after dawn helping her. Now, I had a small pack of teenagers sprawled across my house. Nik and Theo had claimed the spare room. Xander and Olivia were snuggled together on the couch. Samantha had taken the middle of the living room floor for herself. But in Gabby's bedroom, my daughter lay in Roman's arms.

The pair of them were still dressed and on top of the blankets, so I didn't bother waking them. So far as I cared, the kids had earned this. They'd proven themselves trustworthy, and I could only guess that they'd all been worried. If a little contact helped prevent last night from becoming a trauma they'd have to overcome, then my daughter could sleep in her beta-mate's arms. I knew I could trust her again.

So, after getting clean clothes for myself, I headed back out. My first stop was the clinic. Surprisingly, the glass from the shattered doors had already been cleaned up. Jesse and another wolf were currently in the process of hanging new doors, and Bridget was making checks on the kids. Sampson was curled up in the corner as a wolf, but someone was missing.

"Where's Evelyn?" I asked, realizing that I'd completely forgotten about getting her formula.

Bridget turned to me with a smile. "The Chimorys put her up last night. The Parnells had the formula she needed, and the Johnsons had some diapers their daughter has outgrown. Now, if you can convince Sampson that he's off guard duty, then he can go get some sleep."

The old wolf just lifted his lips in a snarl, but his growl sounded half-hearted. "Can I at least get you a blanket to lie on, Sampson?" I asked.

He just huffed and tucked his nose back under his feet. Evidently, that was a no. Tossing my hands in the air, I gave up. The grumpy - but actually sweet - old man wasn't why I was here. I needed to talk to Jonah, because it was now Sunday, and he was going to be a very sick boy soon enough.

Tapping on his door, I slipped into the room to find him flipping through a magazine. "Hi, Elena," he said.

"Jonah?" I asked, moving to the little chair beside his bed. "I want to call your mother and tell her you're ok. If you'll let me, I'd like to bring her here, but we can't let you leave yet."

"Why not?" he asked.

"Because when you turn, it's difficult to know where you are. A lot of converts die that first night for reasons that are easily preventable. Getting hit by a car is the main one. See, the moment the moon comes up, you're going to run. You have to catch it, and you don't even know why, but nothing will stop you from running, and you can't recognize the things you're running through - or across."

"So you're going to lock me in here?" he asked.

"No," I assured him. "Wolf's Run was made for wolves. You'll turn, you'll run, but the gates will all be closed. The pack will guide you to the trails, and we'll keep you moving until you're so exhausted that you'll be able to find your human body again. The problem is that in a few days, your fever will hit. You will become aggressive, and this disease is passed through bites, blood, and sexual contact."

"What?" he asked.

"Condoms work," I assured him. "But we can teach you all about that stuff when you're feeling better. For now, I just thought you might want to tell your mother that you're still alive, and give me the chance to explain all of this to her as well."

"She won't believe you," he insisted.

I just ducked my head and laughed once. "Oh, I probably know that better than you do. I also know that she deserves to know. Leave explaining it to me. All I need is her number."

He gave in and recited it. I promised I'd be back soon enough, then headed back to the waiting area. Sampson looked up, but Bridget was there waiting for me.

"Well?" she asked, pushing the phone toward me.

"Here goes nothing," I decided, typing in the number.

It was answered quickly. "Hello?" a woman gasped.

"Michelle Sims?" I asked.

"This is her."

"My name is Elena, and I'm at the Wolf's Run medical clinic. We have your son. He's fine. Jonah is currently being checked by our local doctor and - "

"Where?" she asked.

So I gave her the address. "Do you need me to send someone to get you?"

"No, I'm on my way. That's only like ten minutes from me."

"Just tell the guard at the entrance that you're here for Jonah," I told her. "They should be expecting you and will give you directions through the community to the clinic. I promise you, though, that he's going to be just fine."

"Thank you," she breathed, and then just hung up.

It didn't take long for her to arrive. A tired little sedan pulled up, shut off, and a woman in her late thirties jumped out, wearing clothes she'd clearly had on for days. She also didn't walk to the door. The woman ran, and Jesse pulled open the half-hung door to make sure nothing barred her way.

"My son's here?" she asked as she barreled into the waiting room.

"He is," I promised, catching her by the shoulders when she tried to go down the hall. "I'm Elena, and there are a few things you need to know."

"You said he was fine!" she snapped.

It was Bridget who answered that. "Medically, he is," she assured the frantic mother.

"But?" Michelle asked, looking back at me.

I just gestured to one of the chairs, indicating that she should sit down. "I don't know you, and I'm sure this is going to sound insane, but there are a few things you need to understand." In that moment, I completely understood why Ian hadn't told me what he was until he had no other option. It would've been so much easier to put this off. "Michelle, he's been infected by a disease that no one believes in. It's going to change him, and we're going to help him through it, but there isn't another doctor in this town who can help except for Bridget here."

"What does he have?" she asked. "And how did he get it?"

And here was the hard part. "He was bit by a wolf," I told her. "The disease is called lycanthropy, and I warned you that you would not believe it, but just hear us out, ok?"

"How did he get bit?" she asked, latching onto the most mundane part of that.

Bridget just moved to stand before her. "Michelle, this disease? It's considered to be fantasy, but it's not. It's a retrovirus, similar to HIV or Rabies. There is no cure, but it can be managed. It's also contagious. Any exposure to his blood, his body fluids, or such could infect you as well, but you need to understand that some people choose to be infected. The downsides are minimal, mainly the initial exposure. The benefits include an overactive immune system that leads to improved health overall. Do you understand what I'm saying?"

"My son has AIDS?" she asked.

"No, not AIDS," Bridget assured her. "He has lycanthropy, one of the mutations of something called therianthropy." She looked at me, then nodded.

"Michelle," I said, "he's going to become a wolf."

"What?!" she scoffed. "This isn't funny. Do you even have my son, or is this some bad joke?"

So Sampson sighed and pushed to his feet. Michelle's head whipped around to see him, and her eyes widened, but before she could say anything else, the old man shifted to his human form, standing there in all of his glory, shielding his pelvis with both hands.

"It's real, we're werewolves, and your boy's a pretty good kid." Then he shifted right back.

Michelle was breathing too hard. She hadn't even moved, and I'd half-expected her to run. Instead, she simply stared at Sampson as if trying to make the hardest decision of her life, but I could see the panic attack building. Clearly, so could Bridget.

"Let me give you something to make this easier," Bridget said, pulling a small syringe from her pocket. "Just a little sedative to help with the anxiety, Ms. Sims."

Michelle didn't try to stop her. Instead, she pointed at Sampson. "That dog was a man."

"Wolf," I corrected, "and yes he was. Michelle, Jonah is going to do the same thing. We've already talked to him about this, and we're going to make sure that he comes through the initial conversion without any problems. Our doctor knows all about this."

"Why?" she asked, looking up at Bridget.

"Because I'm a wolf too," Bridget said. "So is Elena. Pretty much everyone here are wolves."

"Like they were saying on the news?" she asked. "But I thought that was a hoax. That girl said she made the video."

"She unmade the video," I explained. "And the boy shown in it is why no one got shot that day. He's a sophomore, and his best friend got shot making sure the girl who took credit didn't get hurt. That girl is completely human. The rest of us aren't anymore."

She jiggled her head in a nod. "Ok. So, what do I need to do? What if they come hunting for him?"

"You," I told her, "need to go see your son. He will complete his turn on Friday, right around one in the afternoon when the moon rises. You won't be able to be there, but you can wait from inside one of the houses. We have plenty of people willing to explain the entire process to you, ok? And we have almost a week to answer all of your questions."

"Thank you," she breathed, and Bridget led her away.

Soon enough, the doctor came back. "Well, he was happy to see her. She's overjoyed, so I'm glad I gave her a little something-something."

"Is that even legal?" I asked.

Bridget just shrugged. "At this point, I've broken so many ethical laws, I'm just doing what's right for us." Then she gestured back to the room. "So, what are you going to do about them?"

"The mom?" I asked. "Ian and I decided to offer them a house here. Jonah said something about bills being tight, and the last thing we need is a convert trying to hold down a full time job plus school. It's just safer this way."

She nodded. "And the other two?"

I sighed. "I have no idea. They won't be able to go back to normal lives, right?"

"Doesn't work that way," she agreed. "At least they don't have as many complications. Mia said she lived alone and her apartment is probably defaulted. Christian is here for college, lives in the dorms, and already called his roommate this morning. Said he met some girl, gonna take an impromptu vacation, so don't think he's missing. So that's covered."

"Ok," I breathed, weighing all the possibilities. "I'll have to talk to Ian and Ashley, because we can't keep giving away houses. Still, we also can't just toss them out in the cold."

"You've got time," Bridget assured me. "And the entire pack is making sure this crowd is cared for. I've got more help than I know what to do with. But, all of that aside, I have one more question."

"Ok?"

She just pointed at my left hand. "Where'd that come from?"

A grin immediately took over my face. "So, um, I'm getting married again."

Bridget gasped and hugged me hard. "Oh that's great!" she squealed. "You going to do a wolf wedding with all of them?"

I nodded. "Yeah. I didn't even know such a thing existed, but they all want to be my husband, and I like that idea better, so we're doing two. First, I'll get married here as a wolf, and then a year later, we'll have the official and legal ceremony where I marry Ian."

"Mrs. Langdon," she teased. "So, are you actually changing your name?"

"Yes!" I promised. "Castillo is my ex-husband's. I only kept it because it matches Gabby's."

"Ah." She was nodding with enthusiasm. "And Gabby? What does she think?"

"I haven't told her yet, but they asked her permission, so she knows it's coming. And Ian's going to legally adopt her."

Bridget gasped at the cuteness of that. "Ok, he is officially the best Pack Alpha ever. I mean, you're the best Alpha Female, but yeah. I'm so glad I moved here, Elena."

"Maybe be one of my bridesmaids?" I asked. "I want Gabby to be my maid of honor, though. The rest of the Sisterhood should be the bridesmaids."

"Done," she assured me. "And we'll all make sure that Gabby doesn't do anything too crazy." Her eyes moved over to the door. "Or that I don't."

I just mouthed, "Jesse?"

Bridget nodded in that universal way of saying she was definitely going there. "Have you seen his little ears?"

"Yes," I assured her. "My god, they're so cute. And the spots?"

"You two know I can hear you, right?" Jesse asked.

I just turned back to him with a smile. "Get used to it, Jesse. Oh, and it works better for you when you pretend like you can't."

He chuckled at me. "Yes, Alpha. And congratulations on the engagement. I'd better get an invite."

"The whole pack will," I promised. "After all, I have to invite my family."

CHAPTER 60

Over the course of the next week, all of the damage was repaired. I tried to take care of those three converts, but I just felt like I couldn't be everywhere at once. Finally, Bridget kicked me out, saying that I had a Sisterhood for a reason, and they had this. It was my first lesson on learning how to delegate. Ashley promised there would be many, many more.

Because somewhere in all of that mess, I'd become an alpha, and the whole pack had noticed. When Friday finally came around, I was the one who ordered the gates locked, but I wasn't leading the run. That was Ian, and Gabby was back at his hip, keeping pace easier than I could ever imagine. Me? I waited at the fire with the pack members who couldn't run, David, and Michelle Sims.

Once again, Ian's truck was backed up as close to the fire pit as we could get, and we spent the time listening to the howls and chattering while toasting marshmallows. It didn't take long before the first person dropped out, but he was not at all what Michelle was expecting. Theo came out of the woods dragging his toes and leaning on Nik. Evidently our newest convert wasn't quite as ready to run as he'd expected.

"Alpha," Nik said the moment he was in human form. "He's done, but the wolves need a little help keeping track of three converts, so I need to head back out there."

"I got him, Nik," I promised, hurrying to the truck to grab a blanket.

Nik shifted and bounded back into the woods, but Theo just flopped down on his side and began to pant. The whuffing, grumbling noises he was making could only be translated as cussing out his new body. With a laugh, I tossed the blanket over him and squatted down, but that was more than Jonah's mother, Michelle, could take.

"That's a tiger," she said.

"And a... Are you sixteen, Theo?"

He nodded, making another of those soft noises.

"A sixteen-year-old boy," I finished. "He just turned last month, so this is his first full moon, and it sounds like the new ones are pushing the pack hard."

"You have a tiger in the pack?" she asked.

David chuckled. "Yeah, three of them now. And three bears." Then he paused. "Huh, and a triplet of foxes, too. Seems three is our lucky number or something."

"Just worked out that way," I explained to her, before looking back down to the boy. "You ready to shift back?"

"Can I..." Michelle stopped herself.

"What?" I asked.

"Pet him?" she finished weakly. "That's probably very rude, isn't it?"

Theo just rolled back to his feet, heaved himself up, and made his way over. When he was close enough, he shoved his head against her arm just like every cat I'd ever known. Awe filled Michelle's expression, and then she reached over to pet the hair between his ears gently.

"You're so soft," she breathed. "I thought it would be more wiry, or something."

I grabbed the blanket and dragged it back over to the boy. "Change back, Theo, catch your breath, and try not to show off too much skin." Then I told Michelle, "Some people get dizzy if they look."

So she closed her eyes tightly, and Theo shifted. "You're good," he told her before dropping into the closest chair - mine. "And the petting actually feels good. Like when someone gives you a massage or something."

"It's hard to stop, too," David admitted. "I promise that I know my wife isn't a pet, but when she lays her head in my lap? I still play with the hair at the scruff of her neck the way I used to with a dog. They all say it's ok, though."

"So when they're, um, like that?" Michelle asked, making some vague and fumbling gesture. "Like animals? They don't think like animals?"

"Nope," David promised. "We think the exact same after the first shift. Keep in mind, when we turn the first time, we're all running a fever. A bad one."

"Jonah was at one-oh-seven," Michelle told him.

David just nodded. "Pretty normal. But you know how you feel when you're very sick? Almost like you're drunk? It's worse. Then you have the new senses, and they're impressive. Our animal bodies move differently because the joints are set at different angles, and that makes the first time like a very bad acid trip. Somewhere along the way, we figure out what's going on, then we start to enjoy it, and when we're tired enough, we can change back. Since this pack has so many alphas in it, that's all but guaranteed."

"We've also done it a few times lately," I added. "My daughter, myself, and then Theo. Now we have these three."

"This is all amazing," Michelle breathed as she turned to the others. "And you two are human?"

"I'm trying to get exposed," Sasha said. "My husband and I want kids, but I know that if I'm pregnant and get this, I could lose the baby before I turn. So I want to turn first, but I'm not as brave as our Alpha Female."

"Completely unfair," Theo grumbled.

"I know!" Sasha agreed. "You get this on your first try?"

Theo just held up two fingers. "Second. Um, and I kinda wanted to be a wolf back then, but I think I like being a tiger better."

"I've been trying for months," Sasha told him. "Nothing."

"I'm going to get bit," Emily announced. "Not yet. I mean, we've had so many lately, and I'm thinking probably this summer, but my husband and I talked about it. I think Elena had the right idea. Get bit at the last minute, have a short infection, and then run."

"Let me know when," I told her, "and I'll run with you."

"Thank you, Alpha!" she said.

Michelle just waggled a finger at them. "Ok, what's with the 'Alpha' thing?"

"Her title," David explained for me. "Ian is our pack

leader, and he not only inherited the position, but proved that he deserved it. Think of it like the president. She's the first lady. Since the whole titles are Pack Alpha and Alpha Female or Alpha Mate, everyone has shortened them to just Alpha for centuries. So, they get the same title, but it's a Mr. and Mrs. thing. In our pack, however, they both deserve it."

I smiled at him. "Thanks."

"Not lying, Elena. And with all the changes? I think it's a good thing that we have a strong pair as our leadership. Gabby's probably going to be a busy girl, too."

"And speaking of that," I said. "Can I speak to you in private for a moment, Michelle?"

She got up and followed me, but I didn't miss how her eyes kept going back to the trees. "He's going to be ok, right?"

"He is," I assured her, stopping at Bridget's car to lean against the hood. "He's also never going to be human again, Michelle. What Sasha and Theo were talking about? Being exposed by sex. Theo gave his boyfriend one blow job. Well, two, it sounds like. That was all it took, and now he's a tiger. Jonah will never be able to have a normal relationship with a normal human woman again. If he tries, she'll become a wolf. He can use condoms, but he has to do that every single time."

"He should anyway," she reminded me.

"Even when he's forty and married," I countered. "Not just right now while he's in high school. This thing? It doesn't go away. He'll have a need to be near his pack, too. Right now, that's us. No, he doesn't need to stay, but the two of you are welcome to."

"What do you mean?" she asked.

"Do you own your home?"

She shook her head. "We're renting."

"Then move here." I gestured around us. "Let him have access to the trails, be around his own kind - and others - and have access to people who can help both of you when he has a problem."

"I'd love to," Michelle said, "but I can't afford this place. Elena, the god's honest truth is that I'm a month behind on rent, and I need my son to work so we can just scrape by. I work at a pharmacy. I'm not the pharmacist, I'm just the cashier, and that's not enough money to live on."

"How do you feel about answering phones and sending emails?"

She gave me a strange look. "It's kinda what I do every day. Why?"

But I kept going. "Calling people and telling them they can't have what they asked for?"

"Pretty much my current job," she assured me. "Why, Elena?"

"Because Wolf's Run was a test. It succeeded, and now we're looking at expanding. That means I won't have time to be the Alpha Female, a mother, a wife, *and* the Leasing Agent. I've already talked to the Langdons, and they agree with me. We'd like to offer you a job, Michelle. It's eighty thousand a year with free rent. The hours are insane, you will be asked to put up with things that are literally inhuman, and you'll have to figure out how to turn all the rich, spoiled humans away, but it's a good job. It used to be mine."

The woman lifted a hand to her mouth and had to look away because her eyes were getting misty. "Why me?" she asked.

"Because everyone deserves a second chance. What you do with it is up to you, but I know what it's like to be a single mom and desperate. I was once where you are now. This, Michelle, is a clean slate. Living here will be the most magical and simultaneously mundane experience of your life, but it's a good home. These are good people. If nothing else, the job will give you the chance to get back on your feet, get your son through high school, and then decide what comes next, right?"

She sniffed, wiped her eyes, and then looked at me with a timid smile. "Are you at the 'comes next' part?"

I just nodded. "I'm marrying the five men of my dreams. My little girl has the kind of fathers I can be proud of." I laughed once. "And me? I figured out that I did all of this to become a strong woman, but I'd kinda been that way the whole time. Now, it's your turn."

"If my son makes it through this," she decided, "then yes. I'll gladly learn anything I have to. Thank you so much..." She paused, then added, "Alpha."

"Elena's fine," I promised. "Also, we do wine at Ashley's place on Thursdays. Oh, and we're looking at getting shirts, because we are officially the Sisterhood of Being Too Old for That Shit. Well, this shit!"

"I know," she agreed. "I think my son's going to give me a heart attack. But what about the others? Jonah wasn't the only one that man bit."

"No, but Evelyn's starting a daycare for the pack children. Christian's in college. Mia? If she's not struggling so hard, she might be able to do the same. They're all staying, Michelle, along with five others from that pack before it was disbanded. You see, this place?" I turned to look at her. "We're going to make it a sanctuary.

Tigers, bears - we even have a lion interested, which will round things out nicely, I think."

"Lions, tigers, and bears?" she laughed.

I nodded. "And foxes and some wolves. Yeah. See, we wolves have it pretty good. We're a pack. The others? They rely on us to help, because they're scattered out there, desperate to not be discovered, and some of them would do anything just for the chance to scratch their back on one tree. They're desperate, and we can help. I need people in that office who understand what that feels like."

"I do," she assured me. "I want to say more than you can understand, but it sounds like you've been there."

"Yeah," I agreed, "and my pack helped me even before I knew what they were. Now it's time to give the next ones a chance."

And then the first set of howls broke out, announcing a successful hunt. My lips curled into a smile, and David jumped up just as a red wolf ran into the clearing. That was Lane, and his head swiveled around for a moment before it landed on me. Immediately, he shifted.

"Elena, we need you. Christian's running hard and still not done, but Jonah's just about ready. He's also scared, so we don't want to push him."

Without thinking, I began to pull off my clothes, but Michelle had heard that too. "What's happening?" she asked.

"He needs a mom," I told her. "Not a big bad wolf, but someone to make him feel safe." I shoved my pants to the ground, pulling my shoes, socks, underwear, and pants off my ankles together. "It's ok. I got this. It's what pack does for each other."

Then I shifted, racing after my mate to make sure that Jonah knew he no longer had to fight. We were done with that. This was our home, our safe place, and I was not going to let anything happen to my pups. Not Gabby, not her betas, and not this new boy who would be a good addition to the pack.

Lane and I reached them just as Ashley knocked the boy off his feet. Kim immediately dropped her weight on him. Bridget shifted to grab his legs, and I headed right for his head, finding my human body at the exact moment I reached him.

"Hey, Jonah," I said, looking into his eyes.

And I could feel it. That power. That ability to ease him out of this. It was right there, begging for me to use it, so I did. I leaned on him gently, giving him my eyes to hold onto like a lifeline even as I gently petted his head.

"We got you," I promised. "Now comes the hard part. You made it, Jonah. You turned, but now we have to get you to turn back, ok? Nod if you understand me?" He nodded his muzzle. "That's perfect. But the trick is that you can't push. Don't shove your human body away. You need to reach for it. Strain, trying to pull it to you, but don't fight it. Just look right into my eyes, and remember what it was like to have knees, and fingers, and even thumbs. That's it. We got you. You're completely safe, but you have to really reach for it."

His form began to blur, but his eyes didn't blink. They held mine, so I leaned just a little more. This was my pup. They all were, and I could help him find this. As his body lost its shape a little more, the boy finally figured it out, and the next part happened in a rush. His body almost dissipated and then shifted, resettling into the shape he knew best - that of a teenaged human boy.

"I did it?" he asked.

And I didn't care if anyone else was watching. I bent down and hugged the kid, holding him against my shoulder. "Welcome to the pack, Jonah. You're going to be a strong wolf, and I think your mother's going to help us a lot."

Then Ian's hand stroked down the back of my hair, making me look up at him. "You got him? I need to catch the other one."

"I do," I assured him. "And Michelle said yes to the job."

He grinned. "Good. Pax and Trent are with Mia. She made the shift back. Have Lane carry Jonah to his mom." Then he looked over. "Seth?"

"I'll chase him down," Seth promised. "And if we can't stop him, Vic or Lev can."

Ian bent to kiss the top of my head. "It's a good day for the pack. I'll be done soon, Alpha, but until then, take care of our pack."

"Always," I promised.

EPILOGUE

Roman dropped me off at the office after school. I headed inside, waved to the new lady at the desk, and kept going toward the back. The office that had formerly been Henry's was now my mom's. It was just past Ashley's, but I paused to stick my tongue out at her as I passed. Then I swung around the door frame and into Mom's space.

"Hey," I said.

"How was school?" she asked.

I nodded and dropped into the chair before her desk. "Jonah's doing good. The story is that he and his mom had a big fight, he went off to hang with some friends, but they punked him and left him high and dry. Took him a bit to suck up and call his mom, but everything's good. How's Michelle working out?"

"She's learning," Mom assured me. "But I'm curious about why you're here."

"Ian texted, saying I was supposed to wait for him." I just shrugged.

And right on time, my Alpha-Dad walked into the office. "Hi, Michelle," he said.

"Afternoon, Alpha," she called back.

Mom and I both listened to his steps as he came closer. "Ash?" He paused. "I need you for this too."

"Of course you do," Ashley groaned, but the sound of her chair squeaking meant she was following.

Then he stepped into the office and took the chair beside me. "Ok," he said, not even waiting for Ashley to get there. "Dad just closed on the abandoned apartments. That means we're going to have construction going on next door. I need both of you to make sure the pack knows to be careful about shifting while they're around. Looks like night hours only for a bit."

"It's done?" Ashley asked.

Ian just held up a finger. "And we got the land behind the trails. Downside, we have to pull down the walls. The upside, however, is that means twenty-five more acres of untouched land to run in."

"How many houses?" Elena asked. "On the apartment side, I mean."

"Fifty," Ian said. "And that's why I needed all of you in here. This is a big decision, but we have two options. First, we can keep leasing like we have been. But the second option is that we can stop blindly leasing to any wolves who apply, and start looking for those who need sanctuary. Doesn't matter what they are. If they can work with us, learn how to accept a pack, and are willing to do their part to help the next, we'll find a way to get them a house."

"How's the budget?" Ashley asked.

Ian slowly bobbed his head. "We're doing ok. Dad's going to make a few outside investments, but most of the houses are paid in full. We're a bit short on capital after that investment, but with the monthly rent we're making, I think we're going to be ok. Not great, and we certainly aren't going to get rich, but we're going to be making a significant profit."

"We'll need criteria for leasing," Mom pointed out. "It's easy to give some kind of sob story, but how do we verify most of this?"

"We use my covenant," I said. "My betas and I worked hard on it. And I know it's not all official and legal yet, but Henry can fix that, right? I mean, we figured out levels of need and how they rank compared to the others. It's a little complicated, but we were kinda going for a blueprint of how to make this work again."

"The one you showed me?" Ian asked.

I nodded. "Yep. We even talked to Vic to see what the bears thought of it, but Nik and Zaria helped, so that's three others besides just wolves."

Ian looked at Mom and then Ashley. "What do you think? No final answers, and I'm not holding your feet to the fire. I just need to know what page we're on."

"I like the sanctuary," Mom told him. "I mean, isn't that what we did with the kids from Damon's pack?"

"They're not kids, Mom," I reminded her.

"None of them can drink," Ashley countered, "so they are kids."

That just made me roll my eyes, but Ian was grinning at me. "I'm with you on this, Gabby."

"See!" I said.

Ashley groaned at me before she finally answered Ian's question. "I'd like to do the sanctuary idea too, but there are a few more hoops to jump through."

"And we can make that happen," Ian promised. "But if this is the course of action we'd like to take, I was thinking about calling Ethan and Alison, and seeing if they're interested in making a Wolf's Leap up in the Northwest. I'm pretty sure we're not the only place that has shifters in need, and I just..." He looked at me. "Maybe it's being a dad, but I kinda feel like being a Langdon should mean something."

"How?" Ashley asked. "I mean, the idea is great and all, but the logistics of it?"

"Well," he continued, "if we bring the twins - " He looked over at Elena. "Real ones this time. My middle siblings." Then back to Ashley. " - Down here, they can see how we run this. I'm sure theirs will start smaller, but so did ours. Besides, I'd kinda like the two of them here for our wedding anyway. And then, if this all works out, Elena and I can fly up there to help them set it up."

"And who's running the pack?" Ashley asked.

Ian just pointed between me and his sister. "Gabby's my backup and you're Elena's. It would be a weekend, and most of my betas would be here."

"I kinda like it," I said. "I mean, Nik said that before they came here, he and Lev could never shift, and they had to hide what they were, and that it was pretty tough. If one of them messed up, they had to move, and evidently having tigers roaring in the bathroom counts as messing up. Why should anyone have to live like that?"

"I'm with her," Mom said. "I think we can do this. I think we *should* do this."

And then all of us turned to look at Ashley. She just backed up to lean against the wall and lifted both of her hands with a grin on her face. "I tried to play the Devil's Advocate, but I'm out of arguments. Wolves have been so successful because we do have packs. Why can't we become like the Templars of the shifter world, right?"

"Like, guardians?" I asked.

She nodded. "Bring it full circle, Gabby. Pay it forward. All of that. We can do this, so why shouldn't we?"

"It'll be your pack next, though," Ian reminded me. "That means more work, more responsibility, and you'll have to balance all of this with not just high school, but college too."

"I can do it," I promised.

"I know you can," he assured me.

But Mom held up a finger. "I have two completely unrelated questions to this, but since I have you all here, now's as good a time as any." Then she looked at me. "Gabby, would you be my maid of honor twice? For both weddings?"

I nodded. "Yes! Of course, Mom."

Then she looked at Ashley. "And will you be a bridesmaid?"

"Definitely," Ashley promised. "And I'll even hire strippers for the bachelorette party, and - "

"No," Ian said. "Just no. Stop right there. I will have no strippers on my territory."

"Oh, we can go to a bar," Ashley promised.

"I can't," I reminded her. "No fair!"

"No strippers," Mom told her best friend. Then she held up a hand and fake-whispered, "But we'll talk about this more at your place."

"Deal," Ashley fake-whispered back.

Ian flopped back into his chair and threw up his hands. "Is it going to be like this for the rest of my life?"

"Pretty much," I told him. "Aren't you glad you proposed now?"

"Kinda am," he assured me. "And to think, when you moved in next door, I tried to talk Ashley out of this. Now, I've got an amazing fiancée, and a pretty decent kid."

I huffed. "You know what that deserves, right?"

"I'm scared," Ian admitted.

So I just leaned back and groaned out, "Dad! Stop picking on me!"

"This," Ashley said, wagging her finger between us. "This is what you call happily ever after, Elena?"

"Kinda is," she said. "And it's your fault for moving me into a house with wolves next door, but I swear I don't mind at all."

Books by Auryn Hadley

A Flawed Series - co-written w/ Kitty Cox

(Contemporary Romance): *In Progress*

Ruin

Brutal

Vicious

Cruel

Wicked

Deviant

Contemporary Romance: *Standalone Book*

One More Day

End of Days - Auryn Hadley & Kitty Cox writing as Cerise Cole
(Paranormal RH): *Completed Series*

Still of the Night

Tainted Love

Enter Sandman

Highway to Hell

Gamer Girls - co-written w/ Kitty Cox

(Contemporary Romance): *Completed Series*

Flawed

Challenge Accepted

Virtual Reality

Fragged

Collateral Damage

For The Win

Game Over

The Dark Orchid (Fantasy Poly):

Completed Series

Power of Lies

Magic of Lust

Spell of Love

The Demons' Muse (Paranormal Poly):

Completed Series

The Kiss of Death

For Love of Evil

The Sins of Desire

The Lure of the Devil

The Wrath of Angels

The Path of Temptation (Fantasy Poly):

Completed Series

The Price We Pay

The Paths We Lay

The Games We Play

The Ways We Betray

The Prayers We Pray

The Gods We Obey

Where the Wild Things Grow (Paranormal Poly):

Completed Series

Magic In The Moonlight

Spell In The Summertime

Witchcraft In The Woods

Wolves Next Door (Paranormal RH / Poly):

Completed Series

Wolf's Bane

Wolf's Call

Wolf's Pack

About Auryn Hadley

Auryn Hadley is happily married with three canine children and a herd of feral cats that her husband keeps feeding. Between her love for animals, video games, and a good book, she has enough ideas to spend the rest of her life trying to get them out. They all live in Texas, land of the blistering sun, where she spends her days feeding her addictions – including drinking way too much coffee.

For a complete list of books and to receive notices for new releases by Auryn Hadley follow me:

Amazon Author Page -
amazon.com/author/aurynhadley

Visit our Patreon site
www.patreon.com/Auryn_Kitty

You can also join the fun on Discord -
https://discord.gg/Auryn-Kitty

Facebook readers group -
www.facebook.com/groups/TheLiteraryArmy/

Merchandise is available from -

Etsy Shop (signed books) - The Book Muse - www.etsy.com/shop/TheBookMuse

Threadless (clothes, etc) - The Book Muse - https://thebookmuse.threadless.com/

Also visit any of the other sites below:

My website -
aurynhadley.com

Books2Read Reading List -
books2read.com/rl/AurynHadley

- facebook.com/AurynHadleyAuthor
- amazon.com/author/aurynhadley
- goodreads.com/AurynHadley
- bookbub.com/profile/auryn-hadley
- patreon.com/Auryn_Kitty

Made in the USA
Middletown, DE
07 December 2024

66355304R00336